FAMILIAR STRANGERS

THE SECOND BOOK
OF THE TREVU TRILOGY

By

F J WARREN

Best Wishes

Fj Warren

Front cover design courtesy of Justin Hubbard

This novel is entirely a work of fiction. The names, characters and incidents portrayed in it are the work of the author's imagination. Any resemblance to actual persons, living or dead, events or localities is entirely coincidental. F J Warren asserts the moral right to be identified as the author of this work.

ISBN 1846853117
978-1-84685-311-1

British Library Cataloguing In Publication Data
A Record of this Publication is available
from the British Library

Published 2006

by Exposure Publishing
An Imprint of Diggory Press
Three Rivers,
Minions
Liskeard,
Cornwall,
PL14 5LE
UK

WWW.DIGGORYPRESS.COM

ACKNOWLEDGEMENTS

The author wishes to thank her family and friends for their encouragement
before, during and after the completion of this work.
Particular thanks go to Joan, John, Jane and JT for
all their hard work on my behalf.

Special thanks to Iris, Linda, Jennifer, Susan and especially
Justin for his enthusiasm and invaluable assistance.

For May

CHAPTER 1

THE four children stood before their father with all but one of them staring in discomfort at the floor. They were mindful that upon occasion he could lose his temper with them if their behaviour irritated him, but it was a rare occurrence. However, they were all aware that he was scowling and this did not bode well for them. The eldest child, a boy of about ten years of age, raised his eyes from the contemplation of his shoes and glanced quickly at his parent, and in so doing, his bruised face and cut lip were obvious for all to see. The youngest, another boy, never raised his head at all and neither did his sister although she was trying desperately to hold her torn dress together, hoping to make herself look less bedraggled. His other sister, her hair ribbons pulled loose and the skirt of her dress ripped from the bodice and dragging on the floor, held her head high and gazed proudly at her father; if she feared the consequences of their recent actions she did not show the slightest sign of it.

"Well," said their father, patiently but in a firm voice, "I'm waiting. Who amongst you would like to be the first to explain your damaged clothes and George's appearance?"

His bruised and battered son raised his face again, his curly black hair flopping over his creased brow, but he could not think of how to explain his damaged countenance and kept his peace.

"Harry Pendray said I was a black bastard," the girl with the loose dark brown hair and ripped dress announced defiantly, "so I hit him. Then he pulled my hair and his brother Dick pulled my dress and it ripped so I hit him as well. Then George came up to us and told Harry he was not to miscall me so and Harry told him he was a filthy black as well, just like his father, and he hit George and knocked him down. Then George got up and hit Harry, then Dick hit George and I kicked Harry and he tried to hit me but George knocked him to the ground but Dick kicked my leg and made me cry out so I hit him with my book and he started to cry and he ran away." She paused for breath before continuing: "Then Harry said my grandfather was hanged for killing people and I told him it was a lie and . . . and . . ." then for the first time her lip quivered and a single tear ran down her cheek, "and then he said . . . he said . . ." she sniffed and lapsed into silence.

Their father waited patiently for his daughter to recover her composure.

"He said . . . ?" he prompted gently.

"He said my father was a black bastard too and he got me on a white woman and had to take me in to his family because nobody wanted a blackamoor in their home and Trevu children are blackies anyway and . . . and then Grace hit him with her book and he pulled her dress and ripped it and Ben kicked him and told him to leave us alone so he tried to hit Ben but George stopped him. Then they had a big fight and George won because Harry could not fight as well as George and then Harry started to cry and ran away and shouted he would tell his father on us. Then we came home and you saw us as we tried to cross the garden trying not to be seen and shouted at us to come in here at once to explain to you why we . . . why we look like this," she finished firmly but at the look on her father's face she finally lowered her gaze and mumbled: "and that was what happened . . . all of it."

There was an uncomfortable silence; the four children, with their heads bowed, did not look at their father but made surreptitious glances at each other and waited apprehensively for whatever punishment their father would impose upon them. Grace, unable to bear the tension any longer, began to cry, which immediately set Ben off. Their father, Paul, sighed, got up from his chair, and gave his handkerchief to Grace, he found Benjamin's handkerchief screwed up in a ball in his breeches' pocket and, after shaking it out, put his hand under the boy's chin and began to wipe his face. After completing this task, he turned his attention to George and, suggesting that Miss Clavering would be the best person to tend to his hurts, told them all to go to the nursery and that he would have words to say to them later.

"Yes Father," they mumbled in unison and turned towards the door but before they could reach it, a smiling young woman, with chestnut ringlets and laughing hazel eyes, opened it. She was holding a baby of about six months in her arms, and, on taking in the scene, stopped in the doorway with an expression of horror on her face at the sight that met her eyes.

"Children! - my dears!" she exclaimed and then distressfully, "Oh, George! ... dearest your face, Daisy your dress, your hair, Grace ... whatever has ... dearest Ben, stop crying darling. Come, stop now sweetheart." However, poor Ben was unable to control his emotions and ran towards his mother, burying his head, with its mop of curly black curls, in the skirt of her dress, sobbing uncontrollably. He was soon followed by Grace, still holding her torn dress together. George and Daisy moved silently towards each other and George took his sister's hand, squeezing it for comfort and support.

"Chloe," Paul began quietly to speak but found he had to raise his voice to be heard above the noise of the crying children, so he said her name again and she raised a bewildered face towards him.

"Take the children upstairs to Miss Clavering and when you have settled them come back to me. It is important that we talk," he said composedly.

Chloe, trying hard to wipe the bewildered look from her face, merely said "Yes dear," and shepherded the children from the room.

Paul Trevarthen turned to gaze upon the garden once again. He was a tall, well-built man who was in his early thirties but gave the impression of being much younger because of his black, curly cropped hair and his lean features. His skin was not black, as the Pendray children had stated, but it was obvious that he was of mixed race. Large brown eyes set under slightly arched brows, a thin nose, well-formed, high cheekbones and a full mouth blended together into a remarkably handsome face. When he smiled, which was often, females of all ages felt their hearts melt. To his credit he was just as unaware of the effect his appearance had on members of the opposite sex as he had been as a raw young man taking his first steps into adulthood. His path had not been easy, his appearance was not always received with pleasure, but those who had fallen under its spell had never lost their respect and adoration of him. Adopted into his father's household, almost from birth, he had known no other home. His stepmother had adored him and he had always thought of her as his true mother. When she died it had broken his father's heart and his own. After some years his father had married again and this time he had married Paul's real mother, Sardi, the daughter of an ex-slave. In spite of her humble beginnings and her dark, exotic skin, she had become a successful businesswoman. She had built up a business based on the supply of materials and had designed and made fashionable clothes for the highest in society. She it was who had been responsible for acquiring the property in London and Bristol and, through hard work and determination, she had accumulated her great wealth. His father, Redvers, had been the richest landowner in the locality due to the wealth that he had derived from Trevu, his farm and his mine, Wheal Sankey. Consequently, as their only heir, Paul was immensely rich and owned properties in his native county of Cornwall, as well as his mother's houses in London and Bristol, but he rarely left his home. Through his own efforts he had become famous as a translator of Latin, both poetry and prose, and although he had no need of the income he had derived from this occupation he had always written; his published works numbering more than a dozen. He had married in his early twenties and with his wife Chloe they were the proud parents of six children. Daisy, the bold girl who had told him about the fight was his daughter by another woman, Dorothea Petherick. He had imagined himself in love with her for many years, only to realise that Chloe, the shy young girl that he had first met in his mother's fashion house and had married on the understanding that he was not in love with her, was his only true love. He had met Dorothea again and they had given in to temptation. That night had taught him a valuable lesson: how blind he had been not to recognise that the woman he truly loved was his wife, Chloe. After the deaths of both his parents he discovered that he had a daughter but he had no wish to take the orphaned child into his home. It was Chloe, his forgiving wife who had wanted Daisy in their family; he was too afraid and ashamed to acknowledge her existence publicly. That had altered when he discovered the distressing circumstances that his daughter experienced in the orphanage, where she had been placed before her mother's death. He sighed. It had been difficult enough for them to appear before the servants with Daisy when she had joined their household five years previously, but they had done it and whatever the servants had to say about this circumstance never came to their ears. Only Hannah, their cook and housekeeper, had felt emboldened enough to make any pronouncements on the matter. Paul had entered her kitchen and, bravely, and with hardly a pause in his speech, had told her who Daisy was and how she had entered the family and why. At first it seemed as if Hannah had nothing to say, but when she did speak she began a homily that had almost reduced Paul to a state of childhood, such were her words of condemnation. After her withering comments to him, she began to praise Chloe and pointed out how like his father's first wife she was, taking into the house her husband's by-blow as Penelope, his stepmother, had so bravely done in his own case.

"You'd a kept she in the orf'nage I bet," she told him scornfully and when he bowed his head, unable to look her in the eye, she merely said: "Just like Redvers 'imself." She sniffed and flapped her cloth at him in irritation, as if he was still the cheeky young boy forever raiding her kitchen to steal her baking.

"Tidden the liddle maid's fault. Tis the grown ups should knaw better," she sighed, and then in a more conciliatory tone: "but rest assured Paul, she'll come to no harm from me or any of the servants, I'll see to that. But don't 'e go thinking you can go back to your old ways and 'op into bed with any piece that do take yer fancy, 'cos I will 'ave words to say to 'e an' no mistake." She shook herself, and folded the cloth, placing it on the table. Then went forward and, catching hold of his arm, squeezed it, looked up into his discomforted face and with a twinkle in her eye, said: "Well, aren't 'e goin' introduce me to the liddle lamb? I d' knaw full well 'ow to welcome by-blows to this house after all," she laughed gleefully and was rewarded with one of Paul's beaming smiles. Daisy, like her father before her, was soon a welcome addition to the knot of children that regularly found their way to her kitchen and to her welcoming heart.

Penzance society had kept their opinions to themselves and had not dared to bar their doors to the Trevarthens. Position and money had safeguarded his family from social dishonour and the knowing glances that he had sometimes caught being cast in his direction were a mixture of disdain and amusement. He and his wife adopted his daughter and named her Marguerite, but no one used that name and she was always known as Daisy, the name given to her by George the first day she had arrived in the household. People were well aware that the child was his own daughter, her lack of a white skin proclaimed her heritage for all to see. Chloe received much unlooked for sympathy, but she told everyone how proud she was of her new daughter and not one of their acquaintances had the nerve to ask either of them of the circumstances that had brought the little girl into the world. Rumour had expanded to fill the gap left by their lack of explanation. Soon rumour was given some facts to chew upon, as inquisitive matrons contentedly counted back on their fingers and quickly arrived at the well-publicised appearance of Paul Trevarthen and his famous speech at Oxford. Mrs Sampson rifled her box room and was finally justified in her determination to hoard every newspaper she had ever bought. The relevant passage was devoured by the residents of withdrawing rooms the length and breadth of Penzance and when they saw the name, Dorothea, they sighed and nodded knowingly to themselves. No wonder Captain Petherick had tried to kill Paul Trevarthen that night.

"Damn lucky his wife forgave him," muttered Squire Tregurthen to his own wife during breakfast one morning. "Still, old Redvers was a bit of a devil that way. 'Like father, like son,' as they say."

"Nonsense, Tregurthen! To my knowledge Paul has never been known to fool around with other women around here since he married that dear little girl. I suppose he must be allowed one lapse," acknowledged his wife reasonably, "and if there was one woman he would be unable to resist, it would be Petherick's daughter. Remember that dreadful incident at our ball after all."

Her husband nodded in agreement, "and at the hanging. I thought he was just chicken hearted but I can see there was more to it now. Guilt, obviously," he mused.

"Well dear, as I said to dear Mrs Carter only the other day; if there is one man in the county who can get away with that sort of indiscretion it is Paul Trevarthen. With all his money and position, who would be the first to shut the door to him after all?"

"True, my dear, very true," he agreed and took a deep draught from his tankard of ale, then burst out laughing. "There are plenty of women in this town who would not shut their doors but would throw open every one of them in their house, if they thought they could get that particular young man into their bed."

"Quite, dear, but hardly the subject for the breakfast table," remarked his wife pointedly.

The Squire coughed and begged pardon. Being a man not given to understanding woman in general and his wife in particular, he presumed that the fiery blush that had surmounted her cheeks was because of his forthright speech. In fact he had unknowingly discovered that his own wife was yet another of those females who, in spite of her advanced years, would have willingly cast aside all her inhibitions, for one look of admiration from Redvers' handsome son.

Time passed and Paul's indiscretion had been accepted, but until today he had been unaware of exactly how much of his past had been pieced together for the amusement of local society. Aunt Caroline had been right after all, he surmised. After his return from Bristol with his daughter, he had called upon his father's only sister at her home and had admitted to her the circumstances of Daisy's birth, expecting and receiving her censure afterwards. When her temper had cooled, she told him that the truth would be discovered soon enough and asked what would he tell the poor child when she asked who her mother was and, "heaven forbid that she shall ever know; why her grandfather was hanged!"

Paul had closed his eyes upon that question and shuddered, but replied that he hoped that an explanation would never be required of him.

Caroline Crebo sighed and shook her head, "Don't fool yourself Paul. She will be told soon enough. You are not beloved by all. There are enough husbands and families who hold a grievance against you, or have you forgotten your behaviour before you married Chloe? They will take their revenge on that little girl, mark my words if they don't."

His aunt's prophetic words had come true and Molly Pendray's husband had gotten his revenge for being cuckolded by Paul all those years ago. He bit his lip; if not Pendray it would have been some other, he reasoned. After all, there was no one to blame but himself as usual. He had spent enough nights with other men's wives to stir up plenty of hatred and time had only served to fuel their smouldering fires of revenge. His past actions and misdemeanours were coming back to haunt him with a vengeance. His heart ached that his dearest Daisy should be made to suffer for it and that his other children should be made to endure for his sins also. He was still thinking in this vein when he heard the door open and Chloe's gentle voice call his name.

He turned to face her, a guilty look on his expressive face.

"George has told me what happened and what the Pendray children have said," she announced composedly. Her normally laughing face had a worried expression and a pair of sombre hazel eyes regarded her husband pensively.

He hung his head and remarked shamefully, "I'm sorry, Chloe, that it has come to this pass. I suppose that I should have realised sooner that it would happen. Aunt Caroline told me that something like this would transpire, only I determined not to believe her."

She sighed, "It is never wise to disregard Aunt Caroline. She knows the ways of the world far better than a poor innocent like you, Paul, will ever understand it."

He grinned ruefully, "That's true, Madam Wife," he admitted, but his face registered his concern as he continued: "but what will we tell them now, particularly Daisy? I cannot lie to her Chloe. She has a way of looking at me in the same way Father did and I was always at a loss when he attempted to coerce me into giving him an answer. I could only get away from his questioning by losing my temper, turning tail and retreating to my room with all possible speed. Following that example would not be a sound way of answering the questions that Daisy is going to ask of me, if not immediately, at least before many days have passed. She is forming them in her mind at this very moment, I have no doubt."

Chloe sighed and nodded in agreement.

"Do we explain everything to such a young child? Would she understand it all if we did?" she asked.

"Most probably," sighed Paul. "Daisy has a quick mind, although I am never sure just what it is she is thinking. George wears his feelings on his face at all times, it is a simple matter to fathom his thoughts, but Daisy is quite different."

"George is not the only member of this household who cannot hide his thoughts," she laughed and was relieved to see a smile of admission from Paul.

"You said only the other day that maturity had improved me beyond all measure. Have you forgotten already?" he queried, an eyebrow raised.

"Why no, husband, but like any good wife I have been known to flatter to deceive if it should suit my purpose!" she retorted archly.

Paul pursed his lips. He studied her face for a moment, then walked towards her and took her in a crushing embrace. "You are the veriest minx, Madame Wife," he said thickly and, lifting up her chin, looked lovingly into her laughing eyes, "but I love you more than life itself and know full well that whatever we have to face, you will stand by me and support me through it."

"Silly boy," she laughed, "and yes, you may kiss me if you wish, and then we will put our heads together and think how best to explain to the children the reasons that brought about the fight today."

He smiled and, bowing his head, he kissed her passionately. Then he took her by the hand and they sat on the settle, turning their thoughts to the seemingly insurmountable problem that faced them.

"Well, I presume that we will have to be as honest with them as their understanding will allow. Do we tell all four of them or just George and the two girls?" he asked.

"There is no point in telling Ben," said Chloe wisely, "he is far too young to understand."

"Well, in that case, how much of the truth do we tell them?" he enquired, "and how am I to explain to Daisy that her grandfather did indeed perish on the scaffold as the Pendray children said he did," briefly he closed his eyes and shuddered at the remembered image of the struggling man fighting his fate on that terrible day. Chloe squeezed his hand in a gesture of support. He smiled grimly, but it put heart into him nonetheless and he planted a light kiss on her chestnut curls.

"Perhaps we should tell Daisy first, for it concerns her most particularly, and then explain to George and Grace afterwards. We cannot possibly tell all the particulars to them, so that will be easier to bear," suggested Paul hopefully.

Chloe looked at her husband thoughtfully, and then shook her head, "Paul, dearest Paul. Daisy will confide in George the moment they are on their own. Those two are so close and share all their schemes and secrets."

His wife continued in her firm voice: "What we have to do is to tell them as much of the truth as they will understand and as gently as we can, then to explain that we love them all equally and pray that they do not ask any awkward questions. If they do," and she sighed, "then try to keep that expressive countenance of yours under control for once."

"There will be questions, my dear, and you know as well as I from whose lips they will be issued," he told her bitterly.

"True, but we will have to face that when we come to it. We will take them on one side after they have had their tea and between us we will begin to explain Daisy's history," she affirmed composedly.

An hour later and Paul, standing with his back to the fire, wished that the floor would open up and swallow him. His three eldest children had listened wide eyed but in silence as, speaking alternately, Chloe and himself had explained, as delicately as was possible, the circumstances of Daisy's arrival into the family and that it was true that her maternal grandfather had died in the way that he did. George looked worriedly at Daisy; but she stared impassively at her father throughout. When, finally, their tale was told, Chloe and Paul exchanged nervous glances and waited, as composedly as they could, for the questions that they knew were going to be asked.

"Did you love my real mother?" asked Daisy boldly.

There was a long silence but, summoning up his courage, Paul answered his daughter in as steady a voice as he could muster:

"For a long time, but then I realised that I loved Mama more and that I should never have been a bad husband to her," he answered her truthfully.

"Why did my grandfather try to kill you? If he loved my mother as much as you said he did, he should have loved you as well because she loved you," observed Daisy logically, a small frown appearing upon her face.

Paul coughed nervously, but before he could reply he heard Chloe say: "Your grandfather did not like people who did not have a white skin. So he found it an impossibility to like your father."

Daisy stared at her father for a long while and then said: "So the Pendray boys were right and I should not have hit them."

"Daisy, all of you, listen to me and listen well. If anyone tries to hurt you in any way because of your colour, or what you say or think, then you have the right to defend and protect yourselves. It is not right for one person to attack another in the way the Pendray boys attacked you and you did no wrong by trying to protect each other," he told them earnestly.

"Do you still love me, Papa, in spite of everything?" asked Daisy, her voice quivering.

"Dearest Daisy," cried Paul in an anguished voice, "of course, I love you. I love all my children equally and so does Mama," and he opened up his arms, and went down on his knees, and Daisy let out a small sob, throwing herself at him and gripping him tightly. Grace rushed forward and, throwing one arm around her sister, placed the other about her father's neck and sobbed happily. George walked to his father's side and gave him a hug, then turned and surreptitiously wiped a tear from his face, hoping that no one had noticed. Then Chloe was on her knees beside her husband and the children; they turned to her and hugged and kissed her whilst George buried his face in her neck, knowing she would not say anything if she felt his hot tears on her skin because she never had. Daisy was the first to stop crying, but she turned and looked her father full in the face, telling him with great composure that he was never to be a bad husband ever again, for Mama was the best mother in the whole world and he had no reason to go off to be with other women.

Paul, hopelessly attempting to smother the unlooked for smile that was playing on his lips, hung his head and promised Daisy that he would never be naughty in that way ever again.

"I should think so," admonished Daisy fiercely and added: "grown ups should know better," unconsciously echoing Hannah's sentiments.

He knew his wife's laughing eyes were fixed on his face, but because of the children he dare not catch her eye and kept his head bowed.

When Lizzie knocked on the door of the nursery to tell them that Bertram Pendray had called and wished to see Mr Trevarthen, the children lapsed into silence immediately. Daisy raised her chin at her father and gave him a cool stare, but she had nothing to say. Paul, smiling calmly at his children and saying he would be back later, got up from the floor where he had been tickling his youngest son, Charles, and headed for the door.

Bertram Pendray, cap in hand, stood awkwardly in the splendour of the withdrawing room. He was a man of about Paul's age but he had a heavily tanned, weather-beaten face, with callused and worn hands and a spare, sinewy body, which proclaimed that his work was of the outdoor variety. The smell of the sea and stale fish that clung to his clothing identified him as one of the local fisherman. He shuffled his feet and was not looking forward to the interview that he had requested, but he was determined to have speech with Mr Trevarthen. He turned as the door opened and watched resentfully as the tall, dark skinned man he had called to see strode into the room.

Bertram pulled his forelock and bowed his head.

"Evenin' sir," he mumbled bitterly.

"Good evening, Mr Pendray. I presume you have come to talk about the fight between your sons and my eldest four children that took place this afternoon." He paused and regarded Bertram with a serene and quiet face.

"I never told 'em to pick a fight with your children sir," began Bertram, defensively. "They jes' felt a bit uppity after a day in school, an' I've belted 'em good and proper fer the trouble they caused," he paused and then continued, not attempting to keep the bitterness out of his voice: "I 'spect you've given yours a good 'ammering too. That liddle bold faced maid of yours started it my 'Arry said 'cos she 'it 'en furst afore mine 'ad 'it any of yours." He regarded Paul from beneath his lowered brows, a paradoxical expression of submission and belligerence on his features.

"I have admonished them, yes," Paul agreed quietly, "but I have also pointed out that they have the right to defend themselves."

"Amonished them. Wha'd' that mean?" queried Pendray, "Four a' yours pitched in on my two, after all."

"Your boys were verbally abusive to Daisy, and then to George and then, from what I have been told, continued to abuse myself and other family members. The fight that ensued was a defensive action from my children against yours, from what I understand of the matter," answered Paul, trying to remain as calm and diplomatic as he could under the circumstances.

"Humph!" snorted the fisherman disgustedly, "My Molly said I was to watch out fer yer sweet talking ways." He made as if to spit on the floor, thought better of it, and swallowing hard, continued with an angry snarl:

"You'm the master 'ere, Paul Trevarthen, but that don' give 'e the right fer they brats a' yourn to attack who they d' fancy 'aving a go at. My boys might 'ave bin a bit loose wi' their tongues but they was only tellin' them like it is, after all. Everybody roun' 'ere d' knaw 'bout you and yer ways. People don' forget," he ended viciously.

Paul set his lips in a firm line and regarded the fulminating man thoughtfully. He felt his temper rising but knew full well that he needed to control it. Bertram was justifiably aggrieved; Paul's dalliance with Molly all those years past had given him just cause for complaint. Pendray's boys had not been brought up to admire either Mr Trevarthen or his children and Petherick's execution for murder had only added to the scandal that surrounded Paul's own existence. Daisy's appearance had given the scandalmongers in the locality additional cause for much derision and merriment. The Pendray children had only given voice to what was known by a number of people in that area, although they had used their knowledge to abuse his children. They had been offensive about their colour as well but, even if he had wanted to, there was nothing Paul could do to alter that.

"As I see it, the position is this, Mr Pendray," answered Paul quietly, "the children do not like each other. Mine will continue to defend themselves if they feel threatened, in fact I have given them my permission so to do, and yours will probably continue to be abusive to the ... er ... "Blackies of Trevu". Have I that right?"

Bertram's face suffused with red and he lowered his eyes, making as if to study the pattern on the carpet in order to hide his embarrassment. Paul heard a mumbled: "Yessir," from deep within the collar of Bertram's coat.

"I will not have my children apologise to yours for what took place," Paul said. Drawing breath and continuing in a firm voice he added, pointedly: "but neither do I expect any apology from your boys for, as you yourself said, they are only giving voice to what they have no doubt heard from certain people in this locality."

The fisherman kept his still red face lowered and only raised his eyes briefly to flash a malevolent look at his wife's former lover.

"I think," continued Paul urbanely, "that it will be best for both families if no more is made of this matter. Do you not agree?"

Pendray raised his face at that and regarded Paul suspiciously. He agreed, but with reluctance, and then added: "My missus is afeard the boys will be made to suffer fer it at school, yer missus bein' a gov'ner an' all."

"I can assure you that Mrs Trevarthen would never use any influence of hers to damage the education of any child. She is a great believer in giving children the opportunity to advance themselves through education and training. Not every child has the good fortune to be born..." and here he paused thoughtfully, but continued strongly: "...or accepted into a family with money and comfort, after all."

"Humph," muttered Bertram in agreement, "I s'pose yer in the right of it there. My boys are doin' well at school. They 'edden no fools, missus an' me wouldn' want 'em ... wouldn' want 'em punished fer what they did to yours."

"Rest assured, Mr Pendray, no one in my family will do anything to attempt to ruin their education, and I will stress to my children that the matter is closed and they are not to enter into any more altercations of such a nature:" but added for effect, "unless provoked, of course."

"Shall we shake on it, Mr Pendray, and draw this meeting to a close. I think we have said fairly all that we can on the matter," he concluded before extending his hand towards the fisherman.

Bertram regarded Paul shrewdly for a moment and then, wiping his hand on his somewhat grubby jacket, shook hands awkwardly, touched his forelock again and headed for the door. Paul preceded him, politely opening it for him, and walked with him to the main door to show him off the premises, all the while making, for a farmer, quite intelligent and well-informed comments on the state of fishing that was being experienced by the local men at the moment. On the steps Mr Pendray turned and offered Paul some gratuitous advice.

"I should watch that maid of yours, that Daisy. She's a forthy one an' no mistake," and touching his forelock again, he replaced his cap, then turned on his heel and strode jauntily away.

Paul watched his departure thoughtfully and then returned to the nursery. Five pairs of eyes regarded his entrance - four worried children and their equally worried mother - but for once he was completely the master of his features and, getting down on the floor again, recommenced his tickling of his youngest son.

After a period of silence Daisy could bear it no longer and blurted out:

"Well? Did you hit him, Father?"

"No Daisy. I did not hit Mr Pendray and I would appreciate it if, in future, you could refrain from hitting people as well, unless you have just cause, naturally," he said quietly, without raising his eyes from the gurgling baby.

She regarded him coolly for some moments before shrugging her shoulders and muttering only a disdainful "Humph!" by way of comment. Then she turned to George and they continued to play with his fort of toy soldiers until Nurse came to tell them it was time for bed.

CHAPTER 2

A YEAR had passed and the two fathers encountered each other again, but under sadly altered circumstances. This time they met as they entered the churchyard at St. Martin's, each man carrying floral tributes in their arms and forlorn expressions on their faces. At the beginning of spring Penzance had been devastated by a strange sickness that had attacked its victims without mercy. It made no distinction between rich and poor and enveloped all with equal venom. In Paul's household the first to succumb was Hannah's husband Ned and, in spite of her careful nursing, he swiftly died. Then Hannah, weakened by loss and age, was enmeshed in its snares. Paul was at her bedside, along with all of her children, when she died and shed his tears unashamedly with her offspring. She had been as a mother to him for as long as he could remember and his heart ached at her loss. At the end she had opened her eyes, smiled upon her children, and called them by their names, then without so much as a pause had turned her face to Paul and, smiling upon him, had said quietly: "Master Paul, my liddle lamb." Then she let out a long sigh and without complaint died. As if Hannah's loss was not enough hurt for him, the sweeping sickness turned its claws upon Paul's children. Ben, sweet, happy, smiling Ben, took ill and died almost immediately. Rocked by his death, Paul and Chloe watched helplessly as two more of their children succumbed. Their latest baby, a girl of five weeks, stood little chance and the youngest son, Charles, only now beginning to talk, was soon struggling to live. Paul and Chloe pleaded with the harassed doctor, but nothing could be done and their youngest son breathed his last barely a fortnight after the sickness had first reached Trevu. Theirs was not the only household so devastated. Some families lost every member from around their hearth. Chloe, desolated, but stronger than Paul could ever be, held her family together in her tenacious grip, and determined that they had to lift up their heads and go forward. Her private thoughts she kept to herself, her husband never knew the agony she suffered at the loss of their children, so wrapped was he in his own personal anguish. So now Bertram Pendray and Paul Trevarthen found themselves face to face once more. Bertram held a limp bunch of bluebells and campions in his gnarled hands and Paul's arms were full of flowers picked at random from Penelope's garden. They nodded awkwardly to each other and, as Bertram had to dress only the one grave, he left Paul at the Trevarthen plot, performing his sad task, and went to the side wall where his dearest Molly slept under the shade of an old oak. He had come back from sea to be told that she had taken sick and had died within two days. His brain was still reeling from the shock of losing her although six weeks had passed. As he prayed, his eyes wandered idly over the churchyard and could not fail to notice the abundance of new plots that were dotted here and there and the many tokens of fresh flowers that nodded their heads in the gentle breeze. He became aware of the sound of a man sobbing quietly and turned to see Mr Trevarthen on his knees also, but with his hands over his face. Bertram shifted uneasily and wondered if he ought to go over and say anything. "Best not interfere with a man's grief," he thought to himself and, bidding an unspoken farewell to Molly, he rose to his feet. Turning away, he walked slowly towards the churchyard gate.

However, instead of taking the road that led back down to his little house he stopped, hoisted his sparse frame onto the churchyard wall, sat, and waited patiently. He had not so long to wait and looked on as the other man carefully shut the gate behind him.

Clearing his throat he said distinctly, "Sorry fer 'e sir, an' yer missus. Dreadful thing, losing children like that."

Paul smiled grimly and sat down beside the widower before he said: "Thank you Mr Pendray, and I am most sorry for the loss you have suffered. A good mother and ... and wife. I can imagine the sorrow you and the children feel."

"Thank 'e sir," said Bertram who, genuinely touched, had need of his handkerchief, a rather grubby looking specimen, which he blew his nose into and dashed across his eyes hurriedly before returning it to his pocket.

"How do you go on without her, to see to you and the children? It must be very difficult for you," asked Paul and after a slight pause he added: "Bertram."

"Well sir," replied Bertram slowly, "my sister 'ave 'ad the misfortune to lose 'er 'usband in the Wheal Mary roof fall a couple of month's back, so she lost her cottage on account of it belonging to the mine so she and 'er children 'ave moved in with me. We're fair crammed but it 'edden too bad and she's a good cook and careful with the money, so I'm doing all right there sir," and he shot a look at Paul's sad face; and as much as he grieved for his wife did he understand the look of utter devastation of his companion.

There was another long silence, which was broken by Bertram.

"My 'Arry come 'ome from school in tears, yes'day, sir," he said and added: "all 'cos of your maid, Daisy."

"Not fighting again I hope, Bertram?" asked Paul with a long sigh.

"Not this time, sir, no," he replied, "See my 'Arry do miss 'is mother something fierce and so he was a'sheddin' a few tears when your maid saw 'en. She come right over and put 'er arms roun' 'en, so my Dick said, and told 'en not to be sad because she would start to cry too on account of 'er 'Annah and Ben and the babies and she give 'en 'er own kerchief to wipe his face with. He told my sister over tea that 'e thought that was some lovely thing fer she to do." He shot another look at Paul's face and caught him wiping a tear from his eye, so he coughed discreetly before adding: "and so do I, Mr Trevarthen."

Again there was silence, broken only when both men sniffed loudly.

"Thank you, Bertram, for telling me that. Every crumb of comfort helps to lift the burden of sadness does it not?"

"I d' believe so sir, I d' believe so," and then after some quiet reflection he eased himself down from the wall and said: "Best we make our way 'ome sir, back to the livin' an' leave our loved ones to res' in peace."

"Yes," sniffed Paul resolutely and coughed before saying: "You are quite right. We have to move on."

They turned and walked together until the path forked and, after a moment's hesitation, they stopped and faced each other, shaking hands warmly before going their separate ways; Paul Trevarthen to an emptier house than he could ever have imagined and Bertram Pendray to a fuller one than he could ever have wished.

During the school day, only one child now occupied the nursery and Miss Clavering and the child's mother took turns to look after him. Both women were trying not to be overprotective of the little five year old, but he was a determined enough individual to bulk their attempts to mollycoddle him. Consequently Miss Clavering, who had busied herself with replacing George's soldiers in his fort, was distraught upon discovering that little Jack was no longer playing happily with his bricks on the mat and had completely disappeared from her view and, in all probability, from the nursery as well.

"Master Jack," she called worriedly, "Stop fooling Nurse. Come now, Master Jack," and then hearing no reply she cried aloud as a rising panic began to grip her: "Master Jack!"

Chloe heard the raised voice and hurriedly shut the door of the linen press, the contents of which she had decided to check for something to do to occupy her mind, and picking up the skirt of her dress, rushed towards the nursery.

Miss Clavering, now in floods of tears, managed to blurt out that Jack had disappeared and both women searched the nursery high and low, but with no success. Chloe sharply ordered Miss Clavering to stop crying at once.

"He cannot have gone far. Go down and get Lizzie and Davy to come up and help us search for him and any other servant that you set eyes on. He must be in the house somewhere," she ordered.

Miss Clavering rushed down the stairs, heading for the kitchen, as fast as her jelly-like legs would allow. In the hallway she met her master returning from the churchyard. Resuming her sobbing she managed to say that Paul's precious little boy had gone missing and that she and the mistress could not find him. Paul rushed up the stairs to the nursery and found Chloe, with the upper half of her body leaning out of the window, apparently talking to someone in the garden.

"Chloe!" he said in a raised voice, but noticed that she was waving her hand in a gesture to tell him to be quiet. On reaching her side he discovered that she was not, as he had thought, conversing with one of the workmen outside, but was talking quietly to the sought-for child himself. Master Jack had taken it upon himself to climb through the open window and out along the branch of the sycamore, whose thin branches brushed against the wall of that side of the house. Paul's heart almost stopped with fear; Jack had crawled halfway along the branch but he did not appear to wish either to go forward or to go back. Instead he gripped the branch tightly, but with a determined look on his face. Whether of fear or of bravado, it was difficult to tell.

Paul, his heart thumping in his chest, assessed the situation as quickly as he possibly could. The branch supporting Jack's weight would in no way offer the same support to Paul's giant frame. The tallest man in the locality could not make any attempt to rescue his son by climbing out on to the branch. His son could not be encouraged to climb back into the house, along the branch, because he could not turn around. Jack would not or could not go forward, seemingly fixed, as if by glue, to his little area of the sycamore tree. Telling Chloe in a harsh whisper to keep Jack talking and not to let him get distressed, he rushed from the room, almost knocking Davy down in his hurry to get downstairs.

"Davy! Thank God! Go down to the yard and get hold of a couple of the men. Bring me the long ladder from the bottom stable and take it around to the old sycamore tree by the nursery window," he ordered brusquely.

"Can't do that, sir. Daniel got'n over to the lower farm fer cuttin' off they old bough's off the . . . ," but Paul interrupted him rudely, and shouted: "Well get the short one from the tack room and get someone to help you bring it up here!"

"Up 'ere, sir? But 'ow do 'e . . . . ?"

"Just do it Davy and be quick about it!" he shouted in exasperation.

"Yessir!" responded Davy swiftly and turned and ran off to complete his task.

Within a very short space of time, Davy, panting heavily, and with the new stable lad bringing up the rear, brought the short ladder into the nursery. With Paul's assistance they passed it out through the window, anchoring one end in the tree and the other on the ledge of the nursery window.

"Will it take my weight, Davy?" Paul asked anxiously, hastily discarding his coat.

"Yessir. 'Tis a good strong 'en that ladder sir," and he launched into a long speech, which no one bothered to listen to, on the subject of ladders and the merits of the one his master was about to climb out on in particular.

Paul took a deep breath and, on his hands and knees, began to edge himself slowly along the bridge that had been constructed beside his son's precarious perch. It took time and nerve, and it was a long way to the ground. Smaller branches brushed against his face and scratched at it as if attempting to pull him from the ladder, but gradually Paul drew along side Jack, reached out and, catching hold of him by his shirt and breeches, gently encouraged him to let go of his hold on the branch.

"I'm 'fraid, Dada," said little Jack, his bottom lip wobbling.

"No need to be afraid, Jack," said Paul in what he hoped was a confident tone, "I've got you. You won't fall, so let go of the branch and I will lift you onto the ladder and help you back to the nursery. Come now, do as Dada says."

Slowly Jack's grip relaxed and he allowed himself, with only the smallest of whimpers, to be plucked from the bough and found himself on the ladder with his father.

With one arm firmly holding his son to him and the other gripping on to the ladder, Paul tortuously negotiated the route back along the ladder until he was able to pass Jack to Chloe's outstretched arms.

When he had got himself back into the nursery he found that he was shaking and had to make a great effort to control himself. He helped Davy - still singing the praises of not only the ladder but now Paul as well - pull the ladder back into the nursery, where the two servants lifted it onto their shoulders and returned it from whence it came.

Wiping his sweating face with his handkerchief, Paul gulped down several deep breaths before turning to his son, now struggling to free himself of his tearful mother's enfolding arms. He got down on his knees, caught hold of Jack's arm and pulled him around to look at him. A petulant looking face, with angry brown eyes, stared back at him.

"Why did you do such a silly thing, Jack? You could have fallen and hurt yourself badly," Paul told him, giving him a little shake, (and trying to keep the anger out of his voice, which the fright of seeing his son in such a dangerous location had given him).

"I was lonely," whined Jack. "There's no one to play with anymore and Nurse said -" and here he looked at Miss Clavering for confirmation before he turned back to his father, "- that Ben, Charlie and the baby were in the churchyard so I was going to climb down the tree and go play with them."

The effect of this speech on the grown ups in the room was frightening for such a small boy. Miss Clavering began to wail loudly, his mother gave a little scream and stuffed her handkerchief into her mouth to stop herself from crying out again and his father drew in his breath sharply as if he had been kicked by a horse, and cried, "Oh my God! No! No!"

Jack watched in horror as his father's eyes filled with tears and then suddenly found himself pulled roughly into Paul's arms, hearing his father's voice in his ear saying brokenly:

"They are in the churchyard Jack but you ... you can't go and play with them because ... because they are all asleep and they cannot be woken," he whispered hoarsely and made a sound like a sob.

"Why? Why can't I wake them up?" moaned Jack, "I'm lonely. I don't like playing by myself."

"I'm sorry Jack, I'm sorry but it cannot be. Believe me, Dada would give anything to make things different and to have them back here with us again but I ... I can't. We are all lonely now," and he gave a great sigh. Paul used his sleeve to wipe his eyes and as they focused on the discarded bricks he took a deep breath and said resolutely: "Shall Dada help you to build a house with those bricks on the mat."

"Oh, Yes please, Dada," the now smiling child cried with excitement, "a great big one with windows, lots of windows and a bridge and a . . . ." and pulling himself from Paul's embrace he waved his arms to help explain the plan of the structure that he wished to see built.

Chloe removed the handkerchief from her mouth and motioned Miss Clavering to dry her eyes and to close the open window. Then she smiled bravely at her husband and son, now employed in setting the bricks out in a grand design, and left the room. She walked quickly down the stairs and headed for the back parlour, which was bathed in light as usual, and settled herself down in Redvers' old chair by the fire. Then, and only then, she dropped her head in her hands and sobbed and sobbed.

A month later, Paul was about to enter Samuel's bookshop when he noticed Bertram Pendray and his eldest son staring into the window at some of the books displayed there.

"Hello Bertram. Hello Harry. Nice to see you both again," he said.

"Mornin' sir," said the fisherman and his son acknowledged him before asking if he was going to go into the shop.

"Why yes I am," answered Paul, "are you?"

"I just wanted to know if they have any books on ships and sailing. Or even a book about Admiral Nelson," said Harry enthusiastically, "but ... but we ... we can't ..." and he stopped and looked apologetically at his father.

"Money's too tight fer things like books 'Arry. Clothes and food are more important," his father told him roughly and muttered that they had best be getting along.

Paul, thinking quickly, asked if Harry would like to go into the bookshop with him as he had to look for some books he wanted himself.

Harry's face lit up immediately and Paul stopped the boy's father before he could refuse by saying: "If you've got some business to see to Bertram, Harry can stay with me, and you can pick him up when you've finished. I'll keep an eye out for you."

Bertram looked worried, but realised that Mr Trevarthen had offered out of kindness and so he pulled his forelock and said he would be back before the hour was up.

Once in the bookshop, young Harry could hardly contain himself, such was his excitement. After making enquiries of Mr Samuel, Paul discovered the location of the books that interested his young charge, and led him to the relevant shelves.

"Oh my gar!" Harry breathed rapturously, "Jes' look at 'em all, Mr Trevarthen sir, jes' look."

"My gosh, yes Harry. There are lots of books here and no mistake," he smiled fondly, appreciating as only a fellow bibliophile could, Harry's delight at the sight of the rows of entrancing books set out before the young boy.

"I'll leave you to look through them as I have to look for some books over here," and as he turned away he added: "but mind now; you are to let me know if you find something interesting."

"Oh yes sir, I will, I will," said Harry excitedly and began at once to browse along the titles.

When Pendray returned he found Mr Trevarthen and Harry just about to leave the shop. Paul had several books in the crook of his arm but his son was empty handed.

"Hello, Bertram," said Paul, "I hope we haven't kept you waiting?"

"No sir, jes' got 'ere meself. Well 'Arry bes' be goin' on. Mr Trevarthen's a busy man. Say yer thanks and we'll be on our way," ordered his father.

Mr Trevarthen interrupted him to say that as he was going home in his curricle he could quite easily give them a lift.

"It will be a bit of a squeeze but I think we can all manage," he told them with a smile.

Bertram tried to decline, but Paul would not take no for an answer and to be honest the fisherman was glad not to have to walk all the way home. His son was even more pleased. Perched up in Mr Trevarthen's curricle would be a rare treat indeed. On the way, Paul asked if Bertram would object to Harry reading a book for him.

"I am so busy with the one's I need for a book I'm writing I just haven't got the time to read it at the moment, and it is such an interesting subject. Harry noticed it and pointed it out to me. It looks most fascinating." he informed him and smiled over the top of Harry's head into Bertram's eyes.

"I don' knaw 'bout that sir. He might damage it, sir. Ours is a small house, not much room," but he found it impossible to refuse either Paul's smile or his son's pleading look.

"Harry will look after it, never fear, Bertram," Paul informed him.

"What sort a book is it, sir?" asked Bertram after a while.

"Um - it's about boats," said Paul lamely, but was interrupted by Harry, who told him that it was not about boats at all but ships, explaining, with great excitement, about the different types described in the book.

"Thinkin' a buying yerself a ship are 'e sir?" enquired Harry's father and looked at Paul with a mischievous grin.

He was answered by Paul's hearty chuckle and they continued on their way with wide smiles across their faces. When Paul stopped the curricle to let them down outside their little cottage, Bertram reached up to shake Paul's hand and looked into his face. Harry, his eyes shining, was clasping a large, leather bound book to his chest.

"Thankee sir. Kind thought, a kind thought indeed. We'll be careful with 'en, don' worry 'bout that sir," he said earnestly.

"My pleasure Bertram, I'm pleased to know a fellow book lover. Take your time over that book Harry. I shan't want to look at it for a long while yet," and the two fathers shook hands before Paul turned his curricle and headed back along the road that led to Trevu.

That night, in their bed, Paul held his wife in his arms and told her the tale of his meeting with the Pendray's outside of the bookshop.

"That poor little chap loves books," he said, "but what chance has he to look at any but the ones we have at school? I felt much sympathy for him, 'tis such a shame."

"I know dearest," she answered quietly, "but we have only a limited amount in the school and 'twould not be possible to provide so many topics for all their differing interests. We have not the room."

"That is undeniably the truth," he replied with a sigh.

"Unless we set up a library of course," she announced thoughtfully.

Paul started as if he had been stung.

"Chloe! That is the most brilliant idea," he shouted, and began to elaborate on the details. Chloe listened as he talked, a small smile quivering on her lips. Slowly, the sadness of their loss would ease, she knew, but hopefully getting Paul to interest himself in setting up a library would help to take his mind off his sorrow.

After a while she became aware that he had lapsed into silence.

"Paul?" she asked softly.

"Yes, my dearest?"

"I thought you had fallen asleep, as you had stopped talking," she told him quietly.

"Not quite," he whispered, and kissed her lips and then began pulling gently at the ribbons of her nightgown, before he asked her tentatively: "Would you like ... ? It ... it has not been because I ... I no longer loved you. I have been so distraught that ... Do you wish ... ?" but his questions and explanations were destined to remain unfinished as Chloe gently pulled him towards her.

"Silly boy," she breathed and he gave a loud sigh and then silenced her with another kiss.

CHAPTER 3

MR SAMUEL provided a list of subjects and books suitable for starting a library for Mr Trevarthen as he had requested. Mr Armitage, the headmaster of his old school, also sent him a list based on the school library and, with Paul's own extensive knowledge, the beginnings of the library were established. Squire Tregurthen had told him about a suitable property in Penzance that was coming up for sale and after a visit to his lawyer an offer was made on his behalf for the house. The owners, surprised and delighted by the amount that had been offered, accepted with alacrity. Chloe watched contentedly to see her husband fired with enthusiasm for the project and, although there were still days when Paul woke to a black despair, he was managing to control his depression and she found the strength to keep up his spirits, acknowledging that the effort needed to do so acted as a balm for her own sadness.

Paul set the masons and carpenters to work as soon as the property became available. Every room had row upon row of shelves lining the walls. Down the middle of the rooms, depending upon their size, lines of free-standing bookcases were set up to take even more books, and there were tables and benches set out at one end to be used for those wishing to study the books on the actual premises. However, in the midst of ordering and setting the workmen, carpenters and masons about their business and wrestling with sheaves of papers detailing lists of books, Paul still made time each day to play with Jack in the nursery and they grew closer together because of it. It was Paul, and not his wife or Miss Clavering, who discovered that Jack possessed a talent for drawing. At first the little boy produced only crude images, but soon Paul became aware that he had a good eye and could reproduce recognisable portraits of the things he saw around him. His father encouraged him and asked Jack if he would make him a new picture every day. So Jack proudly showed Paul his work daily; they sat on the floor together with his son's little body leaning contentedly against his father's large frame and explaining, with expressive gesticulations, the picture before them. Paul's eyes glowed with love and admiration for his little son and Jack gazed adoringly at his father in return.

When Chloe began to eat her dry toast one morning, Paul could not stop his tears from filling his eyes, such was the mixture of emotions that he felt at the prospect of new life coming into his home after the loss of so many of his precious loved ones. His wife took him in her arms and cradled him gently as if he was the very babe that was even now growing in her body. After a while, he drew away and smiled sheepishly into her eyes. Her answering smile swelled his heart with love and his body with an intense calm.

"Oh my dearest, dearest love," he whispered.

Fondling his curls, she placed her forehead against his and sighed.

"A long, hard road, Paul, for both of us, but we have travelled this far and I think our past troubles have only strengthened the love we have for each other." she said quietly, and taking his face between her hands she kissed him gently, then she smiled and tweaked his nose and said, with a giggle, "My lovely, adorable silly boy."

He caught her hand and kissed her fingers, "Hussy!" he said, reverting to his private pet name for her, and lifted his head. She watched with a feeling of immense relief to see his mischievous smile back on his face after its long absence.

Aunt Caroline had accepted an invitation to stay and she arrived in Paul's carriage, which he had always taken the trouble to send to Truro for her to travel in. Paul dismissed the servant and helped her down from the carriage himself. Although she was ageing and moved more slowly than in the past, she still possessed no small measure of disdainful elegance. She smiled up at him, affectionately, for she had such a fondness for him and he was such a handsome man. They had battled long and hard when his stepmother, Penelope, had died when he was only sixteen and she had come to stay at Trevu with her three daughters, but they had become fast friends with the passage of time. Caroline was there when Daisy's mother, Dorothea, with her father Captain Petherick, the man who made his fortune sailing the seas with his cargo of poor black slaves, had attacked him at the ball at the Tregurthen's. She had helped him through that dreadful experience with more kindness and consideration than he would have believed she could have possessed. It was Caroline who had been responsible for bringing his real mother back into his life and, although he resented that action in the very beginning, he would be the first to acknowledge that by so doing she had set his feet upon the path that had led to his meeting with the young, shy girl who was to become his wife and his one true love. For that his gratitude knew no bounds.

"Paul, your new coachman is inclined to spring his horses," complained that strong willed woman loudly, well aware that the servant could hear, and announced in an even louder voice: "if he were my servant I should have him turned off."

"I'm sure you would Aunt," said her nephew placatingly, "but you know me well enough by now to know that I would never follow such an action."

"Humph!" she snorted derisively, watching as he smiled at the red faced man and thanked and dismissed him. Then, taking Paul's proffered arm she entered the dark hallway to his home and the house that she had grown up in. Chloe came towards her with her arms outstretched and kissed her fondly on her cheek.

"Aunt, how lovely to have you here with us again. It is such an age since you last came to stay. How are the girls and all your grandchildren?" she asked merrily.

"Well, they are all well, and Sofia is in an interesting way again," and she glanced questioningly at Chloe with one eyebrow raised, "and methinks she is not the only one to be so blessed."

Chloe laughed, the colour rising in her cheeks, and Caroline glanced at Paul and saw him grin broadly.

She patted Chloe's hand, "Best thing that could happen, my dear," she said softly, "for both of you."

The sound of the children's laughter could be heard from the garden as Paul escorted his aunt into the withdrawing room, he seated her on the settle before telling her he would bring them in later for her to see.

"Good," she said, "but let me recover from the journey first for heaven's sake, I beg of you." And then, to ensure that he would not forget, said, with a sharp tone to her voice: "Perhaps you will be good enough to have a word with your coachman, Paul, before he takes me home?"

"Yes Aunt," said Paul obediently, "Shall I go and reprimand him at once or may I take tea with you first?"

He smiled mischievously at her and she struggled to keep an answering grin from breaking out on her lips.

"Probably it will be for the best if you have something to eat first, Paul. 'twould not be right if you should not have the strength to perform your duty," and she flashed him her own look of pure mischief, rarely seen by any other than her adored nephew.

"You are right as usual, dear Aunt, and I assure you that I will have words with William, the coachman, and ensure that your return journey is memorable only for its comfort and not for the pace at which you travel," and he executed a deep bow, gracefully.

"I had frequently the need to tell you what a rogue and a devil you were, Paul, in your youth," she said, "your poor wife has much to bear from you, I can well imagine."

"Yes Aunt," replied Chloe, sitting down beside her and entering into the spirit of the game, "he is a sad trial to me. I thought maturity would come with age but sadly I have seen very little sign of it."

"Fiddlesticks," returned Paul, swiftly, and then assuming an almost saintly manner he remarked: "I believe myself to be most mature and not given to childish and frivolous behaviour," and added prudently: "any more."

At that moment there was a knock on the door and Lizzie came in, bearing the tea tray with a small plate of cakes on it. Putting it down on the small table, she began to pour the tea.

Clearing her throat, Lizzie mentioned that she had to apologise on their cook's behalf that there were so few cakes for their enjoyment. With her eyes firmly fixed on the master she said: "Mrs Gurney is at a loss to explain zactly where the first batch she cooked disappeared to, but she can recall that Mr Trevarthen 'ad called in to the kitchen to ask 'er 'ow the new stove was workin'. Twouldn' 'til after 'e left she noticed the one's she 'ad coolin' wouldn' there no more."

Paul attempted to look innocent, but the three women were not fooled, so he blithely said: "Well I did share some of them with the children."

"Not many found their way to the poor dears, I'll warrant," retorted his aunt sharply and, although Lizzie stifled a giggle, Chloe allowed herself to laugh aloud.

The following day, Paul accompanied his aunt to Inez Carter's for a social call. Mrs Carter, as mentally alert as ever, was almost bedridden and had not left her home for two years. However, she still reigned supreme as the doyenne of Penzance society and that tight little circle took their lead from her in all things. Even the Squire's wife deferred to her. She greeted Caroline and Paul with delight. Caroline had been the sister of the young man she had promised to marry, Jack, who had gambled away a small fortune and had finally killed himself. Inez Carter's strength of character had allowed herself to go forward from that disaster and, after a suitable period of mourning, she had married a local landowner of great moral rectitude. Seizing every opportunity that presented itself, she had made sure that their daughters married only the most suitable of husbands. She had always acknowledged that it was to Caroline's credit that she had turned Paul from almost a social outcast - purely because of his birth and colour - to a young man of considerable charm and the most desired bachelor in the neighbourhood. Mrs Carter smiled fondly at Paul as she had done from the moment he had entered Penzance society as a shy, gauche young boy. She had conveniently forgotten that when he was a young child, protected and sheltered by Penelope and Redvers as he had been, she had been in the forefront of those ladies who had passed many hours at social gatherings, deriding the fact that Redvers' by-blow should ever have been accepted into his home. A coloured child, taken to its heart by the great Trevarthen family, had sent ripples of shock around the surrounding area. Bosoms had swelled with indignation and tongues had wagged unmercifully. In those days, Paul had been made aware that he was not thought the right sort of person for these families to mix with. Then his stepmother, Penelope, had died. Those same malicious crones found their collective conscience had been smitten with guilt at her death and, somewhat surprisingly, with greed. They felt guilt because they had treated Penelope, Redvers and Paul with such disdain and greed on realising that the father was a very wealthy man and his son would inherit everything. That gave Paul the highest of positions in society and his lack of a white skin had become an irrelevance. Along with others, she had thrown her daughter at him, but to no avail. Paul's heart could not be won as easily as that. The hearts of the ladies - young and old - that came into contact with him were not so reserved, but it took the quiet, shy, clever and extremely strong Chloe to win Paul as her trophy.

Still smiling at him, Mrs Carter felt her own heart beat faster; he had been and still was so very, very handsome.

"Dear Paul, what is this that I am hearing of you?" she asked teasingly. Paul returned a slightly apprehensive smile. One never knew with the redoubtable Mrs Carter exactly what subject she would be bringing into the conversation.

"Best to enlighten us, dear lady, for I do declare we are all in a twitter of anticipation," giggled her other guest, the young Mrs Hudson, who raised her smiling eyes at Paul speculatively.

"The Squire's wife has informed me that Mr Trevarthen has taken it upon himself to found a library, dear Mrs Hudson, for the good people of Penzance. I must say I am most impressed with your thoughtful action, Paul. Such a literary luminary as yourself would be by far the best person to open such an establishment. Your knowledge will be invaluable in setting up this concern. However," and fixing him with an uncompromising stare she continued firmly: "I would hope that you propose to have, on your shelves, books that will improve the lower classes, educationally and, if I make so bold, morally."

"Of course, dear Mrs Carter, I shall be most careful with my choice of books. I had thought, if it would not be too tiring for you, if you could give some of your precious time to perusing some of the religious works for me. Your understanding of such matters would, I am most certain, far surpass my own humble knowledge. I could never hope to reach the heights of morality that you have so studiously observed throughout your admirable lifetime," replied Paul, with one of his sweetest smiles.

Inez Carter, completely unaware that any sarcasm was intended, was thrilled to be so particularly thought of by such a well-educated young man. Life had become difficult of late, with the encroachment of all her infirmities, but to be so highly regarded gave her an immense sense of pride. She tapped the back of Paul's hand with her closed fan and smiled at him indulgently.

Caroline heard a simpering giggle from the young lady at her side and turned her head to observe her. Not the finest complexion, she noted, but a pretty enough woman. Auburn ringlets, under a chip bonnet, surrounded an oval face, a turned up nose, bold blue eyes and a rather thin lipped mouth. She had been introduced as the wife of the new Preventative Officer who had been recently stationed in Penzance from Yorkshire. Since being presented to Paul she had hardly taken her eyes off him, answering the few polite remarks that he had made to her in a breathless voice and always accompanied with her nervous giggle. Caroline and Mrs Carter exchanged understanding smiles. Paul's appearance had a similar effect on most impressionable young women. She felt a twinge of sympathy for the silly girl and attempted to ask her about her husband's occupation.

"Oh! Please don't ask anything of me. For sure I have no idea exactly what he does and he has given up trying to explain to me. I know he is here to try and catch the wreckers and smugglers. The smuggling trade has lessened somewhat since the blockades with France have ended, he says, and they are turning to wrecking to bolster their nefarious incomes. Apparently, there are whole gangs of men from Breage and Germoe who make their living from this dreadful trade and the miners of Camborne have no compunction in doing to death any poor seaman who tries to protect his cargo. It is unbelievable; but he told me that a boat was wrecked on the Godrevy rocks, and one poor seaman, managing to save his life by getting himself ashore, was threatened by a rough fellow with strangulation if he did not cease his attempts at halting them from plundering his boat. Only fancy! Their womenfolk act in the same manner and use their garments to secrete the smaller items of plunder about their person." Then she turned to address Paul directly: "Gerald, Mr Hudson my husband, says that I am not to worry about him, but at his last posting in Yorkshire life was so much more pleasant and I never had to fear that he would ever come into contact with such rough people. They do not trouble to kill the preventatives if at all possible, you know. Is that not most dreadful, Mr Trevarthen?"

"Indeed, Mrs Hudson, most dreadful," replied Paul, but did not offer any further comments upon her story.

This did not deter Mrs Hudson, who, having found her voice, decided to regale the company with various anecdotes about her previous existence in Yorkshire and how she had wept for almost a week when she found that they had to leave their home and friends to come to such an inhospitable part of the country.

"We are not all inhospitable, Mrs Hudson, I can assure you," said Mrs Carter somewhat coldly, "although I can well imagine that your poor husband will be kept most busy in these parts. The lower orders have always had a rather ambivalent attitude to law and order. Myself, I never employ servants unless I have knowledge of their antecedents."

"I wish that I had had your information, dear Mrs Carter. Gerald was most discomforted when he discovered that I had inadvertently taken on a relative of that dreadful smuggler, Joseph Bolitho, as my maidservant. 'La, ma'am,' he told me, 'why not send a notice to the gazette of all my movements!' Well, you can imagine how devastated I was. I cried and cried and only stopped when Gerald promised to buy me my new bonnet," she simpered and turned to Paul again: "Do you think it becomes me, Mr Trevarthen?" she asked, directing a limpid gaze at him.

"I am sure that you look becoming in all your bonnets, Mrs Hudson," he replied, with his charming smile.

"Oh!" breathed Mrs Hudson, "what a delightful turn of phrase you have Mr Trevarthen. Quite a man for the ladies I've no doubt," and she tittered nervously.

"Mr Trevarthen is a happily married man, Mrs Hudson," said Mrs Carter, rather severely and discomforted that young lady with a very prim and direct stare.

"I ... I ... What I mean to say is ... The lesser sex so enjoy to be praised and charmed and ... and Mr Trevarthen is ... is so charming," she ended lamely.

There was moment's awkward silence, then Paul gracefully asked after Mrs Carter's grandchildren, a favourite subject of that doting grandmother, and in no time at all the company found out all they wished to know of all the assorted progeny that her daughters had produced between them.

"Your eldest, Paul, must soon be ready to continue his education at your old school, I presume." intoned Mrs Carter, in a matronly manner, "I'm sure, like his father, he will be a credit to that famous establishment."

Paul tried hard to cover his astonishment. In truth he had not considered sending George to Helston. The thought of it appalled him; not only because his house felt so empty now, with three of his children taken from the family so suddenly, but because his own schooldays had been so abysmal.

"Your pardon, Mrs Carter, but I have not given any thought to sending George away at this present time," he replied after a slight pause.

"Of course, Paul, of course," and she leaned over and patted his hand sympathetically, "It has been such a terrible time for you both. The sad loss of so many of your dear ones, and all taken from you so suddenly. Another year spent at our school will do George no harm, and I am sure that you are quite capable of adding to his education yourself, with additional lessons, if you see the need of it." She smiled upon him in a doting way and continued to pat his hand.

On their return to Trevu, Caroline brought up the subject of George's education again. They were all seated in the withdrawing room and Chloe looked up from her sewing when Caroline told her that Mrs Carter had wondered, not if George was to go to his father's old school, but when.

Chloe glanced quickly at Paul and watched him shake his head resolutely. She was going to announce her agreement with her husband, but Caroline forestalled her.

"It is no good to shake your head, Paul. George cannot remain at your school for ever. Admirable though the education provided there is, you are well aware that the standard could never hope to compete with the one he would receive at Helston. Apart from that reason he would meet the sons of the finest families in the county. He needs to be provided with an education which is superior to that which he receives here, both academically and socially." she announced authoritatively.

"I do not dispute that fact, Aunt, but I do not wish for him to leave our home. I can well remember the loneliness I endured during my own school days. I would not willingly inflict that on any son of mine," he replied in a resolute voice.

"An absurd reason for keeping him from having a chance to improve himself, nephew," said Caroline, severely, "for if you keep him here with you, you will deny him much. And don't look at me with your father's arrogant stare!" she snapped, "I am telling you this for your son's good. Resign yourself to the fact that he has to be sent away to school. You do him no favours by not allowing him to begin to accept responsibility for his own life. George needs to be hardened to the life he will have to face. Have you forgotten the struggles you had to endure to establish yourself in even this small locality? A fine thing 'twould be if poor George had not been given the backbone to stand tall in his own right."

"To be sure, Aunt, I am well aware of my struggles to establish myself, as you so quaintly put it. But I say again that I do not wish for George to leave my home, or his family, and go to that place to suffer even a small percentage of the hell that I experienced in the name of education," he told her sharply, an angry scowl settling across his face. Any other member of his family, with the exception of his wife, would have taken note of the expression on his face and the angry note in his voice, and turned from the subject under discussion to other less painful themes. Caroline was made of a stronger heart than that.

"Do not use that tone of voice with me Paul. I am in the right of it and well you know it. There is no man, I will acknowledge, who loves his children as you do, but George will not remain a child forever. As he grows to manhood he has to be prepared for his future and to do that you have send him away so that he may develop into a man capable of ..." but she got no further for Paul had heard enough.

He jumped to his feet, and informed her angrily: "That is enough, Aunt! I will listen to no more on this matter. Allow me to make my apologies but I have work to do." He bowed stiffly to his aunt and stamped from the room, slamming the door behind him, a sure sign to all who knew him how annoyed he was.

"Humph!" said Caroline, nettled by her nephew's behaviour, "Chloe, you will have to do something to curb that temper of his."

"I will be led by my husband with regard to George's education, Aunt Caroline. Paul hated his schooldays. I will not question his judgement in this matter and I would most sincerely advise you to follow the same course. We have had to live through much sadness, Aunt, so I would ask you not to harangue Paul over George's future, and," she raised her chin at Caroline and fixed her with a bold stare: "I will not have you mention to George, either, about leaving his family to go away to school. Have we an understanding, Aunt?"

"As you wish," she sighed, "Never let it be said that I should interfere in the way you wish to conduct the running of your family. There will be nothing more said from me on the subject, I can assure you." She sniffed haughtily and resumed her sewing but pricked her finger almost immediately, a sure sign that her equanimity was ruffled, for she was renowned for setting her stitches most precisely.

At dinner, conversation was minimal and, although Paul and his aunt were speaking to each other, there was a coldness in the air. Instead of joining his aunt and his wife in the back parlour as he would normally have done after dinner, he retired to his room and continued his work on his latest book.

Gradually, the week progressed and, in the face of Caroline's reticence to talk upon any subject that referred in any way to education or to George's future, her nephew began to unbend towards her. At first they were most courtly to one another because of the genuine fondness they shared. Chloe acted as a bridge between their wounded pride and helped in every way possible to smooth over their recent altercation. By the time Caroline's stay had come to an end all was forgiven, if not forgotten and she left Trevu safe in the knowledge that the coachman had received his instructions, for she had heard them given, on the sedate manner in which the journey was to be conducted.

Placing the subject of sending his son to Helston to the back of his mind, Paul continued with his life as before. George it was who was to surprise them all a few weeks later, when his own wishes for his future became known.

CHAPTER 4

BERTRAM Pendray called at Trevu to enquire of Mr Trevarthen if Harry could keep his book for a while longer, as he was attempting to do some drawings of the ships depicted therein and it was taking him rather longer than he had anticipated. Paul, ushering him to a seat in his office, informed him that he had no objection and Harry could keep the book in his possession for as long as required.

"Has he an interest in ships or does he wish to be an artist?" asked Paul, his curiosity aroused.

"Oh, 'e like ships, well enough, sir," replied Bertram, "but 'e 'as always been interested in 'ow they're built. Sits fer 'ours up on the 'eadland watching them go by an' when any of 'em dock in Penzance if 'e can get to see them 'e will."

"Perhaps he will go into the shipbuilding business when he is older. There are numerous boatyards in this county, you could apprentice him to one of them and ..." began Paul, but Bertram's ironic smile stopped his speech.

"No offence, Mr Trevarthen, but when the time comes, an' it wen't be long now, 'e'll come with me on the boat. His education wen't be wasted with all the reckonin' of the catch an' the prices an' he do read beautifully. That will stand 'im in good stead in 'is life. I've no complaints. Best thing your missus could 'ave done fer the children roun' 'ere, starting that school," he said genuinely.

"But surely, Bertram, you would be denying him the chance of great achievements in later life. I have often talked with him and he has many admirable qualities to my mind. 'Twould be such a shame for them not to be used," Paul advised.

Bertram twisted his cap in his gnarled hands and studied Paul's concerned expression.

"Was' your boy goin do, your George? Goin' come home to 'elp 'e run this place, 'idden 'e?" Bertram told him quietly, "I aren't doin' no different with mine, sir, if e' think 'bout it."

Paul opened his mouth to speak, but Bertram was in the right of it, he had to acknowledge. He had merely assumed that at the end of George's time at school he would return to live the life of a rich farmer's son and settle down to life on the farm. The two fathers eyed each other reflectively for a while. Paul shifted his long legs before him and tapped his fingers on the table, looking as if he was giving some deep thought to something that was troubling him.

"Bertram, would you send Harry to me one day after school? I would like to talk to him myself," but he added hastily: "if you would have no objection, of course."

"I'll send 'im up sir, but don't go filling 'is 'ead with dreams. Money pays fer needs, sir, people like we 'ave to leave our dreams be, sir. Now if I was you an' you were me things 'twould be different. I'd 'a sent my 'Arry, Dick as well fer that matter, to that fine school old Cap'n Redvers sent you to. Tha's what e' do if e' can, sir, if you got the wherewithal to do it. But I got to feed all we, my sister's four, as well as my two. Leave 'n be sir. 'Arry knows the way it is, 'e wen't argue with me when the time comes. You bin' a good master roun' 'ere Mr Trevarthen, none of your people ever bin' thrown out of their 'ouses or their jobs either, but if you'd open your eyes a bit you'd see that 'tis a bit different fer mos' folks," Bertram told him solemnly.

"If ... if I offered," Paul began hesitantly, "offered to help you to apprentice Harry or to help in some other ...," but before he could continue further Bertram raised his hand to stop him.

"Appreciate your kind offer Mr Trevarthen, but twouldn' do no good. I couldn' accept it. I've always paid me way, an' what we couldn' afford we didden 'ave see," he stated proudly.

"But you should think of Harry, Bertram. If he is as talented as I believe him to be, he should be encouraged to ..." began Paul, but again Bertram interrupted him.

"Listen, Mr Trevarthen; 'Arry 'idden your boy, he's mine. All your goings on with ... with my Molly was well afore 'e come along, I d' knaw it an' you d' knaw it, but if you was to give we money wha'd 'e think people's goin' say? Redvers' boy got another bastard in the parish, tha's what!" Then as if struck by his boldness he blushed fiercely and, lowering his head, apologised profusely for his thoughtless words. This time it was Paul who interrupted his speech.

"I have much to apologise for Bertram, you do not have to tell me that," he interpolated, then took a deep breath before continuing: "I have caused great distress between a man and his wife. 'Tis too late to ask Molly for her forgiveness, alas, but allow me to beg your forgiveness, Bertram, for the crime I committed against you and your family. I had no idea of the pain I was causing to so many people, or even did I care back then if pain was a result of my actions, even though dear Father and Hannah, bless her, spent many hours trying to get me to mend my ways. My selfishness has caused great heartache to more families than yours, I know, and I have to live with the guilt of my sins. In spite of that I would most sincerely implore you to heed what I am telling you. People may talk but I have had people talk about me all my life. They know by Harry's colour that he is not one of mine. Look upon any monetary gift that you receive as my way of making amends if you will, but don't deny the boy a chance of a good future."

Bertram sighed and shook his head. He had been much moved by Paul's speech and sincerely believed his apology, but his pride was greater than Mr Trevarthen's would ever be, and he could not bring himself to accept his offer.

"Well, 'twouldn' easy fer 'e to come out with a confession like you jes' did. I could tell that by the look on yer face. Thank 'ee Mr Trevarthen. A great man to apologise like that an' I d' sincerely believe 'e but I can't accept any money; to salve yer conscience or to make somethin' of my boy. A man got 'is pride, Mr Trevarthen, and in the past what 'e did, comin' 'tween me and Molly like you did, was a sore trial fer both of us, but as far as I's concerned tha's all long gone," announced Bertram, in a quiet, considered tone.

Paul sighed, but he understood the truth of what Bertram had said. It was easy for him with all his money and position. He did not have to go home to a small, overflowing cottage, in a tight little community and face the sniggers of his friends and neighbours. His perception of scandal and malicious gossip was different from Bertram's. He could hold up his head and look disdainfully at anyone who had the temerity even to look at him in admonishment; wealth and position were his cushion. Bertram's neighbours would not be so obliging. They could and would make his life hell if they so desired and he had no doubt that the children would be ragged unmercifully by their contemporaries. Paul's fine words to his own children echoed in his head as he thought of how Harry and Dick would need to defend themselves against the cruelties of the other children in their village and, no doubt, at the school as well.

"Let Dick and Harry come home from school with George and the girls one afternoon, Bertram, your sister's children as well. They can all play together and then have their tea in the nursery. I'll see they are brought safe home. I'll show Harry my library and talk with him there, but I will defer to you and will not say anything to him or intrigue with him against your wishes. Will you agree to that?" he asked quietly.

His answer was a broad grin from Bertram, who enquired: "Got enough in the larder t' feed my lot 'ave 'e Mr Trevarthen? They d' take some feedin'," and he slapped his thigh and laughed heartily.

Paul grinned and promised that he would inform the cook that a plague of locusts seemed likely to descend upon them in the very near future. They got up and shook hands. As Bertram was about to leave, Paul had one more question for him, asking him abruptly if he would have any objection to calling him by his first name.

"Most of my acquaintances do you know, Bertram. I prefer it so," he said, searching Bertram's face anxiously for any sign of contempt.

"Well I reckon I be 'onoured to sir, um ... Paul, I mean, but I should do the same fer 'e. I d' answer to Bert normally, not Bertram. Tha's fer when I'm in me bes' clothes so to speak," and he laughed loudly. Paul joined in, seeing the humour in the situation at once, and then both men left the office and walked to the entrance door. They shook hands again, but this time their warm handshake was accompanied by broad grins.

When Paul informed Chloe that the children of the Pendray household would be coming to play with their own children one afternoon after school, she looked surprised and gazed at him steadily for a moment, but lowered her head and resumed her stitching, merely making the comment: "That will be pleasant for the children, Paul."

"Bert says I shall have to warn Cook because they have voracious appetites," he remarked and smiled at her, on his guard for her lifted eyebrow.

She did not oblige and so Paul allowed the subject to drop, chattering on for some minutes about the fact that it might be worth training the new stable lad up as a coachman, for he had a good eye for a horse and gentle hands.

Nothing more was said about the invitation until George came home from school with a message; if possible their little visitors would be coming to play on Thursday, immediately school ended. Chloe told him that it would be quite in order for them to come on that day and would George very kindly advise Cook for her, telling her exactly how many children to expect. Perhaps also he would be able to suggest some ideas of the food they would like prepared for them to eat on that day. George, all smiles, headed off towards the kitchen with Grace at his heels, loudly making known her preference for her favourite pudding in case he should forget to mention it to Cook. Daisy made no effort to go with them and was left alone in the room with Chloe. She regarded her stepmother with an impassive face until asked if anything was the matter.

"Why did Father want them to come for tea?" she asked abruptly, "Harry was telling me that he can't fathom it out at all and he said that his father had told them that they had all been invited. If Father wanted to see Harry, why did he invite Dick and the rest of them?"

"What makes you think he wants to see Harry?" asked Chloe, quietly.

"Because he is ... he is fond of Harry, and he always stops and speaks to him if he sees him when he is coming home from school. He lent Harry his book on ships, as well, and Father is very protective about his books, as you well know," she stated boldly.

"Perhaps they have a liking for the same books," said Chloe, cautiously.

"Harry likes to read about ships, and sailing, and talks about admirals like Nelson and Rodney. He can be quite boring if you don't stop him," she stated, and then said: "Father has got a host of books but George says he has none that are all about ships, unless they are Greek and Roman ones, and none at all about Nelson. George has a fondness for books as well so he should know because he often goes into Father's library to read there."

Attempting to change the subject, Chloe asked Daisy if she enjoyed to read books.

"Not particularly, Mama," she shrugged, but continued doggedly: "but Harry does. He will sit and read a book, lost to everybody around him, the same way Father does and if we start to chatter Dick tells us to be quiet because Harry is reading, just in the same way you tell us to stop making a noise if Father has got his head in a book. Myself, I think it strange they should be so similar, don't you agree?"

The impassive face continued to stare at her, so Chloe put down her sewing and looked directly into Daisy's eyes.

"Daisy, what precisely are you trying to tell me?" she asked calmly.

"Nothing," replied the young girl, attempting an innocent demeanour, but she looked a trifle discomforted under Chloe's direct stare.

"Harry is the son of Bertram and Molly Pendray, Daisy, and no other. Have I made that clear?" she said firmly.

"Yes, Mother," replied Daisy, but after some quiet reflection, continued carefully: "I only wondered because Joey Simmons said to Harry that Father had been with Molly Pendray when Harry's father was away on his fishing boat."

"I see," said Chloe, cautiously, "and what did Harry have to say about that?"

"He said he knew about it because Annie Kendal had told him the same thing."

"That was not a very nice thing for him to be told, I'm sure," said Chloe quietly, attempting not to look appalled by the revelations that Daisy was making.

"Oh he didn't mind, he said, because when he asked his Granny Pendray if it was true, she had told him that it was but that the others should not feel so proud, because Father had had Joey's mother and had Annie Kendal's eldest sister as well as certain other woman in Penzance!" Daisy announced triumphantly.

Chloe could not believe what she was hearing and from whom. She struggled to overcome a desire to rush across the room and slap the young girl across the face. She, who had never raised her hand to any child.

"That is not a very nice thing to say about your father, Daisy, and I hope never to hear you repeat it. Do you understand me?" she told her, trying desperately to keep her rising anger out of her voice.

"Yes, Mama," replied Daisy flatly, but continued: "I just thought you ought to know what people say about Father."

"I am well aware that people talk about your father in that way, but all this happened before we married. He does not act in such a foolish way now," she told Daisy with a degree of sharpness in her voice.

"He did with my mother," said Daisy sullenly.

Chloe drew in her breath sharply. "It has been explained to you before, Daisy, about your mother," she answered abruptly.

"Yes," and she sighed and kicked the floor with the toe of her shoe, keeping silent for a long time, but when she did speak she continued without hesitation: "I think you are the most wonderful mother, Mama, for you do not mind whatever Father has done in his life. I hope I can be as good a wife to my husband as you have been to Father when the time comes for me to marry."

For a moment Chloe was surprised into silence, but she got up, walked slowly towards Daisy and, putting her arms around her, hugged her gently.

Neither said anything, but Daisy allowed herself to be comforted. She knew far more than Chloe and Paul ever imagined that she could possibly have known, other schoolchildren had made sure of that, but her father's fondness for Harry had set up such a worry in her mind that for once she could not contain the hurt to herself. She did not want to cause her mother pain, but she had to know if Harry was a brother to her. It was important; she loved her brothers and sisters dearly but when she smiled at Harry it was because she liked him. To have him for a brother would not have made her happy; she was becoming enough of a young woman to understand that.

"Daisy. Dearest, darling Daisy, seemingly the oldest and cleverest of all my children. You are not to worry, Harry is not your brother," said her mother intuitively, "and your father behaves like a perfect husband and father and has so done for a long time now. I am sorry if life is difficult for you at school. Your father would be horrified if he knew the half of what you have told me here today. If you do not like it, would you prefer to leave and study at home or even go to a different school? We would so hate for you to be unhappy."

Raising her grim little face towards Chloe, Daisy said: "They will not chase me away, I'm not going to be upset by their stupid words and chatter," and she stood on tiptoe and placed a kiss on Chloe's cheek, "Dearest and best of all mothers, don't fret over me." Secure in the knowledge that Harry was in no way related to her, she left the room and skipped off to the kitchen to find George and Grace and, possibly, to try some of Cook's baking.

Later that evening, as they sat before the fire in the back parlour, Chloe apparently engrossed in a pattern book and Paul entranced by a book on Pericles, she related the conversation that had occurred that afternoon and watched her husband's face carefully for his reaction. Even by candlelight she could see his face darken perceptively; and his guilty and shocked expression would have looked most comical if the situation had not been so discomforting.

"Oh my God!" he breathed, and was smitten into silence.

"'Tis most unfortunate that Daisy is the one that notices so much," she remarked calmly, "for I am sure it had never occurred to me that your past misdemeanours could be the subject of such gossip amongst the children. Neither George nor Grace has ever mentioned the matter to me, but they must all of them have been told the like tales by those same children. Daisy has developed a fondness for Harry methinks and was most concerned, lest he should be a son to you as she is a daughter."

Stung by guilt, Paul returned more sharply than he had intended that, to his knowledge, no child in the district was kin to him, apart from those that lived under his roof. "Twould be most apparent were they any of mine," he said hotly.

"I have not accused you, Paul, so do not speak so to me because your conscience pricks you!" she returned testily.

He mumbled an apology and, his book forgotten, stared broodingly into the fire. Chloe waited for his anger and, she had to admit, her own, to cool before suggesting that perhaps they had better enquire of the children of what they had heard and talked about with their contemporaries at the school and how best to explain their father's past.

"What a clever idea, dearest wife," flashed Paul sardonically, "and how do you suggest we conduct the interview. Behold your sire, he has bedded half the neighbourhood, gotten a daughter outside of marriage as you well know, but fear not, age has brought wisdom and he now behaves like a perfect gentleman!" and he shut his book with a snap and slammed it down on the small table at his side, his dark brows drawn together in an angry furrow.

"It will do you no good to lose your temper with me, husband," returned his wife severely, "I am merely telling you what has transpired between Daisy and myself today. The conversation was in no way pleasant, I can assure you. It is to be regretted that the subject was as delicate as it was, but perhaps some restraint on your part in years past would have obviated the need for my discussion with her!"

Never had his wife made any pronouncement on Paul's philandering behaviour before his marriage. She had immediately forgiven him his liaison with Dorothea and, in all honesty, she knew full well that she had no cause for concern over her marriage. Where other woman were concerned Paul was completely trustworthy, because he loved her and no other. But this was different, she reasoned, this affected the children. They were the innocent victims, their children and others were having to suffer the slights, the taunts, the innuendoes of her husband's careless past. Glaring at her husband's stormy countenance she determined to continue her homily.

"Now we have become aware of what the children hear at school, you will have to shoulder your responsibilities and talk to them about your past. They must be suffering terribly; children can be so cruel to each other. You have a duty to comfort them and apologise ..." but her speech was interrupted by an extremely rude expletive from Paul:

"And how in hell's name do you suppose that I am to accomplish this feat?" he continued in a raised voice, "Perhaps I should produce a list of all my conquests so that they can determine which families to avoid, or perhaps you would prefer me to go down on my knees and tell them my dear wife has instructed me to confess to them all my past sins, so that they will be aware of the monstrous calamities that can befall them as they approach adulthood. I think not!"

Chloe, now in a blazing temper herself, threw her pattern book at him, but he caught it expertly and threw it across the room in a rage. It crashed against the bookshelves in the corner and knocked an ornament - a blue shepherdess with two sheep, all three of whom wore rather insipid expressions on their faces - to the floor, where it lay shattered into small pieces. He looked guiltily at the broken pottery and glanced up into his wife's eyes. She tried to keep her anger hot with him, but the tension had broken and she giggled involuntarily.

"You look more like a guilty schoolboy than a grown man, Paul," she gasped, trying not to laugh, "but 'tis most fortunate that poor Mrs Carter is unable to visit any more, for that was her wedding gift."

"Well, at any rate," said Paul, defensively, "I never liked it. 'Twas not the most beautiful object to adorn ones shelves with."

He sighed, then got up and crossed to Chloe's chair and, seating himself on the arm, caressed her and softly said: "Forgive me Chloe, both my damnable temper and my past. It seems that I cannot escape it, nor pretend that it never happened. Advise me, dearest, how am I to make all right with the children over this, for I know not how to begin to explain?"

"Tomorrow," began Chloe, after a moment's thought, "after school we will have to have another talk with them. I will take it upon myself to talk to the girls and you must talk to George, man to man. Daisy will have already informed him of my conversation with her, so it will not be such a great shock to him."

"True," he said, and they sat quietly watching the flames in the fire, planning their respective speeches that would be required of them on the morrow.

In the library, George was busy reading a book, and looked up in surprise as his father entered the room. At this time of day he was more often to be found in his office talking to the estate manager, Jonas Hampton, about farming business and the work that was to be done on the farm on the following day. He looked at his father's expression and wondered what it was that was making him look so serious. Carefully, he placed some paper in his book to mark his place and gently closed it. Paul pulled out a chair beside him and sat down. George considered quietly for a moment before asking him if he had committed some menial crime that his father wanted to admonish him for.

"No, it is none of your crimes that I wish to discuss with you" said Paul quietly, and George watched as his father ran his tongue around his lips - a sure sign that he was nervous. Paul cleared his throat and asked him abruptly if any of the schoolchildren had told him tales of the things his father had indulged in, when he was a young man and before he had married.

"All the time," replied George complacently, "It is their favourite game to play with us. Trevarthen's women they call them. They think it is most funny unless it their mother, or aunt, or sister. They don't laugh then."

"Ahem," said Paul, clearing his throat again, "I have had a colourful past George, and I regret what happened then and the pain it is causing my children now, and I might add other children as well. I cannot turn back the clock, but if you would prefer I will employ a tutor and you may leave school, to be taught at home until you have completed your education. Your mother is at this very moment telling the girls the very same thing. We would not wish to subject you to such embarrassment amongst your peers."

George looked worried by his bald statement.

"Do you wish me to leave, Father?"

"Only if that is what you would wish, George."

A worried look slowly crossed George's face, but when he spoke he was perfectly composed: "I do not wish to leave school and all my friends, but I would like to learn more than they can teach me there. The teachers try most hard, but I want to discover more about the subjects that interest me than they can tell me, Father."

"I see," said his father, "so you would prefer me to employ a tutor to teach you at home."

"Not at all, Father," said his son, directing a swift glance towards his parent.

His father gazed at him in surprise, then enquired tentatively if he would like for Paul to teach him himself. He watched George's slow smile cross his face.

"Nor that either, Father, for you will get lost in one of your books and probably forget my lessons."

They smiled at each other in agreement, but Paul considered for a long while what next to say.

"I cannot then see how to improve your situation, George. It would not be possible to employ any more teachers at the school; for they have not the room to teach. The school is almost overcrowded as it is, such is the eagerness of the parents for their children to be educated," Paul noted.

George observed his father and wondered how to ask of him the one question that he had wanted to know the answer to for so long. He adored and respected him but he could, on occasion, be quick to anger and the question that he wanted to put to him was likely to annoy him, perhaps more than any other subject. Daisy had often encouraged him to speak to his father about his problem but he had not her courage. However he saw a chance now; his parent's obvious predicament emboldened him. He realised that he had to take hold of the opportunity offered to him; it might not answer, but he had to ask, because if he did not take this chance at this time he would never again be brave enough to say anything about his troubles to him.

"Why cannot I go to your old school? You are well educated; you had the opportunity to go there. Grandpapa went to Helston, and in turn he sent you. Why am I not allowed to go?" he asked simply.

Dumbfounded, Paul could think of nothing to say in reply. George, relieved at the quiet way in which his father received the news, waited patiently for his answer.

"I did not enjoy my schooldays, George. I was beaten by the pupils and teachers, called all manner of names, made to feel most unhappy. Being away from my family was not an enjoyable experience for me. I would not want you to have to endure that."

"I know that, but for the sake of improving my education I would like to go to Helston, because it would give me the opportunity to study further than ever I will be able to do here," George said earnestly, "but if you do not wish for me to go I will accept your wishes," but to hide his disappointed look, his head bowed, lest his father should see the expression on his face.

A long silence ensued. After some time, Paul placed his hand under his son's chin, lifted up his head, and searched his face with anxious eyes.

"Allow me to think about it George. It is the one thing I had not prepared myself for," he said seriously, "but if it is truly what you would like to do I will arrange it for you," he told him seriously.

"Truly, Father?" cried George, unable either to believe his ears or to contain his enthusiasm.

Paul smiled, although in his heart he did not share George's delight, and vouchsafed firmly: "Truly, George."

"Oh, Thank you, Father, thank you. I never imagined that you would ever agree," he gasped and, leaning over, he hugged his father excitedly and found himself held in his reassuring embrace in return.

CHAPTER 5

A WAVE came over the bow of the boat and caught Paul Trevarthen full in the face, drenching him. He turned to his colleague with water dripping off his black curls and cascading down his dark face, his clothes were soaked through to his skin, but he cared not and he laughed almost uncontrollably. His companion shouted across to him if all was well, and he nodded back with his usual beaming smile. Then they set to work as one pulling in the net, both hoping for a big catch, the one because he had never been allowed to act the part of a fisherman before and the other because his living depended on a good haul of fish. The true fisherman appreciated the worth of his strong companion; alone, he would have needed all his strength to pull the net over the side and into the bottom of the boat, such was the size of the catch, but Paul could easily have pulled in the catch by himself. Working together, and with the newcomer receiving the minimum of instruction, they sorted the catch and threw back any that were too small or not wanted. When they had finally finished, Paul produced a large box that he had stowed in the aft of the boat and, sitting with his back to the bow, proceeded to open it and displayed its contents to the other man, who fetched off his cap, scratched his head and gazed in amazement at the variety of food packed into the container.

"Help yourself, Bert, for have no fear, I certainly shall," said the apprentice fisherman.

In spite of the rocking of the boat, both men had never suffered from seasickness, so consumed their meal with gusto and in a companionable silence. When they had finished, Bert took out his pipe and offered Paul a smoke, but he shook his head, never having been tempted by tobacco. He merely finished the last of the wine and replaced the lid back on the box.

"Mare quidem commune certo est omnibus," breathed Paul quietly, and leaned against the side of the boat, gazing contentedly at the vista before him. His black curls glistened with the spray from the sea as it butted against the boat and cast itself upon him, but he had not a care that he was so wet. He stared in wonderment at the blue of the sea and the purple, grey-green of the land that lay before him and ssighed with pleasure.

"Fancy speech that, Paul. Sounds good but d' mean nothin' to me," observed Bert, laconically.

"Pardon me, Bert, I was merely thinking aloud. A fellow by the name of Plautius said it a long time ago. The meaning of it is: 'The sea surely is common to all', and sitting here I think it is most true. For I have no more a feeling that I am a coloured man in a predominately white country, nor that I am a rich landowner who can buy and sell what he wishes than the least of my fellow man. I have only the sense that I am in the company of a good and honest companion, who has as much right to partake of this view and feeling of contentment as I have," he told Bert quietly.

Bert, blowing a cloud of smoke into the breeze, smiled at Paul in an almost fatherly way.

"You'd make a poor fisherman Paul, if you spend yer time a thinkin' that way. 'Tis a lovely sight to be sure, an' some days I d' think to meself: 'Dammee Bert, yer some lucky fellow to be out 'ere like this with nobody a' tellin' 'e what to do or 'ounding 'e fer money', but then I d' bring meself up short 'cos I d' know that if I 'edden got a good catch, me 'ouse an' all in it is goin' go 'ungry. Tha's a sobering thought. I d' knaw then fas' 'nuff if I'm Bert Pendray or Hadmiral Nelson, I can tell 'ee," and he laughed merrily, but then told Paul seriously: "Watching 'e and the way you d' work in the boat I bet 'e any money that yer folks back in Africa knew 'ow to 'andle a craft. You'm a natural Paul."

"Do you truly think so, Bert?" and he beamed with pleasure, but then a cloud passed over his face. "It's so hard, never to have known them Bert. I used not to notice. When I hear people talk about Father, and sometimes his father and then they go on to talk about the Trevarthens and their lineage and how they have farmed this locality for generations and so on, well . . . well, it's hard, Bert. I knew so little of my mother's family. She knew precious little herself. What I know of her own father, was what he told her when she was a young girl, and, in turn, she told me and ordered me never to forget, for as she said: 'His greatness was more than any man's, for he had suffered so much and still retained his humanity.' Well, as she told it to me, he, my grandfather, was taken from his home in Africa at such a young age he could barely remember anything of his homeland. The memories he did have began when he was enslaved and were all of fear, pain and suffering. On the boat over from Africa they threw so many over the side, the dead and ... and the living that he told her the sight of it never left him. He felt guilt that he survived and they had not, but when the boat landed its cargo he soon knew differently. He found himself sold to a plantation, and discovered himself in a hell of another sort, for there they were beaten and worked 'til they dropped. Then the ownership of the plantation changed and the new owner was most enlightened. Well, enlightened for those times. He had some of the slaves taught to read and write. Others, the older ones, were taught trades. It was in his interest - the owner told them - to have well trained slaves. Of course he did not tell them why, but Grandfather knew; for it kept up their value. They had a new overseer who explained that they wanted happy slaves, they could even marry if they had a mind to," and looking up he caught Bert's momentary look of surprise. He smiled at the irony of it, and then explained: "Slaves for free. They didn't have to buy if they could breed their own. The food improved and with it their health. After all, the more they could work and do, the more they were worth, if you understand my meaning, Bert," and he looked up and saw the other man regarding him compassionately. "Grandfather, who had been given the name Samuel Brown by the first plantation owner, was put to work with the estate carpenter. He progressed well and it soon became apparent that he could produce better work than his teacher, so his value increased, and he was sold to a boat builder.

After a while, his new owner sold him to a ship's captain and the next thing he knew he was on a ship bound for England. He was still a slave, of course, but he was deputy to the ship's carpenter. In Bristol, having no more money left to bet with, his new owner, the ship's captain, lost him in a game of cards. It was a lucky hand for my grandfather though, for the man who had won the card game, a Mr Tucker, would not consent to having slaves work for him and he was made a free man. He went to live with him and with that gentleman's influence he got a job in the docks. My grandmother worked as a serving maid for Mr Tucker and, obviously, lived in the same house. She had lost all her family in a fire and Mr Tucker, who seemed to have been quite a philanthropist, had taken her in, along with the boy who had lived in the house next door. After a few years, Grandfather asked Mr Tucker if he could marry Grace, my grandmother. Not only did he consent, but he rented a cottage for them close to the docks. My mother was born and Grandfather worked hard to pay for her education. When Mr Tucker died, Grandfather paid the rent out of his own wage, and my mother found herself employment with a local dressmaker. Then Grandfather was killed in an accident, Grandmother died within six weeks, my mother lost her employment because the dressmaking business had been sold and the new owner would not employ a ... a black, and so she took employment with a family who were coming to work in Cornwall. That's how she came to meet Father and ... and I think the local gossips could supply you with the tale of what happened thereafter."

There was a long silence, during which Bert shifted uncomfortably but he looked up and gazed directly at his companion's downcast expression. In acknowledgement, Paul gave him a grim little smile, but he could not hide his sadness.

"Told anybody else that story 'ave 'e Paul?" Bert asked, solicitously.

Slowly Paul shook his head, "No, Bert, strange to say I have not, not even my dear wife. To honour Grandfather, I will tell the children one day but not yet, they are too young, although sometimes they seem older to me than I will ever be," and he smiled fondly.

" 'Preciate you d' honour me with the tellin' of it Paul." He shook his head, but after a while he snorted derisively and said: "When you was a young buck, I used to look at 'e goin' by, wi' yer good clothes an' ridin' yer fine 'oss and think to myself, 'That bleddy boy got everythin', then when you 'ad my Molly I could a' killed 'e an' no mistake, fer what you did near damn well killed me. But Molly an' me ... well we put it behind we, made a go of it. Wouldn' much else we could do, you bein' Redvers' son and we bein' who we were, and there were plenty a' we folks in the same mess. You'd bin' some busy chap back then, Paul, I wouldn' the only man you made look a damn fool. Then you went to Lunnun with yer mother. You come 'ome and kept yer feet out from other's men 'ouses, played with a few a' they fancy pieces down Penzance a' course, but we'd all done that at sometime or 'nother. Talk was you was goin' marry John Williams' maid, 'e that was mine captain over to Wheal Sankey, but she moved away. Then yer missus to be, only we didden knaw it then, came down from Lunnon with your mother fer the Christmas. Dammee Paul, but she was some pretty young maid, back then," and he paused for a moment before saying, thoughtfully, "Still is. The men roun' 'ere breathed a sigh a' relief when we seen she on yer arm, I can tell 'e. You might not a' known it but she 'ad you caught sure 'nuff. After, you an' she married and set up 'ome together up at the big 'ouse. When yer children come along an' all seemed settled. Then that Petherick turned up an' did 'is best to kill 'e. My gar' that was some thing I can tell 'e. You was talked 'bout fer months! After yer folks passed away everything went quiet fer a while and we jes' used 'ave a yarn 'bout what you was like in the old days, never knawin' 'bout what you'd got up to with Petherick's maid that time. Some said if it wouldn' fer the fact you an' she couldn' marry you'd 'a never bin' like you was wi' the women, and wouldn' 'a upset so many 'a we 'usbands. Some a' they same men couldn' believe when yer maid, Daisy, turned up nor that yer missus took she in the way she did," and he paused reflectively for a moment, his eyes staring at the clouds out to sea, before taking up his tale again. " 'Twouldn' 'til I got to knaw 'e Paul, that I began see life 'edden bin' easy fer 'e. Money don' bring happiness when all's said 'n done, but I didden unnerstand that then. You was rich an' we was all near 'nuff as poor as could be but then I got knaw 'e Paul. After a while, I didden notice the colour a' yer skin, just got to notice the way you 'ad a good word t' say to everybody. Yer workman wouldn' 'ear a word said 'gainst 'e. Now see tha's a strange thing, Paul, 'cos the other masters roun' 'ere wouldn' thought that well of. Now you tell me 'bout yer grandfather, a man you never 'ad the chance to knaw but 'e's a man you got a lot of love fer, tha's obvious. I'm luckier than you Paul, fer I grew up in my grandfather's cottage, and when I was a lad all my grandparents was still livin'. I knew all my family, an' there were a mighty few of 'em most cantankerous I can tell 'e, but I never had look out at the world from behin' a skin the colour a' yours. I knew who I was from the minute I was born. I dunno' what it feels like not to belong somewhere Paul. Like I jes' said, life wouldn' easy fer 'e, I can see that now," he sucked on his pipe again and then said: "'Es Paul, in spite a' everythin' I bin' damn lucky, an' I'd like thank 'e fer 'elping me knaw it."

His companion looked gravely at him for a long while and then, leaning forward, held out both his hands and caught hold of Bert's gnarled hand, clasping it warmly in his strong grasp.

"I have many friends Bert, but few of them would I call true ones. For a man, who I know to my shame that I had wounded so badly, to accept me as a friend with all my shortcomings, does me great honour, and I would have you realise how much your friendship has meant to me these past months," said Paul wholeheartedly

Bert placed his other hand firmly around Paul's, looked up into his sincere eyes and smiled genuinely at him. His companion smiled back in return. After a moment they resumed their positions in the boat and turned their gaze out to sea, both thinking their private thoughts. The boat rocked them both gently and equally for a long while, until Bert said that they had best be getting back.

"Wind's gettin' up Paul. We'd best make fer port, won't be long fer a storm d' get up judgin' by the way they clouds are skuddin' in over there," and he pointed to a spot behind Paul's head.

Paul turned and watched as a group of angry, black clouds began to form along the horizon. He turned and, seeing Bert begin to set the sail, got up immediately and went to help him. The wind took the small sail and blew them into port as if they were the merest thistledown. They seemed to Paul almost to bounce over the top of the waves and the wind, blowing hard behind them, took any words they could say away and flung them out across the sea and scattered them across the depths, so if they needed to communicate they made hand signals to each other. Bert looked thoughtfully into his friend's smiling face and felt a twinge of pride beyond his understanding that his colleague should have unburdened himself to him. When they entered the port, Paul could hardly believe that they had travelled so quickly and informed

Bert, with his boyish enthusiasm that was such a part of his charm, that he had found the speed at which they had travelled a most exhilarating experience.

"I would be most honoured if you would have me on board again," and he grinned mischievously as he continued: "Cap'n Pendray, for I have enjoyed myself hugely."

Bert laughed at him and told him to make haste, for they had the catch to unload.

"I'll 'ave to see what sort a' job you can do with that task afore I decide if I d' need a happrentice," he told his friend mockingly, "but this be thirsty work Paul. Shall us 'ave a tankard afore we 'ead fer 'ome?" he asked hopefully.

"Damn fine idea, Bert," replied Paul in high good humour.

So within a short while the two men entered a local ale house. used almost exclusively by the fisherman of the area, and Paul ordered two tankards of ale. They stood at the bar, Paul dwarfing all present, and slowly began to chat companionably to various of the men standing in the room. At first the other occupants had whispered amongst themselves to see the Master of Trevu, Mr Trevarthen no less, in their midst and wearing such old clothes, but Paul was renowned for his sunny personality and it was not long before he found himself being ribbed by some of the older fisherman. He was in a jovial mood and hoped that his companions would not find it too patronising when he ordered a round of drinks for all those present. They accepted gratefully and without the slightest sign of reluctance or contempt.

"Yer missus won't 'ave 'e within a mile a' she night," one old man, with an arm missing but a jaunty smile on his face, told him as he sipped his ale.

"And why not?" asked Paul good-humouredly.

"Cos 'e do smell like a St. Ives fish wife tha's 'ow," he quipped and the whole knot of men burst into a gale of laughter at his expense.

"Well," replied Paul, unabashed, "I shall have to jump into the stream on the way home to make myself smell more presentable."

"Take more 'n a dip in that liddle, tiddley stream out by you to get rid a' the flavour of the sea, my lad," laughed the old man, wiping tears of laughter from his rheumy eyes. This produced an even louder burst of laughter and from then on Paul found himself the butt of much of their salty humour. He took it all in good part and was in no way averse to giving the men back some of the same.

Into all this merriment strode another tall, well built man. He could not match Paul for height, few men ever did, but he was a fair giant of a man nonetheless and had a decided air about him, so several of the men turned, looking respectfully at him and quite a few of those touched their caps and called a greeting to him. He was possibly in his early thirties although it was difficult to tell his age, for he carried himself so well and had hardly a line to his face, so unlike most of the working men in the inn. Dark brown curly hair, high cheekbones, a short, straight nose, deep blue eyes and a slightly mocking smile gave him a strangely distinguished appearance. He was attired in better clothes than any of the men around him, including Trevarthen himself, who had dressed in the clothes he habitually wore if he went with the men to work on the farm. Walking up to the bar the tall man glanced around the room, mentally noting all present. The landlord, Josh Pascoe, presented him with a drink and waved aside his half-hearted attempt to pay.

The newcomer greeted some of the men present before turning his attention to the Master of Trevu.

Looking Paul up and down, his gaze finally rested on his face and he studied him impassively before saying: "Evenin' Mr Trevarthen, sir. Bin fishin' 'ave 'e sir, fer you d' certainly smell somethin' powerful from where I'm standin?"

Paul grinned but greeted the man with a certain amount of reserve: "Good evening, Mr Bolitho, and yes you are in the right of it. I have spent the day fishing on Bert's boat. And I have been informed already of the fact that my aroma is rather pungent by various of our drinking companions."

Joey Bolitho threw back his head and laughed and asked Paul if he was intending to give up writing and run away to sea instead. This produced another round of laughter, but Paul smiled and waited for their laughter to die away, before replying that he had attempted to try his hand at fishing because Bert had wondered if he might not find the experience enjoyable.

"An' did it prove enjoyable, sir?" asked Bolitho, never taking his eyes from Trevarthen's face.

"Very, Mr Bolitho. But I fear I may never have the opportunity ever to go fishing again. According to what these kind gentleman have been telling me, at any rate," he added, with an unmistakable twinkle in his eye and a mischievous smile on his face.

"Why's that then, sir?" asked Joey, a similarly mischievous smile, quivering on his own lips.

"Well, I have been informed, most sincerely, that if I cannot lose the smell of fish from about my person, my spouse is like to bar me from the house, at the very least," said Paul, and the whole room exploded with laughter, including Joseph Bolitho who laughed as loud and as long as the other men.

He clapped Trevarthen on the back, in a fashion reminiscent of old Squire Tregurthen had been wont to do when Paul and the Squire were both younger men, but Paul was not in the least offended by the good humoured action and merely grinned back at Bolitho. Meanwhile Bert had drained his tankard and suggested to Paul that they had best head for home.

"I'll come up fer a chat sometime, Bert. Got one or two things I'm minded to talk over with 'e," Joey Bolitho told Pendray, but he kept his eyes on Paul's face, searching intently for any response.

Paul schooled his features into what he hoped was a fair imitation of his late father's impassive stare. It was best he knew nothing of some of the things that happened in the fishing community, particularly concerning Joseph Bolitho and his smuggling activities.

"Wastin' yer time Joey, I wen't change me mind an' you d' knaw it," said Bert firmly.

Bolitho merely shrugged his shoulders and, wishing them farewell, turned to speak to the old one-armed fisherman. This old salt chatted happily to him, for he had known him from when Joey had been a babe in arms, and only lifted his hand and head momentarily to wish farewell to Pendray and Trevarthen as they left the inn. He turned his gaze back to Bolitho and carefully noted the features on Joseph's face that resembled his mother. A saucy, brown haired wench as the old man remembered her, with those magnificent blue eyes of hers out of which her son now gazed sardonically upon the world. She had turned plenty of heads in they days, he remembered fondly and she was generous with her favours, so when she fell for the baby that turned out to be Joey no one had been surprised. The father could have been any man of among a dozen, but no one name had ever been linked to Joseph Bolitho's to stand for his sire. Knowing Sally's fondness for sharing her bed, she probably had no clear idea which of her various suitors held that honour herself. As Joey grew to manhood, there were suspicions that he was this man's son or that gentleman's bastard but he resembled his mother closely, so no conclusions had ever been drawn. Until today old Edwin had wasted a fair amount of thought upon it himself, but now he was convinced that he had finally been given the answer. They were not so much alike after all. Few people would notice the similarity, but he had the advantage of knowing all of Sally Bolitho's men. She had lived in the cottage across the lane from him and there had been no back door. He would sit and watch them knock at her door and he could see them leave after their allotted time, wishing often that he could be of their number if funds would allow, for she was such a handsome wench. He supped his ale meditatively and watched her son from under his bushy brows as Joey laughed with this man or greeted another until, at last, he was sure in his mind that he knew full well which man it was that had started Joey in his mother's belly. It was not the name that sprang immediately to his mind, but then he remembered the bay mare; this particular fellow had always a liking for a bay, and that particular colour horse was often seen tied up outside the door of Sally's cottage at night. Seeing the two of them facing each other in the inn, he had noted their similar expressions, the shape of their heads, the way they had of standing straight and tall, with their shoulders back, almost like the military. But then their father stood the same way and he had been a soldier in his youth. The younger resembled his sire most nearly but the elder, he could now recognise, also had a look of his father about him and when seen against his younger brother's face it had been highlighted most particularly, and then there was their very height. He saw and understood what he had witnessed but determined to have seen nothing. "After all," he mused silently to himself, "what good would it do either of them to knaw they d' share a father. The elder 'as made 'is own life, good or bad, and the younger, a likeable young fellow who 'ad suffered 'nuff during 'is time. I shan't open me mouth, an if I ever did folks roun' 'ere would only think I's drunk anyway," and he drained his tankard and looked hopefully at Joseph Bolitho to see if he would purchase him another tankard. Joey smilingly obliged, Redvers Trevarthen's eldest son was as generous in his way as his younger brother had been not half an hour before.

Meanwhile, Paul, completely unaware of old Edwin's discovery, was heading for home in Bert's company. Bert was perched precariously on one of Trevarthen's horses, for as Paul had informed him, it was only fair that he should provide the transport overland if Bert was to provide the vessel to take them on the sea. Both men were in a good mood, Bert because of his catch and Paul's company and Paul because he had so enjoyed himself and he knew and appreciated the value and strength of Bert's friendship. It was not long before their conversation turned to Harry, mainly because Bert wanted to thank Paul for the children's visit to Trevu and to recount the tale of Harry's astonishment at the number of books Paul had in his library.

"Told me you 'ad more books than they got in Samuel' s book shop," laughed Bert and watched for his companion's answering smile. "I got thank 'e Paul fer sticking to yer word and not sayin' nothin' to 'en 'bout not goin' to the fishin' with me," he continued seriously.

"I promised you that I would not, Bert," answered Paul, quietly.

"I knaw, Paul, I knaw, but I bet you was sore tempted, wouldn' 'e?"

"True, Bert, true, but I will not come between a father and his son. You must do for Harry as you see fit. I have not the right to direct you or in any way try to influence your decision," replied Paul, "and if Harry enjoys himself as much as I did, perhaps it will be no bad thing after all."

Bert nodded but remarked, "You 'ad the best of it today, Paul. Fair weather and a good catch. Come to sea on a bad day an' you'll soon change yer mind. Still 'Arry's a good lad. 'E wen't go 'gainst me in this, an' there's no way I can make me fortune in some other trade 'cos I don't knaw nothin' else to do an' I think time is 'gainst me now, anyhow."

"You know me, Bert, I'll never retract my offer. If at any time you wish to accept it you have only to tell me and the money shall be made available to you. Damn it Bert, 'tis Harry I'm thinking of, for I would like to see him do well and given the chance he could be such a credit to you. Don't, I beg of you, refuse my offer out of pride and ...," and here he paused, wondering how much he should say, "and for God's sake don't accept another offer if it should prove in any way likely to bring disaster or danger to you and yours."

Bert turned in his saddle and regarded his companion, with a momentary look of suspicion on his face.

"Don't seem to me that you be as ignorant of what do go on roun' 'ere as you d' make out, Paul, but listen to me an' listen good: There are some things that it don't pay the likes of you to knaw. A man like Joey Bolitho 'idden 'fraid a' nobody. Fer all your size 'e'd slit 'e from yer guts to yer gizzard as soon as look at 'e if he thought you was a danger to 'n. That ol' Customs Officer set man 'pon man after 'n, an' 'ow he did it I don't knaw, but Joey 'ad 'em marked soon nuff and he 'ad 'em all put goin'. He's a damn smart chap, Paul, so don't go thinkin' you can better 'e 'cos you can't an' neither can any other. Tha's 'ow he never danced to the hangman's tune like most of 'em 'ave done who tried 'is game roun' 'ere," and then noting Paul's look of concern he continued in a softer tone: "I've never had no doin's with 'n Paul, but I've bin' sore tempted, time out a' mind, fer 'tis easy money when all's said 'n done. Molly kept me straight. Too afeard lest I should end up in the 'angman's embrace, she was. With me gone she an' the boys would be thrown out the 'ouse in next t' no time. I got a 'ouseful think of now, Paul but I don't want lose no more than what I 'ave already. So rest easy, I'll say no to 'n this time too, but ," he suddenly laughed dryly, and then continued bitterly, " 'tis getting 'arder to do. 'E's like you, Paul, in a funny way. When he d' talk to 'e you can feel yerself wantin' to give in to 'n. 'E d' turn on the charm jes' like you an' the next thing you d' find yerself sayin', ' 'Ess Squire, I'll see to it fer 'e sir, don't 'e worry.' " He stopped speaking as he noticed the hurt expression on Paul's face.

"I'm sorry if that's the way I appear to you," said Paul brusquely, "It is not what I intend, I can assure you," and he dug his heels into his mount's flank and cantered off, with his dark frown furrowing his brow.

Bert watched him in surprise for a moment and then shouted at the top of his voice to his erstwhile companion, now approaching the crown of the hill, "An' Joey got yer blasted temper too, you great silly 'eaded larrap you!" He watched as Paul slowly brought his horse to a walk and then waited for Bert to catch up with him. The fisherman, not an accomplished horseman, managed to encourage his mount into some semblance of a canter, and soon caught up with Paul. Bert glanced cautiously towards him and found a rather sullen expression had settled on Paul's face.

"Bit testy aren't he, Paul?"

Paul hung his head before speaking, "I'm sorry Bert. I know I'm too sensitive and easily offended. The one thing my life has been short of is true friends, people who genuinely like me, who care nothing of my colour, or money, or position. I should not have reacted so stupidly to what you said. I am a fool not to have . . .," but Bert interrupted his speech abruptly.

"Paul?"

"Yes, Bert?"

The only answer was Bert's hand extended towards his friend. Paul smiled a sheepish grin and immediately put forward his own hand and they shook on it to end the quarrel.

"Now," ordered Bert, "stick that great grin a' yours back on yer face, an' les' be gettin' 'ome."

Paul laughed out loud and they resumed their journey, with Bert making rude comments about the smell emanating from his companion and Paul returning his insults just as forcibly by remarking that his poor horse was having great difficulty in interpreting the differing instructions he was receiving from his rider.

"Stick a sail on 'n and I'd soon show 'e 'ow good a 'ossman I could be, you cheeky beggar you!" he responded and the sound of their bellowing laughter resounded around the valley, causing some rabbits to thump their feet in alarm and show their scuts as they hastily abandoned their feeding grounds and headed for the security of their warrens.

CHAPTER 6

CHLOE opened her eyes to see her husband's worried expression on his face. She smiled to reassure him and received her reward to see his relieved smile break out instantly.

"Well?" she asked proudly.

"She's beautiful," whispered Paul, "just like her mother," and he leaned forward and kissed her tenderly. At the same time the baby made her feelings known and produced a thin wail from her crib, so her father got up and gently lifted her and, talking softly to his new daughter all the while, passed her to her mother's waiting arms.

She settled happily for her feed and after a while Chloe lifted a contented face to Paul and asked after the other children.

"They are all quite excited, especially the girls. George was most grown up and shook my hand and congratulated me quite formally. Grace and Daisy can hardly contain themselves, so anxious are they to see her," he informed her with a smile.

"And Jack?" she asked, with a slight frown.

Paul pursed his lips and wondered what to say. He considered that the truth would be the most politic and so told her that Jack had looked at him disgustedly before asking: "Why do we need another girl?"

Chloe giggled, but felt for Jack's position as she muttered softly: "Poor Jack," and then let her daughter clasp her finger.

Paul got up and informed Chloe that he would send Lizzie to her with some tea and that Miss Clavering was no doubt hovering outside the door at this very moment, waiting her chance to attempt to take charge of their latest arrival.

"It never fails to amaze me how fanatical childless women can be about babies," whispered Paul.

"Sshh . . . Paul. She has a heart of gold and loves our children as if they were her own, as you well know," said his wife quietly.

He nodded and looked shamefaced for a moment.

"You are right dearest," he replied contritely, but within a moment his beaming smile was back on his face, "I'll make amends and call our daughter after her," and moved toward the door: "so Alice she shall be. You have my permission to tell Nurse. I do not wish to be present for I am sure she will only dissolve into tears upon my chest as soon as she is informed that she is the dear infant's namesake."

"Out, husband!" ordered Chloe, desperately trying not to laugh, but her happy smile never left her face as Paul blew her a kiss and left the room to go in search of Lizzie, and to procure the tea that he knew his wife would be so pleased to receive.

A few hours later, Paul was about to take charge of his horse in order to ride over to the lower farm when he saw, out of the corner of his eye, young Harry Pendray striding up the drive towards the house. Passing the reins back to the stable lad he hailed the boy and turned to walk towards him.

"Good mornin' Mr Trevarthen sir," called Harry, with a smile, and turned his steps to meet Paul.

"Father sends his apologies but he can't take you fishin' next Wednesday 'cos he got some work on. He'll come up after he gets back and let you know when you can go out with 'en again." he said, and took a deep breath, glad to have got his message off his chest.

"Oh!" said Paul, somewhat surprised by Harry's announcement, for Bert rarely missed an opportunity to take his boat out, as he needed to keep an income flowing in to cover the expenses of his large household. "Well, thank you for coming over to let me know, Harry. Will you stop for a glass of lemonade and something to eat, or have you to get home?"

"Father and Aunt Emily said I could stay if I was asked," replied Harry, and then added hopefully: "Do you think Daisy would ... I mean ... would George and the girls like to see me or are they busy too?"

Paul put his hand on Harry's shoulder and turned him towards the house, informing him that all the children would be pleased to see him, but warned him that the girls would talk of nothing but babies, for that very morning they had been presented with a new sister.

"Oh, that's ... um ... lovely sir," said the boy, and then added worriedly: "George won't want to talk about babies, will he sir?"

"Shouldn't think so, Harry," said Paul, desperately suppressing a grin. "He's pleased he has a new sister, of course, but I expect he will have had enough of the girls' squeaks and squeals by now and will be mightily pleased to have another fellow around to talk to."

He noted Harry's relieved look and, opening the door, they were fortunate to be met by George, about to cross the hallway with the intention of heading towards the kitchen.

"George! Just the fellow we were looking for. Harry has some time to spare and is in need of company. Can you entertain him, do you think?" Paul enquired.

"I should say so, Father," beamed George, "Daisy and Grace are in with mother and the baby and when they get back they will talk of nothing else all day. Jack is still pouting because it is a girl and not a boy and as for Nurse, well," and he rolled his eyes heavenwards in a most comical expression, "because Mama says the baby is to be called Alice, especially after her, she keeps sniffing and blowing her nose and carrying on like that." and shrugged his shoulders in disgust.

Turning to Harry, Paul smiled and said: "Methinks, your arrival is most welcome. You have saved George from what appears to be a most trying situation."

George laughed merrily, then called to Harry and said: "Come on Harry. Let's see if Cook has anything she can find for us to eat. I don't know about you but I'm fair famished." and taking him by the arm led him down the stairs to the kitchen, and Paul listened to their excited chatter as it faded away from the hall.

Lizzie appeared from the dining room and beamed at Paul, congratulating him on the new baby for possibly the third time that morning. He politely thanked her again, then asked her to inform his wife that young Harry Pendray had called with a message from Bert for him and would be staying for a while to play with the children. He smiled again and asked if it would be possible to lay an extra place for Harry at lunch.

"Certainly, sir," Lizzie beamed, and headed off to the kitchen to arrange it.

Paul retraced his steps and returned to his horse, now being patiently walked by the stable lad, thanking him for his kind offices he took possession of his mount and, setting off at a smart trot, headed for his destination with a happy heart and a smiling face.

It was a frosty morning and Paul's breath steamed as he greeted Bert, who was standing on the threshold of his cottage, waiting for him to appear. He closed the door behind him, took the reins that Paul was holding in his hand and, after a little difficulty, succeeded in hoisting himself onto the horse's back. Getting himself into an upright position, he noticed in the early morning light what appeared to be a small white handkerchief knotted into the horse's mane. It caught the slight breeze and fluttered gently. Bert turned a puzzled face towards his companion, and raised an eyebrow in enquiry and said, "Wha's that fer?" pointing with one finger at the piece of cloth.

"Why, 'tis your sail, Bert. You said it would improve your equestrian skills, did you not?" Paul told him, and flashed his white teeth in a grin of wicked humour.

"Humph!" grinned Bert in response, "Cheeky Beggar! I 'ope there's a good swell out to sea. That'll wipe the smile off yer face soon 'nuff."

With their customary visit to the inn now a recognised part of their fishing days, Bert produced the handkerchief in front of the other men and recounted the tale to them, and there were gales of laughter at his expense, as he knew there would be. However, when he told them how his companion had had to hold on to the sides of the boat with both hands, for fear of being thrown into the sea, as Pendray had sailed around the rocks just off the coast, knowing there would be a good swell there, the laughter trebled and this time it was Paul who suffered the men's jibes. Bert laughed and joked with them all, apparently unconcerned with the fact that, in spite of all their efforts, they had landed yet another poor catch.

Chatting companionably to old Edwin. Paul noticed Joey Bolitho entering and watched him stride to the bar, with his normal disdainful swagger. Even the Master of Trevu never displayed his authority the way that Bolitho did, not that Paul was envious, more intrigued at the way people deferred to such a man. Slapping a handful of coins on the bar, the smuggler ordered another round of ale for all those wishing to fill their tankards. There was a prolonged silence as vessels were quickly emptied all around the room. Paul sipped meditatively at his drink and, encountering Bolitho's look of enquiry, smiled but merely shook his head.

"The last time I went fishing with Bert, I arrived home slightly in my cups and my wife was not best pleased," he explained ruefully, "for we had visitors. The sight and smell of me, combined with what she so charmingly referred to as 'an idiotic grin', did not endear me to her and it was to be noticed that our guests left quite soon after I put in my appearance."

"Spend the night in the stable, did 'e sir?" asked Edwin Nance laughingly.

"None of your damn business," returned Paul swiftly, with a grin.

Joey smiled at him and commiserated that that was one of the joys of matrimony, a state that he had never experienced.

"Dunno why," Edwin told him, "plenty a' women bin' after 'e."

"Never found one that I wanted to marry," Joey announced, then added coldly: "well only one, an' she 'ad her eyes on another man so she wouldn' 'ave me. She couldn' stomach my wild ways, anyhow. Too prim and proper fer me she was," and he raised his eyes to look at Paul, who was given the strange impression that he was being regarded with the merest hint of jealousy. He had no idea why, because the women he had bedded in his youth could certainly never be described as prim and proper, although some of them would no doubt have crossed Bolitho's path for he had been - and still was - quite a ladies man, if the reports of his nefarious activities were to be believed. So he convinced himself that he was imagining it and put it from his mind as Joey turned away from him and began to converse with Bert. Paul had no wish to pry, but he found it impossible not to hear what was being said, and what he did hear put a chill in his heart.

" 'Preciate your trouble, Bert," he heard Bolitho say, and out of the corner of his eye he saw him slip a small leather purse into Bert's pocket.

Bert merely nodded, but said nothing and raised his head to see if his friend had been watching. Anticipating what Bert had been about to do, Paul had turned quickly to Edwin Nance and asked him what the circumstances were under which he had lost his arm.

Edwin began to launch himself into what could have been a lengthy explanation, when all heads turned as another person entered the inn. A rather nervous young man, with large protruding blue eyes and a mass of ginger hair, stepped into the room. He held his left arm against his body and it was immediately apparent that he had a withered hand, which he was attempting to conceal against his grubby and worn shirt. He hung his head and walked to the bar, ordering himself a drink and obviously trying not to draw any more attention to himself than was necessary. Bolitho moved away from him, appearing not to notice and continued to converse quietly with Bert. The new drinker put his right hand into his pocket to take out his money to pay, but unfortunately as he placed the coins on the bar, to enable himself to count out the exact amount, one rolled off the edge and fell to the ground. Joey looked down quickly at the floor, quietly replaced his tankard on the bar, and obligingly stooped and picked it up for him. Holding it between finger and thumb he held it towards the young man.

"Best not throw away yer money, lad, 'specially a guinea piece," and he raised his cold, shrewd eyes from his study of the coin and looked full into the blushing face of the impoverished man.

"I ... I ... won it," replied the nervous fellow defensively, and held out his hand for his coin.

Joey raised an eyebrow and stared impassively at him.

"Won it?" he enquired coldly.

" 'Ess, Mr Bolitho sir, I ... my cousin ... my cousin well 'e a ...'e a got a dog fer fightin' an' we took 'en up Bezurrel and put 'en to Michael Eva's dog an' ... an' I backed my cousin's dog to win an' ... 'an 'e did 'an ... an' I won a guinea," he said nervously.

"Your cousin?"

" 'Ess sir ... uh ... Fred Eustice over to Boswedden."

51

"Ah!" said Joey softly, and dropping the coin into the young man's shaking, outstretched hand, remarked: "I see! Fred's old white 'n tan terrier, I 'spose eh?"

" 'Ess sir, 'ess tha's the one sir," he gulped nervously, and grabbing his tankard tried to drink his ale without spilling any, so badly was his hand shaking.

"Likky?" called Joey, to a somewhat bent individual leaning against the bar in the far corner.

" 'Ess Joey?"

"Fancy a stroll?" asked Joey, and looked back at the boy with the withered hand and smiled, almost angelically. Paul could not suppress a shiver, but hung his head impotently.

Likky finished his drink and wiped his arm across his craggy face, picked up his hat, squashed it down over his head so that it covered part of his face, and headed to the door. Joey made his farewells and they left the bar, to be followed a few minutes later by the nervous young man who almost threw his ale down his throat, such was his haste to leave the inn.

A gloomy silence fell amongst the normally convivial group and it was not long before Paul and Bert also departed and headed for the stables to collect their horses.

On their homeward journey, Paul looked at Bert's sombre face, but had nothing to say until they reached Bert's cottage.

"What will happen to him, Bert?" he asked sadly.

"Wha'd d' 'e think 'ill 'appen, Paul?" replied Bert viciously.

"But he's only a boy, Bert," he protested, "Surely . . ."

"Ferget you've ever seen 'n Paul. He's a goner sure 'nuff. You don't win a whole guinea coin in a bet roun' 'ere. Most a' we never seen a guinea coin, Paul," he said angrily, but he could not look his friend in the eye.

"But the dog? It could have happened couldn't it?" urged Paul desperately, "and he's got that withered hand."

The fisherman sighed but said remorsefully: "A withered 'and! 'E's got more than that! 'E's got Lucy Nankivell's youngest maid in the family way over to Zennor so 'e's to marry she next week; 'e's got a widdered mother with 'ardly any sense lef', poor soul, an' she only got 'e fer support but 'ess, 'tis true 'is cousin 'ave got a dog sure 'nuff."

"Then maybe it was as he said and he is not what you all think he is."

"Seen Michael Eva's dog 'ave 'e, Paul?"

Paul shook his head.

"Fred Eustace's terrier is so old 'e couldn' catch a rabbit if it come up to 'en and died in front of 'en, but Michael's dog would take yer arm off sooner 'n look at 'e," Bert told him quietly.

"But . . ."

"Ferget it Paul," said Bert gently, "Comfort yerself with the fact that the poor beggar 'idden goin' knaw what 'it 'en." Shaking his head sadly, he walked up the path to his cottage without a backward glance, but he stopped with his hand on the catch, then turned and slowly retraced his steps to stand again before Paul. He looked into his face for a long while before finally saying apprehensively: "There's people 'ereabouts rely on Bolitho, Paul. They don't want no trouble jes' 'cos some silly, bleddy boy saw a way to make some money by sellin' 'iself to the preventative man. An' don't 'e worry 'bout they 'e's goin' leave behind; Joey'll make sure they get enough money t' live on. 'E wen't let them starve, Paul. 'E's good that way."

"Good! You call what Bolitho does 'good'!" scoffed Paul in disgust.

Bert sighed, turned his face away and headed back towards his house. He called over his shoulder: "I'll ... I'll give 'e a shout Thursday night, if I'm goin' go Friday."

But there was no reply from his companion, who merely turned his horse and set off for his home, pulling the now rider-less beast behind him by the reins. As Bert watched him go, a feeling of immense sadness welled up within him.

"Poor sod," he remarked. But it was unclear, even to himself, if he was referring to his friend or to the young man with the withered hand.

"Well?" shouted the angry man, as he surveyed the now quiet room. His boots and spurs had rivulets of water running down them, his coat had large drops of rain on it and when he removed his soaked hat it exposed his sandy, wavy hair, which was thinning slightly on the brow of his head. He puffed out his ruddy cheeks and tapped his foot angrily on the floor. Then he sucked in his breath over his somewhat flabby lips and his cold grey eyes slowly came to rest on Paul's tall frame and, finally, on his face. Paul found himself wishing that he had refused to go with Bert and had stayed at home with his wife and new daughter but when he had been asked, Bert's worried expression had drawn on his sympathy. It was not Bert's fault after all and Paul would not let what had happened the last time they went fishing destroy the men's friendship.

So both men had set off for their day's fishing and they had landed a good catch that had bought them a lot of pleasure, even though the weather had turned against them and so they had arrived at the inn, full of Paul's cook's good food but dripping with rain water and salt spray. The usual crowd were there, including Joseph Bolitho, who was leaning against the bar with his back to the door. He had turned slowly to face the gentleman who, hardly a minute after Paul and Bert's entrance, had strode into the dark, smoky room. An insolent grin had settled immediately on Bolitho's face:

"Sorry, we can't be of more assistance, Mr Hudson, sir, but I think you'll find there's not a man 'ere can tell you anything," he had replied evenly to Mr Hudson's demand for information about the disappearance of a certain young man, known as Nick Glasson.

"One of you must know something! He was known to have been at this inn a week ago because he was seen by the butcher's daughter leaving these premises at precisely this time of day. Since then no-one has seen him, and let's face it, gentleman," he shouted angrily, "a boy with that colour hair and a withered hand to boot is a damn difficult sight to miss, isn't it?"

"If you say so, sir," answered Joey insolently and sipped his ale, before remarking to the landlord that it was a particularly fine brew today.

"Damn the ale!" shouted Hudson angrily and asked again if anyone had seen Glasson. His answer was a complete silence.

So now he had turned to Paul and there was not one present who did not think that he was the weakest link in the tight little group ranged against the preventative. Bert could feel the sweat on the palms of his hands and hoped desperately that his friend would be spared an interrogation by Hudson, but he could never have imagined the fiendish hell that Hudson was actually to put Paul through.

Mr Hudson made a mocking bow to Paul and said arrogantly: "Mr Trevarthen, sir. What strange company you do keep for a gentleman of your position?"

"I find them not strange, Mr Hudson, and I am honoured to be counted a friend in their company," replied Paul disdainfully, and he eyed the man coldly and succeeded in discomforting him with his cool expression.

Hudson thought quickly. He had to concentrate on Trevarthen for he was the one man there who was out of place; he was not naturally of their number, and he determined to get him to admit to what he knew. The Preventative Officer regarded the dark face before him and attempted an ingratiating smile before saying: "I have a little tale that concerns you, Mr Trevarthen, most particularly and bears some relation to the search for Nick Glasson as well. Would you like to hear it?"

"If you wish to recount it to me, Mr Hudson, I see no reason for me to refuse to listen to it," replied Paul steadily.

"Most kind of you sir, most kind," replied Hudson, and inclined his head. "Now where shall I begin?" he enquired hypothetically.

"At the beginning?" suggested old Edwin and there was a perceptible snigger from many of the room's occupants.

"What an excellent idea, old man," replied Hudson, not in the least abashed, and the ripple of laughter stopped immediately. He looked around the room again before resting his cold eyes on Paul's face for the second time.

"As you know, I have not been in this locality for a twelvemonth so I have been acquainting myself, not only with the area, but with the numerous records that we like to keep on the ... er ... comings and goings hereabouts. According to those self same records; a few years back we had in our employ a gentleman by the name of Samuel Jenkins, who was proving himself most useful to our task. So good at his job was he, that when a well known local personage, of considerable wealth and high position I might add, was threatened by a certain gentleman who bore him a grudge, Jenkins it was who was instructed to follow the gentleman with the grudge and to report his actions and to know at all times where he was situate." He watched Paul's face for any reaction, but nothing altered, so he continued, in a silky tone: "Well, apart from keeping his eye on the known leader of the local smuggling gang," and here he switched his gaze to Joseph Bolitho, but that gentleman was still smiling insolently at him, so he turned again to Paul and watched intently for the change of expression that he felt sure he would catch on that man's face. "Now, where was I? Oh yes! Well he dutifully followed his prey and reported back his every move. The last report he made on that gentleman was that he had taken the stage back to ... now where was it again ... Ah yes, I have it now ... Southampton." Still there was no change of expression, but Bert, and Bert alone, leaning with his head bowed towards Paul, noticed his friend tighten his grip on the handle of his tankard. He felt his heart begin to beat faster and wondered how long it would be before his companion opened his mouth.

"There was to be a dance held at Squire Tregurthen's on the evening of the day following New Year's day in 1810. A lot of the local gentry were to attend, including the aforementioned well known personage and his wife and parents. It appears from what transpired afterwards that the man who bore the grudge had returned, and was about to inflict a great calamity on that gentleman and his family. We discovered, from inquiries that were made at a later time that Jenkins and the said man were drinking in a certain inn not a mile from here. Unfortunately for Jenkins, there was another gentleman also in the establishment that night," he paused for dramatic effect, and then continued: "it being none other than the - than the devilish rogue who was the leader of that smuggling gang. Jenkins was the first to leave the inn and we do not doubt that he was on his way to warn the authorities of his sighting, of both of his ... er ... quarries, shall we say, for he would have received double the remuneration with such a report. Quite soon after, the smuggler and his..." and here he snorted derisively, flicking a glance at Likky Skewes as he did so, "... his friend left the inn also. Samuel Jenkins never made a report, for he was never seen again. But it is to be supposed that he was disposed of by a person or persons unknown who would have had an interest in keeping him from passing on any knowledge of their whereabouts and their proposed actions on that night, the night when almost all of the law abiding citizens of the town would be in attendance at the Squire's ball. An ideal night for them, with no one abroad after all," and here he attempted a knowing grin but, casting a swift glance around the assembled company, he received no response. "As to the gentleman with the grudge, it was to be an hour more before he left the inn, but later that night he held up the carriage of his own particular quarry, murdered a Sergeant of the militia, injured the coachman and attempted to murder the young gentleman that he was seeking." Watching Paul intently for any reaction at all, Hudson had sight only of an impassive countenance and a blank, unseeing stare from the large brown eyes. "Providentially for the young gentleman, for he and all his party were unarmed, when the shot was discharged he was pushed aside by his brave mother and so she it was who, selflessly, took the full impact of the blast. But she did not die then, gentleman. No, not then, but this devoted mother suffered cruelly for many months because of her injuries. Can you imagine how terrible it must have been, gentleman, for her son, her only son, to have to witness her long and painful struggle for life. But think, gentleman, think! If only Jenkins had made his report, if only he had not been, as we believe he must have been, murdered!" He noted the sharp intake of breath but, almost unbelievably, it had not come from Trevarthen, his face was still like a mask. 'Damn!' he thought, 'it must have been one of the others,' but he was coming to the end of his tale, so he determined to finish strongly. He cleared his throat and continued, in his insinuating voice: "If only the message had got through, that poor gentleman's mother would no doubt be alive today, for she was of no great age, and that poor, anguished young man would not have had to suffer the guilt, the guilt that we can be assured that he feels, feels even to this very day, sirs, because it was well known that he loved his mother dearly, and it was her great sacrifice that had saved his own life. If only," and here in the midst of his speech he took one careful stride towards Paul, continuing in his dramatic style: "if only Samuel Jenkins had been allowed to live. What would that man feel, what would any man feel, if he discovers that, but for the almost certain activities of the leader of the smugglers that very same night, all would have been so very, very different."

During the long silence that followed, some of the men shuffled their feet awkwardly, and a few coughed in embarrassment, but not a word was uttered. Hudson waited, knowing that the tension was rising unbearably in the little room, until finally he asked again, but this time only of his own particular quarry.

"Well, Mr Trevarthen, have you anything you wish to impart to me now?" and he smirked, convinced that his tactics could not have failed to have weakened Paul's resolve.

"Mr Hudson," said Paul, quietly.

"Yes, Mr Trevarthen, sir?" swiftly responded Hudson, hardly able to contain his excitement at what he was about to hear. He felt, as well as heard, the sigh of fear that had swept over the assembled company. 'At last,' he thought to himself, 'at last the great Joseph Bolitho has been snared and I'm the man that has done it'.

"It is with great regret, Mr Hudson, that I can in no way assist you in your quest for answers but," and Paul's angry scowl rested for just a few seconds on his face, "I can assure you that I found your tale most interesting and its significance has not been lost on me." Again the impassive expression was back on the face that regarded the preventative man without a tremor.

At first, Hudson stared at Trevarthen with a look of complete shock, then his colour rose in his face and he began to pant as if he was unable to get his breath. He stepped forward angrily to face Paul and raised his riding whip as if to slash him across the face with it. He stopped himself from actually hitting him, but he could not stop shouting into that bold, shuttered face: "Damn you, Trevarthen, damn you! What sport do you think you have of me, sir, eh?" and in his wrath he broke his whip across his knee and threw the two halves into Paul's face, before turning in fury and striding from the room.

For a moment there was no movement and no sound, then Likky left his post and loped silently across the room. He watched from the doorway and then turned to Joey and said, bluntly: " 'E's gone," before returning to his tankard and taking a great gulp of ale.

Voices broke all around Paul, but he heard not a word. Bert leaned over and clasped his arm, but he took no notice and merely stared impassively at the door. The one voice he thought he could not bear to hear sounded beside him: "Well, Mr Trevarthen, you surprised we there an' no mistake. That's worth a drink fer sure. What will it be?"

Paul looked away from the door and found Joey Bolitho standing at his side, an expression of arrogance and, he thought, what might have been regret, on his features. He looked down into the face of the slightly shorter man with a look of pure disgust, "Nothing Bolitho! I want nothing of you, for there is no one thing that you can ever do for me, and anyway," he ended viciously, "they sell nothing here, to my knowledge, that costs thirty pieces of silver!"

Something flashed in the dim light from the door and in a moment Joey's blade was in his hand, but Likky had him by the arm, and was whispering urgently to him: "Not 'ere, Joey, not 'ere!"

Paul had not altered his stance but he did drop his eyes and gazed at the knife, before lifting his head and coldly staring his would-be attacker in the eye without a tremor of fear.

"But for your knife, Bolitho, perhaps my dear mother, as Hudson said, would still be with me today," he remarked coldly.

Bolitho looked discomforted, a rare occurrence, but it was only for a brief moment, "I'm sorry fer 'e Trevarthen, truly I am, but rest assured, I never ... I never knifed that man, you 'ave my word on that. The Trevarthen's kept their scandals as quiet as they could. If they 'ad put the word around that yer fancy piece's father was after 'e, 'e would have been put goin' by any number of people roun' 'ere and that's a fact."

"Best be goin', Paul," said Bert uncomfortably, because his friend's face was no longer blank and now registered not only his anger, but a disdainful scowl that stared at Bolitho without flinching. He hastily caught Paul by the arm and attempted to lead him towards the door but Joey, angered by the expression on Trevarthen's face, pushed Bert away and then poked Paul in the chest with his clenched fist. "I warn you, Trevarthen, you've kept yer mouth shut today, but if you open it in future it will be fer the last time, Trevarthen of Trevu or no, understand me?" And, because Paul snorted at him in disgust, he punched him in the chest in anger and lost his normal, cool control, shouting: "Keep yer bleddy mouth shut, you 'ear me?!"

"I heard you," hissed Paul coldly, "now get out of my way for, of a sudden, the air has a most foul smell in here."

"Damn you!" swore Joey and swung his arm to hit Paul, but his intended victim was before him and caught him such a blow on the chin with his own fist that it knocked him backwards against the bar. Bolitho, unbalanced by the force of the blow, fell on to the ground with a loud crash, as tankards and jugs were jolted from their positions and crashed down around him, spilling their contents over the floor. There was a shocked and terrified silence and no one moved except for one man. Bert, reacting like lightning, grabbed Paul by the arm and pulled him through the door, shouting at him to: "Run, you stupid sod, run!" and still holding his arm dragged him off to the stables. He got them both mounted on their horses somehow and, whipping his own and Paul's into a frenzied gallop, they did not stop until he felt that they had left the inn and the town far enough behind them.

On the road the sweating horses stopped and leaned towards each other, almost as if to commiserate the one with the other at their unlooked for beating. Bert's lungs were still burning in his chest and he leaned over his horse's neck, taking in great gulps of air. When he had almost recovered, he raised his gaze to Paul's face and his heart sank. His friend sat immobile, staring at the far horizon and all the while tears followed one another down his face. There was a long awkward silence until, finally, Bert leaned over, took the reins from Paul's motionless hands and, kicking his horse on, led his friend slowly in the direction of Trevu. He dismounted at the fork in the road and, going around the side of Paul's horse, placed the reins around the mount's neck and put them into Paul's hand. He then took his own mount's reins and tied them to Paul's stirrup. Only then did he look into his friend's face.

"Keep out of town Paul. Let 'is temper cool, fer 'eavens sake. You dun' 'en down day good an' proper an' 'e wen't ferget that. I'll go in Penzance in the mornin' and when I find 'en, and find 'en I will, I'll speak to 'en fer 'e. Wen't be easy, Paul I knaw that, but you kept yer mouth shut like the rest a' we did, so 'Udson'll think you be one a' we now and I'll make sure Joey sees it that way too." he told him quietly.

"What good will that achieve? It will not alter any of the events that he has been responsible for."

"It'll save you from bein' spitted, you bleddy fool, tha's what!" shouted Bert.

"Do you think I fear that?" scoffed Paul.

"No, I don't think you do, but I do, Paul! I do fear fer 'e, an' yer dear liddle missus and they children and all the people roun' 'ere that d' rely on 'e. Joey's temper 'll cool, and 'e's a big enough man to laugh at 'iself so 'e'll get over it. But I knaw I can 'elp and I will, dussen you worry!" replied Bert earnestly.

"Why should Joey listen to you, Bert? He's afraid of no man. Have a care, lest it be you that gets his knife in your belly." replied Paul, not without a note of concern in his voice.

"Don't 'e worry 'bout me, my 'ansome. Joey need another favour off me now. If I tell 'en that you'll still keep yer mouth shut jes' like me that'll be good enough fer 'en, he wen't lay a finger on 'e and you can 'ave my word on that," he vouchsafed.

"Ha!" snorted Paul, "What have you got that is of any use to Joey?"

"I got two things, Paul. I got a boat that 'e's sore in need of, 'cos of it's size and speed. I can get in and out of they liddle coves faster than many seamen roun' 'ere." he answered swiftly and not without some pride.

"And the other thing?" enquired his friend softly.

"Ah! The other thing," he replied, and nodded his head sagely, "Now tha's something Joey Bolitho want above all others."

Paul raised his eyebrows in enquiry.

"I got a cousin tha's gone an' got 'isself a grand new job. 'E's bin' picked 'special by the new man 'cos 'e d' think 'e's jes' the sort a' chap 'e bin' lookin' fer. Our Mr 'Udson bin' an' appointed our Richard 'Enry as one of 'is new special agents. Tha's one a' them Joey wen't want t' kill, at any rate!" and he laughed loudly and long, but joylessly, for there was no mirth to be had in the joke.

CHAPTER 7

BERT kept his head bowed and merely mumbled that he would return when Mr Trevarthen was at home.

"Nonsense, Mr Pendray," ordered Chloe sharply, "Please to follow me, and Lizzie, you may shut the door if you please." She turned, walked steadily across the hall and opened the door into the withdrawing room, waiting as Bertram Pendray walked nervously into the room behind her. She marched over to the settle, turned and sat down, looked up and ordered her guest to shut the door and then to sit on the opposite settle.

"I be dirty, Mrs Trevarthen, ma'am. I 'idden dressed fittee an' ..." began Bert, anxiously, but was cut short.

"Mr Pendray, you will please do as I say for, I am sorry to have to inform you, I am not in the best of humours today," and she glared at him, her eyes sparkling in such a way that it only added to her beauty.

" 'Ess ma'am," said Bert quickly, and lost no time in seating himself where he had been instructed. Keeping his head lowered, he nervously turned his hat around in his hands, but had nothing to say. He thought himself a fool for coming. His appearance was going to cause trouble between his friend and his wife that was for sure, but he needed to see Paul. He could have waited outside, or gone to the stables to enquire after the master's whereabouts but he assumed Paul to be at home. Mrs Trevarthen's voice cut through his thoughts like a knife. He forgot that he was trying to hide his face and looked up guiltily.

"Is there anything I can procure for you, as it would appear that you have been in some sort of accident, Mr Pendray?" she asked crisply.

"No ... n ... no Mrs Trevarthen, ma'am. This is nothin." and he smiled, but winced immediately because of the pain in his face. His left eye was forming a large bruise around it, his cheek was also beginning to darken and his nose and lip still had blood running from them. He took out his handkerchief and wiped his nose, fearful lest the blood ran onto the carpet and left a stain. He coughed apologetically and offered: "Fell on me boat," as an explanation.

Chloe raised her eyebrow, "Truly, Mr Pendray? I would have thought a seaman more sure-footed than that! No doubt you tripped over some object or other."

"Yes, ma'am." he replied, but he continued to look guilty.

"My husband appears to have met with a similar accident, for he tells me that his bruised hand came about from an accident on your boat as well." she said brusquely and regarded him steadily, watching as Bert's face flushed red to the roots of his hair.

"Did 'e ma'am? I mean ... 'ess, ...'ess ma'am, 'e ... 'e did fall over on me boat." said Mr Pendray and he assayed another smile.

"Oh dear!" said Chloe in mock dismay, "I did not realise he had fallen, for he told me that he had trapped his hand. Perhaps he hit his head instead. That might possibly explain his confusion, might it not, Mr Pendray?"

"Please ma'am," implored Bert, "I'd rather come back another time or if you could send Paul, I mean Mr Trevarthen, down to see ..."

"I will not be lied to by my husband, Mr Pendray," she fumed, "and I will have the truth out of him, never fear." She seemed to be struggling to control herself and after a moment said purposefully: "I have not attempted to deter him from your fishing trips for I believe them to be beneficial to him. I would rather he made a friend of you than many another, but if you believe that I am fool enough not to realise that something extremely serious has taken place, then you are sadly mistaken."

"Mrs Trevarthen, don't ask the truth of me or of your husband either," he pleaded, " 'Tis not the sort of thing fer a woman to know."

Her eyes opened wide in shock and he made haste to erase the false impression he had given.

"We didden do anything like ..." he began hurriedly, then said simply: " 'Twas a fight, Mrs Trevarthen, tha's all, jes' a fight. A fight with a man we d' knaw. 'Tis all sorted now, never you fear."

She studied him for a long while and under her straight gaze he wished himself anywhere but where he was at that moment. Finally he heard the big front door bang shut and Lizzie Opie's rather high, nervous voice followed by a long silence. He heard the sound that Paul's familiar long stride made, then the door was opened and in the doorway stood the errant husband and Bert's dear friend. His face was a mixture of shock and worry, and he looked from his wife to Bert and back again, but uttered no word.

"Paul, dearest," said his wife, in a cold voice, "do shut the door. As you can see we have a visitor and he has been waiting most particularly to have words with you."

Paul came in, and after shutting the door behind him, advanced into the room. Looking into Bert's ravaged face he said: "I apologise for not being here to greet you, Bert. We'll go to my office, and we can talk there?"

"You will do no such thing, Paul! You will talk here and in my presence for I will know the truth of this!" cried his wife, angrily.

"I will not!" shouted Paul as he turned to face her, his face an angry scowl, "It is a matter between Bert and myself alone, and I will not have my wife interfere ... involved in it. Now, if you will excuse us we will ..."

"I will not excuse you, either of you, until I am told what has transpired. Bert has already informed me, and I do believe him, that you were both involved in a fight with some other man. What a tremendous fight that must have been, to be sure, for you, dear husband, appear to have fought your particular battle during yesterday and poor Mr Pendray's injuries appear to have been sustained this very morning," she announced hotly.

There was an awkward silence until finally, Bert cleared his throat and said quietly: "Yer 'usband knocked a man down 'cos they 'ad a bit of a row. Well, I didden think it would be a good idea to let it simmer so I went in to Penzance this morning to try me best to make things right with 'en, the bloke Paul 'ad a row with see, 'an well he didden take kindly to me to start off with but 'tis all sorted now. There 'idden goin' be no more fights, Mrs Trevarthen, 'tis all finished now and tha's the truth."

"Did you fight with this man, Paul?" Chloe asked, and tilted her chin at her husband, staring at him coldly.

"Yes, I lost my temper and knocked a man down. That is the truth, but I will not tell you more and I beg you not to ask of me that which I am not prepared to explain." he announced in a quiet, considered voice.

Chloe continued to stare at her husband for a long while, but she had received an answer of sorts and she knew from the way Paul had spoken that his version of the truth contained elements of what had happened. Bert's explanation had been equally vague, but between the two of them she had a partial account of their activities. With that she was prepared to be content. So she stood up slowly and brushed down her skirts, then said in her controlled voice: "If you will excuse me, Paul, Mr Pendray, I wish to visit the children in the nursery." and as she came up to Bert, now on his feet, she turned and, facing him, said gently: "I am most relieved that my husband has such a good friend, but I implore you to do your utmost to steer that mad husband of mine along a more temperate path. I do hope, most sincerely, that your hurts will soon mend, Mr Pendray," and she extended her hand towards him. He hastily wiped his hand on his jacket and, wincing as he smiled, shook her hand.

"Certainly, ma'am. Don't you fret 'bout that, Mrs Trevarthen ma'am. 'Twill be all right from now on, believe me." he announced.

Paul waited some moments after he had closed the door behind his wife before turning to Bert and saying: "I assume he was not best pleased to see you, from the appearance you present. I am sorry, Bert, that you should have received such a beating on account of my hasty actions."

Bert shrugged his shoulders, "Couldn' 'spec Joey to welcome me with open arms, Paul, but after 'e'd knocked me aroun' a bit 'e quieten'd down an' 'e 'idden goin' make a move on you or nothin' like that, so we 'em got no worries there."

"No worries there!" mused Paul, "Where have I worries then, Bert?"

"Nothing bad, Paul, he jes' want a favour tha's all." said Bert worriedly.

"A favour? What sort of favour?" he asked.

"You 'old a dinner party, on a certain date, an' amongst the people tha's invited is a particular gentleman an' 'is wife." he looked up at Paul's face and noted his disgusted expression.

"I need not ask who that would be, I presume?" he said sardonically.

Bert hung his head and mumbled, " 'Twas the bes' I could do, Paul, under the circumstances. No man 'em never knocked 'n down afore, like you did. An' afore a gaggle of 'is mates too. That didden please 'en either."

Paul sighed, "So I am to be besmirched by his intrigues too, am I?" and he swore.

Blushing heavily, Bert began to apologise but Paul angrily cut him short: "Why could you not have accepted my money, Bert? See what your damn pride has brought us to! Too proud to accept fair money but glad enough to take hold of foul. I wish to God I had never met you!"

His friend flinched at that, for it gave him more pain than all of his cuts and bruises combined, but he continued bravely.

"Fergive me Paul, I didden ever think it would d' turned out this way. I told 'e what 'e was like with the charm 'n all an' I didden think no one would find out. I never bin' caught. I'm too smart fer they, an' now, 'cos of me cousin, I d' never go out without I d' knaw zactly where the preventative men are."

He turned away, and picking up his hat from the settle, said slowly: "I'll be goin' now Paul, but next week I'll see 'e fer fishin' as ..." but he got no further as Paul interrupted him by saying angrily: "Oh no you will not! I will never fish with you again, Bert. I'm sorry for it but that all has to end now."

Bert sighed and faced his friend again, "I'm some sorry Paul, but Joey says you'll be on me boat next week, barring bad weather of course, same as usual. An' we're to go fer a drink after, like we d' do. 'Udson got 'is eye on we now see. Joey don't want make 'en more su'picious than 'e be already. 'E said to tell you 'e'll 'ave a liddle chat with 'e so I'm warnin' 'e now Paul, keep yer temper with 'en this time fer all our sakes." Paul said nothing, his feelings were writ large on his face, so Bert turned slowly and shamefacedly and proceeded towards the door. He opened it and said his farewells, but only silence answered him, so he made his solitary way across the hall, and let himself out of the house and turned homewards. The ache he hid in his heart far outweighed any of the pain of the injuries that were so obviously displayed on his body.

Dinner was a quiet affair that night and Paul made no attempt to keep up a flow of conversation. Normally his wife and himself would have chatted happily together, and teased each other and laughed, but tonight they sat in almost total silence. When they retired to the parlour Paul picked up the book he had been reading, shifted his position in his chair - the better to see the print from the light of the candles - and began to read. Chloe regarded him silently, and holding her peace she picked up her stitching but, after setting a few stitches, dropped it again, and spoke to her husband in a quiet and composed way: "Paul, have you placed yourself in danger because of your actions, for it seems to me that Mr Pendray was most concerned about you when, judging by his appearance, he should have been the one to be the most apprehensive on account of his own condition?"

Paul looked up from his book and studied his wife's face. He had seen many emotions on that so-pretty face today. There were smiles, laughter, anger, and now worry. He could not believe what had happened to him in such a short span of time. Going from a decent, honest, gentleman farmer to a smuggler's helpmate in one short step seemed so unbelievable that he almost refused to accept it. There was no possible way he could explain to Chloe that his prized fishing jaunts could have led him to such a catastrophe. His good name now lay fouled in the dust, and he knew there was no way back for him. To save his friend he had lied, and now he would have to keep on lying to preserve all that he held most dear. But what appalled him more than anything else was the knowledge that he had become the puppet of the man whose actions had, albeit indirectly, led to the death of his mother. None of this could be related to Chloe, no hint of the distress that his pride and his honour, and most importantly his heart, were suffering. So he squared his shoulders and said gently: "I foolishly lost my temper with a local chap who is inclined to settle all his arguments with violence, but Bert felt honour bound to attempt a reconciliation, and despite his appearance, Bert has indeed accomplished his aim. I am not in danger, neither will I be, for the man in question has accepted that I have a hasty temper on occasion, but am like not to lose it with him again for he knows now, because of Bert's actions, that we have no need to inflict violence upon each other."

Chloe sighed, "I will ask no more, Paul, and I will accept your explanation. But take care, dearest, for methinks some of the company you keep are not the sort of people that it would be wise to mix with. They are not all as honest and upright as Mr Pendray after all."

He sighed but merely said: "No my dear, you are, as usual, in the right of it."

The following week, the two friends sat in the boat as usual, the catch on board and stowed ready to be unloaded when they reached the port. While they had been busy working everything appeared as normal as usual, but now they ate their food in almost total silence.

"When we d' get back, Paul, we'll need make a better show a friendship than what we be doin' now," observed Bert, "Mr 'Udson is busy makin' lots a visits t' the inn. 'E's waitin' to catch 'e off guard, you or another, but 'tis you 'e's got 'is sights on 'cos you 'idden truly one a' we so me cousin bin' tellin' me."

"Never fear, Bert, I'll play the game for you and Mr Bolitho. Hudson will have nothing from me, I can assure you," he said flatly.

"Thanks, Paul," said Bert humbly, "but you d' knaw I never wanted this. You be too good a man t' be mired by all the mess I bin' an' got meself in."

Paul sighed, "Not much other that I could do, Bert, for there is no way I will see you and your family damaged if I can help it in anyway whatsoever." And after a moment's hesitation he held out his hand and Bert, smiling for the first time that day, grasped it and shook it warmly.

So when they were in the inn consuming their ale, they gave the impression of being the good friends that they still were. Mr Hudson came in and decided to partake of a tankard, with all the nonchalance that he could muster. He chatted awkwardly to one or two of the men present but made no attempt to converse with either Paul or Bert, although he had acknowledged them both. Everyone present was awaiting the entrance of the one man they felt sure would arrive before long. They were not to be disappointed. When he did enter, closely followed by Likky, he nodded to Mr Hudson, and flashed an insolent smile in his direction. All present were aware that the tale of the altercation had reached Mr Hudson's ears, for he had spent some time of every day since that fateful afternoon, either pacing up and down outside the inn or, as today, inside it. He watched Bolitho like a hawk and had the pleasure of seeing him make his way towards Trevarthen without straying from his line. What he saw next was not what he had anticipated at all. Bolitho slapped Trevarthen on the back, then laid his arm across his shoulders in a most friendly way and said laughingly, in a loud carrying voice: "Next time Paul, I'll knaw better than t' wait t' see what a man you can be with yer fives. 'Ell's bells, Paul, I thought you'd knocked me to kingdom come when you planted that facer on me. First man ever t' 'ave floored me I can tell 'e. No 'ard feelins', eh Paul? I'll buy 'e a drink fer it an' no mistake. C'mon Josh, you knaw the score!" Turning to the landlord he reached into his pocket and threw down a handful of coins in his usual extravagant fashion.

The Preventative Officer could not believe his eyes. Bolitho appeared to be on the best of terms with the man, even to be embracing him in what looked like, to Gerald Hudson at least, an almost brotherly fashion. So friendly with the same man, who, it had been reported to him, had fought with him only a week previously. Joseph Bolitho was not a man to fight with and to expect to receive from him the slightest morsel of forgiveness. He knew full well, because he had made it his business to know, that the two protagonists had not had any meetings during the intervening week. So perhaps all was as it seemed; that they were friends was obvious, as they were not adverse towards each other. After all, it would not have been unusual for two such well-matched men to square up to each other out of pure enjoyment. He sipped his ale slowly, a puzzled look on his face. He watched as Trevarthen and Pendray appeared not in the least put out with Bolitho's friendly comments to them and accepted quite happily the drinks that were provided for them. Josh Pascoe, the landlord, approached him and asked if he would like a drink, at Mr Bolitho's expense. Hudson blinked in astonishment before puffing out his cheeks and saying rudely: "No I bloody well would not!" and picking up his new whip and his hat, stalked from the room in high dudgeon. As before, Likky took up his post and when he pronounced that all was clear, Bolitho removed his arm from about Trevarthen's shoulders, and in so doing released the grip of his hand that he had been pinching firmly into the top of Paul's arm.

There was an expectant silence in the room, all the spectators present awaiting events just as Hudson had done.

Joey leaned on the bar and studied Paul's face impassively, his previous carefree smile completely gone.

"Don't 'e ever do that to me 'gain Mr Trevarthen, sir, 'cos you wen't live to tell the tale if 'e do!" he hissed malignantly.

"Then I would advise you to take care not to provoke me in future, Mr Bolitho." replied Paul in a calm voice, and sipped his ale unconcernedly.

Bolitho looked astonished for a moment, and some of the watchers present drew in their breath sharply, but then he threw back his head and laughed loudly and genuinely before slapping Paul's back again. "Well, you're a cool one an' no mistake, Mr Trevarthen," but then added in a soft undertone: "I'll send 'e word, Mr Trevarthen, when I need you to arrange my little - uh - diversion." Then he laughed again, said farewell to the group of bemused, and in some cases disappointed bystanders and, nodding his head at Likky, they left the inn and disappeared down one of the alleys that led off the yard.

There was an excited gabble from the men present, mainly about the fight and Paul's obvious fighting prowess in relation to Bolitho's. Old Edwin watched Redvers' son shrewdly for a while before saying: "You was lucky there, Mr Trevarthen, sir, fer 'e'd a killed 'e on the spot if 'e'd wanted to. Nasty man, old Joey, but t'aint bin' all his fault."

"Hardly a blameless life, though Edwin, would you not agree?" asked Paul, bitterly.

"Blameless, 'ell no!" snorted Edwin, "but 'twouldn' all 'is fault like I jes' told 'e. See 'e's like you," and he nodded at Paul's look of surprise, "if you'll fergive me impert'nance. 'E wouldn' born to a wedded couple either, but 'e wouldn' took into 'is father's 'ome like you was." He sighed, and took another sip of his ale, before continuing in a reflective tone: " 'Ess, the poor beggar never stood a chance at all, what with 'is mother bringin' 'ome any man with 'nuff money to pay fer 'er favours. When he was old 'nuff t' not do much more 'n stand 'e was thrown out the door as 'er bedfellows were dragged in. Poor liddle beggar use be sittin' under the window 'owling while 'is mother was inside makin' a livin' with 'er body. An' if 'e made too much racket ol' Sally use' come out, with 'er clothes 'anging off 'er most times, n' ¹scat 'en roun' the 'ead till 'e went quiet." He glanced up at Paul before saying quietly: "Growin' up like that didden do 'en no favours."

"How do you know all this?" asked Paul, intrigued.

"Lived right 'cross the road from she tha's 'ow. Lot a' nights, Mother, God res' 'er soul, used 'ave 'im in an' give 'en a bite to eat, an' mighty glad 'e was to 'ave somethin' in his belly fer Sally, 'is mother, couldn' care whether 'e 'ad food or no. 'E 'ad some damn 'ard life. Tidden to be wondered at 'e's the way 'e is. Anythin' 'e 'ad 'e stole, 'cos if 'e didden, 'e wouldn' 'ave 'ad nawthin' 'ardly."

"I cannot condone his lifestyle, Edwin, or to forgive his murderous activities," announced Paul stiffly.

" 'Course not, but like I jes' said you 'ad the 'vantage of 'im. A father an' a proper home t' grow up in. An' 'e's open 'anded fer all 'is terrible ways, fer if there's a widder an' children that needs food or money or a sick man that can't work, an' 'e knaws 'bout it, 'e'll see them right. There's many a folk roun' 'ere wen't 'ear a word 'gainst 'en. Sad case, sir, look as proud as you d' like, but if it 'ad been you instead of 'e 'an 'ad start off like 'e did what sort a' man do you think you'd 'a bin'?" and he stared boldly into the eyes of the Master of Trevu.

For a moment, Trevarthen looked uncomfortable, but then he sneered: "One who would rather die than take his path."

Edwin snorted at him. "Easy 'nuff fer you say! I bet you've never known 'unger in yer life! You never 'ad grow up lookin' at every man's face and wonderin' which one was the one that made 'e with yer mother. Never 'ad a mother who'd rather be pleasurin' some man than tendin' to 'e," he mocked, then shook his head and continued sadly: "an' in spite of all that 'e growed up thinkin' the world of 'er. Broke 'is 'eart when she was killed," and he took up his tankard and emptied it.

"Killed?" enquired Paul, as he automatically placed the money for another ale against Edwin's tankard.

"Thank 'e sir, thank 'e," said Edwin, and touched his cap, before continuing: " 'Ess killed. Some fella she brought 'ome turned nasty and beat 'er pretty head in. Joey it was who foun' 'er, poor beggar. 'E wouldn' no more than ten or 'leven 'spose, can't 'member zactly. Anyway they caught the man an' 'e was put in the lock up but 'is mates said 'e was with they, so after a while they 'ad let 'en go."

"What an appalling thing to have happen to you, and at such a tender age" said Paul, and even in his hatred he had sympathy for Joey then. "What happened to Joey after this awful catastrophe?"

"Well, 'e got thrown out the 'ouse 'course an' 'e had fend fer 'iself. Tha's when 'e started go wrong good an' proper."

"Perhaps if his mother's murderer had been brought to justice it would have been easier for him," remarked Paul contemplatively.

Edwin smacked his lips together after taking a welcome drink from his now full tankard. He wiped the froth from his bristly top lip before saying softly: "I never said 'er killer wouldn' brought t' justice, sir."

---

1 ¹Scat: Hit or beat

"But he was released," protested Paul, frowning.

"Better fer 'en if 'e wouldn'. They foun' 'en down the bottom of Jennin's Lane with 'is throat cut, an' full a' stab woun's with 'is own knife stickin' out 'is 'eart," he announced.

"Joey?"

"Well 'e turned up at our place covered in blood, any rate. Mother 'ad 'en in an' washed 'en off, burnt 'is clothes on the fire an' dressed 'en up in one of our Davy's shirts. Then she put 'en bed in with we an' made we say 'e 'ad bin with we all night. When the justices turned up we stuck by our story an' said 'e 'edden lef' the 'ouse since the af'noon afore. Ol' Joey never fergot we fer doing that. We 'em never bin' rich but we never went 'ungry from then on, not if Joey could 'elp it any rate. 'Twouldn' long after that Joey thinks to rob a smuggler, by the name of Barnaby Rickard. Damn silly thing fer 'en to try to do fer Rickard, a big fellow an' no fool, 'ad 'en tied up in a trice an' took 'en home with 'en. Bleddy good job too fer he wouldn' 'ave lasted much longer livin' 'and to mouth, like 'e was. Barney trained 'en up to watch out fer 'en, like Joey got Likky t' do. They was some brave team an' no mistake an' built up a load a business. Well Rickard made a pile a money an' when he'd made 'nuff fer 'is needs 'e give up the smugglin' trade an' Joey did too. 'E was after this maid that 'e wanted marry but she wouldn' 'ave nawthin' do with 'en on account of 'is bad ways, although some d' say 'twas 'cos of 'er wantin' some other man. Anyway 'e went up 'Ampshire live with Barney an' 'is missus, but the poor beggar couldn' settle. 'Twouldn' long afore Joey come back 'ome, an' tried 'is luck with this woman 'gain but 'e didden 'ave no joy an' then she upped an' moved away. Well, by she doin' that it did fer Joey. See, trouble was, Paul, poor ol' Joey didden knaw no other life, an' with no wife keep 'en straight, twouldn' long afore 'e took over the smuggling gangs that Rickard 'ad bin' runnin' an' tha's what 'e bin' a doing ever since, " and he concluded his tale with another long drink from his tankard.

Paul looked broodingly at his own almost full tankard, the ale that had been bought for him by Joseph Bolitho but which he had not touched since the smuggler had left the inn.

"You know that I cannot forgive him, Edwin, and why," he said dejectedly.

" 'Ess sir, I d' knaw. But 'e's cut to the soul at what 'appened I could tell that, 'specially when you think 'is own mother was murdered too, an' when 'e 'eard 'Udson's tale to the end 'e was lookin' fair sad fer Joey. After all 'e didden never 'ave no argument with 'e Paul, or yer fa . . ." but here he stopped as if he knew not how to continue.

Paul frowned in puzzlement and prompted, "Or my what?"

Edwin it was who now looked uncomfortable, then after a moment's thought said brightly, "Why yer family 'course."

Paul nodded, accepting without question Edwin's statement.

There was a long silence, during which Paul stared meditatively at nothing in particular and Edwin managed to finish his drink, noisily smacking his lips together. More money passed across the counter toward him and he made another exclamation of thanks to the provider.

Bert, who had been listening quietly to Edwin's story, regarded his friend silently. Something puzzled him about the old man's tale; not what he had related, for most of the men present knew the story of Joseph Bolitho's blighted beginnings, but the way in which it had been told to Paul. Almost as if he had been trying to make peace between the two men. He shook his head. Old Edwin was a great man for a yarn, one of the best at telling a tale. 'I'm gettin' carried 'way with the silly ol' fool's story,' he thought to himself and smiled grimly. Still, it would do no harm if Paul showed less antagonism to Joey in public. They were not free from Hudson's suspicions yet, any of them.

"Goin' on now, Paul?" he asked quietly.

Paul merely nodded and, his ale still untouched, wished all farewell, nodding his head to Edwin as he strode from the inn with Bert in his wake.

Old Edwin watched them depart thoughtfully, then drained his own tankard before pulling Paul's tankard towards himself and taking a drink from it. After all, he reasoned, the buyer would not have begrudged it to his old neighbour, even if Joey's own nearest relative could hardly bear to soil his lips with it.

CHAPTER 8

CRATES of books littered the hallway of the house that Paul had adapted to be a library. Most of the shelves had already been filled; books had been arriving since before the first shelf had been put up, but there were still more arriving every day and, as he had spent the previous day fishing, he would be kept busy today arranging all the books that had accumulated. Normally he had the help of Mr Samuel's new assistant, a very earnest young man, who rushed to complete Paul's every request and was more than ready to run from one end of the house to the other to place any tome in its correct place. Paul admired and appreciated his enthusiasm but, because his employer had himself received an order of books, he was needed at the bookshop and was not available to help Mr Trevarthen.

Paul sighed in resignation, took off his coat and got down to his work and, after checking the order against his list of books on the invoice, was soon happily working through the various titles and allocating them to the groups of books that he was stacking in to their respective sections, in tall piles on the floor. When he had sorted all the sections, he lifted as many as he could from a certain pile and, carrying them to the appropriate room, began to place them on the shelves, taking his time in order to place them correctly. Tall and strong, he could carry a large amount and soon the piles of books in the hallway began to dwindle steadily.

"Should not be long now before the Library opens its doors." he mused in a soft voice, but he had still to appoint a librarian and a team of assistants. He would have to turn his mind to that soon. Into his thoughts he heard a woman's voice, calling his name distractedly.

"Mr Trevarthen, Oh! Mr Trevarthen, sir. Please sir, where are you?" it said in an urgent tone.

Recognising the voice at once, he hastily dropped his book and descended the ladder he was standing on, then headed out of the room and down the stairs to the hallway. Miss Clavering stood before him, pulling at her handkerchief nervously with her sombre bonnet sitting lopsidedly on her normally neat coiffure, which itself had strands of her mousy brown hair fallen loose and hanging down over her frightened face.

"Miss Clavering, why whatever is the . . .?"he began to say, but she rushed upon him, crying out hysterically and shouting: "He's gone. He's gone sir. I had him by the hand, but I just had to drop it for one moment to take my money out of my purse and when I turned around he'd . . .." She stopped and burst into tears. Fear gripped Paul and he caught her by the shoulders, "Who has gone?" but in his heart he knew which one of the children would have been holding Nurse's hand and, more importantly, which one would take the slightest opportunity to free himself from her presence.

"Master Jack," she sobbed, "I was in the apothecary's and I had the arnica cream in one hand and I needed to take out my money and . . ." but it was all too much for the poor woman and she slumped down on a chair and burst into racking sobs.

"Have you looked for him?" asked Paul desperately, and watched as she nodded her head vigorously, "Everywhere," she sobbed, "but when I could not find him I came here."

"Stay here," he ordered abruptly, "for if anyone should find him they will surely bring him to this house." and he shrugged himself into his jacket and rushed from the house into the street, not even bothering to shut the door behind him.

Jack had stopped running as soon as he thought Nurse had been lost. He hated having to go with her to the town. The other children could stay at home but they did not always want to play with him, so Nurse often took him with her on her shopping trips. "The outing will do you good, Master Jack, and you will be able to see lots of nice things." she would say firmly. Well, that was a lie because he never got to see nice things as she went from shop to shop, buying potions and powders, or items of clothing, like socks and comforters and sometimes, - and he frowned at the thought of it - she would make him stand still and hold a shirt up against him to see if it would fit. He hated that worse than anything because if there were women in the shop, they would always stop and stare and say things like: "Oh! The dear little boy. Isn't he handsome? Just like his father. Look at those eyes." and lots of silly things like that. Some would even pat him on the head. He would scowl, and then Nurse would tell him to smile, and to say: "Thank you ma'am," but the worst of it was that she would never listen when he said he wanted to go somewhere interesting, or to stop and look at something that had caught his eye in the street. Oh no! It was always: "Come on Master Jack, stop dawdling" or "Come here and let me wipe your nose," and she would grab hold of his nose firmly between the folds of her handkerchief and would not let it go because she would tell him to 'make a big blow, now, Master Jack,' and when he did as he was asked, albeit reluctantly, she would screw his poor little nose almost right off. He skipped along the alley, thinking of all the horrible things she made him do and felt most pleased with himself that he had escaped her clutches. A large, brindled dog ran in front of him and gave him only a cursory glance but, undaunted, Jack ran after the animal calling out: "Doggie, doggie!" to him. When the dog stopped and turned, Jack had almost caught up with him and held out his hand but he stopped abruptly as the dog curled back his lips and showed his teeth in a snarl. He let his hand fall and the dog, with a final departing growl, loped silently away. The little boy was not feeling quite so confident now. He looked about him and something about the dark, smelly alleyway began to frighten him. On either side of him were shabby little houses, with small windows, which seemed all the while to be looking at him and threatening him. Trying to look bold; he was marching along the alleyway's length when a door at the side banged open and a horrible looking sight met his eyes. A large man came shambling through the door and almost fell upon him. He had matted hair, a pockmarked, unwashed face and his eyes seemed to roll around in their sockets. His clothes were dirty and worn and his boots had holes in the toes, but the smell that emanated from his person was disgusting, worse than the midden in the farmyard and little Jack's nose wrinkled up in distaste. Out of his unfocused eyes the frightening apparition saw Jack and tried to grab at him, but he moved quickly out of his reach.

"Com' 'ere ya' liddle bastard!" the man swore and tried again to catch the boy but Jack, who had no intention of staying anywhere near to this terrifying person, took to his heels and fled. Halfway down the alley he missed his footing on the slippery cobbles and crashed to the ground, spoiling his clothes and cutting his hand on some broken glass. He got up hurriedly and, believing the horrible apparition to be close behind him, ran blindly on. When he got to the end of the alley, he found he was in an open space, almost like the farm yard at home, and then he heard someone laugh and turned his face into the sun to try and see where the sound had come from. Blinking into the light and screwing up his eyes in an attempt to see properly, he could make out three men standing in an archway and when he looked more closely he realised the one with his back to him was his father. So he breathed a sigh of relief and ran towards him calling: "Dada! Dada!" as loudly as he could. The trio stopped talking and the tall man whirled about to face the little boy that was heading so purposely towards him.

Jack panted up to him, reaching out his little arms, but he stopped dead as he looked up into a stranger's face. It was not his father after all, although he was a big tall man like his father and in some way he looked like him, but his hair, and his eyes, and his skin were all the wrong colour. Jack drew in his breath sharply and backed away, tilting his chin boldly at the man, even though he felt his lips tremble.

"Well, well..." said the man unemotionally, but then he grinned, "Who 'ave we 'ere I wonder?"

"Tha's easy 'nuff knaw with a skin like 'e got. Tha's Trevarthen's youngest boy, well his youngest livin' one any rate," said one of the other men, nonchalantly, "Anyway, c'mon Joey, bes' be goin' on."

"What 'e mean, bes' be goin' on? Can't leave the poor liddle beggar 'ere! Anythin' could 'appen to 'en. Looks a bit roughed up anyhow." said the tall man and he held out his hand to Jack. For a moment the little child looked too frightened to move, but slowly Jack edged forward and tentatively held out his own hand towards the familiar stranger.

" 'Ello!" said his new friend, "What you bin' a' doin'," and he laughed genuinely and then said, "Not fighting, I 'ope."

"N . . No sir, I fell and cut myself. A dog growled at me and a horrible, smelly man tried catch me and . . . and I runned away and then I fell over . . . and I cut my hand. Look!" and he held it out trustfully for the man to see, "and then I come out here and I saw you and I thought you was Dada and I runned towards you but . . . but you wasn't my Dada and . . . and . . .," he sniffed and desperately tried not to let the tears that brimmed in his eyes fall down his cheeks.

"Well, no matter, young sir. We'll find yer Dada, don' 'e worry." the man informed him with a reassuring smile and, as he spoke, he took a white handkerchief from his pocket and expertly bound the boy's hand with it before asking him where he thought his father might be.

"I don't know," gasped Jack, now there was no stopping his tears and he sobbed uncontrollably.

The stranger looked exasperated, but his friend told him Trevarthen would be at the Library. Bert had said he should have gone yesterday instead of going out fishing, so he would have to work at the Library all day to make up for the time he had lost.

"Well, you come along a' me young fella and we'll soon 'ave 'e back with yer father." said the tall man. As Jack continued to sob and showed no inclination to move, he bent down, lifted him into his arms and started to walk off with him, holding him firmly in his reassuringly strong grasp.

"I'll catch 'e later Likky," he shouted over his shoulder, "at 'ome if I d' get 'eld up findin' the boy's father. I 'spec 'e's tearin' roun' Penzance lookin' all over fer 'en."

So his two friends, grinning all over their faces at the sight of the great Joey Bolitho playing nursemaid, departed and headed off towards the lower end of the town. The tall man took a short cut and soon Jack recognised the familiar sight of Chapel Street, so with his big stride the man directed his steps purposely towards the house that was to become the town's Free Library. He was making pleasant conversation with the boy, who was quiet but for the occasional sniff, when, on turning the corner, the boy's father almost collided with them.

"Oh Jack!," he cried, "Oh my precious boy!" and he held out his arms as Jack was passed over into their safe haven and burst into tears upon his father's shoulder quite unashamedly. Paul, his eyes closed in relief, breathed deeply and hugged his son to him, rocking him gently to reassure him. Slowly he realised that his son's protector was standing before him and, opening his eyes, found Joseph Bolitho's eyes observing the scene, with perhaps a satisfied look on his face, he could not be sure. It was always difficult to know what Joey was thinking.

"Thank God you found him, Mr Bolitho. I was out of my mind with worry lest he had been in an accident, or worse," breathed Paul in a relieved voice.

"Well, I think 'e've 'ad a fall an' cut 'iself but nothin' too bad, but he come runnin' up to me shoutin' 'Dada' at the top of 'is voice," he remarked and he laughed jovially. "That made Likky and Seth laugh I can tell 'e."

Paul blinked in amazement while the smuggler explained that the poor chap had the sun in his eyes and probably thought the first tall man that he saw was his father.

The first moment of relief over, Paul began to thank his son's saviour, but Joey cut him short.

"No problem, Mr Trevarthen, sir, couldn' leave the poor liddle chap after all. 'E'd a never a foun' 'is way back all this way. 'Spose 'e run off when you wouldn' lookin'. Easy done."

"Well he did run off, the young devil," said Paul and he smiled at Jack and gave him a little shake, "but he was not with me, but with Nurse, who is no doubt still howling fit to burst in the hallway of the Library at this very moment." He then bethought himself to admonish Jack most severely for running away from Miss Clavering and for causing her such distress.

Jack hung his head, but mumbled something about not liking old ladies patting his head and telling him he was just like his father and things like that.

"And Nurse wouldn't let me look at a dead cat in the road, even though I said please, twice!" he argued reasonably. His father and the other man burst out laughing at that, so the little boy laughed too and then hugged his father happily and kissed his cheek. Joseph Bolitho smiled at them, but felt a sharp pain in his chest at the sight of their affection, almost as if his own knife had pricked him. 'Silly fool,' he thought to himself, and then said he had better be getting along.

"No!" said Jack, in a determined little voice, "You come too and then you can tell Nurse I wouldn't no trouble because if Dada says I'm no trouble Nurse always says Dada is be . . . b . . . sotted with me and that I must have been naughty because I always do things I shouldn't do," and he wriggled until his father released him. When he was on the ground again, he took Joey by the hand quite confidently and proceeded to tell him that Nurse had said Grandpa Redvers had told her that Dada had been a little devil too when he was a boy.

Paul and Joey exchanged gleeful grins, but then his father said that he could not expect Mr Bolitho to go out of his way for him, as he was a busy man and no doubt had things to do.

Jack looked absurdly downhearted, but raised a face to Joey that was a picture of sorrowful entreaty and asked simply: "Please, Mr Bytho, please tell Nurse for me."

There were lots of things Joey Bolitho had been quite adept at refusing to do in his life, but the pleading look in the boy's eyes unmanned him and he bent down to look into Jack's face and said: "All right, young Jack, but if ever I 'ere that you run off like that 'gain' I'll get yer father to give 'e a good 'ammerin'."

"He won't do that 'cos he don't hit nobody." said Jack positively.

"Oh he don't, don't he? Well 'e 'it me once and I'm a . . . a friend of 'en, so don't be so sure 'e won't thump you one if you don't be'ave. You 'ear me?" he told Jack, and turned and winked wickedly at Paul.

"Yessir!" said the boy promptly, eyeing them both with dawning respect.

As they approached the Library, Miss Clavering could be heard in the street, such was the commotion that she was making. One or two worried passers by were standing in a little group outside the door, wondering whether to go in or not. Upon Paul's arrival they dispersed after his brief, smiling explanation, whilst Jack led Mr Bolitho into the hall and presented himself before his distraught nurse. The little boy was immediately clasped to her bosom and showered with even more tears. He raised his eyes at his rescuer and such was his expression that it induced a smile from him. It was explained that he had come to no harm and that he had been brought back most safely, and " 'Ess, 'e'd not bin any trouble an' 'ad behaved 'iself perfectly" Bolitho vouchsafed to the nurse. For this affirmation Joey received a beaming smile from the runaway, so after ensuring that Jack's cut hand was cleaned properly, Miss Clavering wiped his face, then cleaned and adjusted his clothing - amidst much moaning - and told Mr Trevarthen she would take his son home immediately.

She commanded her charge to thank Mr Bolitho for taking such good care of him, so Jack promptly released her hand and ran over with his arms outstretched, innocently expecting Joey to bend down and pick him up as his father would have done. Joseph Bolitho looked swiftly at the boy's father, who nodded his head, so he did indeed reach down and swept Jack into his arms, receiving a tight hug and a large kiss on the cheek for his trouble.

"Mind you do what yer told now, else you knaw what!" he told Jack in a severe voice, but one that was not completely devoid of warmth.

After their departure, Paul walked up to the smuggler, held out his hand unreservedly and waited patiently. Joey looked at Jack's father for a moment with his impassive face, but he extended his own hand and smiled.

"I owe you a handkerchief, Mr Bolitho, and, methinks, a lot more besides for the lower part of this town is not the most salubrious area in which such a young boy should get lost," said Paul.

"Don't worry 'bout 'e Mr Trevarthen, 'e'll do all right," replied Joey, "Mind you, I shouldn' fancy 'avin' look after 'en fer long. Look like 'e's a bleddy devil when 'e want be," and he laughed out loud.

"He certainly is that Mr Bolitho, and I have much sympathy for poor Miss Clavering, for he does his utmost to avoid her control at all times. Luckily, he will be at school soon and they will have the unenviable task of controlling him," said Paul fondly.

" 'E's not a bad lad, 'e jes' got a bit bored. Pity you a . . . pity they children to you died like they did," he remarked gently, and he looked up and caught Paul's forsaken expression.

"Yes, you're right, Mr Bolitho," said Paul, sadly, "for he lost the two brother's that were the closest to him in age. When they . . . died, he would be forever going off to look for them, because he could not understand that they would never be coming back to play with him." Trevarthen kept his face lowered but Bolitho saw a watery glimmer in his eyes, so he said, brightly: "Still, you got another liddle one now, fer 'en to play with."

There was an uncomfortable silence, then Paul sighed, sniffed, and laughed dryly, before saying: "Unfortunately, she is not the brother that Jack hoped he was going to have."

"Tcha! Poor soul," said Joey and his shoulders began to shake and catching Paul's eye, he was relieved to find an answering twinkle in them and both men had a quiet laugh at poor Jack's expense.

"I'm sorry, Mr Bolitho, you will have to excuse me but I ought to finish this before I leave," said Paul, and indicated the small piles of books left in the hallway, "for I have still more to put away upstairs, as I had to leave them when poor Nurse arrived in such a panic."

Joey looked around him, then bent and picked up one pile and said: "Well come us on then, or else you'll be 'ere all night." Paul blinked in surprise, but it had been a long day and even his love of books was beginning to wane, so he smiled, picked up another pile and led the way upstairs.

It was Joey's turn to look surprised when he saw the row upon row of books, ranged upon the shelves. When Trevarthen was again at the top of the ladder and engrossed in what he was doing, he called down, unthinkingly, to his new assistant if there was a book called, "The Canterbury Tales," in the small heap that lay on the table. A sudden thought struck him that it was unlikely that the smuggler had ever learnt to read, but after a moment he heard a succinct, " 'Ess," and when it was passed up to him with the comment: "Bit immoral fer roun' 'ere, Paul. Make a few a they biddies pop their stays if they was t' read this, 'specially what that Wife 'a Bath's tale got in it," Paul almost fell off the ladder, such was his surprise.

"How do you know that?" asked Paul incredulously.

"What 'e mean, 'ow do I knaw that? 'Cos I read the bleddy thing, you fool, 'ow did 'e think I knaw," said Joey testily.

Paul was so surprised at the fact that Joseph Bolitho could even read, that he could not help but stare rudely at him. The smuggler's impassive expression came down on his face immediately, but his voice was full of irritation as he said: "You 'ent the only man roun' 'ere, Paul Trevarthen, can bleddy read!"

Paul's face darkened with a flush of embarrassment, and he mumbled awkwardly: "My apologies, Mr Bolitho, I . . . I had no idea. I wasn't even sure that you could actually read until just now, when I asked for that book, let alone that you had gone to school."

For a moment it looked as if he would have to sort his books on his own, but Bolitho, his temper rising, swallowed hard and then announced that he had not attended school, as unlike,- "Mr Trevarthen, I never 'ad a father t' send me to a good school, but, in me youth, I was very friendly to the vicar's wife over to Sithney an' she very kindly taught me to read. I went see she regular fer years an' we both benefited greatly, if you d' knaw what I mean," and he tilted his chin defiantly. Paul tried, he did indeed try most diligently, but he began to chuckle and then to laugh loudly, and as his companion's face began to perceptively darken with anger, he managed to gasp: "Damn me, Joey, but that's a damn enjoyable way to learn your letters! You have the advantage of me there for I wish I could have learnt mine in the same fashion," and he put up his hand to wipe the tears from his eyes.

A slow grin crept across Joey's face and he joined in with the merriment, but after a while they stopped laughing and resumed their work, and so it was not long before they had put the last book in its place. Paul asked, in a reserved, shy voice if his assistant would like to look around and, on receiving his assent, he conducted Joey on a tour of the Library, going into details on all the different rooms and how they were divided into different sections. The questions that were asked were all relevant and intelligent and the smuggler surprised Trevarthen by asking if he had any of his own books on the shelves. "I read a bit a' that one 'bout the chap with the elephants goin' over some mountains. Now 'ang on. I'll get it in a minute - Alps, tha's it, 'e went over the Alps."

"Hannibal?" said Paul helpfully.

" 'Ess, 'ess," said Joey excitedly and he raised a smiling face to Paul and continued: "I was over to Squire Tregurthen's on some . . . er . . . business an' I saw it on the shelf so I picked 'en up an' 'ad a bit of read," and noticing Paul's eyebrows raised in surprise he said: "Well, who the 'ell did 'e think bought the stuff I d' get in," and then laughed at his shocked expression and shook his head muttering: "You're some innocent liddle soul aren't 'e?"

Paul smiled ruefully, "Well, to be honest, Joey, I must admit I am, for Chloe is forever telling me that it is so, and also that it is what comes from spending too much time with my head in books. But as to having my own books here, I thought it would be rather grandiose of me to put my own works on the shelf, so I have not done so," said Paul honestly.

"Bleddy fool!" commented Joey succinctly. By this time they had reached the hallway and Paul fished in his pocket for the keys as they prepared to leave.

"A drink, Joey, for all your efforts on my behalf today?" asked Paul, sincerely.

74

Joey stared at him in astonishment, but then surprised him by saying quietly: "No, don't be seen in yer good clothes with me. 'Tis all right when you're with Bert an' yer mates an' look like one a' they. Yer peers can accept that, you bein' a bit odd like and goin' out fishin' like you d' do, but you shouldn' be seen with me in the better taverns an' we 'ent goin' walk together all the way through town to get to Josh's place."

"I care not," said Paul stoutly, "for I will acknowledge my . . . my friends wherever I am and in whatever garb I sport."

"Tha's a pretty thing say, Paul, very pretty, but our friend Mr 'Udson will be up yer place in next to no time if 'e see we two walkin' together through the town an' 'e'll go through yer cellars an' stables fer days looking fer contraband," he explained, smilingly.

"Well, he won't find anything," vouchsafed Paul.

"No tha's true," admitted Joey, " 'cos yer workers will 'ave less t' do with me than their own master would like to do," and he laughed at the discomforted expression on Trevarthen's face. Clapping him on the back, he gently propelled him through the door. After another handshake they wished each other farewell and turned and took their separate ways.

On the way home, Paul stopped his easy canter and set his horse at a walking pace. He was deep in thought and when he came around the corner where his mother had suffered her mortal wound, he stopped for a moment and cast his mind back into the past with a sombre expression on his face. Having to pass the place every time he went to town had always given him a feeling of despair, but it had been a long time ago. He had learned to live with it, but Hudson's tale had appalled him as he realised its implication. Worse than that was the growing feeling of warmth he felt for Joseph Bolitho.

"By rights I should hate the man," said Paul to himself, "but there is much about him that I admire." In his mind he saw that poor boy with the withered hand and felt his disgust well up within him. He heard again Old Edwin's tale and felt sorrow for Bolitho all over again. Then all that had happened that very afternoon and the friendly way his son had reacted to Joey. Thankful though he had been to have Jack returned to him, in his heart he felt distressed by the sight of his son in Bolitho's arms. Then the surprise of discovering about Bolitho's reading abilities and the fact that he had done business with Squire Tregurthen, and on a regular basis. The day of the hanging, that very hypocrite had talked delightedly about having Joey and his accomplices hung. "Hanging out like their mother's washing!" he had said. Paul shook his head. He was unable to understand all that he was finding out about Bolitho and still nagging at him was the feeling that this one man had a value to him; that his importance to Paul far outweighed his past actions. He conjured up an image of Joey's face in his mind: the blank, impassive way he had of looking at people, the way he stood straight, tall and proud, that mischievous smile - there was something about him that unnerved him. "Like looking at a ghost, almost." he thought and he laughed aloud and shivered, but his horse was startled by the noise and shied and broke into a canter. Paul made no attempt to rein him back. The past was the past; his mind thought only of his happy home as he pushed his horse into a gallop in order to cover the last part of his journey the sooner.

CHAPTER 9

"I so wish I had been able to attend, but my poor health, being what it is, made it an impossibility," announced Mrs Carter sadly, "Everyone was there, I am told. Did Mr Trevarthen make a speech?"

"Yes, well, no, not at all. He said nothing about his own part in it, merely introduced the Librarian, a Mr Pawley. A most refined gentleman with a very quiet way of speaking, and indeed is so exactly one's idea of a librarian, that one cannot imagine that he would have been fitted for any other employment.

Naturally, Squire Tregurthen made a speech about Mr Trevarthen and the way he had set up the Library, and mentioned quite a bit about his scholastic abilities and his good works. Poor Mr Trevarthen looked most discomforted. There are other staff employed at the institution, for indeed 'twould prove impossible for Mr Pawley to be capable of attending to the whole establishment on his own. There are so many books! Mr Trevarthen must have spent an absolute fortune on those alone! There are whole rooms devoted to differing subjects, far more than my poor abilities could ever hope to understand but I was able to take out one of those famous romances, Sense and Sensibility no less. And Mr Dennis took out a delightful book on fishing, so our evenings will be spent in much quiet contentment. Now I have talked quite enough, dear Mrs Carter, for I have to make some purchases from Mrs Martin's. She has the most wonderful jonquil sprigged muslin and I would so much like to have a dress made for dear Charlotte in it, for with her colouring, it would suit her admirably." still chattering happily, Mrs Dennis rose to her feet and promised Mrs Carter to call again soon.

After her departure, Mrs Carter had not long to wait before she was again receiving visitors; Not only her dear Mr Trevarthen, but accompanied by his wife and their sweet little baby. Chloe explained that, knowing Mrs Carter would not be able to come to Trevu to see little Alice, they had thought it only proper that they should bring the baby into Penzance especially for Mrs Carter to see her.

The old lady beamed with pleasure and, when Paul carefully placed Alice in her arms, she found she could not stop smiling.

"How kind of you both to think of me, and to go to such trouble for me. My dears, she is most beautiful, and look, look!" she cried excitedly, "she is smiling at me." Paul and Chloe exchanged their own smiles, for in all probability their daughter was suffering a slight attack of wind, but no matter, for little Alice had given immense pleasure to Mrs Carter.

"We will not be staying long, Mrs Carter, for we do not want to keep Alice from home lest she becomes agitated. She has the most powerful set of lungs. The volume of her crying far outweighs anything the other children were able to produce," laughed Chloe.

"Oh, poor Paul, how distracting for you." said Mrs Carter, sympathetically.

"Oh, I mind not Mrs Carter, for it is so wonderful to hear the sound of a baby crying in the house again." and he leaned over and gently stroked his daughter's fluff of hair with his long fingers. He raised his eyes to his wife's face and his smile was for her alone. She responded in kind but then turned her attention to Mrs Carter and complimented her on her sure touch with children: "For see how peaceful little Alice lies in your arms, ma'am."

"My late husband, God rest his soul, was most impressed with the way I ministered to our own children. Of course, the nursemaids were responsible for the more mundane side of children, but I was responsible for much of their society manners and when they were older the girls relied on me to find them exceptional husbands. I do not think I disappointed them." she said proudly.

"Certainly not, Mrs Carter, for your daughters and their respective families are a credit to you." remarked Chloe and Paul smiled, nodding in agreement. The shallow-hearted Mrs Carter had developed a most sympathetic tendre for Paul over the years and Chloe had to admit that the lady had always been at pains to show her affection for Paul; after the first shock of Daisy's appearance, it was Mrs Carter's determination to continue to accept Mr Trevarthen as a visitor to her home that had enabled the scandal to be accepted, if not with equanimity, at least with some small degree of benevolence.

With a knock at the door, Mrs Carter's maid announced the arrival of more visitors. Mr and Mrs Hudson entered; the lady all of a bustle and the gentleman far more reserved. After greeting Mrs Carter, Mrs Hudson immediately fell into raptures over Alice, announcing her wish that they have children of their own soon, "for they are the most delightful creatures, are they not Mrs Trevarthen?" and she turned and beamed excitedly at Alice's mother.

"Most delightful," agreed Chloe, and frowned down her husband's wicked grin.

Mr Hudson, seating himself with Paul on the settle, remarked to that gentleman that he had not seen him of late.

"Has the enchantment of fishing from an open boat lost its charms for you, Mr Trevarthen?" he asked, brusquely. Chloe, still smiling, noted his coolness but his wife began to chatter to Mrs Carter about children in general and Alice in particular, so she turned her gaze upon Mrs Hudson and answered any of the questions that were directed to her with the best of her ability and with as much equanimity as possible.

"By no means," answered Paul, urbanely, "but I have been most occupied with the Library and found I had to devote more time to that establishment than I had foreseen. However, I hope to resume my piscatorial pursuits as soon as my time allows."

"Bolitho has been keeping a low profile, recently, don't you know. A couple of trips to France and some other activities involving ..." and here Mr Hudson coughed, and lowered his voice to say discreetly: "... a certain lady of notoriously lax morals who frequents the taverns of St. Ives."

"I have no knowledge of Mr Bolitho's whereabouts, Mr Hudson, for, as I have mentioned, I have had very little opportunity to frequent Josh Pascoe's most convivial establishment of late," replied Paul serenely.

"Surely, after the service Bolitho rendered you, you find yourself indebted to him? There must be some way in which you would wish to recompense him after returning your dear son to your bosom. A man like Bolitho would expect a reward, that's for sure!" snorted Hudson, derisively.

"On the contrary, Mr Hudson, I do not think that Mr Bolitho even considered the possibility of a reward," replied Paul, attempting not to sneer, "and he certainly never asked one of me."

"How strange. You were seen leaving the Library together long after your son had returned to your home with the nursemaid. Rather an unusual place for Bolitho to frequent I would have thought," remarked the preventative man, his hard grey eyes continuing to study Trevarthen's face.

"I regret to have to correct you Mr Hudson, we left at the same time but not, I might add, together. Mr Bolitho's assistance was most valuable for he helped me to finish the work I had in hand on that day, allocating certain books to their correct locations. However, I have no knowledge of Mr Bolitho's whereabouts after he left the Library, but I expect you could, if you wished, no doubt enlighten me."

To say that Mr Hudson looked shocked was the least of it, for he assumed the expression of a man who had been hit by a thunderbolt.

"Joey Bolitho helped you to arrange books!" he said incredulously, "Stap me, I never even knew the fellow could read!"

"I know, I was most surprised myself," agreed Paul, "but he seemed remarkably well read. His teacher was most . . . um . . . thorough, apparently."

Mr Hudson studied Paul's face pensively, before remarking with the merest hint of a threat in his voice: "When next you fish, Mr Trevarthen, sir, beware you do not sail too close to the wind. 'Tis most dangerous, so I have been told."

Paul lifted one eyebrow and said derisively: "Your concern for my welfare is most intriguing, Mr Hudson. I thought not that you worried so much for me."

"On the contrary, Mr Trevarthen, your welfare is one of my main interests, for I have noticed that the company you keep and the friends you have are quite often the very people that I am most interested in." replied Hudson, coldly.

His dark companion smiled collectedly, before commenting that perhaps Mrs Carter was unaware of Mr Hudson's suspicions towards her good self.

His adversary smiled serenely back, before commenting: "Vastly entertaining Mr Trevarthen, but take care, lest your wit should rebound on you. There are those hereabouts would not like to think that a personage of such high social position as yourself should be entangled with the sort of riff-raff with whom I have seen you conversing."

"Fear not, Mr Hudson, there are . . . er . . .personages in this town who, from my first appearance here, have always considered me to be one of those very . . . er . . . riff raff to which you refer," replied Paul, without a hint of malice.

"My! How you gentlemen do chatter!" broke in Mrs Hudson, and both men turned to face her. Chloe noted that, whilst her husband's expression was as passive and innocent as ever, the Preventative Officer looked rather annoyed by his wife's interruption.

"Paul, dearest, I think it is time we took our leave, for I cannot believe that Alice will remain in her present contented condition for much longer and I fear she is like to deafen all here when she wakes," said Chloe with a smile. Paul rose to his feet and they began to take their leave of Mrs Carter and the Hudsons. Mr Hudson bowed to Mrs Trevarthen and remarked that he hoped to meet her again before long.

"Perhaps you and your good wife would care to visit one day, Mr Hudson, for you wife has expressed a desire to see our children and we hardly ever come into town with them." said Chloe, and looking up caught a fleeting glance of anger on her husband's face.

"Delighted, I'm sure," said Mr Hudson, promptly, "My wife and I would be honoured to call upon your good selves, for my dear wife, . . . um . . . and myself too of course, will be enchanted to meet your children, and I will be gratified to resume my conversation with your husband. I feel sure that he has much that he can tell me."

He found himself subjected to one of Mrs Trevarthen's direct stares and felt his colour rising in spite of himself. She smiled calmly and responded: "Then I hope, for your sake, that he does not bore you, Mr Hudson."

"Bore me, ma'am?" he asked, puzzled.

"Why yes, Mr Hudson, for once my dear husband talks of books, then I am afraid there is very little anyone can do to stop him." and she smiled quizzically at him. He had the oddest feeling that Mrs Trevarthen was laughing at him, but dismissed it from his mind. Women were such uncomplicated creatures after all.

The Master of Trevu stamped his foot angrily. His wife lowered her head over her stitching but preserved her silence.

"Well?" snapped Paul, "why in hell's name did you ask them to call? Not to ask of me first was bad enough, but to baldly invite them in such a way that I cannot now cry off!" and he stomped angrily across the room and flung himself into his chair.

"I will not answer your questions until you stop swearing in that obnoxious way," she replied calmly.

"Oh! You won't, won't you? Well, hear me, Chloe! I do not wish to have to converse more than I need to with that damned man, and as for his insipid fool of a wife!" He kicked at the pile of logs in the corner of the hearth, sending them cascading across the floor. "I would as soon sit and talk to a monkey!"

There was a lengthy silence, broken only by her husband who kicked at another log angrily. He had his dark scowl on his face and he was not in the mood to be either charmed or cajoled by his wife. Chloe was well aware of that, but she was also aware that although she may have annoyed him by asking the Hudsons to call upon them without consulting him first, there was something more, something that he was extremely worried about. Perhaps even afraid of. She preserved an innocent front, and continued her stitching. After many years of marriage, she had realised that her most successful ploy in getting her husband to tell her what she wanted to know was not to ask him directly, but to wait for him to tell her himself. His anger was always his first defence, she had merely to bide her time, she reasoned. So she made no reply.

Sadly she had miscalculated for once as, annoyed by her silence, her husband sprang out of his chair and stood in front of her before announcing harshly: "I shall not ask of you again, Chloe, for I will have an answer. Now, tell me why in bloody hell did you invite them here?" She winced, but continued to set her stitches until the embroidery was ripped from her hands and thrown across the room. Never had she seen her husband in such a temper before, and she felt a small quiver of fear in her stomach. For a moment she was too shocked to move, but the next instant she was on her feet and dealing her husband a hefty blow across his cheek. Immediately, Paul raised his hand to hit her back but, realising what he was about to do, turned from her and crossed the room, then grabbed hold of the mantelpiece with both hands and stared down into the fire, breathing heavily.

"How dare you?!" shouted his wife, her good intentions gone. She could not believe that Paul had been about to hit her, he who had never raised his hand to either her or the children. "If I wish to invite someone to this house I will, and you shall not deny me, husband or no! You have never objected to any invitation that I have ever issued. Now, of a sudden, I am no longer allowed to invite my friends . . ." but Paul spun on his heel and scoffed: "Friends! What damn friends? You had never met Hudson's wife until today and as for that blasted husband of hers . . ." and he stopped and took a deep breath. "Wife!" he said angrily, "You have no idea of the trouble that you have caused me by your thoughtless actions!" and he turned his back on her.

"You are in the right of it, husband! I have no idea why I have been subjected to the worst display of temper that I have ever seen from you, but well I know it is more than the fact you think the wife stupid and the husband . . . and the husband a threat!" she asserted.

Paul whirled around, his angry scowl displaced by a look of shock. His eyebrows snapped together.

"What do you imply, Chloe, by a . . . threat?" he asked sharply.

"Oh Paul! 'Tis so apparent that you are on your guard with the man, I would have to be the biggest fool an' I could not recognise it!" she answered, recovering some of her composure.

"I cannot tell you why I am guarded in his presence, Chloe, for it concerns another. It is not my affair alone, but I have to preserve my silence in order to protect him," he sighed, then added: "in truth, I have to stay silent to protect more than one."

"I see," said Chloe quietly and took a deep breath, "but surely, you have never been involved in the smuggling trade, so who do you have . . . Oh my God!" she gasped, and lifted her hand to her cheek, " 'Tis Bert Pendray."

Paul let out his pent up breath, but merely said: "Bert and . . . others." He turned away from her and said slowly: "I know so much more now than six months ago, and I am mired to the elbows, and Hudson knows it but he cannot prove it. He has decided to worry me, like a dog with a rat, in order to break me and to make me tell of what I know. Of Bert's part in smuggling, I know only that he has involved himself in that activity, not when nor where, and . . . and I am aware for whom he works."

"Joseph Bolitho?" asked Chloe quietly, and watched as her husband nodded, before continuing: "Was he the man you had the fight with?" and watched as her husband sighed and inclined his head again.

"His reputation goes before him, Paul, for he is a most dangerous man," she observed quietly.

"More dangerous than you will ever know, Chloe, but he is also the man who found our son and brought him back safe and well, and whom little Jack now regards as one of his greatest friends. He is as complex as a riddle with no solution. I am disgusted and repelled by him at one moment, and the next I would wish him a friend, such a bagatelle of a fellow is the man," observed her husband. He thought pensively for a long while and then recounted bitterly: "One of Mr Hudson's agents, a person paid to follow and report on Bolitho, disappeared. Hudson interrogated a group of us at the inn. Bolitho was there along with Bert. Had I told what I knew, and make no mistake, Chloe, I knew enough for Hudson's needs, then Bolitho would have been taken. Bert would not have stayed out of either man's clutches if that had happened and, with Bolitho arrested, his associates would have vented their anger in the way they knew best. Not only Bert's family would have suffered at their hands but also mine, and with no witnesses Bolitho would have to have been released. Do you understand now the consequences of your thoughtless actions today?" he asked, then shook his head and, turning away, slumped into his chair and stared broodingly into the fire.

Chloe lowered her head, "I'm sorry, Paul, if I had known I would never have issued such an invitation." and she crossed the room and bent to retrieve her embroidery. Resuming her seat, she threaded her needle, but she could not resume her stitching.

During the silence that followed each of them had time to reflect upon the argument that had just taken place. Paul had been full of tension from the moment Hudson had walked into Mrs Carter's withdrawing room. Chloe had been aware that something was wrong, but nothing could have prepared her for the revelation that her husband had just made. She had been so pleased when Bert and Paul had started their fishing trips, for she realised that the one thing her husband lacked was male companionship. His greatest friend, Peter Fleetwood, they rarely saw as he worked abroad for such long periods of time. His oldest friend was in the army and, after fighting in the Peninsula Wars, was now stationed in London with his family. Her husband was in regular contact with both of them but he rarely saw either. He disliked to leave Cornwall and if he could he would avoid the necessity. He much preferred the company of his wife and family, but she understood that he needed the dynamic fellowship of men. Going about the farm had been of help there but, although on the best of terms with his workmen, he could not make a friend of any of them as he could with Bert Pendray. Bert was independent of Paul, for he worked for himself and, therefore, they did not have a master and servant relationship. Paul benefited greatly from the physical exercise of fishing but more than that he enjoyed the fisherman's companionship. He had a fondness for Bert's children and she knew, for he had told her, that he had offered monetary assistance to his friend for his children's sake, but Bert's pride had not allowed him to accept the gesture. Obviously, Bert's attempt to better his circumstances was to avail himself of the money that could be made from smuggling. So Paul had become involved, albeit reluctantly in Bert's intrigues, and now she had brought down upon his head a meeting that he had no wish to partake in. He had good reason, for it could prove to be a potential disaster to not only the Pendray family but her own as well. Then there was Joseph Bolitho, a man she had never met or even seen, but a man she had been told so much about. A character of such known cruelty that, when her husband had confirmed that the person who had indeed rescued little Jack from danger was indeed that infamous gentleman, she had given an involuntary shiver at the thought. Now her husband had to protect not only his friend but Penzance's most notorious criminal as well! She found it impossible to believe that her beloved Paul should have become so embroiled in such a catastrophic situation, but so it was.

While these thoughts went through her mind her husband stared at the fire, for he had much to contemplate as well. His biggest fear was that by a word or deed he should implicate his friend in the smuggling trade. He was terrified that he would be responsible for causing Bert's downfall, for he could not imagine how he would be able to extricate his friend from the justice that would be so surely meted out to him. Then Bolitho's justice, what of that? Joey would not allow any man his freedom if they reneged on him, he was well aware of that fact. He saw again poor Nick Glasson and shuddered at his imagined end. He was revolted by Joey's complete disregard of the poor lad's right to exist but, from Joey's point of view, he had to keep informers quiet and to put an end to their life was the most certain way he knew of doing that. If Paul, in his turn, should become one of those informers, however inadvertently, what would happen to him? He had an honest man's fear of death, but there was more than that to be afraid of. He could not imagine Joey hurting his family, but he could not deny that Joey had the most vicious of tempers. He felt himself grow cold at the thought. No, Joseph Bolitho, the great paradox, was not the man to cross swords with. Bert had warned him time and time again of that fact, but then his thoughts returned to their talk in the Library. Surely such a gifted and intelligent man would not do harm to an enemy's family. Various Roman Caesars sprang to his mind, along with the crimes that they participated in. Were they not gifted and intelligent too? He sighed loudly.

Chloe looked up and caught his eye. He smiled grimly, and asked quietly: "Well, Chloe, my wisest counsel, what advice have you for your most troubled husband?"

"I have been considering the problem Paul, and hope I have achieved some sort of solution. Mrs Hudson has expressed a desire to see the children, and so she shall. She will also see the thing that my husband does better than anything else?" and she smiled as Paul raised his eyebrow in enquiry. "She will see what a family man I have for a husband, for the children will be forever with us during the visit, and I defy any man, let alone Mr Hudson, to have a sensible conversation with you when you are displaying all the tendencies of an idiot, as you are like to do when playing with your offspring."

Paul laughed and admitted that her solution might answer. "It is my only hope, for if I am alone with that man I will have great difficulty in keeping my face and actions under my stewardship." He sat watching her, a feeling of reassurance creeping over him. Imagining the scene of the withdrawing room full of his energetic brood, he smiled to himself. It would answer, for Hudson could not, in all honour, attempt to question him, especially if the girls would go through their not inconsiderable repertoire of songs. Grace and Daisy both had very pleasant voices and enjoyed singing. All the children played the piano, including little Jack, whose efforts required far more practice than he was prepared to give to it. He grinned broadly at his imaginings for Hudson would, he knew, hate every moment of the visit. After a moment he stood up and walked towards his wife, gently removed her sewing from her hands, pulled her to her feet and into his arms and held her to him. "Well, have you any other . . ." she began but he merely said: "Quiet! I have talked enough." and proceeded to kiss her fiercely and passionately, and in between his kisses he offered her his abject apologies for his actions and his behaviour.

"Humph!" laughed his wife, "You are as ever a charmer, Paul. You never fail to amaze me that, after losing your temper you always try to atone for your behaviour by attempting to have your wicked way with me."

"Not wicked, surely?" he quizzed but availed himself of her hands and, seating himself on the settle, pulled her down to him and began to shower her with passionate kisses whilst his fingers deftly undid the fastenings of her dress. His wife threw back her head and laughed, then returned his passion with fervour. He hoped to God that none of the servants or children should suddenly make an entrance into the room, for he was well aware that their mutual ardour was quite unable to wait for the cloak of night.

"Hasn't been in fer three days," said Josh, "I saw Mrs Wherry an' she said he was lookin' pretty bad. If you's thinkin' of goin' see 'en I wouldn' leave it too long, Joey."

Joseph Bolitho observed the ale in his tankard, but merely nodded. His mind was elsewhere. On the previous night his contraband was almost lost, not at sea but when brought to shore. A party of four preventative men, on returning to Penzance from an unsuccessful foray in Lamorna, where they had been informed that a vast quantity of brandy and geneva was to be landed, came across his men. They should have been later to disembark their goods, but with a sudden storm brewing they had endeavoured to land as soon as possible. To lose both their cargo and their lives would have been a disaster. These poor gentleman were almost taken but, as luck would have it, a group of miners coming home from their work lent invaluable assistance to the freetraders. As a result, two of the preventatives ran away, much bloodied and bruised, one had his arm broken and the unfortunate fourth, receiving a ball in the chest, was not expected to live more than a few days. Bolitho preferred to work unhindered for he had no wish to kill a preventative man. They were often local people, old sailors or army men who were no longer required for service to their country, so were put to use in the customs service. When too old for even that, heaven help them, for their country rarely did. However, if those same customs men interfered with his methods of securing his livelihood, then he was prepared to stop them with whatever means he had at his disposal. He armed all his men, but if they did not wish to kill anyone he did not punish them, their companions would see to that. To be taken meant almost certain death; either press-ganged into the navy, transported or hung. If the men did not look out for each other then they would be lost. Enough men had found that out to their cost. The fellows that worked for Joey admired his skill in avoiding capture; for himself, his men and his cargoes. He paid them well, looked after their families if they were injured, and made sure that the locals who dared to turn informer were despatched with the minimum of fuss and without trace. Last night could so nearly have been a disaster, he acknowledged to himself, so he would have to take more care in the future. Perhaps he should curtail his visits to St. Ives? After all, one wench was much alike another and he would have no trouble in finding some other fair damsel with which to fill his arms. 'No' he thought sadly, 'they were not all the same. There is one, one above all others, who I would give my soul to have.' As he brought his beloved to mind the dull ache that had never left him pulled at his heart. He pictured her again and trembled with excitement at the beautiful vision that the sight of her always presented to him.

"Another, Joey?" asked Josh, quietly, breaking in on his tortured thoughts.

"No . . . no thanks, Josh, I'd best be goin' on. Things to do. Catch 'e 'gain' my ol' mate," he muttered distractedly, and dragging himself back to the present, strode purposefully out of the inn.

He returned to his home, briefly, and retrieving a bottle of his best brandy from under the brick behind the chimneypiece, he made his way to the locality in which he had first seen the light of day. He met Mrs Wherry at the end of the street and she sighed and said sadly: "Not long now, Joey me lad, not long now. Still 'e've 'ad a good span," and she hitched up her basket and headed off to her own home. Bolitho called out as he pushed open the door, but his only answer was the sound of creaking wood. Knowing the house as he did, he knew well where to find his quarry. He had to bow his head low when he entered the linney but there he was, lying on the floor, on some old sacking filled with straw. Years ago, Joey had offered to get him a real bed, but he told him he preferred not to sleep in one because he never had slept on anything else. Creeping towards him, Joey watched the laboured breathing and knew the old man's time was nigh.

The light from the small window shone full into Joey's face as he sat himself upon the floor. He uncorked the brandy bottle, and finding a dirty cup, wiped it out with his handkerchief and filled it with the amber liquid.

"Edwin, 'ey, Edwin! Look what I got fer 'e, my 'ansome? 'Tis my best cargo ever. Try a drop a' this ol' son, this'll perk 'e up," he said with a smile.

Edwin opened his eyes and looked at his companion, and then at the cup.

"Good stuff, Joey?" he rasped, painfully.

"The best," Joey assured him.

Joey propped the old man into a sitting position and presented him with the cup, and Edwin took it in his shaking hand and drank greedily, spilling some down his unshaven chin.

"Damn tha's some good, Joey," he said, his voice noticeably stronger, and he turned his head and regarded his companion with a thoughtful expression on his face.

"I knawed you'd come see yer ol' mate, Joey. Knawed you wouldn' let we die thirsty," observed Edwin.

"Never said anythin' 'bout 'e dyin', now, did I?" smiled Joey.

"Didden' 'ave to, Joey. I d' knaw that fer meself," vouchsafed the old man and regarded Joey shrewdly. He finished his drink, and had the cup refilled. Edwin smiled his thanks, but then fell into a reflective mood and said no word for a while.

Joey shifted his position uneasily. He had no wish to stay longer than was necessary for fear of tiring the old man, but of a sudden Edwin looked up and, staring him in the face, said brightly, "Got a yarn fer 'e Joey. Jes' fer you. I bin wonderin' whether 'tis bes' tell 'e or no, but if I don' you might do somethin' yer goin' regret."

"Go on then, Edwin, I'm listening," said Joey, hoping that it was not to be one of his more convoluted tales.

"Ever wondered who sired 'e Joey? I would a' done if I was 'e. I would 'ave bin' proud sire 'e meself if yer mother would 'ave obliged me but I was never in pocket enough fer she," he remarked, smiling fondly. "She was some 'ansome maid and she knew it, my God she knew it." he looked up and caught his listener's eye. Joey's face wore his impassive expression, but Edwin knew well the turmoil that was raging within him.

"Do you knaw 'is name?" asked Joey, quietly, "Is 'e . . . is 'e still alive?"

The old man shook his head. "Died some years back, but 'e never knew you was 'is boy. Dammee Joey, even Sally 'ad no idea who yer father was! You d' knaw that. I reckon if 'e knew 'e wouldn' 'ave left 'e lead the life you 'ave fer 'e was the sort a' man would 'ave seen 'e right, don' 'e worry 'bout that." he said with a smile and noticed a muscle twitch in Joey's cheek.

"Edwin, if mother didden' knaw an' my . . . my father didden' knaw, 'ow come you do?" he asked, softly.

"Ah! That was the trouble, my 'ansome. You d' look jes' like yer mother, see. I bin' lookin' at 'e fer years and I never could see it, not 'til a few months back. Knawed then, knawed in a minute." and he drained his cup. The smuggler refilled it, but Edwin began to struggle for breath.

" 'Ell's bells, Edwin, don' 'e die now, fer Christ's sake!" urged Joey.

The sick man laughed weakly, but the brandy restored some of his sagging life and he took up his tale again.

"I knawed all Sally's visitors, Joey, couldn' miss 'em. The ones with money use tie their 'osses outside the door. I never missed much, but Sally 'ad so many of 'em, Joey, I couldn' place yer sire. When 'is son come along, a few years later, he never strayed from 'is 'ome again. But still I didden' knaw yer father, nobody did. Then 'is boy come in the inn a while ago. I'd seen 'en in town plenty a' times but never thought no more of 'en than 'e was a damn nice chap. You walked in an' stood talking to 'en. 'E didden' look like you, an' you didden' look like 'e but 'e looks like 'is father see, an' when you was talkin' to 'en I could see you had a look of 'en 'bout you. The only way you could look like 'e was if you 'ad the same father. The more I looked at 'e the more I could see it; the look on yer faces, the way you d' both stand, yer very build. I don' think nobody else will ever notice 'cos I'm probably the only one lef' who can 'member back what use' 'appen over to yer 'ouse. I mind his own father's big bay 'oss tied up outside yer door all they years back. He spent a lot a' nights in yer mother's bed," said the old man, and then he added: "I'm dying boy, so I thought I'd better tell 'e 'cos I wouldn' want 'e kill yer own brother, Joey."

The impassive expression gave way to shock, "What do 'e mean? Kill me own brother!" and then struck by a horrific thought, Joey asked desperately: " 'E 'idden 'Udson's man, is 'e?" The old man shook his head slowly.

"No 'e 'idden anybody's man. 'E's 'is own man. But you'll put 'en goin' fast 'nuff if you've a mind to, 'tho 'e do 'ave no idea 'e 'ave even got a brother," wheezed Edwin, and suddenly he was racked with a fit of coughing and fell to one side, his head lolling alarmingly. Joey leaned over and gently lifted Edwin in his arms. The old man's eyes rolled back in their sockets. Desperately, Joey called his name, again and again, and finally Edwin coughed, and Joey whispered urgently to the old man, "Tell me 'is name, Edwin, 'is name!" He had to place his ear against the old man's lips to hear his final words. Then Edwin's body jerked once, letting out a long rattle of breath before it relaxed in Joey's arms and the old man died. Gently, Joey laid him down on his bed and covered him with his blanket before picking up the almost empty bottle and replacing the cork. He turned and, bending low, headed for the doorway, where he could stand at his full height. Turning, he looked at the dead man's peaceful expression and merely said: "Thanks Edwin," even though Edwin had failed to name his brother at the last. The old man had managed to gasp only the one word, but it was enough for Joey. After all, it was not the most common name hereabouts. He knew now why his erstwhile neighbour had taken years to discover Joey's sire, for it was not the person that most people would associate with the man he had grown up to be. He saw the named man again, in his mind's eye, striding tall through Penzance, caring not what was said about him and his actions, saw the pride in his face in his acknowledged son's character and achievements. He would have liked a father to have shown such a pride in him, but that could never be. Tears stung his eyes as he remembered the coins in the mud, their brief conversations and the first and last painful journey together as he led the sick man along the road from Penzance, to die in peace in his own home instead of on the roadway. If only his father had known who he was, how different his life could have been. But in spite of his regrets, his son felt inordinately proud to know, at last, the name of his sire and, with that knowledge, the name of his brother.

Letting himself out of the house, he met Mrs Wherry heading up the street towards him. He stopped her and told her the news. She smiled sadly but accepted gratefully the money he gave her for Edwin's funeral and for her care of him.

"Did 'e say much at the end, Joey? Fer 'e bin' some quiet these last few days," she asked.

" 'Ess 'e did. You knaw what 'e was like. Couldn' go without tellin' me a yarn," he replied softly, and they both smiled before parting and took their separate ways. Mrs Wherry to arrange the laying out and the funeral and Joey to find himself some quiet area on the cliff top, away from all, so he could ponder over the knowledge and the implications of who he was, at last.

CHAPTER 10

"I wished I had known, Bert, for I would have gone to his funeral. Were there many present?" asked Paul, and took off his hat and wiped the sweat from his brow with the sleeve of his coat.

"A fair few," replied Bert, " 'e bein' a well known chap. No family left a' course. They bin gone fer years, but people was fond a' the ol' beggar none the less, so quite a few made the effort. Joey was there, with Likky and quite a few others, and ol' Josh shut the inn fer an hour and went to see 'en off as well. Mind you, we all went back there an' Joey 'ad put in a fair bit in the pot so Josh did a roaring trade, come end up," and winking at Paul he enquired, "I s'pose we be goin' back there, Paul, as soon as we be done fer the day?"

"Damn right," said Paul, enthusiastically, "for I have such a thirst on me today, I could empty Josh's cellars."

"Well, you'd bes' not, else yer missus 'll be after me as well as 'e an' I reckon she can be a tarter if she's a mind to," and then said hastily, "beggin' yer pardon, Paul."

"Oh! No offence, Bert, and yes you are in the right of it. For someone of such small stature she can be most imposing. I have had to tread carefully on many an occasion." and he laughed loudly and fondly. A fisherman looked up from mending his nets and noted what the two men were doing, all the while listening intently to their conversation. He watched as they unloaded a poor catch, mainly mackerel he noticed, and even then few enough of them. His own plight was similar; the fishing was poor. But Pendray was smiling broadly enough. He bent his head to his task, lest they saw his interest and merely acknowledged their greeting as they passed him, with a gruff " 'Ow do!" as they passed by. He waited until they had almost disappeared from sight before feverishly folding his net and following them at a discreet distance. When they disappeared into the inn, he waited anxiously for a moment, then turned and hurried down one of the alleyways that led in the general direction of the Customs House and in the opposite direction from his own cottage. Carrying his coat and spare boots was an added encumbrance and he swore under his breath: "Damn, I should 'ave gone 'ome furst, get rid a' this lot." But he reasoned philosophically that he would have finished his business soon enough and would soon be on his way to his wife and family. Suddenly, he heard a noise behind him and looked over his shoulder, troubled lest someone was following him, and promptly walked straight into a man who appeared in front of him as if from nowhere. Looking up, his heart froze in fear for, smiling down at him, was no other than Joseph Bolitho. "Joey!" he gasped fearfully, but Bolitho's smile only broadened.

"Goin' the wrong way, aren't 'e, Davy? Thought yer place was down by Newlyn," asked Joey, still smiling.

Fear clutched at Davy Richards' heart, but he thought quickly and said he had some business in the town.

"Sorry, Davy," said Joey and smiled again, "Don' let me stop 'e if you're on business, ol' son," and he stepped aside to let him pass.

"Thankee, Joey, thankee," gasped the fisherman in relief, and he looked up briefly into the still smiling face before hurrying on his way.

"Follow 'en, Likky," said Bolitho quietly, apparently into thin air for there was no one to be seen, "I'll knaw what business 'e's on, an' with whom, afore I 'ave to act."

A shadow detached itself from a darkened doorway and proceeded to follow Davy at a discreet distance, ducking from view every time that the man glanced furtively over his shoulder.

Joey, meanwhile, was no longer smiling but was taking his easy strides in the direction of Josh's inn. When he entered, Bert and Paul were deep in conversation with Saul Tregonning and, as he approached, he heard them mention Edwin's name and knew they were talking of the funeral because the words, "good crowd" were spoken. As he neared them he ordered his customary round for the 'boys' and nonchalantly slapped his money onto the bar.

"Joey," nodded Bert in greeting. Paul turned and looked at him enigmatically for a moment before greeting him in turn.

"Bin chasin' anymore runaways, Mr Trevarthen?" laughed Joey quizzically.

"Not in Penzance, Mr Bolitho, no, but we had damn near to take the tack room apart on Friday, when Jack decided to hide there from his poor nurse. We were to have visitors and she rather stupidly informed him that he would be required to be washed and combed before being attired in his best clothes. Whether it was the word 'washed' or 'combed' that decided him to take to his heels I know not, but he certainly set the house about its ears when he disappeared."

"And did 'e look presentable when 'e met Mr and Mrs 'Udson?" asked Joey, softly, and found himself on the receiving end of a long, cool stare.

"Most!" was the sharp retort.

Joey threw back his head and laughed and then slapped his companion on the back, which only added to that man's discomfort.

"Mrs 'Udson's new maid said her 'usband 'ad a face like thunder when they come 'ome. Apparently, 'e didden much enjoy 'aving to spend the 'ol af'noon 'aving . . . now what did a' say? . . . 'Trevarthen's brats', tha's it, entertaining 'im. 'Is missus was most abrupt with 'en 'cos she said they was most accomplished children, what with their playing the piano and singin' an' she thought even the liddle boy with the scowling face was mos' adorable. I knew that 'ad be Jack, sure 'nuff. So our poor ol' preventative man 'ad a wasted af'noon by the sound of it. You're to be congratulated, Mr Trevarthen, fer yer cleverness." he remarked and laughed again.

"My wife suggested that, as I had no wish to spend the afternoon conversing with a man I disliked, the children would prove a useful distraction, as indeed they did." he commented, and then wondered if mentioning his wife's part in the scheme had been a wise idea.

"Your wife knaw of yer . . . uh . . . aversion to this gentleman then, Mr Trevarthen?" Bolitho asked shrewdly, but not coldly, Paul noted with reassurance.

"Mr Bolitho, my wife is a remarkably clever woman. What she does not know of she will guess at and she is rarely in the wrong with her assumptions." replied Paul, not without some pride.

"True 'nuff?" enquired Joey, but before Trevarthen could reply continued:

"I always thought 'e luckier than mos', Mr Trevarthen, an' now I realise it. I should like to meet 'er fer I'm sure she would be worth the knawin'."

"Unfortunately, or perhaps fortunately, that is a situation that is unlikely to arise, Mr Bolitho, for you do not frequent the same houses." replied Paul, frostily.

"Mmm, possibly," mused Joey, " at least, not at the same time." He grinned at Trevarthen's look of discomfort but merely said: "Please to tell 'er from me that I appreciate 'er efforts on 'er 'usband's behalf fer knawin' 'e's got a clever wife behin' 'en takes a load a' worry from off me shoulders."

"I cannot imagine that I could ever be a worry to the great Joseph Bolitho, could I?" asked Paul sardonically, and glanced coldly at him.

"I use' think 'e were, my 'ansome, but I knaw differen' now," the smuggler informed him softly, and Paul received a most unusual stare, a mixture of pride and affection.

"I know how to keep my mouth shut, Bolitho! You have no worries there, and I do not have the inclination to make of Hudson a friend or, if I could have helped it, would I even have wished him for an acquaintance. After all, I met that gentleman here first, and his interest in me was occasioned by the interest he had in you at that time, an' I remember correctly." he informed him evenly.

"Ah, don' be so touchy, Trevarthen, I d' knaw 'e fer no enemy of mine, don' 'e worry. An' I'll keep that damn man from off yer back as bes' as I can, never fear," and he turned and looked up as Likky appeared in the doorway and made a sign to him with a slight nod of his head.

Joey signalled back similarly, and drained his tankard. "Nice see 'e again, Trevarthen. Tell Jack 'e better be behavin' 'iself or else I'll want knaw why. See 'e all 'gain boys," he called out to the other men, and amidst loud farewells and waving of hands, he strode purposefully from the room. Paul noted in particular the way he had hitched up his knife that lay in its sheath in his belt and for some odd reason he felt a shiver run down his spine. Bert was asking him a question, so he turned politely and began to converse with him. Soon his apprehension was forgotten as they discussed a particularly amusing sight that they had seen from the boat that afternoon. Country dwellers so rarely looked out to sea when they engaged in their passionate frolics, no matter how much care they took to hide themselves from anyone on the land.

From the top of a stunted elm tree, Daisy and Harry viewed the surrounding countryside. Smoke, curling gently from the chimney of the Pendray cottage, drifted across the valley and disappeared on the breeze that was blowing inland from the sea. The wind ruffled Harry's fair hair as he stood up on the branch and pretended that he was an admiral looking out to sea. Daisy watched him and smiled secretly to herself.

"Why do you always have to do with ships or the sea Harry? Whenever I am with you that is all you seem to be talking about," asked Daisy, her feet swinging idly.

Harry shrugged his shoulders, but said: "Well, 'tis what I like to talk about best, Daisy, you know that. Anyway, you never want to speak about girl things so I suppose you don't mind at all. Do you, Daisy?" and he sat back down on the branch and gave her thigh a comradely slap as if she were her brother, George.

Daisy studied her leg for a moment and then sighed and said: "No, I don't mind, Harry."

"I've got something of great importance to tell you Daisy," he volunteered cautiously.

"What's that then, Harry?" she asked, and busied herself with stripping the bark from a branch with a twig so that her face was hidden from his view.

"Well, I'm to leave school soon and go to work with my father for he needs help full time with the boat, you see," he looked up but he could not see her expression, only the sweep of brown curls hanging loosely from the confines of her bedraggled ribbon. "He had hoped that he would be able to keep me at school longer but . . . well, if I can help him maybe he could take the boat out more often and make more money. You see we . . . we are not very rich, Daisy, for Aunt Emily has no money of her own and with her four children, it is difficult to manage. I don't actually mind, Daisy, but I shall miss your company. But . . . but we shall still see each other, at church on Sundays and perhaps of an evening if we are not fishing on that day." He waited, nervously, for Daisy to make her reply.

"I . . . I shall miss you Harry, for I think you my greatest friend but . . . but I do understand that . . . I mean, I know . . . I . . . your family . . . Oh Harry! I shall miss you dreadfully!" she said sadly, but kept her face turned away.

There was a long awkward, silence, and Harry heard a distinct sniff from Daisy, but thought it best to pretend not to notice.

"Shall we get down now, Daisy, and see if we can tickle some trout in the stream?" asked Harry, apprehensively.

"Why yes, Harry, that would be such fun," replied Daisy, turning her impassive face towards him and allowing him sight of a small tight smile.

On the way down the tree, Daisy ripped her dress but Harry was the more concerned, and when they got to the bank of the water course, she knelt down and got mud on the front of it as well. They were unsuccessful in their attempts to catch any fish and, when they had decided it was time to return to the cottage, they walked slowly back, but did not have a lot to say to each other. George and Dick arrived with some sticks and furze that they had gathered for the fire. Mrs Bosanko thanked them both but was most concerned that Daisy's dress was in such a state, and would have attempted to clean it if Grace had not told her that it was often the case that Daisy spoiled her clothes, for she much preferred to play like a boy.

"You are not to worry, Mrs Bosanko," she said, reassuringly, "for if Daisy did not dirty her clothes, Mama would think she had not enjoyed herself." and she turned towards her sister with a smile. She was somewhat surprised not to have an answering smile in return, but assumed that Harry and Daisy had argued about something and took no more notice than that of Daisy's blank, closed expression.

The Bosanko girls were most keen to show off the new skirts and petticoats that had been made for them by their own hands with the help of Grace's dextrous fingers and her guidance. Mrs Bosanko hugged and kissed Grace with delight and much respect, then extended her arms to Daisy. Daisy smiled as best as she could and allowed herself to receive the same attention, although possibly with less enthusiasm, for Daisy was not like her sister, after all.

When the carriage arrived to take the Trevarthen children home, they said their goodbyes and George and Grace both noticed how quiet Daisy was on the journey home. On arrival at Trevu, they both headed off to find their mother but Daisy went off on another quest, as she knew where to find the object of her search at this time of day. When she arrived at the door she paused for a moment and then dutifully knocked. When the voice bade her enter, she opened the door and stepped resolutely into the room. She tried to look composed, but she fell victim to her overwhelming sadness and so it was a sobbing daughter that threw herself into her father's arms. She blurted out her troubles between choking sobs, as Paul gently smoothed his hand over her head and curls, and held her in his reassuringly strong embrace. When finally her crying had stopped, they talked for a long while and, although Daisy's sadness had not dissipated completely, she felt better for talking to someone. She reached up impulsively and kissed her father before thanking him for his kindness. She also returned his handkerchief for, as usual, she had lost her own.

"I am sure that you will not mention this to anyone else, Daisy, but I did offer money to Mr Pendray to help him with his household finances, but he is a proud man and, quite rightly, refused to accept my offer. If I could I would do my best to make this easier for you, Daisy, for Mr Pendray told me that this would have to happen at some time in the future. He has tried most hard to extend Harry's time at school, but with his sister's children in the house as well it has been most difficult for him. However, it is not as if Harry is to go away from here and you will still be able to see each other, for I shall certainly do nothing to keep you from enjoying each other's company."

"I know, Dada, but I will miss Harry so much for I have no other friends like him in the whole school!" she sighed.

"I understand, my little sweetheart," he commiserated, "but perhaps it will not be so bad as you imagine. I shall have to think of something that you can do that will help to occupy your time between your meetings with Harry. Would you like to ride with me after school, or perhaps I could teach you to drive my curricle? Although perhaps it would be wisest if I were to begin with the pony and trap."

She looked up into his face sadly, but attempted a smile. "Will you teach Grace as well?" she asked slowly.

"Well," said Paul artfully, "I would offer, but I truly think she has not the aptitude for it that I am sure you will show."

He was rewarded with a proud smile.

"Do you truly believe that, Father?" she asked, glowing with pleasure.

"Oh yes," he said, and it was not actually a lie, for Daisy did love her boyish pursuits so and therefore, he reasoned, she would be the one to be far more interested in learning such a skill. In this he was proved correct, for his daughter was most adept at handling the pony and trap, so he swiftly moved her on to controlling a team of horses pulling the farm cart. He did not use his usual team - a rather sprightly pair of matching chestnuts - but his reliable old bays that did not mind at all that inexperienced hands were attempting to guide them along the country paths. When her father suggested that she might like to take Harry up in the pony and trap and drive him around the lanes, with Paul mounted on his grey hunter beside her if needed, she could not wait to hitch up the pony, such was her excitement. So in spite of the impending doom that was to fall upon her, occasioned by the loss of her friend from school, Daisy's new interests went some way to compensate her. To have her father's undoubted admiration gave her no small feeling of pride as well.

When next Paul went fishing with Harry's father, he mentioned that Daisy had been quite downhearted to think she was to lose her friend. He thought that Bert was not going to reply at first, but then he said: "I d' knaw Paul, but, there's a fair few mouths to feed in our 'ouse. Tidden easy an' I won't 'ave anything off you, so don't even bother to offer," he replied quietly.

Paul sighed, but tried determinedly: "I thought perhaps that you might like to do some work for me on the farm? I could pay you well."

Bert sat back and regarded him shrewdly for a while, "An' what sort a' work would that be Paul? Fishing in yer river, perhaps?"

His companion looked uncomfortable, but before he could think of some occupation that would occupy Bert, the wind shifted suddenly and they had to work hard to bring the boat around, so there was no further opportunity to talk for a while. It was not until they were leaving the quayside that they had time to continue their conversation and it was there that Joey found them both preoccupied with their talk. He waited for a moment, but as Bert turned his head away, exasperated at Paul's continued attempts to help him, he seized the moment and greeted both men in a jovial manner.

"Thought you two would have nothing left to say to each other after a day's fishin'?" he laughed, and caught sight of Paul's perturbed face, wondering exactly what it was that had so put him out of countenance.

" 'Ow do, Joey." greeted Bert. "We be goin' t' Josh's if you've a mind to come fer I think Paul an' me 'ave talked 'nuff," and he raised his eyes to his companion's face. As it was apparent that he would not give way to Paul on the matter, his friend sighed, turned to Joey and merely said: "Good day, Mr Bolitho."

"Tell 'e what, Mr Trevarthen sir, would 'e mind if you was to walk on ahead a' we, fer I 'ave a small matter I wish to discuss with Bert 'ere?" asked Joey politely.

"No. Not at all," replied Paul, not wishing to have knowledge of their conversation, and turned and strode away, informing them over his shoulder that he would purchase their drinks for them.

"Right you are, Mr Trevarthen, sir, most grateful," Joey called out, and watched the retreating figure until he was well out of earshot.

" 'Ad a row, with 'en Bert?" he asked.

"No, no! Tidden no row. The poor beggar keep tryin' 'elp me financially. 'E got a fondness fer me eldest an' want get 'en apprenticed to a boat builder fer me, or else want me take money to keep 'en on at school. I bin' tellin' 'en ever since I said 'Arry would 'ave leave school that I won't do it, but 'e won't give up," said Bert and shook his head sadly.

Both men turned and began to walk slowly in the direction of the inn. It had never occurred to Joey that Bert had ever been offered such assistance from Paul but when he thought about it, it was just the sort of thing that he would do, for he was a man renowned for his generosity.

"I got a job comin' off that will do 'e nicely, Bert. That'll 'elp 'e out a bit if you'll take it on fer me," Joey asked quietly.

Pendray sighed and began to shake his head. "'Tis becomin' a risky business, Joey. Ol' 'Udson got it into 'is 'ead that I'm the man to watch. The customs men 'ad their boat not thirty yards from we day an' was watchin' we pullin' our nets in, an' it wouldn' fer the sight a' seein' the Master of Trevu gettin' 'is 'ands dirty, I can tell 'e."

"I knaw, I knaw but I'll watch out fer 'e. You think 'pon what I said, Bert. I'll make sure you get a fair rate fer it, don' 'e worry 'bout that, pard'," urged Joey, but by this time they had reached the inn and no more was mentioned on the matter.

CHAPTER 11

MOST unusually the whole Trevarthen family, with the exception of Alice, who had been left in Miss Clavering's enraptured care, were together in Penzance.

George's new suit was not quite ready for collection from Mr Murdoch's, the tailor's, so as Paul had to visit the Library the whole family were making their way in that direction when Jack, whose hand was resting happily in his brother's, had his attention drawn by the appearance of a man he knew well. Letting out a gleeful shout of "Mr Bytho!" he dropped George's hand and took off across the road in the direction of that gentleman, who he had spotted closing the gate of a large imposing residence, the back entrance of which led onto the road.

A carriage, bowling smartly down the road, would have been his downfall were it not for his father's presence of mind in swooping down upon him and grabbing hold of the back of his coat, immediately arresting his progress. Jack, thwarted, let out a howl but Paul had scooped him up into his arms and would not let him go.

"I want see Mr Bytho!" screamed Jack, angrily, thumping his little fists on his father's chest to vent his temper.

A voice behind him telling him to behave himself made him stop immediately, and he caught his breath on a sob, as he turned around in his father's arms and looked into the face of the man he had been trying to reach. He smiled cajolingly but he received no answering smile. His hero regarded him sternly, so Jack lowered his eyes and attempted a penitent expression.

"I shall 'ave words with you in a moment, young man," said 'Mr Bytho' and Joey turned his attention to Paul, greeting him pleasantly with a small nod of the head, and the words: "Mr Trevarthen, sir."

Paul shifted his son so that he held him firmly in one arm and replied: "Mr Bolitho," and nodding his head in turn began to introduce his family to him.

George regarded him in awe, for the lads at school had so many tales to tell of that gentleman's outrageous scrapes and adventures. Grace smiled coyly and dropped a curtsey, Daisy obligingly curtsied in turn but lifted her chin and looked at him impassively, something he found rather disconcerting, although he could not fathom why. As for Mrs Trevarthen, her warm hazel eyes took in everything about him and the slight smile on her kissable mouth entranced him so, that he, a practised ladies man, was almost lost for words. He swept off his hat and executed a perfect bow, but as he raised his eyes to her face he was intrigued by her slight frown and the way she had of looking so directly at him. 'Almost as if she is looking into my soul,' he thought. Turning back towards Paul and his youngest son with a slight flush on his face, he heard Paul say: "-and of course you have already been introduced to Jack. Or more correctly he had introduced himself to you." He looked down at Jack, who had now wriggled himself out of his father's arms and was standing by his side, but this time with his hand held most firmly and, encountering Jack's palm being held out towards him, was instructed to look at his scar.

"I shall do no such thing, Master Jack, until I 'ear an apology from you to yer parents fer yer behaviour 'ere today," said Joey grandly, "fer I told 'e last time you was to behave yerself, did I not?"

Two large, doleful eyes were raised to his questioner's impassive face, then Jack nodded dumbly and was heard to mumble something.

"I beg yer pardon?" enquired Joey, and his lips twitched, and Chloe noticed what charm that added to his features.

"I said I's sorry Dada an' Mama," and he looked up into Joey's face and added, "very sorry," for good measure. He watched as Mr Bolitho looked at his father and then his little heart leapt with glee to see both men smile at each other.

"Right you are," said Joey, then bent and held out his arms, receiving a delighted child into them. He stood up with Jack in his arms and examined Jack's scar, of which that young lad was most inordinately proud, with all the due care and attention that such an emblem warranted.

" 'Tis a rare sight to encounter you in the town with all your family Mr Trevarthen, sir," said Joey conversationally, after nothing more could be found to be said about Jack's hurts.

"Not quite all, Mr Bolitho. The youngest has been left at home for, as you can well imagine, looking after Jack is an accomplishment in itself," replied Paul with a laugh, and then proceeded to explain that they were making their way to the Library if it would please him to accompany them. He attempted a refusal but turned immediately when he heard Mrs Trevarthen's voice, its tone precise but pleasant, say: "I would like to take this opportunity to thank you, Mr Bolitho, for returning little Jack to his father when he ran away from his nurse. We were most grateful in your assistance, not only to Jack but to ourselves, I can assure you." and Joey felt himself almost a young man again at the sight of her smile.

"Not . . . Not at all, Mrs Trevarthen, ma'am, my pleasure," came his stumbling reply and hastily turned away from her, for he was sure he had a flush forming on his cheeks. 'Damn!' he thought, 'am I to fall fer another of that man's women,' but her husband was asking him a question, so he began obligingly to talk of something that had occurred the last time they were in the inn together as they proceeded on their way to the Library. At the entrance, Jack was replaced on the ground and was told again to behave himself in future and that, the next time they encountered each other, he hoped he had done nothing that he deserved reprimanding for. Jack looked doubtful but smiled anyway although he was disappointed that his friend would not be coming into the Library with them.

"Perhaps Mr Bytho can come to tea one day, like the Penjay children?" asked Jack hopefully of his father, but even he noticed that there was a constrained silence for a moment.

"Mr Bolitho would be most welcome," he heard his mother say after a slight pause, "but I imagine he is such a busy man he would have great difficulty in finding the time to come." Mr Bolitho and her husband both looked at her gratefully, although there was just a hint of regret on the former's face.

"Very kind of you Mrs Trevarthen, ma'am," he replied and bowed again, "but you are in the right of it. I'm sorry, young Jack, but don' look so downhearted fer I 'spect we'll meet up 'gain 'fore too long," and impulsively bent down to receive a parting hug from the disappointed young lad. With a pat on the back for Jack, and a bow and a wave he was gone, taking his easy stride towards the bottom of the street and off on his own business. Chloe watched him as he walked away and turned to her husband, who was looking at little Jack, holding on to his father's hand tightly and waving furiously with the other at the disappearing figure. Something about the man intrigued her. She did not know what it was and thought of asking Paul what he knew of the man but, decided against it at present and kept her own counsel.

That evening in the back parlour, Paul responded to her question about Joey Bolitho's past and recounted Edwin's tale. She looked most sympathetic, but he did not hesitate to point out that Mr Joseph Bolitho had been suspected of killing, or causing to have killed, a great number of people. He considered telling her that one of those killed might, if he had been given the opportunity to deliver his message, have saved them all from the horrific night they endured through Daisy's grandfather's attempt to kill him, but thought better of it.

"I realise that he is a most appalling man, but I must admit that he has a great deal of charm, in spite of all his atrocious ways, and I should imagine women find him quite irresistible," she said, her head buried in her stitching.

"Oh yes, you are quite in the right of it there, Chloe. He has no qualms about being a monster one moment, yet can turn on such charm the next. Men are not indisposed to his appeal and Bert found it impossible to refuse to work for him. As for women; well show me the women who does not find him irresistible," remarked Paul, studying the fire broodingly. He turned of a sudden and looked at his wife, but she appeared to be absorbed in her embroidery, so he warned her quietly: "Don't fall under his spell, Chloe, for I warn you he is a most dangerous man. Death seems to follow him wherever he goes."

She kept her head lowered but said composedly enough: "I shall do as you say, Paul, but there is something about him and I must admit that, like Jack, I am disposed to like him in some strange way," and out of the corner of her eye she saw a worried frown cross his face. She would have enjoyed to continue her game, but raised her laughing face to him and said: "but I think my own husband would have something to say if I showed too great a partiality towards the man."

"Damn right, he would have something to say, madam!" and he sprang out of his chair, placing his hand under her chin, tilted up her face and studied it closely, "even if he were well aware of what the devil of a tease his wife could be to him." For answer she giggled. He looked at the clock to ascertain the time and, pulling her from her seat, he headed for the door.

"But Paul," she laughed, "I must protest for it is far too early for us to retire. The servants will talk."

"Let them!" he announced hoarsely and, pulling her into his arms, kissed her longingly, before lifting his head and once again studying her face.

"And," he announced authoritatively, "methinks, you will have little enough to protest about 'ere long."

"Pooh!" she laughed wickedly at him and, slipping from his grasp, fled from him and ran towards their bedchamber, hotly pursued by her laughing husband.

George's first letter to his parents was full of the new friends he had made at school and, although his father read it over and over again, he could find not one word of despair or regret in it. He did say that he missed them all dreadfully and that he sent them his dearest love, but as this was followed by a description of the history teacher - a poor man with a twitch, which all the boys found hysterically funny according to George - and was preceded by his description of the surprisingly good food that was served to all the chaps, 'and plenty of it too!' he enthused, his father was given the distinct impression that his son's experience of Helston was going to be vastly different from his own.

Chloe looked as grateful as her husband that their son appeared to be enjoying school and she knew full well that Paul had arranged for Mr Armitage to keep a careful eye on her son and his exploits. Daisy and Grace missed him dreadfully at first, particularly Daisy because her brother had been in all her schemes and plots from such a young age, but her father was busy with his plans to teach her to ride and she occupied herself quite well with that. There were moments when two such volatile temperaments as they shared butted up against each other, but there was a lot of good humour in their exploits and Daisy never complained if her horse unseated her, but merely got up from whatever spot she had landed in and remounted her horse. Paul's admiration for her grew as he witnessed her tenacity.

Grace made herself busy with her sewing and, as she had made a special friend of Mrs Bosanko, made no objections whatsoever in accompanying Daisy to the little cottage; she to talk and sew and Daisy to wander off with Dick and Harry, to engage in pursuits that would have brought pleasure to their absent brother. Daisy it was who successfully caught the adder, which they proudly brought home for the others to see. The consternation the sight of the snake caused was most comic amongst the little gathering of females, but luckily Bert arrived at that moment and took the offending creature away to dispose of it. "Please not to kill it, Mr Pendray," said Daisy earnestly, "for I caught him at his slumbers and he made no attempt to bite me." He assured her he would do no such thing, but warned her and the others that they were not to pick up such a creature ever again for it was most poisonous. Daisy hung her head and looked most contrite, as she apologised for putting him to such trouble and for upsetting the household. He smiled back at her and told the child her apology was accepted, receiving her rarely seen but quite entrancing smile in return. As he headed off to the woods with the poor adder in the bottom of a sack, he thought how like her father she looked when she smiled.

Dropping the snake carefully on an open space and keeping his legs well away from it, he was gratified to see it slither off into the undergrowth and, after waiting for a moment, he turned and walked back through the trees in the direction of his home. He had come from a meeting with Joey Bolitho and he found himself in quite a quandary. Joey had a cargo of brandy sitting in the Isles of Scilly awaiting collection. It had been brought from France in easy stages so as to avoid detection by the Customs Officers. It had been landed first in the Channel Islands by a French cargo ship that often made the trip from France to St. Peterport. From St. Peterport it travelled, along with a few dozen sheep, to St. Mary's and was even now sitting in the vicar's spare bedchamber in Hughtown. If Bert could collect it and deliver it to the little cove that they used for the bulk of Bolitho's transactions, he would receive a good payment for it, enough to enable poor Harry to continue for a while longer at school at any rate. It was risky using the same cove, but Joey had set up a distribution network along the whole route. If at any time they suspected that the preventative men were about, there were any number of places or people who could make brandy casks disappear in the wink of an eye. It was good brandy too. Joey could be sure of a good market if he could only get it landed. He needed Bert's services for that, as his boat was the sturdiest vessel in the little port and her master by far the best at handling his craft. His knowledge of the locality was second to none and his seamanship could not be bettered. Bert was still undecided, but Joey was using all his charm and was desperately attempting to persuade him to land his catch.

By now, Pendray had almost reached the door of his cottage and looked up as he heard a team coming down the lane. He saw Paul sitting in his familiar curricle, with his bays in hand, coming down the lane at a spanking pace. He reined up beside Bert and greeted him warmly.

"Hello, Bert. Thought I would pick the girls up myself tonight. The bays were in need of a run so here I am. How was the fishing today?" said his friend as he swung himself down from the curricle with his usual athleticism and held out his hand to Bert. They shook hands and talked for a while about the fisherman's catch and laughed at a tale of Nat Roscorla's that Bert recounted to him. The door opened and the girls came out, followed by the other members of Bert's household. Daisy's eyes lit up immediately when she saw the curricle, but Grace was not quite so enchanted until Mrs Bosanko said pointedly what ladies the girls would look in such a smart turnout. Grace beamed with pleasure, for she looked as neat as a pin. But Daisy, in her normal manner, had succeeded in giving the appearance of someone who had fallen foul of a footpad, so bedraggled did she look. Grace immediately secured the seat beside her father, but Daisy was not in the least abashed at having to sit on the outside. It was much more exciting, she considered, especially if their father made his horses go at a good speed. When they were all on board, they happily waved their goodbyes to the Pendrays and Daisy called to Harry that she would see him at school tomorrow. After turning the equipage, Paul tipped his whip at Bert, then cracked it expertly over the horses' heads and the curricle and its occupants surged forward on their homeward journey.

The following day Bert gave Joey a brief nod as he arrived at the inn and Bolitho breathed an inward sigh of relief. He had his man at last.

CHAPTER 12

THE wind whipped his coat around him as he pulled on the rope, but Paul Trevarthen determined to save as much as could be saved of the hay. The sudden storm had taken them all by surprise and Jonas Hampton had ridden into the farmyard, shouting at the top of his voice for the men to come and save the hayricks. Every able bodied man dropped what they were doing and began to run towards the mowhay where all the ricks had been set up. It had been a poor crop; heavy rain had meant that drying the hay had been particularly difficult that year. They had all worked hard to save what they could to provide winter fodder for their animals. Even then they had sent more livestock to market than was normal. Their neighbours had done the same and consequently their sale had produced lower returns. Now, if the storm meant that their ricks were to be blown apart, they would have to send even more livestock for slaughter and the resultant drop in their value would have to be borne as best it could. For Paul Trevarthen it would not be a problem - he was a rich man - but there were many farmers who wept that day as they tried their hardest to tie down their ricks to save their struggling farms. Throwing the rope back over the top of the rick would normally have been an easy matter for Paul, but even he had difficulty against the force of the wind. Working in teams the men, all from the farm and some more brought out from the stables, battled hard against the ferocious gale. Jonas had them all well organised and at last he was satisfied that their handiwork would hold against the vicissitudes of the storm.

"I believe we done 'en, sir," he told Paul as they surveyed the tightly roped ricks lined up like soldiers against the force of the opposing wind.

"Well, I certainly hope so, Jonas, for I would not wish to do that again. See the men rewarded for their efforts on my behalf today, I am most grateful," he shouted above the howl of the wind.

In spite of his discomfort at the outrageous weather, Jonas smiled. He would acquiesce to Paul's command, and wondered how many other masters would think to reward his men for their endeavours, but he merely shouted in reply: "Certainly, I will do that Paul, for they have worked hard, every one of them."

Paul nodded his agreement, and with a wave to the men, called out his thanks and made his way back towards the house. Once indoors, he divested himself of his sodden coat and, shrugging himself into a dry one, told Davy to send the carriage for the children today, for they could not be expected to walk home from school in such conditions.

"Blowin' in 'ard today, sir," nodded Davy, "I dunno' when I can remember such a storm afore."

"Quite, Davy," agreed Paul, heading off to the kitchen to dry himself before the fire and possibly to inveigle some hot pies out of Mrs Gurney, the cook.

That lady managed not only to provide sufficient pies but also some hot mulled wine. Paul assuaged his appetite and his thirst, and thanked her warmly before retracing his steps to the hall and making his way to the back parlour. Chloe was busy arranging some flowers in Penelope's glass vase, the one his father had purchased when he was a child to replace the predecessor that his son had broken. He smiled to himself as he remembered the enjoyment he had had with his little bow and arrow and the scrapes he had got himself into by deploying it around the farm. His wife looked up and smiled back at him as he came through the door.

"Are the ricks safely roped, Paul?" she asked.

"Yes, thank God. Now, I had best return to my book for I do not at all fancy another hour out in that storm," he said.

"It is just as well you could not go with Bert to fish today after all, for you would not have been very comfortable in this foul weather," she remarked, wisely.

"I should think all the sane fishermen are safe in harbour today, for 'tis not the right conditions to take to sea in," he said, then turned on his heel in surprise when he was interrupted by a furious knocking at the door.

"Come in," he called, and the door opened immediately. Framed in the doorway was a most unusual sight for Trevu. Nat Roscorla, breathing heavily, made a garbled greeting to Chloe but, not waiting for her response, turned to Paul and cried, " 'Tis the Winsome Lass Paul, she's bein' battered on yer rocks. Get some men and tackle, 'cos 'e's a goner sure 'nuff if 'e don' get some 'elp soon."

"What!" cried Paul, "Why in hell's name did he go out in such weather?"

" 'E didn't go out in it, 'e's comin' 'ome in it," shouted Nat, " E's got a cargo up fer delivery to Winnerd's Cove but 'e'll never make it 'cos 'e's bin blown in t' yer rocks. 'E's 'olding 'er fer now but 'e's 'eavy loaded Paul, tidden goin' be long fer 'e's done fer!"

Paul, without bothering to ask more, rushed out of the door, catching hold of Nat's arm as he did so. As they ran for the stables, Nat gasped the explanation that Seth had seen Bert as he himself headed for harbour trying to outrun the storm. All the fishermen knew which cove Bert would have to head for, it was the only one safe enough on that treacherous coast. Even then Paul knew how difficult it would be to land the boat safely. Many a time he and his farm hands had been called to the assistance of various poor souls, who had been driven on to the group of rocks that projected out into the sea from the sandy beach. In calm weather they were quite easy to circumnavigate, but with the wind blowing hard onshore and a heavy swell you could be cast upon them in the blink of an eye. Shouting instructions as he ran, he ordered up ropes and the farm cart as well as the assistance of the already tired men. Pulling his horse from the stall he threw himself on to its saddle-less back and pulled its head around using the halter, for he could not wait for his stable lad to prepare the creature for him. He grabbed a rope from the hook on the wall and looped it over his shoulder.

"Follow in the cart, Nat," he shouted and kicked his horse in the flanks and galloped out of the yard. All the way to the cove fear gripped his heart. Nat had said Bert's boat was heavy laden, and he knew well that his cargo would not be fish, for he would not wish to land those at Winnerd's Cove. The wind and rain lashed at him, as if whipping him in punishment. He should have stopped Bert. He could have done it in some way if he had persevered, not given up and let Bert fall into Joey Bolitho's clutches. Now here was one of the few people that were close to him, in danger of losing his life on Paul's own doorstep and all because of that damned man. He could have wept, such was his impotence in the face of nature's anger. The countryside sped by around him and soon he was at the top of the cliff, where were assembled carts and shays and various beasts. As he looked down he saw a group of men; some standing forlorn and others gesticulating wildly, but all of them were looking out past the huge rollers that were pounding themselves against the rocks and beach. In the midst of all the furore was a small boat, being pitched and tossed like a piece of driftwood, a prey to the elements. Paul could see the struggling figure, grimly trying to defeat the waves and bring himself home safe. In a moment he had jumped off his horse and was running down the steep little path, heedless of any danger to himself, for if he had fallen it would surely be to his death, so sheer was the slope.

He ran towards the group on the beach and recognised every one of the men assembled. In another place and at another time they had all laughed and joked together, but today there were only grim faces to be seen. He caught sight of Seth Mankee and headed towards him, struggling to keep his pace in the cloying sand. When he reached him he put out his hand and steadied himself by gripping Seth's shoulder, and gasped: "Can he make it?" and watched in horror as the man turned and sadly shook his head.

"The wind 'll throw 'en on yer rocks, Mr Trevarthen, sir. 'Twill break 'er back, sure 'nuff," and he spat in disgust.

"Can no one get to him, swim out or something?" Paul panted desperately.

"Swim out? Swim out in that surf? Only a hidiot would even think of it fer 'tis death sure 'nuff," he said.

"I can make those rocks, for I learnt to swim here as a child. Bert could jump off his boat and swim towards me, with a rope around me, and your men pulling you can get us back to the shore. It will mean losing the boat, but that is a small price to pay," urged Paul.

"You learnt swim in a sea like that did 'e, Paul?" Seth asked derisively, pointing at the boiling surf. "You'll be throwin' yer life away, a bleddy fool thing do an' Bert wouldn' thank 'e fer it."

Heedless to Seth's words, Paul was busily tying the rope around his waist, his discarded coat lying on the wet sand. With the knots secure he started to take off his boots, still deaf to Seth's protests and entreaties. Some of the other men came up to them and tried to persuade him not even to attempt such a fool plan. Then suddenly, above the howling of the storm, they all heard a splintering crash and watched in horror as Bert's little boat was thrown against the rocks by the furious sea. The mast was broken and the rudder lost: Bert was doomed, for now he had no way of controlling his boat. Every fisherman there knew it would not be long now. They heard Paul gasp: "Oh my God, no!" and then he was gone, running blindly for the sea, with the rope paying out behind him. There were shouts for him to come back, but all present knew he would not.

" 'E won't come back alive," said Nat, who had arrived just in time to see Paul wade into the surging waves, "Bleddy fool!".

Meanwhile Paul's legs were being sucked out from under him, so strong was the current, so he dived into the water and struck out strongly for the rocks. He was not the fastest of swimmers, but he had great strength and he would need every ounce of it if he were to get to those rocks. Even as he swam, he realised he would have to land himself on the shore side of the outcrop, for fear the boat came down on him if it were caught on the waves and thrown on to the rocks. He swam on, pounded by the surf, his lungs bursting in his body but he would not swerve from his goal. Waves crashed over, around and on him, beating at him as if he were a felon being lashed. He looked up as he took a lungful of air and noticed how close the rocks were. In a moment he felt a sharp pain in his leg as a jagged edge, hidden under the water, ripped open his flesh. Heedless of the pain, he heaved himself on to a ledge and lay still for a moment, trying to get the strength back into his beaten body. The roar of the angry sea put real fear into his heart and he thought of his beloved Chloe and all his dear children. He was consumed by sadness, but he was here now and it was up to him to save himself and Bert, so in the teeth of the gale he stood up, the better to catch sight of the boat. There was a splintering crash and the next moment the bow of the boat rose up before him and was held up like a black avenging angel over him. His heart was stirred by past emotions and present dangers, but his body took over and he clambered across the rocks and climbed up the side of the boat. He looked wildly around, calling Bert's name until he saw him in the stern of the boat, trapped under the roped barrels of his cargo, seemingly unconscious. On reaching him, Paul began to pull feverishly at the casks and, loosening them from their stays, threw then over the side of the battered boat. He fell to his knees and, grasping Bert around his chest, pulled him free. His head was bleeding and his right arm hung awkwardly, possibly broken, Paul could not be sure.

"Bert! Bert!" he shouted desperately, and felt a surge of relief as he saw Bert's eyelids flicker. Slowly his eyes opened, then widened in surprise at the sight of Paul's concerned face staring down at him.

"What you doin' 'ere, you bleddy fool?" he asked weakly.

"Come to bring you home, you mad idiot," said Paul, and grinned at him.

"We'll never make it, Paul. I broke me arm. You get off now afore it's too late fer 'e to save yerself. Please, Paul, please do as I d' say," he pleaded, "Think of yer family, you silly sod."

"I'm thinking of both our families," shouted Paul, and he undid the rope from his body and payed out a long length of it before reattaching himself to the lifeline and then knotting the extra length around Bert's waist. He stood up and heaved Bert to his feet and, half dragging him, edged his way to the side of the boat. Holding on to his friend he determined to leap off the boat and into the water, and the only place he could do that was at the stern, where the water was already pounding against the little craft.

"We'll have to jump for it, Bert, but look:" he shouted above the roaring crescendo, "our friends are ready to pull us safe ashore," and he turned and smiled at his friend, receiving Bert's smile in return.

"Yer some stupid fool, Paul, but the best friend a man could wish fer. Thankee, Paul, thankee fer ...." but his words were abruptly taken from him as, before they could throw themselves upon the sea's mercy, the timber of the boat jarred under their feet and the boat was sucked from its cleft and drawn back into the sea. They both lost their footing, but Paul held hard to his friend and would not let him go. Thrown back against the deck, and with the boat once again pitching and tossing on the waves they lay huddled together, when a wave of such intensity picked up the little craft and flung it down on the rocks with all the venom that the sea could muster. With spars of wood splitting and splintering all around them, she broke her back. Amidst the howling of the wind and the crashing of the timbers, Paul looked up into his friend's face, as if the sight of it was all he needed to restore him to safety. Bert smiled back, then the surf rained timbers and casks down upon them in another attempt to dash them into pieces. Paul covered his head with his free arm, but even then he sustained a heavy blow to his left temple and in the cold was aware of the warm blood running down his face. Bert was lying with his head lolling on his arms. He must have been hit too, thought Paul. Then a tremendous wave plucked them from the remnants of the boat so suddenly that they were thrown into the sea and Paul, holding fast to the lifeless Bert, began to swim as best he could for the shore; unable, even in this, his moment of greatest extremity, to release his grip on his dear friend.

Back on shore a line of men, composed of fishermen and Paul's farm hands, had formed around the rope and had watched in wonder and awe as they saw Paul reach the rocks. They witnessed in mounting horror the sea's vicious retribution on the little boat, but when Nat shouted: "They're in the water!" they took up the strain on the rope and began to pull steadily for the shore.

Unaware of the two men who were running towards them, they kept up their steady pull and did not stop even when a voice shouted: "Who the 'ell tried to swim out to 'en?"

" 'Tis Paul Trevarthen, Joey," gasped Seth, to the tall man at his side.

"What!" cried Joey, aghast and then cried angrily: "Why in bleddy 'ell didden nobody stop the young fool?"

" 'E wouldn' listen, Joey," cried Seth, in a scared voice, "We tried stop 'en 'onest," and looked in wonder at Joey's distraught face. The face of a man who could kill and smile at the same time had never appeared to Seth in the guise it wore now.

'Don' like losin' such a good cargo 'spose,' thought Seth in the midst of all their frantic attempts to save the men, 'tight fisted bastard!'

The desperate swimmer could be seen slowly approaching the shore, hanging on to his companion. But he was tiring fast and he would not leave hold his friend, the better to save himself. Twenty yards from the shore his head sank from their view, but they pulled on and Joey, heedless of his clothes, rushed into the water and, catching the rope, began to pull as strongly as any man. Suddenly, a wave caught the desperate pair and spewed their bodies on to the beach. Some men at the front dropped their section of the rope and rushed forward. Paul's hand was fixed firmly into the knotted rope around his friend's waist, so they had to pull both men up on to the beach together. They lay in a heap, twined together like tangled seaweed until Joey's knife flashed and he cut the cords that bound them together.

When they moved Bert, his head lolled back awkwardly and there was not a man present who did not realise that Trevarthen had struggled to bring home a dead man, for poor Pendray lay on the sand with a broken neck. His failed saviour lay lifeless on his back, his body cut and bruised, with blood pouring from his head and body, forming a dark red, ebbing pool on the sand.

Seth shook his head sadly, "Two good men gone," and he removed his hat.

"No! It can't be!" shouted Joey, desperately and stood astride Paul's inert body, almost like a tiger defending his catch, and shouted for the men to help him turn him over for, in spite of his own strength, the man could not be turned by one person alone, no matter how great was his need.

When they had got him face down in the sand, Joey placed his hands around Paul's waist and pulled him up with all his strength, so that his head lay on the sand but his middle was about two feet above it. Joey shook him violently but nothing happened, the body was still lifeless, but he would not give up and tried again. Of a sudden, Paul wretched and water and blood poured from his mouth, spreading out onto the sand like a liquid cloak and then disappearing, leaving only a pink stain behind.

"Slap 'is back, somebody," yelled Bolitho, frantically, and Jonas Hampton dealt his master three hefty blows in the middle of his back. For answer he heard his master cough, and then moan, and then he began to wretch again. When they thought he could be sick no more they laid him down on the sand. Joey dropped to his knees beside him and shoved his hand inside his shirt and said in a relieved voice, "His heart is beaten' boys, weak, but 'tis beatin'." An incongruous cheer came from the little group of men and then Joey began to issue instructions and they rapped off his tongue so fast that soon every man there was put to work. The tallest and strongest were detailed to get Paul to the top of the cliff and on to one of the wagons to be taken to Trevu. Joey, still kneeling, finished knotting his handkerchief around Paul's bleeding head before releasing him into their hands, then another detail of men were ordered to take up Bert's body and convey it to his cottage.

"Go with 'em Nat," he said, "and stay there until I come or send fer 'e." Then the rest of the men, Paul's workmen included, were given the task of collecting the casks.

"Get every one of 'em ashore an' stowed on to the carts, then take 'em into town or to a place where they will be well hidden, but not on Trevu land. There are forty to be found an' I want none missed, the broken ones as well as the sound" and he swept them all with his hard stare, "fer if the preventative catch sight of even the merest part of one of 'em they will 'ave Paul Trevarthen fer smugglin', you mark my words." He sent Seth to Penzance to fetch the doctor, and gave him money, in case the man would not come without payment, then he turned to helping the men collect and count the casks. When they were accounted for and hidden on the carts, they all left the beach and made their way to the top of the cliff. Slowly, with every surging wave, the Winsome Lass cast her broken body on the beach and lay in tattered remnants upon the sand.

Joey, now alone, sat his horse at the top of the cliff and stared out to sea. His lips moved but no sound was made, and he gave the impression of a man lost in prayer. After a while he dragged his hand across his eyes, turned his horse towards the road and, when he had reached it, headed for Bert's little cottage. He stayed for over an hour, and when he left he had only a few coins remaining in his pocket. The sight of the orphaned boys had cut him to his tarnished soul and he had great difficulty in keeping his voice under control. Dick and Harry sat side by side by the little fire, desperately watching their father as if, at any moment, his body would give a sudden start and he would be miraculously returned to them. Emily Bosanko sat in shock, staring at her brother's body as it lay stretched out on the table from where they normally ate all their meals. Her girls clung close beside her and all of them were crying. When he left, the sound of their sobbing followed his footsteps down the little cottage path and echoed in his ears. Remounting his horse, he sent Nat home and took the fork that led to Trevu. When he arrived, his horse was taken by one of the stable lads who had helped to carry his master home.

"Doctor's in the 'ouse now sir," he informed Joey, "but Mrs Trevarthen, 'ave said if you was to turn up you was to go in, sir."

"Thankee," said Joey, composedly, and walked slowly towards the house. As he arrived, the door was opened and Dr Dunstan appeared in the doorway, on the point of departure. He recognised Joseph Bolitho at once although he personally had never had any dealings with the man and, striding forward, took him by the hand.

"Well done, sir, well done," he said, "for in my opinion you may have saved Mr Trevarthen's life."

"May 'ave?" asked Joey, anxiously.

"Terrible injuries, sir. Bad concussion, broken ribs, severe loss of blood from the cuts on his body and methinks he has still a lot of water in his lungs. When he arrived he was in a poor condition. Constant care and careful nursing may pull him through, let us hope so for his poor wife's sake. Well done, again, sir," he said, touching the brim of his hat in salute, headed towards his carriage.

Joey slowly advanced towards the door and hesitated before it, but of a sudden it was opened and he looked down into the anxious face of a red-eyed servant.

"Mr Bolitho, sir," said Lizzie and dropped a quick curtsey, "Mrs Trevarthen says I was to show you into the withdrawing room if you called sir. Please to follow me," and she led the way across the hall and into a large, tastefully furnished room with an inviting fire burning in the grate.

"Shall I bring you something sir?" she asked politely, but he shook his head and she excused herself, leaving him alone to his thoughts. He stood in front of the fire and spread his hands to the warmth, only then realising how cold and wet he still was. His boots were sodden with salt water and his breeches covered in wet sand and blood. His jacket was also wet with the rain that had been pouring down upon him, for he had given his cloak to Nat to cover Bert's body with and had forgotten to reclaim it when he was at the cottage. He did not want it back anyway, for although it had covered Bert's body it could not cover his own shame. He knew, like none other, how he had cajoled and coerced Bert into making that voyage. How he had turned on his charm until the poor, desperate fisherman had been unable to resist. For a moment he felt bitterly angry that Bert could not have accepted the gifts that Paul had insisted on offering to him. The door opened quietly behind him. So wrapped up in his thoughts was he that he did not hear it until a voice made him turn sharply on his heel with a guilty expression on his face.

"Mr Bolitho, sir," said Chloe in a quiet but determined voice, and she stared sadly into his face, "I believe I have you to thank that my husband has been returned alive to me."

He could think of nothing to say, but she continued in her soft voice: "We are hoping and praying that he will prosper, but the doctor has been rather pessimistic, although he has assured me that a man of Paul's strength and stamina stands more chance than most of . . . surviving his injuries," and then her courage failed her and she gave a small sob. In a moment he was by her side, his arms outstretched. But he dropped them to his sides again, because he could not bring himself to touch his brother's wife, even in the moment of her greatest distress. She looked up into his face and, summoning up her courage, asked if he wished to see Paul.

"Of course, he is not awake for the doctor has had to drug him, for fear he move about and damage his poor body the more," she said with only a slight tremor in her voice, but a tear sparkled in her eye as she explained: "He was awake when they brought him in, but he knew me not." She gave another little heartbroken sob, but quickly she took out her handkerchief and wiped her eyes and blew her little nose. "Forgive me," she said, "I am a little overwrought."

"Why ma'am, 'tis most understandable. But I came only to see 'ow 'e . . . 'ow Mr Trevarthen does. I would not stay," and he held out his hand to her with the intention of taking his leave, so unsettled was he to be alone in her presence, and his heart ached within him to see her stricken countenance.

She smiled bravely at him but merely said: "Please to follow me," and turned and left the room. He followed behind her as she led him up the staircase to the bedchamber where her husband lay.

Miss Clavering got up from the bedside at their entrance and, hastily wiping her eyes, quietly left the room.

Chloe walked up to the big bed and, seating herself in the recently vacated chair, motioned the smuggler to go around to the other side. In the shaded candle light he had a good view of the damage that Trevarthen had sustained in his vain attempt to save his friend. His head was heavily bandaged but the side of his face was heavily bruised. Where Trevarthen had knotted his hand into the rope was also bandaged, for it had been severely cut and bruised. Joey could not see but he knew that the broken ribs would have been bound and he knew that Paul's left leg had been badly gashed, for there had been blood pouring from the wound when he had been pulled ashore. He realised that Paul had been heavily sedated, for he lay motionless, but even then he understood the doctor's concern for his patient was having great difficulty breathing.

"When first I knew him," said Chloe softly, a wistful smile playing on her lips, "he caught pneumonia and lucky we were to save him, for he was most dreadfully ill. He survived, our doctor told my Grandmother, because he was a fit and strong young man. My fear now is that his poor battered body cannot do him the same service should he suffer such an illness now. He was most dreadfully cold, you see, and although we have done our best, with hot bricks all around him, we cannot keep him warm," and she reached her hand across the covers and clasped Paul's large hand with her little one, as if to pass her strength to him.

"We must hope fer the best, Mrs Trevarthen, ma'am, and I knaw full well that he will receive no better care an' attention than that 'e will receive in 'is own house," said Joey gently, with as much reassurance as he could muster.

"I d' knaw that the one thing yer 'usband loves above all else is 'is wife an' family. 'E'll fight to stay alive fer 'e Mrs Trevarthen, never you fear," and as she looked up he gave a reassuring smile, and she felt heartened by his confidence.

"I'll be goin' on now Ma'am, but if you 'ave no objection I shall call again to see 'ow 'e goes on," he said quietly.

"None at all, Mr Bolitho, you will be most welcome," she said and stood up to shake his hand, "and thank you again for all you have done for Paul, tonight, for well I know 'twas your actions that saved his life. I would be most grateful if you would take Paul's cloak, for I can see that you are badly soaked and to travel back to Penzance in this storm will only add to your discomfort. I can if you wish have the carriage brought out for you."

He was touched to the heart by her concern for him, when her own husband lay so ill beside her, and it almost unmanned him but he plucked up as strong a voice as he could muster and said, quietly: "Mrs Trevarthen, you concentrate 'pon Paul and don't fret yerself 'bout me. I shall do very well, but I will 'ave the cloak fer I would not wish to get even wetter. I shall see meself out, Mrs Trevarthen, ma'am, but if at anytime you d' need anything please do not 'esitate to call 'pon my services." He shook her hand and bowed his head towards her. With one long, last glance at his poor, battered brother he let himself out of the room and left Trevu, returning to his own home, a sadder and a wiser man.

CHAPTER 13

THE crushing pain in his chest intensified as he drew breath sharply, and he opened his eyes and realised himself in his own room, lying in his warm bed. The nightmare horror of the sea was ebbing away from his brain, but he felt in great distress and wanted to remove himself from the room and go to the cove, for he felt that there was something there that he was needed to do. He attempted to rise from his bed but his body failed him, for it seemed it had no strength in it. He turned his head on the pillow and noticed someone sitting by his bed with a book in their hands. His eyes widened in shock when he realised who it was who sat so quietly at his bedside. The person got up, crossed the room and tugged twice at the bell pull before returning to the chair and sitting down again.

Paul tried to speak, but his throat was so dry that the words would not come, so he continued to stare in disbelief at the man who sat smiling back at him in a calm and reassuring fashion.

"Awake at last, Mr Trevarthen, sir. We 'ave bin wonderin' 'ow long it would be," and then, noticing that Paul was trying to talk, he stood over him, lifted him gently in his arms, placed a cup against his lips and helped him to take a drink. He gently lowered him against the pillows and, at that moment, the door burst open and his excited wife stood in the doorway, breathless, with a flush on her glowing cheeks and a smile on her lips. She rushed across the room to her husband's side, grasped his hand and, smiling through her tears, said simply between her sobs: "Oh Paul! Oh Paul! My dearest, most beloved," and she cast her head upon his shoulder and wept uncontrollably. He whispered her name hoarsely and she looked up and caressed his unshaven face with her hand. Joseph Bolitho, not wishing to impose, moved slowly to the door and left them alone, carefully closing the door behind him. He began to walk towards the stairs but, just as his foot was placed on the top step, a shout made him turn and look along the corridor.

"Mr Bytho! Mr Bytho!" shrieked Jack excitedly and ran towards him with his arms outstretched.

Joey raised his finger to his lips, and immediately the little boy stopped his shouting, but continued to run towards him. Bending down, he picked up the boy and walked along the corridor, holding him in his arms in the direction from which Jack had run. He met Miss Clavering, looking fraught, as she rushed from a large room to his right. She gave a sigh of relief but Joey did not attempt to relinquish his burden. However, when he informed the nurse that Mr Trevarthen had awoken and his wife was with him, she promptly burst into tears and would have been unable to take charge of the little boy in any case. She returned to the room with her handkerchief deployed over her face. Jack, unsure of what was happening, lost his delighted look and turned a frightened, nervous face towards Joey. He smiled at him reassuringly and carried him into the nursery. Paul's eldest daughters sat sombrely with their stitching lying idle in their hands. They looked up nervously as he entered with their brother in his arms, but their faces lit up when he told them that their father had awoken and seemed to know his surroundings.

"May we see him?" asked Grace, but Joey advised her to ask her mother.

"'E won't want much in the way a' visitors just yet," he said kindly and added reassuringly: " 'E's still too poorly but it won't be long fer 'e's up an' about 'gain, you mark my words. Strong chap, yer father."

"Can I see him too?" asked little Jack, not wishing to be left out.

"Only if 'e be'ave," said Joey, in a severe tone.

"Yessir," replied his young charge and then asked hopefully if 'Mr Bytho' would like to see his pictures.

Joey accepted, expecting nothing more than a succession of childish images but, like Jack's father before him, he was surprised at the quality of the work produced. He was busy conversing with the girls and placating Jack at the same time, when the door was opened by the children's mother. For a moment she caught her breath to see her children sitting happily with Joseph Bolitho, but then she realised that, in their eyes, he was a different person from the one that their father and mother knew. He looked up from admiring Jack's picture of a puppy and smiled in return at her happy face.

The girls left his side immediately, rushed towards her and asked when they could see their father, promising to be well behaved and not to distress him in any way. Hugging them to her she told them quietly that their father was still too weak at present, but once he began to feel a little better they would be among his first visitors.

"And me," called Jack from his seat on Joey's knees, not wishing to be left out, and defensively he added: "I will be good."

His mother laughed at his angelic expression and Jack immediately chuckled back in response. He climbed down from his 'Mr Bytho's' lap, ran to Chloe and grasping her skirts he hid his head in its folds. She bent over and tousled his black, curly locks, and at the same time Joseph Bolitho stood up and came towards her, a curious expression on his face. Again she felt unnerved by being in his presence, for there was something about the man that she found most unsettling.

"I'd best be goin' on now, Mrs Trevarthen, ma'am, now Mr Trevarthen 'as begun 'is recovery. I could tell by 'is face that 'e didden 'spec' see me by 'is bedside."

"Nonsense, Mr Bolitho! Your assistance has proved most valuable, for your strength, both physical and mental has proved most inestimable these past few days," she asserted. "And you will take some lunch with us before ever you leave this house, I can assure you!" and she smiled up into his face.

He smiled back, hoping that his giddy admiration for her did not show too obviously on his face.

"Come children, we will all dine together today, for Jonas is very kindly sitting with your father. He is asleep once more, for he will need much rest before he is able to get up and go about amongst us again," and she turned and led the way down to the dining room. Little Jack caught hold of Joey's hand and skipped along at his side, but lowered his voice when they passed the door that led to his father's bedchamber.

Chloe directed Joey to sit beside Jack at the table in the dining room - much to that young boy's delight- and in consequence his table manners were impeccable throughout. With the girls sitting opposite Joey, it was probably the closest the man had ever come in his life to dining in a family group. As they chatted excitedly around him, a great sadness came over him. During the past week he had spent much time in contemplation. His life could have been so different if the mother who knew of Paul's existence had also known of his, for he realised he would have been welcomed into the house as openly as his brother had been. The servants had shown their love for their master, but the older ones had also talked fondly to him of the old master and his first wife. They had all remarked that Penelope's kindness and love had shown itself again in Paul, he who was of no blood relation to her, and they marvelled at the strangeness of it. There were kind words a plenty for his real mother, Redvers' second wife, but she had been and would remain in their eyes something of an exotic. In her way she had been just as kind, but those who had known the first Mrs Trevarthen never lost their devotion to her and Sardi could not match up to their regard for Penelope, whom they considered to be the most saint-like woman that they had ever known. They talked to him of Redvers too, but they were unaware of the gladness that filled his heart as they reminisced. He would so like to have known him better, talked more with him and ultimately been recognised by him.

"They loved each other dearly, the ol' master an' 'is boy," remarked old Davy fondly one day, as he sat sucking on his pipe. He was sitting outside the stables and Joey had fallen into conversation with him as he was on the point of leaving Trevu.

" 'Annah 'Endra, she that used be the cook 'ousekeeper to 'ere, always use' say Redvers 'aving a son at last was the makin' of 'en. 'E never looked at another women after that. No, soon as young Paul come along, he stayed 'ome nights with 'is missus. Never looked to stray 'gain. 'E loved she somethin' fierce sure nuff, and no wonder fer she took young Paul in as if 'e was 'er very own. The Cap'n was some proud of she and when she died the poor beggar didden' knaw what 'it 'en. Lucky 'e 'ad Paul 'elp 'en through it, tha's all I knaw fer 'e was 'it pretty bad, I can tell 'e," said the old man, then knocking his pipe against his boot, got up and brought the conversation to a close by offering to assist Mr Bolitho to mount his horse. Joey had smiled and refused his assistance, but he rode home that day with his head full of stolen memories of his father, and they brought him pain and joy respectively.

Now he sat at Paul's table, amidst his family, but could claim no part of their life unless it was as the beloved husband's and their devoted father's rescuer. The sands of time had ensured that, for him, there was no way to be recognised as even a small part of their family's existence. If old Edwin had taken over thirty years to discover who Joey's sire had been, then he had to acknowledge that there would be no other who would be able to do the same. Unlike his brother he did not resemble Redvers in looks. Paul, even with his brown skin and his mother's brown eyes, looked like his father. Those arched eyebrows and his long, thin nose, combined with his high set cheekbones. His beaming smile was in no way like his father's more closed countenance. But he could, if he wished, even assume that face, for he had seen him with just such a look that day as they had stood in the inn and listened to Hudson's tale. Staring sadly at the wine in his glass, he felt his sleeve tugged and heard an urgent: "Mr Bytho" from the little voice at his side. He turned and smiled down into Jack's face, then raised his eyebrow and looked momentarily severe at the suggestion that had been made to him. There would be no way for him to be allowed to take Jack into town and so he told him that his place was here amongst his family, especially now because his father was not well. Jack looked suitably chastened and to emphasise his authority Joey looked at him severely, with only the merest hint of a smile on his face. Turning away, he looked at Mrs Trevarthen as she sat in her place at the table and their eyes met. She was staring at him in a most strange way and he turned his face guiltily from her. He, who had always thought that he could never be outfaced by anyone, because he had burned into himself from his boyhood onwards the idea that the world had nothing to give him and, what it did have to offer, he would have to steal and not be given, even love.

"Mama, when can I go to visit Harry . . . I mean visit the Pendrays again?" asked Daisy suddenly, breaking in on all their thoughts.

"I . . . I don't know, dearest, for I have been so worried about your poor father that I have given them hardly a thought, and that fact alone distresses me greatly for I should do something for them. I know how much your father would want me to if he knew what had happened," her mother replied sadly.

"Have you not told him that Mr Pendray has died, Mama?" enquired Daisy, shocked.

"Not yet dearest. He is much too ill and I cannot for the life of me bring myself to tell him." She looked up suddenly and smiled desperately at Joey: "Mr Bolitho I . . . I know it is a terrible thing to ask of you to do but when next you see him could you . . . could you tell Paul?"

He drew in his breath sharply and she thought for a moment that he would refuse her stumbled request, but he squared his shoulders and replied that he would tell Paul that his friend was dead and explain the circumstances.

" 'Tis best we wait fer 'im to ask, Mrs Trevarthen, ma'am. If I am with 'im when 'e does I shall tell 'im, fer 'e tried so 'ard to save Bert 'twould not be right to lie," said the man who, up until that moment, had lied and deceived his way through life because it was, after all, second nature to him.

She smiled gratefully at him and again he felt his body's dull ache with its longing for her admiration. This woman he would love for who she loved, her husband. The other, the one he had so desperately wanted to marry when she was a young woman, had loved the self-same man. But she had never smiled at him as Chloe had, could never turn to him in admiration for, in her eyes, the one love she saw and had always seen was Paul Trevarthen. For years he had attempted to charm her, make her recognise his love for her but she was as unbelieving of his protestations as Paul had been immune to her desire of him. He found himself smiling as memories of his then-unknown brother came back to him: Bringing him, drunk and insensible, safe home to Trevu after his first encounter with the redoubtable Polly Vingoe, at another time and in another place would have made him laugh out loud. In Penzance he had often the opportunity to hear of his exploits with various local women and to have seen Paul smile a greeting to some poor damsel; never to recognise the ecstatic devotion that was directed at him in return. Bolitho marvelled that his sincerest feelings for women should be directed at the only two that, in his heart, he knew he could never hope to have respond to him in the same way. The first because she wanted only the boy she had grown up loving and who could not bear to accept the despotic Joseph Bolitho as his replacement. The second because she so loved her husband that in that terrible storm he would have moved heaven and earth to save his brother's life, and not just for Paul's sake alone. Even then, in the midst of his fear and panic, he had realised he would never be able to face this woman if he had brought back her husband to her and laid him dead at her feet. His troubled thoughts were interrupted again, but this time it was Grace who spoke:

"Mama, if you were to have a basket of food made up, Daisy and I could deliver it, for I am sure that Mrs Bosanko would be most grateful of it as she must be in dire need. Mr Pendray was the only one to bring money into that household, I know, and now how shall they manage without him?" she asked, and her eyes filled with tears at the thought of it.

Chloe bowed her head for a moment and said she would arrange something, then said in shame: "I should have thought of doing all this before. Paul will be distraught when he finds out, for he so tried to help them."

"Rest easy, Mrs Trevarthen, ma'am, fer I can assure you that money 'as been received by Mrs Bosanko to 'elp her in her time of trouble. If you would wish it I can escort the young ladies to the cottage, fer I will be visiting them this very afternoon and I can bring them safe home again afterwards," Joey said, in a subdued voice.

"I should not ask it of you, Mr Bolitho, but I know my girls so want to go for they have a great fondness for the family," she replied.

"Me come too?" chirruped a hopeful voice at his side.

"No, I'm sorry young sir but you'll 'ave stay 'ere an' look out fer yer mother fer us, you bein' the only man in the 'ouse while yer father is sick an' yer brother is off to 'is school," remarked Joey swiftly, and noticing Jack's annoyed look, promptly asked if he was not capable of doing that for him.

"All right, Mr Bytho, I do what you want but you come and see me when you get back, won't you?" asked Jack, in a disappointed voice.

"Only . . ." began Joey, but was interrupted by his slavish admirer, who completed his sentence by saying: "I know 'Only if I behave myself'," and he sighed, accepting his fate.

His response was so comical that both the girls and their mother burst out laughing, while Joey grinned at him and gently tweaked his ear, which action made Jack smile adoringly at him. So preoccupied with Jack was he that he did not notice a pair of hazel eyes regarding him sombrely from beneath creased brows. There was something about Joseph Bolitho that Chloe was determined to know, and a most strange thought started to show her where to begin to look.

That afternoon, he escorted the girls as promised to the Pendray's little cottage. Her eyes full of tears, Grace handed over a basket of food and also delivered a tied bundle of the children's old clothes.

"Mama says please to accept them, Mrs Bosanko, for Alice is far too young to wear our old clothes and Mama would not want them to go to waste, there are some of George's jackets and breeches as well as his old shirts. Losing Ben means that there is only Jack to wear them and again he is so young. She says it is wicked to keep them in boxes when they would be of use in your family. Mama wishes you to know it is not out of charity that she would like you to have them, but she cannot abide wastefulness and would much prefer you to make use of them. She wishes to tell you how heartbroken she is for you and for your family's loss," recounted Grace. It had been a long and beautifully delivered speech, but at the end of it Grace burst into tears and found herself comforted by a sobbing Mrs Bosanko. Daisy had gone to sit by a very quiet and stunned looking Harry. Reaching out, she caught hold of his hand and squeezed it tightly. He looked into her serious face and began to sob quietly, so she put her arms around him and gently patted his back. Joey sat awkwardly at the table, looking about him at the desolation that he knew he had created. In the past he had always sent one of his henchmen to deputise for him. Rarely had Joey been in the midst of the sorrow and heartbreak that his actions had so often caused. He would arrange a handsome payment and further help if they required it. For the women and daughters, he could often find work at the great houses where he sold his smuggled cargoes but this, this was so different. This was what pain looked like and in his heart he now began to know what it felt like. In saving his brother perhaps he had begun to save himself, who could tell? He spent some time talking quietly to Emily Bosanko and passed over some more money, then it was time for them to take their leave. He noticed how close Daisy and Harry had been during the visit; they had not only sat together but they were close together in spirit. He would have to be blind not to have seen that.

On the way home, it was again a very quiet little group that made their way back to Trevu. He helped the girls down from the carriage and they slowly made their way into the house. They found Chloe in the withdrawing room and told her all that had transpired at the Pendray's and how Mrs Bosanko had sent her thanks for her good wishes, also that she hoped that their father was soon to recover his strength.

"Has he woken again, Mama?" asked Daisy, hopefully, and her face fell when her mother shook her head sadly.

"He is so very weak, dearest. It will take time, you know," she said softly, trying to hide her own fear.

"He will get better, won't he Mama?" asked Grace, her eyes filling with tears.

"Of course, 'e's goin' get better, young ladies, but like yer mother said 'tis goin' take time, an' worryin' yer mother idden the bes' way to 'elp 'er now is it?" announced Joey, and lifting his eyes to Chloe's face, gave her some of his courage with a smile.

Chloe told the girls to go to the nursery as she had some news that she wished to give to Mr Bolitho, adding that she would come to see them later and to make sure that Jack did not leave the nursery.

"Yes, Mama," said Grace and turned to go, but Daisy hesitated a moment and turned to look at Joey, who felt uncomfortable under her gaze. He stood back to let her pass and she marched resolutely past him, following her sister from the room. Turning to Chloe, he asked simply: "You 'ave news fer me, Mrs Trevarthen, ma'am. Does it concern your husband?"

"It concerns both my husband and yourself, Mr Bolitho, but please to take a seat," and she motioned him to the settle and sat herself down opposite to him. She directed her strong gaze at him and studied his face for a long time. He shifted uncomfortably under her scrutiny but said nothing.

"When first I was introduced to you Mr Bolitho, I dreaded having to meet you for I had heard such bad reports of you. The terrible man who will kill rather than lose a cargo, a man who cares for nobody, a man without a heart. Is that a fair description of you Mr Bolitho?" she asked.

" 'Ess ma'am," he answered her directly, for under her gaze he felt compelled to be truthful.

"Then why, Mr Bolitho, have you worked so hard to save my husband's life? What is he to you, that you have thrown your head into a noose for him, you who have never even come close to being caught before? Now you come to his house and offer assistance to him and his family without a care for your own safety. I know, as the girls do not, that Bert Pendray was smuggling for you, and that on his last trip when his body and my husband had been removed from the beach, you set all the men left to clear any contraband and see it safely hidden. 'To save Paul from the 'Preventatives' my workmen have told me. Paul had never anything to do with smuggling before he met you. I have learned of some of the trouble he got himself into by defending and protecting Bert Pendray, and I know that in order to do that he had to protect you, and how much he hated himself for having to do such a thing, for he had no great love of you..." She saw him catch his breath and hang his head, but she continued without a pause: "...but I have had this chance to know you. I have seen you with my husband and the care you have for him, and I have seen you with the children and how hard you have worked to reassure them and to set their fears aside. I have watched your face, your smiles and expressions and I have come to recognise you for more than Joseph Bolitho the smuggler, in fact I have come to see you almost as a family member." She spoke in a quiet, controlled voice, watching as a guilty look appeared on his almost invariably stony countenance. She continued in her pleasant voice, but the sound of it was chilling him to his marrow: "This afternoon when you sat with my youngest son and talked to him, I was most forcibly reminded of the many times that his elder brother, George, and his grandfather, Redvers, would sit and converse, just as you were doing with Jack. Redvers would smile at George in just the same way as you were smiling at Jack, and I wondered why that image should intrigue me so. Then I cast my mind back to when I was a young bride, and how the servants told of Paul and his father and how alike they were, in face and in . . . in other ways. As time went by I learned from servants' gossip that my father-in-law, like my own husband, had a past. A philandering past shall we say? I learnt that, until Paul came into his life, Redvers sought companionship away from his own roof. Surely you would agree with me, Mr Bolitho, that under those circumstances Redvers might have fathered more than one child, perhaps even another son, outside of his marriage bed. And if he did, Mr Bolitho, that this child would grow up, possibly in this locality? If this is indeed the case then this child, when grown, if he had been told of his parentage would seek either to destroy Paul, out of raging jealously, or to hold him more dear than his own life, out of love for the son of his father?" Her eyes narrowed as she saw a heavy blush cover his face and he swiftly bowed his head to avoid her gaze. She regarded him in silence for a long time as if expecting a reply. Watching him, she noticed how tightly his hands were grasped together, so tightly that his knuckles showed white.

Realising that he would not speak, she took a deep breath and then announced firmly: "Would you like me to tell you what I think my news is now, Mr Bolitho?"

He kept his head bowed and said nothing, but he knew he was in the presence of someone who, in spite of all her cares and worries, had sat and painstakingly pieced together what he had so recently thought would never be discovered. Again there was a long silence, but finally he raised his head and met her gaze squarely.

" 'E does not knaw an' I would prefer 'e never finds out. Our father never knew of me existence, you see, an'..." he paused before continuing quietly: "...I never knew meself until me neighbour died a few weeks ago. It took 'im many years to discover it, but when 'e saw me with Paul 'e knew then, fer to 'im we 'ad a look of each other. I look like me mother. I only resemble yer 'usband and me . . . me brother in build an' expression. 'Tis most unlikely others will ever see it, Mrs Trevarthen, an' I will not use it to damage me brother or 'is family."

She regarded him serenely, "I am so sorry, Mr Bolitho, that you could not have been taken into this household and given your rightful place as Paul has been. Your life would have been so different had it been so, do you not agree?"

" 'Ess, ma'am." he replied solemnly.

"As it is your wish, Paul will never hear from me of your heritage, but if he ever discovers that you are his brother then whatever he wishes to do about it I will comply with, for you are the eldest and you would have the right to be the Master of Trevu," she said.

"No I wouldn', Mrs Trevarthen ma'am, fer I was never recognised and adopted by . . . by Redvers Trevarthen like yer 'usband 'as been and neither 'ave I earned the right to it," he said gravely.

"But the Trevarthens have immense wealth, Mr Bolitho, from the farm and the mines at least! They were all part of Redvers' estate, the rest came to Paul through his mother. I know my husband and if he knew of you and how you stood in relation to himself, he would not see you without that which he considered rightfully yours, Mr Bolitho. I beg of you, make yourself known to him, for he would wish to amend that which should be righted," she said resolutely.

He stood up, strode angrily away from her towards the fire and stood with his hands against the mantelpiece. An action that was so like her husband's that she could not forbear a smile. She watched as he stared moodily into the flames for a long while, then he turned, came back to her and looked down at her from behind his father's now recognisably impassive face.

"I will not 'ave 'im knaw, Mrs Trevarthen, and that is my final word on the matter. There is that about me that you do not knaw, but yer 'usband does, and it would break 'im to 'ave to accept me into 'is family. Trust me in this, ma'am, I beg of you. A long time ago I did something, all unknowin', that destroyed my father and almost destroyed his son. Paul knows of it an' I learned of it at the same time, but when I committed this particular foul deed I knew 'im not fer me brother then. When I found out Redvers was me father, I was told because the man who told me was dyin' an' 'e wanted me to knaw 'bout me past, in order that it might stop me from killin' me own brother. I 'ave killed or caused to 'ave killed a fair few in me time, Mrs Trevarthen, an' 'fore I knew Paul fer me brother I was quite prepared to kill 'im, and to do it without shame or conscience. 'E 'ad survived because yer 'usband was more use to me alive than dead. You don' knaw what you'd be askin' 'im to do in acknowledgin' me. I can't lose me past and stand along side of 'im because 'e would be dragged down in the gutter with me if 'e did such a thing. Leave it be, Mrs Trevarthen, leave it be!" he cried wretchedly, then turned from her and strode across the room to stare unseeingly out of the window. Slowly, she stood up and walked to him and stood at his side.

"You can change, Mr Bolitho, change your life and settle down to a respectable existence. You do not have to live the life you have created. If you do not want to be acknowledged publicly, Paul has enough money to set you up in some respectable position, away from here if you wish. I have seen you with my children, seen the love you have for them. I know there is a good man who had not the opportunity to show the world his greatness. Please, Mr Bolitho, listen to me in this for . . ." but he interrupted her pleading and shouted at her in despair: "No!" then turned to face her with an expression of hurt desperation on his face. She would have said more, but there was a knock at the door and he turned away from her to stare out of the window again. She walked from him and seated herself on the settle before answering. Lizzie entered to say that Jonas Hampton had sent down a message: that the master was awake again and had asked to see her. Chloe got up immediately and headed towards the door, she turned excitedly to see Joey still at his post by the window.

"I'll be on my way now, Mrs Trevarthen. I'll call tomorrow if tha's all right with you, ma'am?" Joey said quietly.

"As you wish, Mr Bolitho," she replied, "but please to remember that you must say your farewells to young Jack before you leave. Lest you wish to lose your heroic stature in his eyes?" and she smiled at him so enticingly that he felt his heart jump at the sight.

He bowed his head in acknowledgement and they left the room and headed up the stairs together. He left her at the door and walked down the corridor in the direction of the nursery. Jack's cry of delight was instantly hushed by Miss Clavering, but she could not stop him from throwing himself into his hero's arms. Before he left, Joey was presented with a picture that the little artist had painstakingly drawn for him of Trevu House. For his age the drawing was of a high standard and Joey thanked him for his gift most sincerely. Jack would never understand the satisfaction that his little gift had given his idol, but was delighted by 'Mr Bytho's' obvious pleasure and the large hug he received. Jack and his sisters said their farewells and Joey bowed to Miss Clavering with great formality, receiving a condescending nod in return. As he again traversed the corridor he paused for a moment outside of his brother's door, wondering if the questions that he knew Paul would have to ask had been raised with Chloe. If she had to tell him she would, for she had the strength for it, but in his heart he hoped that she would not be required to do so, for he felt it his responsibility. Turning, he quietly made his way down the stairs and out of the house. A few minutes later, mounted on his horse, he departed for home with Jack's picture carefully tucked into his shirt, against his heart. He did not want to despoil the image; either of the one that had been so faithfully drawn for him, or - the sight that warmed his heart the most - of the family within the house.

The following day he arrived at Trevu in the middle of the morning and was received in the withdrawing room by a subdued Chloe. She greeted him warmly but seemed preoccupied, so he asked her if there was anything that was giving her additional cause for her concern.

"In truth, Mr Bolitho, Paul is so very quiet and, although he asked of me no question of what has happened, I am so worried of his reaction when he does become aware of Mr Pendray's death. He was most fond of him you see, for Paul, although a man known and admired for the warmth of his personality, does not make friends easily. When . . . when the children died and Mr Pendray's wife also, they were drawn together by their mutual sadness and a bond developed between them. Indeed, were it not for Harry's love of books, Paul would not have set up his Library and when Bert Pendray invited him to go fishing he could not conceal his pleasure in it. Now I fear he will withdraw into his world of books, for all that has been brought to a disastrous end and he will seal another brick into his wall of sadness, hiding himself away with ancient roman generals and orators. It is that looming disaster that preoccupies me, Mr Bolitho, for in spite of all his learning and the pleasure that he obtains from it, I have always believed that Paul needs to do more with his life than sit behind a pile of dusty books," she said.

"He has the farm, ma'am. He loves to work there fer the men 'ave told me of their admiration fer him and what he undertakes," replied Joey, trying to leaven her despondency.

"The farm and the work he does there in no way matches the excitement he obtained with Mr Pendray. The fishing was most important to him, you see," and she gave him her direct look. "The smuggling, and the related aspects of it that he came to know of, saddened him desperately. But his enjoyment of his days at sea in the companionship of Bert and the other fishermen were most beneficial, now all that is lost to him."

"Perhaps 'e will fish from another man's boat, fer 'e 'as acquired strong links with all the local fishermen through Bert," he suggested.

She shook her head, an expression of great sadness on her face.

"No, Mr Bolitho, that is not the answer. You see, he had such a high regard for his friend that no other will be put in his place," she answered gently.

There was an awkward silence. Once again Joey wished he had never requested of Bert that he should have smuggled for him. He had inveigled Bert into working for him because he required such a man for the tasks he wanted done, but he had never foreseen the disastrous consequences that had now fallen on to his brother's head. But his present prosperity was due entirely to his law breaking and, as he knew no other trade, he was again setting out to defraud the Government. Last night in Penzance, he had been followed by Hudson for the whole of the evening and his foresight in sending Seth as his deputy to meet the ship's captain - that he had done so much business with previously - had been providential, for his next project would need careful planning. Without the Preventative Officer's presence it would be a most effortless exploit, however he could feel the man's hot breath on his neck and he knew in his bones that before long he would have that man out of the world, as sure as the sun rose every morning. Even with his experiences over the last week, he could no more turn from his trade than could a blacksmith become a dancing master. Suddenly a knock at the door heralded the arrival of Lizzie, who announced that the master was awake and wanted to see his wife and, as he was in the house, Mr Bolitho also.

Chloe rose to leave the room and motioned that Joey should attend upon her husband. He followed in her wake, feeling that he would rather have been anywhere else but in that house at that time. Chloe entered the bedchamber, thanked and dismissed Jonas, then sat herself down beside her husband and caught hold of his hand. Her smile lit up her whole face and he answered it with a weak smile of his own, but that disappeared as he turned his head to see Joey quietly entering the room, who closed the door softly behind him, leaned against it and regarded the invalid with his impenetrable gaze. The two men stared at each other without exchanging a word and Chloe was suddenly aware of the tension in the air. The question that Joey had been dreading to hear was finally asked of him:

"What of Bert, Mr Bolitho, how is he?" asked Paul in his weak voice.

CHAPTER 14

SILENCE followed, but Joey hung his head, saying nothing, so Chloe turned to her husband and told him they would talk of it again when he was feeling better.

"No!" he cried hoarsely but angrily, "We will talk of it now and I would know from Mr Bolitho how Bert is, for it is at that man's feet that I lay the blame for his disaster at losing not only his boat but his good name!"

Chloe saw Bolitho flinch but still he remained silent. Mrs Trevarthen, attempting to placate her husband, stretched out her hand, ran it through her husband's curls and said softly to him: "Paul, you are not well. Do not lose your temper like this for it will not be of assistance to you in your recovery."

"He will tell me what I have asked of him, lest he be too much a coward to do even that!" he said angrily and jerked his head away from her caressing hand, "I would know. Tell me!"

Joey sighed and moved from the door. Pulling out the chair on the other side of the bed he sat down and thought for a moment before saying curtly: "There was nothing you could do, Paul! Bert was dead afore ever you left the boat. When you was pulled ashore 'is neck was broke. You did yer best but you couldn' save 'en."

"Dead! Dead!" he gasped and then closed his eyes, as if that action would make all well again, "You are lying, he can't be dead . . . he had only a broken arm. We were speaking together at the last we . . ." but then he shut his mouth on the futility of it and drew breath painfully.

"I have sent our condolences and provisions to the family. The girls and Mr Bolitho have visited the family, Paul. We can do more for them, for I know you would want that and . . ." but Chloe's explanation was cut short abruptly by her husband's angry voice addressing Joey.

"Can you sleep at night, Joey?" he raged, "with all the death and destruction you have caused? You have killed one of my greatest friends and for what? Your damn greed! Your lawless ways! That poor family! What of them? Your filthy money won't bring Harry and Dick back their father, nor Emily Bosanko her brother, nor I my dear friend," and he caught his breath on a sob and moaned in pain.

"Paul, rage at me when yer recovered. You need to rest now, but I do most sincerely apologise fer what I've done to you an' yer family, believe me in that," and Joey sat with his head bowed at his brother's side.

"Old Edwin told me to feel sorry for you because you deserved my pity, Joey, but I don't feel sorry for you, for I loathe you! I hate everything about you! I want you out of my house and away from my family. If possible I want never to see your damn face again, do you understand me?" he rasped struggling to get his breath.

"No, Paul! This will not be, for you are talking of the man who saved your life. You can despise him as much as you like, but you will not bar him from this house, for without his action in saving you from death when no one else believed you alive, you would not be here now to even feel hatred," his wife said firmly.

Her husband turned to regard her in astonishment. He opened his mouth to speak, but his wife continued in a firm yet placid voice: "Dr Dunstan has brought rumours from Penzance that Mr Hudson has been making enquiries of you, and also that he was most interested to discover that Mr Bolitho was involved in your rescue from almost certain death. If Mr Bolitho is no longer to attend upon us then he will believe that one of you is attempting to deceive him, for it would not be thought at all unusual if the man who saved your life should not call to enquire upon your recovery. Mr Bolitho has called upon you every day since the tragedy occurred. If now he is to be barred from this house then, if I were Mr Hudson, I would certainly wish to know why his presence is no longer required and would then proceed here with all haste to question you about certain matters. In your present weak condition you would have difficulty in controlling your emotions, Paul, I am aware of that, but you must understand you cannot admit to Hudson that you have any knowledge of anything that occurred that afternoon. You cannot condemn Mr Bolitho out of spite for the love you felt for Bert."

"Can I not, madam?" he shouted as strongly as he could, "That man had destroyed my life twice over and still I am to say nothing! And now my wife, the person I adore most in all this world, tells me that I must keep silent?" and he shifted his gaze to regard Joey viciously.

"You must do as you see fit, Paul," said Joey softly, from behind his unfathomable stare. "I 'ave not the right to expect yer mercy another time," and he bowed his head and stared at the floor.

There was a tense silence until finally Paul opened his mouth to speak, but before he could say anything there was a hurried knocking at the door. Lizzie came in on their answer and said worriedly: " 'Tis Mr 'Udson, ma'am, an' 'e says 'e will have words with Mr Trevarthen. I told 'en 'ow sick 'e was but . . . Oh Ma'am! 'E's comin' up the stairs now!" and she turned and looked in fear at the door.

"Say nothing, Paul, say nothing," his wife pleaded with him, then turned as Mr Hudson swept into the room and gave Paul a brief, tight smile.

"Good morning, Mr Hudson. No doubt you have called to offer your best wishes, but as you can see Mr Trevarthen is truly not well enough to have visitors," Chloe said abruptly.

"Is that so, Ma'am? You do surprise me. I must presume that Mr Bolitho is not a visitor in that case?" he snorted.

"You presume correctly, Mr Hudson, for as the man who saved my husband's life, I could hardly deny him the opportunity to receive my husband's heartfelt thanks on being restored to his wife and family," and she smiled at the preventative man and pinched her husband's hand at the same time.

"Mr Bolitho, a saviour of his fellow man?" and Mr Hudson laughed derisively, "Must be for the first time, Mr Bolitho, would you not agree?"

Joey Bolitho raised his eyes to Paul's and said nothing, preferring to maintain his silence.

"Well, well!" sneered Hudson, "The great Joseph Bolitho, smitten into speechlessness. This is a most unusual occurrence, is it not? However, perhaps he would answer some questions of me? You as well, Mr Trevarthen, for there is much I need to know."

From his pillows, Paul regarded his inquisitor with a disdainful look upon his face and merely said: "What is it that you wish to enquire of me, Mr Hudson?"

"On the afternoon of the storm, Bert Pendray attempted to run his boat aground in your cove, Mr Trevarthen, for one reason. His boat was packed with contraband and he would need his friend's assistance to dispose of the contents, for his friend has a large estate and would have no difficulty in hiding a quantity of illicit goods on it. Mr Bolitho, as great an organiser as he has been, was in dire need of help to get his cargo in. My men are searching now, all over this farm and the lower one. They will look through every building you own, Trevarthen, and when they find what they are looking for, and find it they will, I will haul you and Bolitho before the courts and you can swing together till your bodies rot!" he stormed, unable to maintain his pretence of calm.

Joey coughed quietly and said softly: "An' if you don' find anything, Mr 'Udson, what then? Goin' apologise to Mr Trevarthen fer disturbin'' 'en I 'ope?"

"I shall find what I am looking for, never you fear, Mr Bolitho," and he turned to Paul and regarded him steadily. As he began to speak again, two of the three listeners felt the cold hand of fear clutch at them: "But if they do not, I am sure that the man whose own mother lost her life because of Bolitho, and who let him get away with it, would not commit the same mistake again by letting him kill his great friend and still remain silent. Tell me, Trevarthen, and I'll save your neck and keep you out of it. Bolitho is the man I want and only Bolitho. Give him to me, Mr Trevarthen, and I will take him out of your life forever."

Paul felt his wife's desperate pressure on the palm of his hand, and felt but did not see Joseph Bolitho's stony gaze directed at his face. He stared in silence at the Customs Officer, standing so proudly at the foot of the bed: secure in the confidence that this time, having no one left to protect, Paul would tell Hudson what he wanted to know.

So Paul drew a deep painful breath, and began to speak. To hear what he had to say, Mr Hudson had to lean forwards towards the bed, giving the appearance that the three were gathered around the man's deathbed.

"Mr Hudson, you never fail to amaze me, sir," Paul said painfully, drawing in another tortured breath before continuing in his strained voice: "Bert was coming home from the Scillies. There was no contraband on his boat, he was merely returning from visiting his late wife's cousin, she was a Scillonian, or didn't anyone tell you that? The southwesterly that blew up took everyone by surprise, on land as well as at sea. Bert left too late from St. Mary's to make port. He had no option but to try to beach her and my cove was the only one that he could use. It is often used by sailors to beach their boat on, for there is no other cove that offers them such sanctuary. Search my property as thoroughly as you wish, but when you have found not one item of contraband you may return and apologise as Mr Bolitho has recommended." He stopped and gasped for air again before summoning up all his strength and rasping: "Now get out, for I shall do better without sight of your ugly face!"

No one said anything, but Hudson stared incredulously at Paul for a few moments. Then, in a sneering voice that trembled with anger and barely rose above a whisper, he said: "You and your sort disgust me, Trevarthen. Riff raff, you said some people thought of you and you laughed at the knowledge of it. I see you differently. I see a black bastard who has used his money and position to do down the good people around him, trying to play the master and make slaves of honest people. I'll have you in the gutter before I am finished with you, you and that slimy bastard who sits so boldly at your side." During this tirade, the Preventative Officer's face was just inches from Paul's own, now Hudson stood up straight and addressed both men: "Be warned, both of you, I have you in my sights, 'twill not be long before my shot finds its mark!" he shouted.

A quiet voice, steely calm said: "Do forgive me, Mr Hudson, if I do not see you out but I am sure that, now you have no reason to stay, you will be leaving immediately."

"Certainly, ma'am, for there is nothing further that I wish to discuss with Mr Trevarthen." Then he turned to face her and continued derisively: "but as I will be searching the premises, this house included, I expect to be here for quite a while," and he turned on his heel and marched from the room.

Chloe got up and crossed the room, waiting with her ear to the door until she had confirmed that he had gone down the stairs and, on hearing the front door slam, turned away and resumed her seat. She bowed her head over her husband's hand and began to sob quietly, unable to hold back her despair. Paul began to cough, so Joey raised him up and helped him take another drink before settling him back against the pillows.

"They will find no contraband 'ere, 'tis well away from this place, I 'ave made sure of that," Joey announced contritely.

"Is there anything at Bert's cottage?" asked Paul in little more than a whisper.

"No, 'tis well concealed fer we 'ad time to get all well away," and he cleared his throat and said: "Thankee 'gain, Paul, fer standin' by me."

"I did not do it for you, Joey, I did it for Bert's family, for why should his boys have to suffer more than they have to save your damned neck," he whispered angrily. "But my wife is in the right of it as usual, for if you leave now, Hudson will believe us all to be involved in your damned, filthy business!" He began to cough again. Chloe raised her head and, dashing away the tears from her eyes resolutely, got up and began to look through the medicine bottles on the small side table. She picked up a glass and measured out a quantity of dark liquid into one glass, then poured water into another and advanced upon her husband holding both of them. He looked at her and, raising his eyes to her face, asked if the taste of the medicine was so atrocious that he would need the water to help it down. She sighed and nodded, "But it will make you feel so much more comfortable, Paul," she said coaxingly. He heard a chuckle behind him and turned his head to see Joey quickly wipe the smile from his face. As Joey realised that he would be needed he adroitly lifted Paul and, between Chloe's cajoling and his own physical strength, the patient was persuaded to take the potion. The effect was not immediate, but Paul soon began to feel drowsy. He smiled at his wife as she left the room to supervise what was happening with Mr Hudson and his search. The servants would keep quiet, she was convinced of that, for on the day that her husband was brought home insensate, she had informed Jonas Hampton and Lizzie that they were to ensure that nothing of what the household and the workmen heard and saw was repeated to anyone outside of the family. She wanted to be there to give support and encouragement to her staff, and to ensure that Mr Hudson, in his desperation to find contraband, did not overstep the boundaries of his search.

Paul, watching the door sleepily, saw the handle turn. A small, black, curly-haired head looked around it and whispered: "Dada?" Joey rose to his feet but stopped as Paul said softly: "Let him come in, Joey, for I have missed him so," so little Jack was allowed in and he rushed across the room in delight, stopping immediately when he caught sight of his father's damaged face. His smile disappeared and he promptly burst into tears and blubbered: "Somebody hurt Dada!" and then he began to howl in earnest. Joey reached his side, picked him up and began to placate him.

"Now if yer goin' be very quiet - very, very quiet - you can come an' sit with me an' talk to yer Dada," Joey told him softly, "but yer Dada got go sleep else 'e wen't get better." He sat the boy down on his lap and Jack watched his father wide-eyed.

"Mr Bytho?" he asked in an awed tone.

" 'Ess, Jack, what is it?" Joey said.

"Why my Dada got hair on his face?" he whispered.

Paul smiled and listened as Joey told his son that he had not been able to shave but, when he felt better, he would have his face shaved and look like his Dada again.

Jack smiled at his father and then asked: "Will you be better soon, Dada?" and Paul told him softly that he would and that he was not to worry about him. Jack nodded solemnly and then whispered to Joey: "Mr Bytho, can I get on Dada's bed?" but his hopeful expression dimmed when he was told that his father was too ill to have small children climbing on him.

"You wait fer Dada to get better, like I told you, then you can play with him again. Don't you worry, Master Jack, 'e'll be better soon. Now you be very quiet because Dada's goin' sleep now so I don't want no noise from you, you understand?" he said softly into Jack's ear, and the little boy nodded solemnly.

Even Paul had to smile at the incongruous sight of the infamous smuggler soothing his son, but he was so very tired and the effects of the medicine made him drowsy, so he closed his eyes upon the sight of them.

After a short while, Joey and Jack's vigil was interrupted by Chloe's reappearance. At first she looked angry, but Jack held fast to Joey's hand and attempted his most disarming smile. "I have been very, very quiet, Mama, 'cos Mr Bytho said I had to be," he offered in little more than a whisper.

"Well, that is a good boy." said Chloe severely, but she could not hide her smile. "But I think it best that you go back to the nursery now, so say goodbye to Mr Bolitho and come with me," and she held out her hand imperatively. Reluctantly, Jack hugged Joey farewell and got off his lap, then went to his mother and allowed himself to be taken back to the nursery.

When she returned some time later, she sat by her husband's bed and studied his sleeping form for a long while. Eventually she raised her eyes to the man who sat across from her and asked abruptly: "What did Mr Hudson mean, Mr Bolitho, when he said that Paul had lost his mother because of your actions?"

She had to wait a long time for a reply. At first he looked her squarely in the eye, but then he bowed his head in remorse and began to speak in a subdued, and guilty voice:

"One of the people I . . . I killed was the man that was followin' Captain Petherick. I knew nothing of this man's other activities, ma'am, I was just preservin' me own life and me own trade the only way I knew 'ow. This chap, the customs agent, saw me in the inn an' was on 'is way to inform on me so I . . . I . . ," and he looked down and shook his head, but after a moment bravely continued: "Mr Hudson made sure that Paul 'eard about it and took great delight in tellin' 'en, but Paul wouldn' say nothin' 'bout me an' what 'e knew I'd done 'cos 'e knew 'e would pull Bert down if 'e did. But the more 'e tried save Bert the deeper I was gettin' both of them caught in me net, see. All the time I never knew who Paul was, I jes' thought I was some damn smart fellow fer gettin' the Master of Trevu to do zactly what I wanted 'en to. I'm . . . I'm some sorry, Mrs Trevarthen, 'cos I've caused some trouble to me brother an' all 'is family, but do 'e see now 'ow 'e'll never fergive me, no matter what I d' do to try put it right?" and he raised a face full of despair to hers.

"Yes, I understand, Mr Bolitho, and I am afraid you are in the right of it, for the death of his mother I do not think that Paul could ever forgive you." She sighed, caught hold of her husband's hand and, taking it to her lips, she planted a soft kiss on his long fingers. They sat on, guarding the bed and its sleeping occupant in silence, lost in their own private thoughts.

Meanwhile, Mr Hudson, under the watchful eye of Jonas Hampton, went through all the farm buildings of both the lower farm and the farmyard at Trevu. His men were most thorough, but by now very tired for Jonas would not allow them to throw his master's property around. Consequently, they had to lift sacks one by one and not toss them aside with pitchforks and evils[2]. Finding this very strenuous and, burdened by their uniforms, they were soon sweating heavily. Trevu was the largest farm in the locality and had more than one barn and two stable blocks, apart from the carriage house and the cattle byre and pigsties. At the end of two hours, Hudson's men reassembled in the yard and were directed to move the midden. They stared at him in disgust, but their commander stood threateningly in the middle of the yard and they had no option but to obey him. Jonas leaned against the stone wall of the cart house, with a barely concealed smile on his face; most of Hudson's men were ex seamen, few if any of them had anything to do with the land. So when they began to move the midden, they began at the most compacted part of it. After a very short space of time they soon realised that they were making no impression on it, but Hudson bellowed at them nonetheless. After a while, their efforts were proving fruitless and the sheer hard labour required was draining their strength. Each pitchfork wedged itself into the thick, compressed, foul mess and when removed emerged almost like a sword from a body, stained but devoid of any content. Hudson, becoming extremely red in the face, eventually realised the futility of what he had asked his men to

---

2 'evil: A four or five pronged manure fork.

undertake and ordered them to leave off their task. When Jonas repeated Mrs Trevarthen's instructions: that anything moved had to be replaced, his men looked almost on the point of mutiny. But once again Hudson overruled them and, panting with anger and very red in the face, instructed them to return the pile that they had moved. Intending to go on and search the house after their work on the midden was completed, Jonas asked them to kindly remove their boots, for it would not be right to invade the house with all the farm filth that was clinging to them. The Preventative Officer strode towards him with his hand on his sword, but Jonas did not move and pointed out that he was not refusing for the men to make a search, but it would not be right to enter the house in such a dirtied condition.

"I presume you have no objection to my entering the house, Mr Hampton, for I am not in any way soiled with the dirt of this place?" he fumed at Jonas.

"Why, none at all Mr Hudson, sir, please to follow me," he said, almost jovially, and he led the way back to the main door of Trevu's house.

Lizzie met him at the entrance, for she had been watching with interest - and a great deal of merriment - from the side of the end wall of the yard, and had only just returned to her post in the house. If Hudson thought she looked rather pink and breathless he did not remark upon it and stormed past her, making his way once again to the master's bedchamber.

Without stopping to knock, he pushed the door open, and he found Mrs Trevarthen and Joseph Bolitho, still sitting opposite each other on either side of the bed. They both looked up at him in a startled fashion but neither said a word, either to him or to each other. Trevarthen himself was awake and looked more alert than he had done earlier, so Hudson strode towards Bolitho's chair and stood beside him, looking down into Paul's face.

"I have thoroughly searched the two farms and have yet to search the house. However, I have noticed that the one place that seems to be particularly well guarded on this property is this very room. I intend to search it. Have you any objection, Mr Trevarthen, sir?" he almost shouted, such was his frustration at his wasted time.

"None whatsoever, Mr Hudson, but I am afraid you are doomed to disappointment, yet again," replied Paul, almost amiably, and in a stronger voice than he had used before. His smile was wiped from his face, however, as Hudson replied with simply the one word, "Good!" and leaning forward before anybody could stop him, caught hold of Paul's bandaged hand and jerked him forward. Whether he presumed that anything hidden in the room would be secreted away somewhere in the large bed or whether he wanted to establish that Paul Trevarthen was indeed injured, it was not clear, but as a result of his actions Paul could not contain his scream of pain. Chloe was on her feet immediately, reaching for Hudson's arm, but before she got anywhere near him, Joey sprang up from his chair and, surging forward like a pouncing tiger, had Hudson by the neck, pushing him back against the wall. With his impassive face inches from Hudson, he had dropped his hand to his dagger and then went cold in the pit of his stomach when he realised that his sheath was empty.

Paul, stuttering with pain, cried out for Joey to leave Hudson be. He had to call again, for with no knife Joey was now attempting to strangle the man.

"Leave him be, Joey! I order it! Do as I say, leave him be!" he barked authoritatively. For a moment it looked as if the smuggler would not obey him. But slowly he released his grip, let his hand drop to his side and backed away from Hudson with a disgusted sneer on his face, whilst his victim held his hand to his throat and began to cough and gasp for breath. Into this melee strode Dr Dunstan and, seeing his patient sitting in the bed and holding his damaged ribs, rushed towards him, until he became aware of the customs man leaning against the wall in some discomfort.

"What the devil . . . What has happened here? Mr Trevarthen?   Mr Hudson? Well, will one of you tell me what has happened?" he exclaimed.

"Mr Hudson seems to think that my husband is suffering no injury and, believing him to be lying in a bed for no better reason than to hide a quantity of contraband, attempted to pull him out of it in order to find the spoils that he is convinced lie hidden on our property," explained Chloe, her voice shaking with emotion.

The doctor said nothing, but crossed to his patient's side and ensured that he was returned to a prone position in as gentle manner as possible, before turning to Hudson and dismissing him from the room with a jerk of his head.

"One moment, sir," rasped Mr Hudson, still feeling his neck, "I will not be ordered out of this room until I have ascertained that . . ." but he stopped immediately as Denzil Dunstan turned on him and delivered a withering speech about his conduct and behaviour towards a badly injured man. He concluded with a threat that swiftly whitened Hudson's normally high colour: "My old friend, Sir Reginald Bonython, shall be hearing of this and I do not think he will be best pleased when he hears of what has happened here today. Your actions, as I am sure you are well aware, have far exceeded anything that you might possibly consider to be your duty, sir. Now get out and take your men with you!" and catching Hudson by the arm, pushed him out of the room and shut the door behind him. Hudson's footsteps could be heard receding along the corridor and down the stairs. As the doctor returned to his patient's side they all heard the resounding slam of the front door. Dr Dunstan quickly established that, although in great pain, Paul had received no lasting damage to either his ribs or his hand. In silence he dressed Paul's leg wound and re-bound it with Joey's assistance. As the wound on his patient's head was beginning to heal, he applied some lotion to it and determined not to re-bandage it, deciding that if the air got to the wound the healing process would be completed the sooner. After insisting that Paul drank an obnoxious potion, that nonetheless proved extremely effective in relieving Paul's pain, Dr Dunstan then crossed the room and, availing himself of a chair, carried it before him as he returned to the bedside, then sat down before surveying the faces of all present.

"Before I contact Sir Reginald, I think it only fair that I have some knowledge of what has transpired here today. Would you not agree?" he asked, but noted Trevarthen and Bolitho exchange guilty glances.

"Mr 'Udson believed Bert Pendray 'ad a smuggled cargo which is 'idden in this 'ouse or elsewhere on the property. There is no cargo 'ere, Dr Dunstan, and Mr Trevarthen 'as nothing to do with the smuggling trade. I attacked Mr 'Udson in order that 'e should leave Mr Trevarthen alone fer I believed that Mr

Trevarthen would sustain a serious injury from Mr 'Udson's attempt to remove 'im from 'is bed," said Joey and looked at the doctor all the while with his enigmatic mask.

Dr Dunstan leaned back in his chair and regarded him with a shrewd expression, but preserved a silence for a long while.

"Mr Bolitho, I am well aware of your occupation, indeed there is probably no man in this locality who is not, but I will accept your explanation of the events that happened here today. However, be very careful, Mr Bolitho, for Mr Hudson will do his best to implicate you in any smuggling that takes place from now on, for he will not forgive or forget your assault on him to day." Then he turned and addressed his patient: "And you, Mr Trevarthen, sir, will find yourself in serious trouble with the authorities if Hudson can ever find the smallest trace of any illicit goods in or on your property. I will do the best I can for both of you, gentlemen, for Sir Reginald and myself have been friends for many a long year. Hudson's actions here tonight have weakened his position, but he will only strive the harder to crawl back into favour with the head of the service, and Bonython is not averse to success. It will do Sir Reginald's position in society no end of good if he can be praised for capturing the most famous smuggler in the county. But it will damage him considerably if it is found that, in attempting to do so, one of his officers injured Cornwall's most famous author, as well as one of the wealthiest and most admired men in the County. Well, gentlemen, when I contact Sir Reginald is there anything further that you wish me to say on your behalf?" he asked pointedly.

The two men looked at each other briefly and shook their heads, looking embarrassed, then Paul coughed and launched himself into a speech, offering his thanks to Dr Dunstan for his proposed intercession on the men's behalf. The doctor stood up and replaced his chair, then came and looked down at Paul, studying him quietly for a long while.

"You are too good a man to be tainted with this fellow's reputation, Mr Trevarthen, sir," he said sternly and swept his hand towards the smuggler, "but if you determine to remain his friend, I would advise you to encourage him to give up his lawbreaking and to take up an honest profession, instead." He turned his attention to Chloe, bowed and said comfortingly, and in a noticeably gentler tone: "I will call again this evening, Mrs Trevarthen, to re-assure your good self, - and indeed to confirm on my own behalf - that your husband has not sustained any lasting damage after his treatment at Mr Hudson's hands." He issued his farewells and left the room with Chloe, who had taken it upon herself to see him from the house and also to thank him for all he had done and proposed to do on her husband's behalf.

Paul turned his head on the pillow and regarded Joey with a calm expression, at variance with the worried look that was sitting on that person's countenance.

"Would you have killed him?" Paul asked softly of him.

" 'Ess," he replied, without hesitation.

"That's what occurred to me earlier, Joey, and I did not want his blood spilled in my house. As he has now left my property you had best have your knife back. You will find it under my pillow," and he looked into the man's surprised face, unable to prevent a mischievous grin.

Reaching his hand along the sheet, Joey encountered the bone handle of his knife and retrieved it, replacing it in its sheath before asking Paul how he had taken hold of it and why.

"When you lifted me up it was easy enough to reach down and remove it. But as to hiding it under the pillow, that presented more of a difficulty; Jack was of assistance there because you had to get up to go to him," he replied blithely, "and as to why? As I told you: I will have no blood spilled in this house."

"You are only puttin' off the day, Paul, fer I will have 'im!" Joey spat out viciously.

Paul sighed, and then winced as the pain in his chest increased momentarily. They regarded each other warily for a long while, then of a sudden Paul spoke:

"Joey, would you do me a favour?" he asked softly.

"Whatever you would wish of me, Paul," replied Joey, surprised to be asked.

"Get my shaving gear and get rid of this growth on my face for me, for I detest it so," said Paul.

Joey continued to look at him in astonishment, but rang the bell. When Lizzie arrived, he asked for some hot water and, when she returned some minutes later bearing the jug, she was closely followed by Chloe, whose face wore a puzzled frown. When she realised what operation Joey was about to perform on her husband's behalf she was swift to protest, but Joey stopped her, saying that if her husband felt well enough to want to be shaved it was a good sign. She relented and, leaving him to his task, headed along the corridor to the nursery to make sure that Jack was still engrossed in the picture that he was drawing for his father. When Joey had finished with the razor he cleaned it and put it away and, as he was wiping Paul's face, was aware of being scrutinised. He felt a little uncomfortable under his brother's gaze, but said nothing and soon returned to his seat.

"Thank you," said Paul politely, "that feels so much the better. I have not a fondness for beards and as I no longer have a manservant to assist me I was at a loss as to whom I should ask for assistance. Jack's distress at my appearance made me determined to have myself shaved but I had not considered you for the role of barber. However, when you attacked Hudson on my behalf I felt emboldened to ask you. Until that moment I could not be sure that you would not take the opportunity to cut my throat."

Joey grinned in return but said seriously: "I've told 'e 'fore Paul, I'll not be the one to put 'e goin' if I can 'elp it in any way."

"Intriguing, Joey, for you to be so considerate toward me. There must be a reason for your concern," and he raised an eyebrow at him, but Joey only looked discomforted and vouchsafed no comment. He was aware that Paul was continuing to stare at him and looked up in relief when Chloe returned. He observed her face and its entrancing smile as she beheld her husband.

"Oh, Paul, how much better you look! The girls are most jealous that Jack has been to see you, so I have informed them that if you are well enough they may come in for a short while before they have their tea. If you have no objection of course," and she smiled winningly at him.

"None whatsoever. To be honest I have missed them all so much," and as a thought struck him, he asked worriedly if George had been informed of what had happened.

"Yes, dearest, I have written every day to tell him how you have gone on and he has dutifully replied. He wanted to come home but I told him it would be for the best if he should stay at school. When you are better we will send for him to come home for a few days," she said and moved across the room to his side. As she seated herself in her chair, his hand moved across the counterpane towards hers. Joey got up abruptly and told them he had better be leaving for he had some business to see to in the town.

"Will you come tomorrow?" asked Paul.

Joey paused with his hand on the handle of the door. He thought for a moment and then turned with a half smile on his face, telling them that he would probably be unable to make a visit, but if the time was available to him he would come for an hour in the evening. Paul called his name and he lifted his head, looking at him steadily.

"I will have no harm done to Hudson, Joey, for if anything should befall the man, 'een he only sprain his ankle, it will be to you that they look for the cause. Do you understand me, Joey?"

Shifting uncomfortably, Joey said nothing and for a moment it looked as if no reply was forthcoming.

"All right, Paul. It shall be as you request but I am not the man to endure 'is actions. If I find he 'as moved in any way more against you, then I will act and this time you will not stay me 'and," and with a nod to Paul and a bow to Chloe he was gone.

Paul sighed and remarked: "Might as well tell him to shake hands with Jack Ketch as to try and stop him from killing Hudson. I fear for his life, Chloe, for I have a great respect for Joseph Bolitho, although I know he has committed many foul actions against his fellow man. He has committed crimes against myself that I cannot forgive, although the Lord knows I would wish that I could." He gave a long sigh, then cried angrily: "I like him, Chloe, you see, and I know I should not!"

"Why can you not allow yourself to feel friendship toward him, Paul, for he appears to care a great deal for you?" said his wife cautiously.

"It is not so simple to be a friend of Joseph Bolitho, Chloe. If he had not encouraged Bert into smuggling he would be still alive today. The people Joey employs to do his dirty business have no love of it. They want his money so that they can improve their miserable lot, have more food on the table, better clothes on their back, pay the rent, or to keep their children at school." He lapsed into silence as he thought of the orphaned boys in their cottage. Chloe thought he would have nothing more to say, but he continued in a quiet, considered tone: "Joey smiled at a young, crippled boy that Hudson had employed to watch him. We were all together in the inn and we all knew what Joey intended to do to him, but none of us said anything to either warn the poor fellow or, later, when Hudson asked his questions about the boy's disappearance, to implicate Joey. I have never felt so tainted and disgusted with myself as I did that day, Chloe. One word from me and Joseph Bolitho would have been taken and I would have been free from him for ever, but that one word would have put Bert's life in danger. If Hudson had taken Joey, the others would have to be gotten rid of to keep them from talking. Skewes, Joey's helpmate would accomplish that without a qualm. I could not allow that to happen so I lied, and when I did, Joey knew I was as much embroiled with him as the others. He so disgusted me that I hit him. For anyone else to do such a thing to him, and in front of his friends, there would have been no forgiveness but for me there was an amnesty of a sort. I could be used and turned into Joey's puppet. Bert was desperate to keep Harry and Dick at school for as long as he could possibly could. He undertook more and more smuggling on Joey's behalf, and I was powerless to stop him. Bert was a proud man, he could not accept my money for it was a gift of charity, but he could take Joey's because he had to earn it. Well, he has earned his money now," and he gave a long sigh.

"Dearest, do not berate yourself so, I beg of you," and she stroked his arm soothingly. Then her lips curved upwards mischievously and she announced that she would send to Penzance immediately, to employ the services of a reliable barber who could attend upon him on a daily basis, for he looked so much more handsome when he was shaved.

"Wife?" he said softly, with the merest twitch of his lips but an undeniable twinkle in his eyes.

She looked enquiringly at him.

"When I am restored to health I shall make sure that your teasing of me stops immediately, for your behaviour is most outrageous towards my poor self."

"Pooh!" she laughed at him in reply and, leaning over, kissed him lovingly and felt her heart leap with joy at his tender response.

CHAPTER 15

WITHIN a month, Paul was able to go about the countryside with Dr Dunstan's permission. He was still unable to sit a horse for his leg and ribs were too painful to stand the jolting, so the carriage was used to transport him to Penzance and around the estate. With his wife he had visited and consoled Emily Bosanko, and was surprised to hear that Joey Bolitho was still visiting her and the family and was still helping them financially. After staying for little longer than an hour they said their farewells, returned to the carriage and made their way home.

At Trevu Paul informed his wife he thought that he would go to his room and work on some text. Chloe smiled brightly at him, for it was the first time since the accident that he had shown any desire to do any of his translating and she knew full well the pleasure it gave him. Sitting at his desk, however, Paul was unable to focus his mind on the work set out before him and found himself wondering about Joseph Bolitho and his activities. He no longer called as frequently, much to young Jack's disappointment, and when he did it was apparent that he had no desire to talk about himself. To Paul it was obvious that he was again enmeshed in his smuggling and was attempting to avoid contact with himself in order to protect him from the activities that he was engaged in. If he was helping Emily Bosanko then he would need a good income, for Paul knew that the Pendray household was not the only one that the man was helping. He puzzled over Bolitho and his way of life for the rest of the day and, at dinner with his wife, he felt moved to remark that it was indeed strange that Bolitho should have always taken it upon himself to help others, for his reputation did not give one to believe that he was naturally magnanimous.

"I must admit, dearest, that in spite of all my knowledge of his dreadful past I find him a most sympathetic person. After your accident he came every day and sat with you. He was so kind to the children, particularly Jack, and he gave me such confidence and would not let me become down hearted. You were so ill, dearest, I am afraid I did frequently think that you would not survive, but Mr Bolitho would always bolster my belief and he would not let me give in to my fears. To be honest, Paul, I do not truly know how this household would have managed without him, quite apart from the fact that his prompt action when you were pulled ashore undoubtedly saved your life. Dr Dunstan was most impressed with him and was saddened to think that such a man should be wasting himself with his criminal activities," and she sighed and added: "and I can only agree with that sentiment."

Her husband regarded her shrewdly for a long while, but added nothing to the conversation and, after their meal they retired to the back parlour and read quietly to themselves without mentioning his name again. Paul, his head bowed and apparently absorbed in reading his book, was far more engrossed in the problem of his wife and her obvious admiration for Joseph Bolitho. He felt most uneasy that she should admire him so, for in spite of his kind actions on his own behalf, Paul found it impossible to forgive the man so easily. His mother and Bert seemed ranged side by side against this strange man and he had more fondness for them than for Bolitho.

George returned for a few days and helped to lift his father's depression. It was obvious to Paul that his son was thoroughly enjoying his time at school and Mr Armitage had written to him privately that his son was, as his father had been before him, a quite exceptional scholar. Paul was immensely proud to have George so regarded and, smiling with pleasure at the headmaster's comments, he hastened to show Chloe the headmaster's letter. As he was about to cross the hall, there was a knock at the door and Lizzie bustled up the stairs from the kitchen to answer it. Paul paused to see who it was that had called and watched as Joseph Bolitho politely removed his hat and greeted Lizzie pleasantly. Striding forward, he approached Joey and greeted him quietly, then directed him to proceed with him to the withdrawing room. He was aware that the man was regarding him with a reserved expression on his face. Drawing breath deeply, he could only hope that Bolitho was not having problems with a smuggling operation and had come to him in hope of some form of assistance. Then he felt a flush of shame cross his face, for Joey no longer attempted to embroil him in any deception. Indeed, he had not even implemented his request to have the Hudson's dine with them once he had realised Paul's loathing of the Preventative Officer. Entering the withdrawing room together, Trevarthen and Bolitho stood for a moment, both watching Chloe as she turned from the window to see who it was that was entering the room. At once her face broke into her familiar, sunny smile and she crossed the room towards them both.

"How nice to see you again, Mr Bolitho," she said with her hand extended, smiling as he bowed his head towards her and took her hand in his firm grasp.

Paul watched them both, but said nothing. He turned away and walked towards the settle, waiting for his wife to take her seat before sitting down himself.

"Well, Joey, to what do we owe your presence here today? As you can see I am almost restored to health, so I doubt that my wellbeing is the reason for your visit," he said brusquely.

Chloe turned her head at once and regarded her husband with a worried frown. She was most surprised at his abrupt manner and supposed that one of his injuries was paining him. Joseph Bolitho seemed not to have noticed the tone of his voice for his face was devoid of any emotion, but he inclined his head towards Paul and, after congratulating him on the improvement to his health, merely remarked that he was passing and thought it churlish not to call.

Paul regarded him coldly and then said rudely: "How kind," and having nothing further to add, turned to look at his wife. Chloe, smiling apologetically at their visitor, turned away quickly and directed a puzzled look at her husband, but quickly recovered her composure and began to recount to Joey the tale of Jack's latest escapade. He directed a smile of pure enjoyment at her when he heard the trouble that the young scamp had caused to Miss Clavering yet again, but it was particularly noticeable that her husband played no part in the conversation. They were both aware that they were being subjected to Paul's intimidating stare, but for their own reasons chose not to notice.

"Yer friends at Josh's 'ave been asking after you," remarked Joey to the convalescent, his face expressionless, then asked quietly: "They were wondering if you was to call upon them again?"

"I have no reason to visit them," said Paul sharply, "but please to pass on my good wishes when next you see them."

Under Joey's direct stare, he began to feel uncomfortable. At first he thought that no reply was to be forthcoming, but when Bolitho did speak, his words drew a flush of shame from him.

" 'Twas not only meself that saved you, Paul. Those men pulled you through they waves as if their lives depended on it. Now you tell me you 'ave no reason to call. What thanks to give them is that?"

In the silence that followed Paul was aware that, not only was he the recipient of Bolitho's stare, but his wife was also looking at him with a cool expression on her face. But Paul set his jaw and made no reply.

"If my husband does not wish to visit his old friends, I would be most grateful if you would pass on our heartfelt thanks to them for all that they did on that day. I am well aware, for the farm hands have told me, what efforts were made on Paul's behalf to save him, even if he has not the wit to see it for himself!" she remarked sharply.

"I will decide how I conduct myself, thank you, madam!" he retorted, stung, but after a moment remarked that he would think about making a visit to the inn some time in the future, "when riding is not so uncomfortable."

Joey took the opportunity given by Paul's last remark to enquire after his injuries, and drew from him the admission that he was not quite as fit as he had implied.

"Dr Dunstan is of the same calibre as old Simcott for making a man rest. But I suppose he is in the right of it, for I would not want to have anything spoil my recovery now; 'twould be most annoying to have to take to my bed again," he announced begrudgingly.

A smile crept across Joey's face, but before he could answer there was a knock at the door. Lizzie appeared, to inform Chloe that Cook wished to have words with her in the kitchen concerning the menu for the evening meal. Excusing herself, Chloe left the room and the two men were left regarding each other. Paul was the first to speak and enquired of Joey if he had been troubled with Hudson since their encounter in Trevu.

Shaking his head, Joey said: "Keeping away from me. Bonython must 'ave 'ad words with 'en sure nuff." He laughed mischievously, but Paul did not respond. Bolitho did not seem to be at all embarrassed by Paul's coldness towards himself, in fact he appeared to derive much amusement from it. With Chloe no longer in the room his face was more mobile and he chatted quite happily to Paul, who merely regarded him with a cold stare and hardly said a word. What answers Trevarthen returned to any questions posed by him were curt and sometimes monosyllabic. But Joey was not in the least deterred and, as he rose to his feet when Chloe returned, Paul was able to observe the affectionate look that he directed at her as she walked to her seat. When he saw her display her laughing smile in reply to Joey, Paul felt a cold hand clasp at his heart. Never had he seen his beloved wife smile so winningly at any other man. Even their old friend, Peter Fleetwood, a renowned bachelor and a determined flirt, had never received a smile containing such warmth from her.

Surely she was not attempting to tease him by flirting with Bolitho? He frowned, and watched them both with his angry scowl darkening his brow. If Bolitho and his wife were aware of his stare they gave no sign of it and conversed happily with each other, a fact that did nothing to lighten Paul's sombre mood. When Joey rose to leave, his host breathed a sigh of relief and escorted him to the main door. His farewell was merely civil, and he watched his visitor broodingly as he made his way to the stables to collect his horse. When he returned to the withdrawing room and to his wife he studied her face for a long while, before remarking that she appeared to derive great enjoyment from seeing Bolitho again.

"Of course I was pleased to meet with him again, Paul, but it was most noticeable that you were not in the best of humours. Has something happened to disturb you?" she asked innocently and, picking up her embroidery, began to set her stitches again.

"I'm not sure if I have cause to be disturbed, wife, but I would advise you not to be so forward in your greeting to that man," he replied coldly.

At first she looked shocked, but his surprising statement brought forth a hearty chuckle from her and she told him not to be so absurd, for she had in no way flirted with Joseph Bolitho.

Forgetting his original intention of showing her Mr Armitage's letter regarding George's prowess, he stood up abruptly and made his way to the door, a heavy frown on his face. Grasping the door handle, he turned suddenly and addressed her again:

"I have warned you before, Chloe, not to fall under that man's spell. Clever as you are, Madam Wife, you are no more immune to Joey Bolitho's charm than any other woman," and wrenching the door open he strode from the room, slamming the door behind him, leaving his wife staring at his departure in shock and disbelief.

As soon as Dr Dunstan gave permission for him to ride again, Paul took the first opportunity that presented itself, had saddled his grey hunter and rode into Penzance, making straightway for the stables nearest to Josh Pascoe's inn. The cheery stable lad beamed him a smile of welcome as he took Trevarthen's horse, for this particular gentleman had always been his best customer and his enforced absence had caused the young boy's income to dwindle dramatically of late. The return of the gentleman who dispensed his largesse so freely was a most welcome sight indeed to the impoverished urchin. Whistling happily to himself he led the grey to his best stall, resolved to give of his best to such an important resident.

Paul had determined to visit the inn again, but as he strode towards its familiar door he felt out of place, for Bert was no longer with him and he had dressed in his normal attire and not the old clothes he had always worn for their fishing trips. Perhaps, looking as he did, the men that he knew would be there at that time of day would find his appearance strange and he would not be welcomed as he would have liked. Begrudgingly, he knew that Joey had been right when he had advised him to visit them for they had all helped to save his life, but his heart ached with sadness that the position that he attained with them as Bert's friend had been lost forever. Now, they would stop their drinking and stare at him in his fine clothes, as if he had been a stranger lost in the little back alleys of that part of town who had called at the inn to ask directions.

He paused as he heard the inviting sound of the men's chatter and raucous laughter and made to turn away from the door at the last, for he could not face them after all. A soft voice at his back made him jump and he turned and looked guiltily at the speaker.

"Not 'fraid go in to them, are 'e Paul?" asked Bolitho, and his shrewd blue eyes searched Trevarthen's face, noticing his slight darkening flush acknowledge the truth of the question.

"Why no . . . I . . . I merely . . ." stumbled Paul, but he was not quick-witted enough to find a reason to hide behind and merely looked shamefaced in front of his questioner. He had often done so in front of his father when, as a child he had been caught committing some minor crime and found himself before Redvers to answer for his misdeeds.

"Well," said Joey in a reassuring tone, "you've got yerself this far, 'twould be a shame if you d' go away again." Gently he turned Paul to face the door and, slipping his arm through his, firmly propelled him into the inn.

"Look, boys!" he shouted loudly and jovially as they entered the dark, smoky room. "See who I found comin' to call on we again!" and he withdrew his arm and took a step away from Paul. A great shout went up from the assembled men and as one they rushed towards him with their hands extended. In the midst of an excited throng Paul was borne towards the bar. He looked up to see Josh's grinning face and the next moment a foaming tankard was slapped down in front of him. However, he had not a chance to pick it up, for man after man took his hand and shook it in delight. Even a fool could not fail to notice their genuine pleasure in seeing him again and he felt shaken to his soul at the warmth of their greeting. He attempted to thank them for their efforts at saving his life, but not a man would listen to him and many there attempted to buy him a drink of rum or brandy to help speed his recovery, not allowing him to put his hand into his own pocket to buy them anything. Looking over their heads, he caught sight of Joey, who leaned against the end of the bar with a half smile on his lips and responded to Paul's glance by raising his tankard to him. With much laughter, the men began to tease Paul as they used to do, but when Seth mentioned Bert's name a sombre mood descended upon them and they solemnly raised their tankards and drank to his memory. However, their joy at seeing their friend amongst them again brought back their jollity, and soon their excited chatter filled the room and tumbled out into the little courtyard outside of the inn.

There, a tall man with ruddy cheeks pursed his lips and nervously tapped his whip against his boot as he stood in the small yard and stared worriedly towards the inn door. After the shattering interview Gerald Hudson had been subjected to with Sir Reginald Bonython, he did not feel so confident about entering the inn. But although he had been most careful not to make such a fool of himself again, his ambition to capture Joseph Bolitho and anyone else in his circle had in no way been dimmed, so he started forward determinedly. As he entered the room a blanket of silence fell over the excited crowd and there was not a man amongst them who was not annoyed at his entrance, for it had dispelled all their joy at Trevarthen's return. He was aware that every man in the room was staring at him malevolently, but he merely cleared his throat and said: "Good day, gentleman," in as mild as voice as he could maintain, then headed towards the bar and ordered himself a drink. Josh placed a tankard before him with a heavy thud, spilling some of the ale over the counter. Mr Hudson did not look in the slightest part annoyed, but paid for his ale, taking a long draught of it before replacing it on the counter and turning around, the better to survey the crowd that filled the inn. The men stared at him but not one of them spoke, so he cleared his throat again and addressed himself to the tallest man in the room.

"I see you are returned to your customary good health, Mr Trevarthen, and how delighted your old . . . um . . . friends are to see you again, especially Mr Bolitho, for I see he is here today," and he smiled a greeting to Joey and inclined his head slightly, but only received a brief acknowledgement in return. It was noticeable that Bolitho had a slight frown on his brow, an unusual occurrence for he rarely wore any expression on his face, unless it was the insolent smile that he so frequently directed at Mr Hudson. The customs man could not help but feel pleased with himself, for his new agent was a quite exceptional and unlikely bearer of tales and information, but his lowly position gave him access to some of the knowledge that Hudson required. It was also apparent from Bolitho's frown, he reasoned correctly, that Hudson's sudden appearance so soon after Trevarthen's could mean only one thing; that a spy had been set on to Paul and that Bolitho was the one man in the room - apart from himself - who was aware of the fact. Bolitho would have his work cut out to find the agent who had taken the shiny coin this time, surmised Hudson. So many of the men present would not care so much to spy on Joey for fear of sudden death. But Trevarthen would go against no man, so they would feel safe enough to inform on him. Hudson watched as Joey sipped his beer and noticed as his cold, blue gaze swept wonderingly around the faces of the assembled men. He allowed himself a small, self- satisfied smile, then looked up as he heard Trevarthen addressing him:

"I am sure you will be much relieved to know, Mr Hudson, that Dr Dunstan had pronounced me fit to go about again, so I thought I would take the opportunity to visit my many friends. However, you have no need to fear that I shall suffer a relapse, for I have promised my wife to return after only a short visit," and he glowered at the customs man from beneath his black brows.

"Oh, I see you are well protected and I have no worries on that score, Mr Trevarthen," said Hudson in an insinuating manner. "For surely Mr Bolitho will want to see you safe home, such a friend of your family as he has become." He enjoyed to see the look of discomfort that swept across Trevarthen's face at this remark. Satisfied with what he had seen, he finished his drink, headed for the door, and merely waved his whip as a gesture of farewell.

As soon as he had departed, Likky detached himself from the group of men around Paul and left the inn with only a swift glance in Joey's direction. Seth swore long and loud and some of the men made derisory comments about Hudson, but it was not long before their conviviality had returned and soon they were happily drinking, laughing and conversing again, so it was only Paul and one other that noticed Likky's return. Watching out of the corner of his eye he observed as Skewes shrugged his shoulders at Bolitho, which did nothing to alleviate the frown on his accomplice's brow. Looking up, Joey found his brother's eyes upon him but, immediately, his stony stare replaced his worried expression and he returned Paul's gaze calmly. Then, when he observed that the group at the bar was beginning to disperse, he finished his drink and made his way towards Trevarthen. Paul was making his farewells and promising to return before long. He thanked the many men who had offered to take him fishing with them, although he had politely declined all of their invitations. His allegiance to his late friend meant that he was unable to accept another in Bert's place. Turning, he noted Joey at his elbow and found himself in his company when he left the inn. As he headed towards his stabled horse, Bolitho kept pace with him and chatted in a friendly manner about Paul and his family. But all the while Trevarthen noted that his eyes were never still and that, although the smuggler did not give the impression of being nervous, Paul sensed that he was not at ease. When they reached the stables, the stable boy saw them approaching and brought out Paul's horse to him with a wide smile on his face. Its owner grinned back at him and flipped him a coin. The boy caught it expertly and thanked him profusely before looking at Joey inquisitively. Recognising his glance of assent, he disappeared into the stables and returned, hanging grimly onto the bridle of the smuggler's frisky roan. Paul looked surprised that Joey's horse should have been stabled with his for, when in Penzance, it was well known that Bolitho walked everywhere, consequently he stabled his horse nearer to his house and not on this side of town at all. Another coin was caught deftly by the young lad and, touching his cap to Joey, he returned to the stables and disappeared from view.

The two men regarded each other silently for a moment, then Paul announced that he had better be leaving for his home lest his wife begin to worry over him, for this was the first time that he had ridden horseback since the accident. As he mounted his horse, he noted that his companion was doing the same and he frowned in irritation as Joey turned his horse and directed it to fall in step beside Paul's mount. However, he made no comment and the horses walked slowly out of the yard. It was Joey alone who noticed a whisper of sound behind them and he turned to see the disappearing figure of the young boy, hastily running from the stable in the direction of the harbour. For a moment the smuggler did not comprehend the significance of what he had seen, but when he did the horror of it grasped at his heart with a cold hand.

"Oh God, surely not!" he cried aloud, and Paul turned and regarded his stricken face, before asking what it was that had made him call out in such a manner.

Turning to Paul, Bolitho informed him abruptly that he would see him to his home and, in spite of Paul's protests that he was perfectly fit to make the journey on his own, insisted on accompanying him. When they were two miles out of the town, Joey pressed Paul into taking a turning that took them into an unkempt little lane, which led to an old abandoned cottage. At the cottage he told him to dismount and, when Paul promptly refused, brusquely advised him that if he wished to see something that was going to amaze him, he had best to follow his instructions. Paul was intrigued and, after a moment's hesitation, did as he was told. They tied their horses to the stump of an old apple tree in the overgrown garden and headed back towards the road. Hidden from view by the uncut undergrowth surrounding a clump of trees, Paul was directed to watch the road.

"Why should I have need to do that for . . ." began Paul, but in a moment a hand was over his mouth and he heard Joey's voice hiss in his ear, instructing him to be quiet. They had not long to wait before they heard the sound of galloping horses and in a moment Hudson and a detachment of his armed officers flashed past them, heading purposefully along the road towards Trevu. Paul's eyes widened in surprise, but when he turned to face Joey he noticed only the grim little smile that played on that man's lips.

"But how did he know where to follow you Joey, for he left the inn before you and no one followed us to the stables?" asked Paul with a puzzled frown.

"He 'as a new agent Paul, one who told 'im as soon as you and I 'ad entered the town where we were 'eaded, an' when we left 'e told 'im again what road to take in order to follow me. Did it not seem strange to you that as soon as you and I arrived at the inn 'e appeared?" and he saw Paul nod in agreement.

"Do you have any idea who his new man is?" asked Paul quietly, fearing that the answer might name one of those who had been so friendly to him a short time ago.

Correctly interpreting his worried look, Joey assured him that it was none of the men in the inn. Paul sighed deeply with the relief of it, but then another frown appeared across his brow and he searched Joey's face for the answer.

"If you have knowledge of who is not Hudson's agent, then you must assuredly know the name of the person who is," he stated, surprised by the sudden look of discomfort on Joey's face.

"I'm not certain but I 'ave me suspicions," replied Joey, but said no more. Taking him by the arm he walked him back to his horse. Once mounted, Bolitho directed Paul to turn his horse across the road and they took to the fields, making their way back to Trevu over farmland. Upon their arrival, they were not at all surprised to find Hudson's men in Paul's yard and Hudson himself seated with Chloe in the withdrawing room.

"Maybe I'll take 'e up on yer offer, Paul but I 'aven't bin' out shooting rabbits fer a fair few years now. Still, there's a fair number down by yer river an' no mistake," said Joey in a loud voice, then he turned to greet Mrs Trevarthen before making a leisurely bow to Mr Hudson.

" 'Tis a fine day fer a ride into the country, Mr 'Udson, but 'tis a pity you didden tell Mr Trevarthen you was to come a callin' on 'en, fer you could 'ave ridden 'ome with 'en yerself," he observed in a calm voice.

"I had business in this locality, so called in to assure myself that Mr Trevarthen had arrived home safe and well," observed Mr Hudson calmly. He seemed not at all perturbed that he had not caught sight of the two men on the road.

There was a minimal amount of conversation and soon Mr Hudson announced that he had to take his leave of them. Paul politely saw him to the door, but when he returned to the room he was startled to see that Joey was preparing to leave himself. Now it was his turn to catch him by the arm, telling him that he would be a fool to follow the man so closely.

" 'Tis not 'Udson I'm wishful to follow, Paul. I must needs see to another matter," announced Joey tersely. He made to brush past him, but Paul would not let him go, so he swung around to look him in the face and asked to be released.

"I will not," announced Paul stoutly, "for I am well aware that you have the intention of murdering some poor fellow before the sun sets on this day."

"Let be, Paul. 'Tis me duty!" cried Joey.

"Duty! Duty to kill some poor man who has taken money to feed his wife and family! Don't talk to me of your duty you blaggard! Think instead of the poor family he is to leave behind. Have you not done damage enough to the families around here?" and he shook him in temper, unable to contain the hurt and pain within him.

Joey sighed and put up his hand to Paul's, again asking him quietly to release him. When Paul shook his head firmly, he caught at his wrist and applied such pressure to it that the pain of it shot up his arm and Paul, unable to sustain his grip, let him go and stood back from him. He grimaced as he rubbed at his burning arm and swore at Joey, who merely said: "I'm sorry Paul," and turned on his heel to leave the room. On reaching the door he stopped as a gentle voice behind him called his name.

"Mr Bolitho, please. I would beg of you not to do this thing, for the sake of your soul and our regard for you," said Chloe composedly.

He whirled about and stared down at her, noting her large, fine hazel eyes and the soft, sympathetic smile lying on her lips. His own face showed its despair as, once again, he opened his mouth to refuse her request. However, she stood up and came towards him, holding out her hand. He heard her say softly the one word: "Please." Automatically, he raised his hand and for a brief moment grasped hers. She noted in surprise that it shook slightly. He found himself staring into her beautiful face and felt the colour rise to his cheeks. Across the room, Paul began to frown at what he saw displayed before his eyes but he said not a word. The banging of the main door and the sound of children's voices broke the spell in the room. Joey turned away from Mrs Trevarthen and went and stood by the fire with his hand resting lightly on the mantle, then turned his gaze upon the door, which suddenly burst open. Jack bounded into the room and stopped dead when he realised whom it was that stood in the room apart from his parents.

"Mr Bytho!" he screamed in delight, then sprinted across the room without greeting his parents at all and threw himself at Joey.

"Jack!" shouted his father angrily, "How dare you! How dare you to come into a room and behave in that fashion! Where are your manners? Come away from that man at once and greet your mother as your sisters are doing!"

Jack turned from Joey with a shocked face and stared at his father in disbelief, before reluctantly muttering: "Yes Dada," and with dragging feet made his way to his mother, held his face up to be kissed and then hid it and his sadness in the folds of her dress. She tousled his curls and flashed a brief look of admonition at her husband, before bending down and whispering to Jack that he was to go to his father and greet him properly too. When Paul looked down at his son's bowed head he sighed, bent down and, catching up the little boy in his arms, held him close as if he was afraid of losing him. But

Jack kept his arms firmly at his side and would not throw them around his father's neck as he was normally wont to do. The pain of Jack's action cut even deeper into the wound that Paul had inflicted on his own heart. After briefly kissing Jack's averted face, he set him on the ground again and turned from him to talk to Daisy and Grace. Paul then directed the children to greet Mr Bolitho. When Jack held out his little hand, he did not look at Joey until that gentleman had taken it into his much larger one and squeezed it gently. Only then did he raise his chastened face to Joey and returned his understanding smile with a crestfallen one of his own. He heard his father's cold voice informing them that they were to go to the nursery, for Mr Bolitho and himself were engaged upon some business and they did not wish to be disturbed. The children dutifully left the room, but Jack could not resist a look over his shoulder at Joey before leaving; his downhearted expression was not missed by his father. Chloe observed Paul for a while with a cool stare, before returning to the settle and resuming her seat.

After an awkward silence, Paul cleared his throat and turned to Joey, boldly asking him to name Hudson's latest informer.

"Can't tell you 'is name Paul," he replied simply.

"Why ever not? Do you think I would warn him of your intent towards him?" he asked.

"No," replied Joey quietly, "because you couldn' get to 'en as fast as I."

"I will not have you kill another man, Joey. Bert was the last to pay with his life for you and your foul deeds," he announced in a hard tone, his eyes fixed on the smuggler. "There will be no others if you wish to be welcome in this house again."

Joey sighed and, after a moment's quiet reflection, said, "I can't promise not to kill another man again, Paul, fer I 'ave many to think of an' I will not 'ave them 'anged to salve your conscience."

"I ask not for myself you damn fool, but for you! For God's sake, Joey, stop now! Turn from your life of crime, you can be a better man than this!" he urged him, but drew breath deeply as he saw Joey's blank stare settle over his face and knew that he pleaded in vain.

They both turned their heads as they heard Chloe's soft voice gently ask of Joey: "How can I tell little Jack of what sort of man it is that he has made a hero, Mr Bolitho?" and she lifted her worried face to him. Unable to return her stare, Joey hung his head and said nothing, but he shifted uneasily under their gaze. After a while, he lifted his head and stared at Paul before saying abruptly: "It shall be as you d' wish Paul. I'll not kill 'n." He watched the look of relief that flooded his brother's face but, as Paul moved towards him, he strode away from the fire and again headed towards the door. Turning on his heel, he bowed to Chloe and tersely wished her farewell. Then, throwing over his shoulder to Paul that he would see himself out, he hurriedly left the room, banging the door shut behind him.

CHAPTER 16

HE SMILED as the horse thundered towards the steeple ahead of all its fellows. The wind rushed through his hair and he knew that none would catch him now, for his was the best horse and would win this day. Then he would be hoisted high and they would all shout his name and praise him and he would have the money, for he had won the prize. He laughed delightedly as he saw the money pouring from the purse, catching the light, shining and jingling into his hand . . . but it was not his hand. It was too big to be his hand, for it was a man's hand and of a sudden the cheers of the crowd and the smell of the sweaty horse disappeared. He sat up in the straw, wide awake, then blinked in confusion at a face that sported a friendly smile, which seemed at odds with its cold, blue eyes.

"Evenin' young sir," said the calm, cool voice. The man continued to smile down at the dishevelled boy sitting in the straw, then closed his fist around the small pile of coins and the boy lost sight of the bright shiny golden one that had so excited him earlier that day.

"Made a fair bit 'day, lad," he continued and shifted his position slightly from where he sat on top of the feed sacks.

The boy gulped and said: "Lots a' people come town day, sir."

"Rich ones?"

" 'Ess sir," and he nodded his head vigorously.

"An' they come 'ere to stable their horses?" asked the man sceptically.

" 'Ess sir," and the lad nodded again.

The man threw back his head and laughed at that, for they were in the poorest part of the town. But then he considered that Paul had stabled his own horse there, perhaps it was his coin after all? He stopped laughing and frowned at the boy, casting his mind back he again saw the shiny coin flipped through the air that Paul had tossed to the boy. A shilling maybe, but no golden guinea that was for sure. Best to check though, for he would be certain of what it was that the boy had done.

"What did Mr Trevarthen pay you?" and noting his puzzled look, added so that the boy would be sure precisely to whom he was referring: "The dark skinned man."

"A shilling, sir, a shilling!" the frightened lad gasped, then taking his chance he sprang to his feet and bolted for the door. But the man was before him and before he could cry out, a hand was clamped over his mouth and an arm had him firmly pinioned around the chest as he struggled in vain. Looking up into the chilling eyes of his assailant, his own eyes brimmed over with his tears, but the expression on the man's face did not alter one bit. He was lifted off his feet and carried towards the back of the stables and, although he continued to struggle, there was nothing he could do to save himself. He was pushed against the side of the end stall and tried to wrest the strong hand from his face, but to no avail, when of a sudden the hand was removed from his lips. He tried to shout for help, but a rough cloth was pushed into his mouth and he was as powerless as before.

He froze with fear as the man leaned his face towards him and smiled at him. "Not long now, young sir, then all your troubles will be over," and the strong hand gripped him around the neck. He felt a throbbing in his head and everything around him began to go black, until finally his small world disappeared from sight and his little body slumped at the man's feet.

As the man looked down at the crumpled heap he heard her voice again pleading with him; saw his brother's angry and disgusted frown. He shook his head as if to clear everything from his mind except for that which he had to do. Picking up a discarded horse blanket, he threw it over the little body then wrapped it up and tied it firmly with a length of rope. Slinging the bundle over his horse's back, he climbed up behind it and headed out of the town, taking the road for Newlyn and not stopping until he had reached his destination.

A week later, Paul dismounted from his horse and turned to greet the boy as he came from the stable to take hold of the beast's bridle, blinking in surprise to see the bent old man who was shuffling towards him. So astonished was he that he enquired of him if the boy was unwell.

"Dunno, sir," the grizzled individual muttered, "No one seen 'en since Tuesday last. Tha's what d' 'appen when you d' give work to orfans. They bin no good fer proper work," and still complaining he led the horse away without looking back at Paul. If he had done, he would have noted that the man stood rooted to the spot with an expression of shock and horrified disgust on his face. Paul, innocent as he was, knew for certain then whom it was that Joey had suspected of spying on them. Of course, he reasoned with a sudden flash of realisation, for who else had been around to know and note his arrival and also to be aware of his departure from the town? His body was chilled with the cold horror of what the smuggler had so obviously done, the boy's complete disappearance signalled that fact. But to kill such a young lad, surely even Joey could not do that? He felt sickened and did not want to go to the inn, however he felt himself dragged there as if by an irresistible force. He had just begun his journey down the first alley towards the inn when he heard his name called. He turned to see Joseph Bolitho leaning against a door set into the side of a run down cottage.

Paul walked towards Joey and stood in front of him, staring at his calm expression. Of a sudden his hatred rose up within him and his arm swung out, slapping Joey firmly across the face, bracing himself for the blow he felt sure would be returned. He was astonished when Joey made no attempt to hit him in turn, but merely caught hold of his raised arm and, opening the door, pulled him into the cottage and pushed him against the wall.

"How could you, Joey? How could you for God's sake! He was a child, hardly older than Jack!" his brother cried out in despair.

Joey took his hands away from Paul and moved away from him to the window. He looked out, studying the alley to see if anyone was walking down it. Satisfied that no one was abroad, he turned back and regarded Paul with his impassive stare.

"Think I killed 'n do 'e, Paul?" he asked in his quiet voice, and then continued bitterly: "Do you think even I would kill a young lad like that?"

"You . . . you filthy bastard!" Paul stuttered in his distress and temper, "You would not hesitate to kill anyone if it were to suit your purpose! I'll never understand you, Joey! For one moment you will do all you can to help some poor soul that has fallen on hard times and the next you will cold-heartedly kill to save your neck! What sort of man are you to be so evil?" and he continued on, ranting at the smuggler without a care, for he was consumed with hatred at the man's actions.

"My God! I would know the name of the bastard your mother bedded to make you, for you are . . ." but he got no further, for at his words Joseph Bolitho launched himself upon him and rained punches down upon him so quickly that he was caught off guard. When he recovered his balance he returned the blows and both men fought as if nothing would stop them, crashing about in the little cottage and causing the dust to fly up in great clouds round about them. But when Joey heard his brother gasp in pain as his fist caught him in the ribs that had been so recently broken, he stepped away immediately and dropped his hands. Trevarthen, undeterred, came on and attempted to land another blow, but at the last moment Joey stepped aside: Paul's clenched fist thumped into the cob wall of the cottage and before he could turn he found himself pinioned from behind.

"Stop it, Paul, stop it," panted Joey in his ear, "we must not fight. It would not be right. The boy is alive still." When he felt Paul relax in his grip he released him and stood away from him, leaning against the wall and breathing deeply.

Nursing his bruised and throbbing hand, Paul turned to face him, blood trickling from his bottom lip. He gasped at the pain from his damaged ribs and, seeing an old bench against the wall, went over to it and sat down heavily.

After a moment Joey crossed the room, pulled out some rags from the wall, uncovered a hole and extracted from the recess the bottle that lay hidden in it. He crossed over and removed the cork, offering the man holding his ribs a drink. Gratefully, Paul took a gulp from the bottle and coughed as the fiery liquid burnt his throat. Holding the bottle in his hand and still clasping his ribs, he wiped his bloody lip on his sleeve before passing the brandy back to Joey, who took a long drink and then seated himself beside him on the bench.

"Not dead, Joey?" gasped Paul. "You didn't kill him after all?" The other man nodded his assent.

"Spirited 'im away, far from 'ere. 'Ad take 'n out the county but 'e didn' 'ave no family so nobody's goin' miss 'en. Took a boat from Newlyn that was leavin' fer Bristol, an' 'ad spend me time playing nursemaid to 'en 'cos 'e didden 'ave no sea legs, so to speak. Still, once we landed 'e perked up again. I got a friend up country, made 'is money smugglin' years back an' 'elped me set meself up with 'is contacts. Well he went and got 'imself a pretty place in 'Ampshire. Big estate, plenty a' 'orses so I 'eaded fer there with 'en. I was meanin' fer the boy, Billy, to work on the farm or in 'is stables, but when they saw what I'd brought them they wouldn' take no money fer 'is keep 'cos 'e an' 'is missus got no children. Said they'd give 'n a good 'ome with they instead, an' from the way Barney's missus kept grabbing 'old of the poor liddle beggar an' kissin' 'en all the time tha's what it looked like to me. I stayed the night, an' apart from screamin' the place down when she give 'en a bath 'e looked to me like 'e was enjoyin' 'iself. Didden stop eatin' at the supper table and Phoebe put 'nuff food on 'is plate to feed an army. Certainly 'ad a grin from ear to ear when Barney took 'en down to the stables the next mornin' an' got 'en pick out 'is own pony. Jes' kept sayin' "Truly mine, mister, truly mine?!" Plucky liddle devil too, 'cos he fell off three times but kept gettin' back up till 'e 'ad mastered 'en," and he chuckled at the memory of it.

Paul stared shamefaced at his aggressor - who was now sitting with a large grin across his face - before muttering, contritely: "I beg pardon, Joey, that I should have thought what I did and for the . . . for the things I said," and he held out his damaged hand towards him.

Glancing down, Joey took his brother's bruised and bleeding hand in his own and merely pressed it lightly. Then, taking out his handkerchief, he wet it with some of the brandy from the bottle and dabbed at the blood on Paul's lip. Paul winced at the sharp sting as the spirit burnt into the cut on his lip, but he still managed a rueful smile.

"Fer a book lover Paul, you d' fight well," observed Joey, "I must remember that in future." At his words, Paul threw back his head and laughed until his ribs warned him to be more careful of himself.

"I have misjudged you yet again, Joey. Will I ever understand the man you are? I wish it would be so for I should truly like to," he told him earnestly. He was surprised to see the pleasure his words gave to him and the blush that swept up Bolitho's face in a crimson tide.

"Best call on Dr Dunstan while yer in town, Paul, an' let 'en 'ave a look at yer ribs," said Joey after he had recovered himself and nodded his head towards Paul's hand, which was still holding his side.

"Oh, they'll be fine," replied Paul, in an offhand manner, "for I can hardly feel them now." But his lie did not convince Joey and so when they rose to leave, after the alley had been carefully observed for strangers, Trevarthen found himself led towards the top of the town. It was not long before both men found themselves in the good doctor's front room, which he used to see his patients.

The doctor listened to their explanation of a friendly fight and after a thorough examination announced - to Joey's relief - that Paul had sustained no lasting damage, but applied some lotion to his bruises and noted that Joey would probably find himself with a black eye before the day was out.

"Consider, gentleman," said Dr Dunstan as he put the stopper back in the medicine bottle, "your appearance here today. I am not aware that you have ceased your criminal activities, Mr Bolitho and I have warned you, Mr Trevarthen, that keeping Bolitho as your friend does your reputation as an upright member of the community no good whatsoever. People will talk about you, sir, for even those who have dealings with Bolitho make sure that they are not seen in his company, whereas you go abroad with him and care not."

He found himself on the receiving end of a frosty stare.

"If I wish to go abroad with my friends in this town, I damn well will, Denzil, for in my life I have found 'tis more often the common man who would wish to accompany me than those you would call my peers. I am grateful for your trouble here today, please to send me your bill and I'll see it paid," and he shrugged himself awkwardly into his jacket and made to leave the room. But the doctor moved in front of him and brought him to a halt.

"Listen to me, man, before it becomes too late for you to save yourself. Whatever this fellow means to you," and he pointed to Joey, "get him to take up some occupation that reflects a better side of him, for your sake if not his own."

"You have missed your calling, Dr Dunstan!" cried Paul angrily. "For I am sure the Church would make good use of you. Or perhaps the Methodists could find you a flock to preach to!"

"Paul," called a calm voice from the side of the room, " 'e means well. And after all 'tis no different to what you 'ave often told me yerself."

Spinning around to face Joey, Paul looked at him in astonishment, but Bolitho ignored him. Striding forward he threw a handful of coins onto the table. Smiling at him in his charming manner he said: "Les' 'ope 'e listens to 'e one day, Dr Dunstan, but I warn 'e, 'e can be damn stubborn."

Dr Dunstan could not forbear a smile and held out his hand to Joey, remarking: "Indeed, Trevarthen can be assuredly obstinate, so perhaps he will keep on at you until finally you change your ways. For you are wasted as you are, Bolitho, and methinks you are aware of it."

Joey laughed and told him that the Methodists were hoping to build themselves a new chapel over to Marazion, and that he would see the doctor's name was given to the congregation. Paul, looking uneasy, mumbled his farewells - for he was still in an angry frame of mind - and strode out of the house with Bolitho following in his wake. The doctor shook his head, but allowed himself a wry smile and watched as they headed towards the lower end of the town. Physically of a similar build but so different in class: Bolitho the lawbreaker and murderer and Trevarthen of Trevu, the idol of the social and educated classes of Penzance. Still marvelling at the appearance the two men presented, he stepped back and closed the door upon his sight of them.

Meanwhile, the late protagonists decided that they would forgo their trip to Josh's tavern, for the comments that they would be certain to attract about their appearance from their friends could prove difficult to counter. So, they made their way back to the stables to collect their horses and Paul, remembering Joey's remarks of the previous week, suggested that they should indeed go rabbit shooting.

"The lower meadow is quite infested, Joey, and if I do not do something about them soon the cattle will have no pasture to speak of," he enthused boyishly.

The smuggler smiled at him but shook his head.

"What will Mrs Trevarthen 'ave to say to me if I bring you 'ome looking the way you d' do? I shall be shown the door an' never allowed to call again," he remarked with a wry smile.

"Oh! I expect she will understand, for she knows I can sometimes be hasty tempered," responded Paul blithely.

"All right, Paul, I'll go shooting with 'e, but I'll leave 'e to explain to yer wife 'bout our appearance," and he grinned in devilment at Paul.

On arrival at Trevu it was to be expected that, apart from Lizzie, the first person they encountered in the house would have been Chloe. She stared in horror at their bruised and battered faces and listened to her husband's faltering explanation with patent disbelief. She gave an exasperated smile and wished them good hunting and, as they would be gone for the best part of the afternoon, told Joey that, should he wish it, he was welcome to dine with them. He thanked her graciously before following his brother to the gun room and once there blinked in surprise at the number of weapons Paul had ranged about on the walls. He accepted the use of the shotgun that was handed to him in delight, for it was the finest weapon he had ever seen.

"I have them made for me in London," explained Paul, "but as we are of a similar build you should have no trouble," and as he chatted on excitedly about the afternoon's shooting, Joey noted how pleased he appeared to be to be going out on a hunting trip.

"Must spend a lot a' time shootin', Paul, with all these 'ere weapons to choose from," he suggested.

Paul sighed: "Well, no, not actually Joey, for I prefer to have company when I shoot. Father and I used to go about a lot together, but when he died I got out of the way of doing it. Sometimes Jonas and I have had an afternoon's shooting, for if we did not we would be in a bad way with the number of rabbits to be found hereabouts, but that is more like a job of work."

Chloe watched from the window as the two men set off, chatting happily to each other, and could not help smiling to herself. She sighed with contentment at the thought that her husband was unknowingly becoming a friend of his own brother.

On their return, each shouldering a similar amount of game, they headed to the kitchen with their booty, but Mrs Gurney told Paul that unless he wanted to eat rabbit pie for a whole week, then it would be best if they were distributed amongst the workmen.

"I'll see to it if 'e want, Mr Trevarthen, but come tomorrow, after they've 'ad a good soak in salt water. I shall be making pies for you and the household, and of course if Mr Bolitho would like one made 'twill be no trouble at all." She smiled at both the hunters, even though she had noted that the master had pocketed two of her saffron buns that were stacked on the large platter at the end of the table.

They both thanked her and Paul agreed with her suggestion that the unwanted game be given to the men, but Joey graciously refused her offer of a pie, because he would not be at the house on the morrow.

"Manage a beef pasty, can 'e sir, fer I've some to make fer the workmen fer their supper?" she asked.

"Why of course, fer I can stick it in me pocket, no trouble at all," replied Joey gratefully and he smiled at her in a most charming fashion.

She smiled back in gratification and puzzled to herself why it was he seemed so familiar to her, for she was not a Penzance women and had never met him until he had come to Trevu, when the master had almost drowned himself trying to save Bert Pendray. Shaking her head, she continued to knead her pastry and told herself she was being a silly old woman and thought no more of the encounter, for now her head was full of preparations. So she sent for Davy to clean and skin the rabbits she would require and to take away the others for dispersal to the work force.

Meanwhile, Paul and Joey sat in the gun room and disposed of the stolen buns before turning to the task of cleaning their guns. They laughed and joked with each other and Paul happily dismissed his previous worries about his wife's admiration for Joey that had so troubled him before. He almost laughed aloud at his stupidity for his unwarranted jealously. Well, he knew that his beloved Chloe had never looked at another man, nor would she ever, lest he was a fool to her. He watched as Bolitho held the barrel of the gun to the light to ensure that it was clean and then began the task of reassembling the weapon.

"You are a damn fine shot, Joey. Who taught you?" asked Paul conversationally.

"Nobody did, he replied. I jes' picked it up as I went along an' 'ad a few tips from folks 'ere an' there. Bought me first gun off a soldier fallen on 'ard times. I'd made a fair bit of money on a smugglin' trip with Barney an' fancied to 'ave a gun. First time I fired it I blew the top end off 'Arry Semmons' corn rick tryin' to 'it a crow. I must 'ave bin' about fourteen 'spose. Well, 'Arry come tearin' out from the barn, swearin' an' shoutin' and went fer to thrash me." He laughed as he cast his mind back to the scene.

"And did he . . . er . . . thrash you?" enquired Paul, grinning broadly.

"Lord no!" he admitted, "Fer I was too fast fer 'e! But his missus caught me as I cut to run roun' the corner of the farmhouse an' 'eaved a bucket a' slops right over me. God, I stank like a dog fox fer days!" Trevarthen, unable to contain himself any longer, howled with laughter at the thought of it and, when Chloe opened the door a few minutes later, both men were still convulsed by the humour of Joey's story.

She was pleased to see them both so happy in each other's company and was delighted to see her husband to be enjoying himself so, for after the loss of his dear friend she had thought never to hear him laugh again. Once their merriment had subsided, she informed them that hot water and towels had been taken to Paul's dressing room so that they could clean themselves and that the household would be ready to dine as soon as they returned.

The children and their mother were seated at the table when the two men entered the dining room. Jack's face lit up immediately and when his hero took a seat beside him he beamed with pleasure. He shot a quick look at his father, but as he seemed to be in a pleasant frame of mind he turned his attention to his especial friend. From that moment on his tongue did not cease to regale Joey with all the tales of his adventures. When their meal was finished, the covers were removed and Chloe and the children - much to young Jack's obvious disappointment - removed themselves to the nursery, but their father promised the children faithfully that they could come down again later. The two men discussed the day's events happily over their port and when they did eventually leave the table they had consumed between them rather a large amount of it. They had been in no hurry to join Chloe, who had advised Paul that, as the children were to come down before retiring for the night, she would be found in the withdrawing room, but when they did appear it was not long before the children descended upon them. Grace, as usual, was most ladylike and sat by her mother, setting her stitches in a most intricate and beautiful sampler. Daisy sat by her father's side and talked animatedly about her pony and her wish to ride with her father again soon, whilst Jack climbed onto Joey's lap and talked incessantly about a multitude of subjects. There was no one in the room who did not feel a certain sympathy for the poor man, who so patiently listened to each story that was relayed to him. Jack was most in awe of Joey's now blackened eye and stared at it in fascination, but respected his father's command that he was not to touch it, for it would displease 'Mr Bytho' very much. When it was time for the children to retire for the night, their mother went with them to see them all to bed. Meanwhile Joey, full of good food and drink, sat with his long legs stretched out before him in front of the roaring fire, unable to remember a time in his life when he felt so at ease and comfortable. When she returned, Chloe played little part in their conversation, but noted with a satisfied smile on her lips how relaxed the brothers were with each other. Refusing Paul's offer of a bed for the night, Joey rose to leave at about nine and wished Chloe farewell. On entering the hall with Paul he was confronted by Lizzie, who hurriedly descended down into the kitchen and returned with the promised pasty, still warm from the oven and wrapped in a linen cloth.

Walking to the stables, Paul shivered in the cold night air and Joey told him to go back inside, for he was perfectly capable of getting his horse by himself. Still, they talked for a while as Bolitho saddled his roan, after refusing any assistance from the stable boy, and agreed to have another shoot before the month was out. Joey mounted his horse and, bending down, he shook Paul's hand and thanked him, a broad smile across his face, before turning towards the road and making his way homewards at a steady canter. The full moon lit his way beautifully, while a fox barking on the hill to his left and an owl hooting from the small wood behind the blacksmith's cottage added to his enjoyment of the evening. The frosty air bit into him as he sped down the moonlit track but he hardly noticed, for he was so content within himself that if he had to plough his way through a snowdrift he could not have cared. So he travelled on regardless, regardless even of the tall man who stood in the shadows by the end wall of the cluster of cottages that lined the road at the turning that led from the Trevu road. Joey, who rarely missed anything, noticed nothing, because the man stood like a statue. It was a while after the horseman had gone by before the stranger walked back along the farm track to where he had tethered his mount. He had no wish to draw attention to himself should his horse inadvertently whinny, for the air was cold and crisp and the sound of it would have carried to the passing rider. When he mounted his horse, he seemed to have no desire to pursue the rider. Throwing his cloak around his tall frame to protect himself against the cold night, he trotted gently on in the direction of Penzance and his home, where his dear little wife would be waiting for him with more empty-headed tales of how she had spent her day and what she had bought. He would listen indulgently to her, but half his mind would be employed with what he had witnessed that night. He knew he would use what he had seen to tighten a net around the smuggler so firmly, that finally he would be caught. A cruel smile twisted his lips as he savoured the thought of being in the midst of the roaring crowd who would witness his hanging. And the Master of Trevu as well, if he could manage to enmesh him in his trap, for his hatred extended to him as fully as it did to the other. He laughed aloud with delight at the thought of their demise, unable to contain his excitement. A wood pigeon on the branch above him ruffled its feathers in fright at the sound of it and took wing - to take itself away from what it perceived to be a threat.

CHAPTER 17

AT THE end of November, two of the town's most famous stalwarts died. Squire Tregurthen suffered what appeared to be a seizure and fell into a coma from which he did not regain consciousness. Within a week, Mrs Carter finally succumbed to her rapidly failing health and died in her sleep. Both funerals were lavish in the extreme, not only to represent the standing of the deceased but because the respective families had no wish to allow themselves to be seen to be in any way parsimonious. Squire Tregurthen's cortege was undoubtedly larger, but Mrs Carter's coffin had many fine brass fittings and far outshone the one that had been seen less than a week before, making its mournful way along the street towards the Church and the cemetery. Paul, with his wife, attended both the funerals but at Mrs Carter's funeral service his Aunt Caroline was also in attendance; she thought it her duty to be present, for Inez Carter had been known to her for such a long time.

After, they returned to Trevu, Paul taking great care to ensure that his aunt was ensconced close by the fire and that she was protected from any draughts, for it had turned cold and a chill wind blew in from the sea without respite. Naturally, Caroline was pressed into staying for a few days longer than she had previously intended, therefore it was towards the end of her second week in residence when something occurred that shook her aura of respectability to its foundations. Sitting with Chloe in the withdrawing room, both women were engrossed in a pattern book when Paul bounded into the room with two shotguns, announcing to his wife that he had met with Joey in the town and they had decided on another rabbit shoot that afternoon.

"Joey?" enquired his aunt, and raised her eyebrow at him.

"Yes, Aunt, I have fallen into the habit of spending the odd afternoon attempting to control the rabbits in the lower meadow and a fellow from the town comes to shoot with me," he explained, hoping she would make no further enquiry. He should have known that it would not be the case however and, after some firm prompting, finally admitted just who it was who answered to the name of Joey.

His aunt's face registered her horror immediately that the smuggler's name was mentioned. Launching herself into a speech, she affirmed that her nephew had finally lost his senses. For to be known as an acquaintance of that scoundrel, let alone a friend, was to drag the Trevarthen name into the gutter for all time. Paul's mulish expression settled onto his face, whilst Chloe took great pains to explain to Caroline the debt the family owed to Mr Bolitho for his actions on the day of Bert's death.

"Well, you should have given him money, for that sort of rogue is not the sort of person one should encourage into one's house. Your poor father would turn in his grave if he knew what you were about, Paul," she announced scathingly. "You should have had more sense." She then demanded to know if she were expected to meet the fellow.

Frowning at her, Paul announced that in his house his guests would always be made welcome. He added, bitingly, that if she felt that her manners could not extend to meeting those friends he wished to entertain, she could always retire to her chamber. Noting Caroline's swelling bosom, Chloe hastily attempted to defuse the situation, but at that moment came a knock at the door and Lizzie, in her innocence, showed the subject of their conversation into the room. Joseph Bolitho stood on the threshold with a twinkle in his eye and a smile on his lips. But when he caught sight of the grey-haired matron, with an affronted look on her features and sitting so stiffly by the fire, his expression of pleasure disappeared at once and his emotionless mask descended on his face. As it was impossible for Paul not to introduce them, he did so as swiftly as he could in the hope that the two men could leave the house the sooner, whilst his poor wife would be the one left in sole charge of his simmering aunt.

Joey bowed low over Caroline's hand and merely said: "Mrs Crebo, ma'am," in a firm but unemotional voice. Caroline bowed her head, but involuntarily she raised her eyes to Bolitho's face and in so doing she almost gasped in amazement. She found herself looking into the face of a man whose features she could not place, but his expression so reminded her of her brother's, even of his son's, that she stared at him most rudely, until she remembered her manners and hastily averted her eyes. Quickly, she removed her hand from his and plucked at the folds of her shawl in nervousness. Paul was puzzled at her reaction but then assumed that, because of her disgust at his friendship, she was not best pleased to have found herself introduced to such a person. Without even asking his wife, or indeed Joey himself for that matter, Paul announced that Mr Bolitho would be dining with them that evening and attempted a quelling look at his aunt. Caroline, too confused even to frown, kept her head turned towards the fire, so Paul merely squared his shoulders and informed both the ladies that they would be back at sunset. He opened the door and, after Joey had bowed again, both men left the room. Not long after, they heard the front door bang shut on their departure.

Caroline, unaware that Chloe knew full well the relationship that her husband bore to Bolitho, hastily began to talk on mundane matters in a very nervous way. But, although puzzled, Chloe assumed that she had been most put out at having to meet a man she detested, so tried hard to put her at her ease. Although Caroline could have said she was indisposed, she discovered that she had no intention of not sitting down to dinner with the fellow. Consequently, when they found themselves seated at the dining table, this time without the children in attendance - for they would have been far too boisterous for Caroline to contend with - she had time to study him at her leisure. She had time also to study her nephew, who did not appear in any way to realise just what it was that to her was so apparent about the man who sat opposite her. Naturally, due mainly to Caroline's presence and the children's absence, dinner was a formal affair and Joey constantly felt ill at ease, for the woman who sat opposite him had a great look of Redvers about her and he frequently felt himself subjected to her hawk-like stare. Mrs Trevarthen tried hard to keep the conversation flowing but had great difficulty, for the other members around the dining table made little attempt to join in. Caroline was far too interested in attempting to study their guest, without giving the impression that she was paying any attention to him whatsoever. Paul was annoyed with his aunt's very offhand manner, both to himself and to Joey, and that poor fellow appeared to be wishing himself well away from Trevu, for he was not giving the appearance of a man enjoying either the food or the company.

After the ladies retired to the withdrawing room, Joey hastily downed a glass of port and announced his intention of leaving immediately.

"Nonsense!" exclaimed his host, with a sudden frown, and then admitted coaxingly: "for should you leave I shall find myself derided by my aunt unmercifully." He looked up, fully expecting to see a grin on Joey's face, but none was forthcoming.

"Don't vex yourself with Aunt Caroline, Joey, for she is a guest in my house and she knows me well enough to realise that her wisest course is to keep her own counsel in the presence of my friends," he continued.

"She 'idden impressed with you 'avin' me fer a friend Paul," remarked Bolitho, "that's pretty obvious at any rate," and Paul sensed he was not best pleased at her reception of him.

"Come on Joey, another port, to give us both the strength to endure her basilisk stare when we join the ladies," and he grinned conspiratorially, adding: "for I shall need one: I will have to endure much from her once you have left, I can assure you." His mischievous grin raised an answering smile from Joey, so they enjoyed another glass before leaving the dining room and making their way into the withdrawing room. Seeing them both framed in the doorway, Caroline felt her heart contract in fear at the sight of them. 'What if that scoundrel is attempting to worm his way into the household and in some way to depose Paul from his position as head of the family?' she thought to herself. But she then dismissed the idea at once as being quite ludicrous, for there was no way that Bolitho could lay claim to his parentage; you would need to have known the father well to have noted his likeness in his son.

Conversation was desultory, but later Lizzie appeared with the tea tray and Chloe got up to busy herself with pouring the tea. She had only just passed around the last cup, when Miss Clavering knocked on the door to inform them that Daisy had attempted to jump from her chair to the bed and had missed her footing, and was now lying in a heap on the bedroom floor with a nasty cut on her foot. Both her parents excused themselves and went to her assistance, her father to lift Daisy back into the bed and her mother to nurse her injured foot.

Bolitho resumed his seat and coughed nervously, but made no attempt at conversation, only too aware that a pair of hard, dark eyes were fixed on his face. The silence was broken when the redoubtable aunt spoke:

"Mr Bolitho, you appear to have become a great friend of this family. I cannot help but think it strange that this should be so, for I cannot imagine that socially you are welcomed everywhere," she said coldly.

"Quite true, Mrs Crebo, but yer nephew is determined to 'ave me fer his friend and I am most 'onoured by 'is friendship towards me," he replied stiffly.

"I can well imagine that you are," she remarked tartly, and then, determined to know more, added: "and, is it not most unusual, Mr Bolitho, for I have the strangest impression that for some reason you should be well known to me? Absurd, is it not?"

Although he made a great effort, Joey let his mask slip, recovering himself quickly, but not so quickly that Caroline Crebo did not notice his moment of discomfort.

"Quite so, ma'am," he responded crisply and attempted to turn the conversation onto the subject of the weather. But he had never had to contend with Mrs Crebo before and she was nothing if not determined, so he met with no success.

"My brother - Paul's father - always found the weather at this time of year most bracing," she informed him in a severe tone, then continued in the same vein, with every sentence that she uttered containing an allusion to the late Captain in some form or another. Her eyes never left his face and she noted the way in which the man attempted to keep his expression impassive, but she ploughed on relentlessly and shaft after shaft found its mark. When she alluded to Redvers' scandalous behaviour before Paul's appearance into his life, she was aware of the startled expression that appeared on his face. Determined not to lose her advantage, she drew breath boldly and posed a question that she presumed he would have difficulty in answering:

"Does he know who you are?" she said in her abrupt way, convinced, as only a sister could have been, that she was addressing her brother's eldest son.

The smuggler started, and colour flooded into his face. Then he lowered his head and shook it slowly from side to side, before sighing loudly and replying that it was not his wish that the Master of Trevu should ever be made aware of their relationship, for he saw no reason that would involve his need to know.

"Paul is as glad a' me friendship as I am of 'is, Mrs Crebo, ma'am. 'Tis best left at that I believe, 'cos 'twould only cause 'im pain to knaw more," he added quietly.

He encountered a look of surprise, and possibly admiration. But before she had a chance to say anything further, the door opened as Paul and Chloe returned, regaling them with an account of Daisy's injuries and to pass on a request from Jack for Joey to be allowed to his room to wish him goodnight. Quickly seizing his opportunity to get himself away, Joey stood up, excused himself and made his way to see his admirer. Meanwhile, conversation in the withdrawing room revolved around the children until Paul, unable to contain himself any longer, enquired of his aunt if she had been in any way rude to his guest.

"Not in the least, Paul, for I pride myself that my manners are impeccable and know full well how to conduct myself. An' it matters not with whom I am conversing," she added, waspishly. "Such a pity as it is that other members of the family could not have conducted their life in the same fashion," she bemoaned, for her recognition of Joey and his own revelation had somewhat tarnished the reputation of her most beloved, if at one point scandal racked, brother. Thinking about her brother's past, she considered that it was foolish in the extreme to have believed that Paul could have been the only result of Redvers infamous philanderings, for at the time he was the talk of Penzance, such was his conduct. She had attempted to remonstrate with him on many an occasion, and when Paul was taken into the household it had caused a tremendous rift between them that was not healed for many a year. How different it would have been if the other had been the one to have been taken into the family? But then, she thought salutarily, how empty her life would have been never to have known Paul. For to her he had become the son she never had, and as much as she had tried to instruct him in the ways of the world he had taught her far more about finding value in others. His determined friendship with a man of Bolitho's reputation was proof enough of that, for if there was the smallest spark of humanity in any man, Paul would seek it out and treasure it. Therefore it was not strange at all that he should have developed a fondness for the man. And perhaps it would not matter so very much, for Bolitho appeared not to welcome the discovery of who he was, and was so obviously afraid that Paul would one day be made aware of exactly how they stood in relation to each other.

When eventually Joey returned, she attempted to make herself more agreeable to him, earning for herself Paul's grateful smile as he recognised her efforts to set his friend at his ease. Joey determined not to overstay his welcome, for he was not so certain that Paul's aunt would not embarrass him with a thoughtless remark. Although he had the impression that their previous conversation had gone no further, as it was most obvious from Paul's behaviour toward him that nothing had been communicated to him on the subject. He rose to take his leave and, as he bowed over Caroline's hand, he was surprised to find that he was having his fingers tweaked, although her face had only the slightest semblance of a smile on her lips. Raising his eyes to hers, he felt immensely reassured when she announced that she hoped that they would have the opportunity to meet again some day.

"I would 'ope so as well, Mrs Crebo, ma'am, fer it was a pleasure to meet with 'e," he replied with a hesitant grin on his own face. Then turning to Chloe, he bowed his head, shook her hand with great gentleness and thanked her for his meal, then preceded Paul from the room. This time, confused but strangely exhilarated, he rode home at a gallop, consequently he had even less time than before to notice if any one observed his passing along the way.

Aunt Caroline used her remaining time at Trevu to discover all she could about Joseph Bolitho, and by the time she left for Truro, any doubts that she may have had regarding his intentions towards her brother's son had been set at rest. His lifestyle and occupation she found abhorrent. But as long as he made no attempt to embroil her nephew in his nefarious activities she thought that the friendship would in fact be beneficial to Paul, for Chloe had made her aware in her letters how badly her poor nephew had been affected by the loss of Bert Pendray's company.

When it was time for her to leave, Paul ensured that plenty of hot bricks were installed in the carriage, as well as a sable wrap of his mothers to keep the winter's chill from her bones. As he bent to kiss her cheek, he felt the pressure of her hands on his arms and hugged her gently in return.

He noted how kindly she looked at him and smiled fondly in return.

"Dearest Paul," she breathed, "such a treasure as you have been to me," and he could not be sure, but he thought she blinked away a tear.

"Why," he answered, shaken by her warmth to him, "thank you, and I might add you know the regard I have for you, Aunt," and he kissed her again, then took her arm and helped her into the carriage. After making sure that she was comfortably ensconced, he ordered the coachman to depart and stood with his hand raised in farewell until the equipage had disappeared from view.

Sitting at the table in Bert's cottage, Paul smiled shyly at Emily Bosanko and patiently explained the meaning of the papers he had placed in front of her, whilst her two youngest daughters played happily with the two dolls that he had presented to each of them on entering the small cottage.

"Their purpose is to act as a contract between the apprentice and his employer," Paul informed her. "The apprentice will undertake to perform whatever the employer requires of him and the employer will undertake to instruct the apprentice in the skills needed to become a master of his trade. I have chosen most carefully, Mrs Bosanko, and sought out the advice from several prominent men involved in the shipbuilding industry in and around Penzance. They have all confirmed that this is the best boatyard in which to apprentice a boy who has an aptitude to learn, for they encourage their young men to advance themselves and provide continuous schooling alongside the training they are given on the shipbuilding side of the industry. However, it is for you to decide as Harry's guardian, and whatever your wishes should be I will abide by them." Paul sat back in his chair and waited quietly for her response.

"It would cost so much, Mr Trevarthen, sir!" she fretted.

"It will all be paid for, Mrs Bosanko, never fear. There will be no cost to yourself," he assured her.

"But it is so far away. How will 'e live? Where will 'e stay?" and she raised worried eyes to Paul's face.

"I would be honoured if you will allow me to undertake any and all expenses that Harry will incur during his apprenticeship, including clothing, and providing him with an allowance. And as to where he will live, well, that can be accomplished quite easily, for I have several acquaintances in Falmouth who would be more than willing to provide him with suitable accommodation. Naturally, you would expect to see where Harry would live and would wish to visit with him from time to time. There is a teacher at George's school whose son wishes to be apprenticed with the same firm. I thought, if you would agree to it, that Philip, the teacher's son, could accompany Harry when he comes home for the holidays. Then Harry could meet him and hopefully establish a friendship with him," he smiled and continued until she raised her hand and asked him to stop.

"I 'ave a question, Mr Trevarthen. 'Tis a simple one. Why should you wish to do this? Fer Harry or fer Bert?" she asked, studying him carefully.

He looked momentarily surprised, then considered for a moment before replying: "I would like to see Harry given the chance I think he deserves. He's a clever chap and I think he will do well. Bert would not accept anything from me and I accepted that he preferred to provide for his own family, and he had every right to do that. But when . . . when I could not save his life that day I felt that his responsibility had been passed to me. However it is for you to decide, I have not the right to impose my wishes on your family."

"If 'e leaves school and gets a job I would be able to use 'is income, Mr Trevarthen, an' that would be some useful because I cannot live on charity fer ever. Mr Bolitho 'as bin' most kind and you, Mr Trevarthen sir, 'ave been more than generous, but I cannot expect that it should continue," she told him simply.

"I do not see it as charity, Mrs Bosanko, ma'am, for to me it is a responsibility placed upon me when my dear friend lost his life. I am certain that if I had been the one to lose . . . to lose my life then your brother would have done all in his power to help my family in any way that he could. Even in the midst of that dreadful storm, we talked about our families and hoped ourselves saved for their sakes," he said earnestly.

Emily managed a smile, then pushed the papers back towards him. Paul's face registered abject disappointment, so quickly and simply she told him:

"I can't sign it Mr Trevarthen, sir," 'fer I cannot write."

Relief flowing across his features, he quickly told her that it would be in order for her to make her mark, then he could witness it for her. So she stood up and went to find some of the ink and writing pens that the children kept in the corner of the room to practice their writing. When she brought them back to the table, Paul inked the pen for her and she laboriously made her mark. With his signature witnessing her mark and a brief statement indicating that she was Harry Pendray's guardian, the papers were completed.

She went to the side of the room, lifted the kettle and poured the boiling water on to some of her precious tea, which she had spooned into the teapot. A plate of cakes mysteriously appeared from a curtained shelf and was placed on the table alongside the cups, the teapot and the milk. Paul grinned in anticipation and soon discovered that Mrs Bosanko was indeed, as Bert had once told him, a wonderful cook. He complimented her on her baking and she smiled back.

"Can't read, Mr Trevarthen, but I can count and mother taught me to bake an' I can sew a bit," she laughed merrily. Paul noticed how similar she sounded to Bert and felt reassured by the sound of it, almost as if that which he had lost had not completely left his life.

They sat and chatted companionably about Bert's boys and their respective offspring and, when the time came for Paul to leave, he extended his hand and wished her well.

"Of course, I shall call again and I know that Chloe wishes to come to see you, for with only Alice at home during the day she is at a loss as to how to spend her time. If you would not object she would be most pleased to visit," he told her simply.

She hoisted the youngest child onto her hip and smiled up at him, showing the dimples in her cheeks, as she told him that his family were more than welcome in her home.

Later that afternoon, he walked to the cemetery with his arms full of flowers and quietly dressed the graves on his family's plot. He had thoughts and silent words for all of them but some flowers were saved, for he could not leave without making his way to the oak tree by the cemetery wall. He sank on his knees and in silence asked his friend's forgiveness for imposing himself on his family, but assured him that he could not help himself and that he would do everything that lay within his power to help them.

That night after they had dined, he told Chloe that Emily Bosanko had agreed to his wishes and that Harry was to be apprenticed to the finest shipbuilder in Falmouth. She smiled at him and told him that Bert would have been pleased to know of all he was doing for his family.

"I hope that is the case, Chloe, for when he was alive he would take nothing from me," he said worriedly, "and I cannot be sure that what I have done is what he would have wished me to do."

"Paul," she said gently, "he would understand that you would have to help his family, for the sake of your friendship if for no other reason. You are not to fret yourself that you have annoyed his spirit, for I know Bert would be glad to think his dear friend was doing his utmost to see that his family are secure and well provided for."

He smiled at her and said simply: "I pray it is so, Chloe," and he lowered his head. His sadness was apparent as he contemplated the logs in the fire, which burned brightly and sent their sparks racing up the chimney in little showers of light. Chloe left her seat and put her arms around his neck, hugging him gently to comfort him.

The following day being a Saturday, he sent for Daisy and explained to her that Harry would be leaving to go to live in Falmouth so that he could take up an apprenticeship at a shipbuilders. The expression on her face almost made him rip the indentures into tiny scraps, but she nodded at his words and agreed with him that it would be for the best, else Harry would have to follow a horrid occupation that she knew he would have disliked intensely.

"He won't forget me, will he Father?" she asked with her lips quivering.

"Daisy, dearest Daisy, who could ever forget you?" he replied with a brave smile. She smiled resolutely back at him and when he held out his arms to her, she cast herself upon his chest, crying pitifully.

"Damn fine thing you be doin' fer 'Arry, Paul," said Joey as he added another rabbit to his tally. He watched as Paul's dog, Meg, bounded across the grass to retrieve it. Looking up, he caught sight of Paul's melancholy expression, so he leaned over and placed his arm about his shoulder, squeezing it compassionately.

"It is playing on my conscience, Joey, for when alive, Bert would not let me do anything for him of that nature. It troubles me so because I am disturbed that I have gone against his wishes," he said and lifted his troubled face to Joey, who stared calmly back at him.

"Paul, Paul," he said, giving him a gentle shake, "yer not t' feel this way. Bert would not want it. When 'e was alive you nor me 'ad no right to involve ourselves in 'is family. We did tho'. I got 'en smugglin' so 'e could make more money an' keep 'Arry on at school. An' you, you went fishin' with 'en - taking 'Arry's place although you 'ad pleasure from it too. An' you did more than that."

"No I didn't, Joey, for Bert would take nothing from me," he said with a large sigh.

"Course you did, you bleddy fool!" Joey told him firmly.

Paul looked at him and raised his eyebrows in puzzlement.

"I . . . I do not understand you, Joey. What did I do?"

His companion studied him for a while, then announced with a knowing smile:

"You made sure 'Arry would never want fer another book again. You built the bleddy Library fer 'en. You might a told yerself it was fer the town an' the people who couldn' afford buy books like you d' do, but 'twas Bert's boy that set 'e off down the road. So stop feelin' guilty fer yerself. You're too 'fraid you've done the wrong thing fer 'en to think right, you bleddy fool! If Bert 'ad the money 'e would 'ave done the same thing, an' now 'e's gone you've taken on 'is responsibilities. Bert would be damn proud of 'e Paul, an' tha's a fact, cos tidden every man can claim to 'avin' a friend like you," and he took a deep breath as he saw a small and determined smile set on his brother's lips. "Now come on you fool, else every rabbit in the valley will 'ave gone bed fer ever we 'ave the chance to 'ave a crack at 'em."

He dropped his arm from about Paul's shoulders and, sliding his hand down his arm, gripped it firmly and pulled his brother to his feet. Paul looked at him and grimaced sheepishly, then they walked stealthily towards the hedge and along the bottom of the meadow until they came to a sunny spot that they knew the rabbits liked to frequent.

After dinner that night the two men enjoyed the port and the brandy that resided in the dining room and, still having a thirst, sent for some ale from the kitchen. They were happily quaffing their way through it until the Master of Trevu decided it would be a good idea to open another bottle of wine. Paul did not often drink to excess, but on occasion he could and would do so. Joey's words had brought him much consolation and the relief from the worry that he had experienced made him reckless, so he indulged himself. The smuggler was just as happy to take drink for drink with him, for he would have had to have been blind not to have seen that, after his talk of the afternoon, the poor man had found great relief in the sentiments that Joey had expressed. Chloe, sitting alone with her book in the withdrawing room, was informed by Lizzie that the gentlemen were: "looking most 'appy on account of the drink they 'ad consumed" and "should she air the sheets in the spare bedchamber?"

Chloe smiled and nodded her assent, and the two women exchanged a knowing smile. When finally the two men managed to join her in the withdrawing room, one glance at their inane smiles and unsteady gait was enough to confirm her belief that, although Joey was carrying his drink the better, he would still find it difficult to ride his horse to Penzance and hope to arrive in that town without having fallen off at least once. He attempted to refuse the offer of the bed, but it was now Paul's turn to take him by the arm and lead him off in the direction of the stairs, which they negotiated with some difficulty and a great deal of noise and laughter. A nightshirt was laid out on the bed for him and, after a rather loud and prolonged farewell, Joseph Bolitho was left alone to get himself to bed. He managed to do this and sank between the warm sheets. Although the room was spinning somewhat he was not drunk enough not to appreciate the quality of the bed he was lying in, for he had never slept in such luxury and he was aware that he was to spend his first, and probably last night, in his father's house. It gave him a childish pleasure and his face registered his delight as he turned it into the pillow. Sighing deeply, he was soon fast asleep.

CHAPTER 18

"All alone . . . um . . . Likky, are you not?" enquired the smooth but sinister voice at his elbow.

" 'Ess Mr 'Udson, sir, and 'tis only me friends d' call me Likky," he replied moodily, studying his ale and not bothering to lift his gaze to his questioner.

"I beg your pardon Mr . . . ah . . . Mr . . ." replied the Customs Officer mockingly, but then continued with an obvious lie, "but as I do not know your name I am afraid I have no knowledge of how to address you."

Likky took a long drink of his ale and, as he returned his tankard to the counter, announced quietly, lest the others should hear, "Skewes," and he paused before saying resignedly: "Leviticus Skewes." Lifting his head, he glowered at the man standing beside him.

"A most fine name, sir, most fine," complimented Mr Hudson, and smiled his cold smile. "Biblical connotations are so often the sign of grateful parents, are they not?"

"I 'ave no idea sir," pronounced Likky, "fer I'm named after me uncle that was killed in the war 'gainst the colonists."

"Well, I am sure he would have been gratified to see his name carried on in such a proud and noble man," he continued in his oily fashion, but Likky merely snorted his disgust at the man, who remarked again on Likky's solitary state:

"I suppose it is only to be expected that Mr Bolitho should have so little time to spare for his oldest friend, for he spends so much of his time with his new one, does he not?" But Likky would not rise to his bait, so he talked on undeterred and continued to sow his seeds of doubt and distrust, broadcasting them evenly so that they would take root the better.

" 'Tis not to be wondered at, Mr Skewes, for Trevarthen is a most wealthy fellow after all. Bolitho would be a fool indeed, were he not to grasp his hand of friendship, would he not?" and he noted the way in which Likky's shoulders tightened. "He seems to have developed quite a liking for visiting the man's house, although whether it is Trevarthen's money or his wife that interests Joseph Bolitho, it would be difficult to tell, such a fellow as he is." He sniggered crudely before continuing: "Perhaps he has business interests with Trevarthen, for after all his money could be of great benefit to him," and he took a slow drink from his own tankard, watching discreetly as Likky's frown deepened sharply on his brow.

"No need for old friends if his new one could offer him more after all, eh, Likky?"

There was no response and in truth Hudson did not expect one, but he ploughed on with quiet determination and in as friendly a tone as he could muster from the depths of his icy personality.

"Still, Joey is not the sort of fellow to drop an old friend, albeit if his new one has drawn him from his side. Rumour has it he spent the night there, don't you know? But then I expect you would have known that, being such an especial friend to him as you have been," and he watched as Likky picked up his tankard and drained it hurriedly.

"Another, Mr Skewes, sir?" he enquired with his loathsome smile hovering on his full lips.

"Like I told 'e 'tis Leviticus, sir! Likky announced angrily. "Mother called me Leviticus, not Judas!" And cramming his hat on his head, he turned abruptly from him and left the inn.

Walking quickly, he disappeared into the alleyway and, flattening his frame into a deep doorway, waited a full fifteen minutes hidden from view to see if anyone should be following in his footsteps. But no one came along in pursuit of him, for Hudson had no need to follow Likky: his words were embedded deep into the man's mind and could not now be weeded out.

When Joseph Bolitho caught sight of her coming out of Mrs Martin's imposing establishment, he felt his heart contract within him. He stood still like a man turned to stone, but a fire that had never been quenched burned the brighter within him. Watching as she walked up the street towards the apothecary's shop, he determined to follow her and, as he did so, took great care that his neck cloth was neatly arranged and that his appearance would be pleasing to her. At the top of the street she turned her steps to take her into Chapel Street and began to descend slowly, her modest but elegant dress sweeping grandly along as she moved. He thought for a moment about what he should do, then he took a short cut from Market Jew and, on reaching the street that was his destination, began to walk in her direction. When he saw her looking at a display in a shop window he hesitated, so unsure was he of what course to follow. His longing to see her gnawed at him, so he took a deep breath and began to walk purposefully towards her and, when he was by her side softly spoke her name. She started and looked up into his face, her eyes widening in surprise at the sight of him.

"Why, Joey!" she said in astonishment, and when she smiled he thought his heart had melted within him. As he extended his hand, he could feel it shaking with the excitement of the moment. The years had been kind to her for she had changed little; her fine green eyes that looked so clear, her soft skin and the cupid's bow of a mouth that he had always wanted so desperately to kiss. Her dark brown curls were pulled back now and dressed most finely, he noticed. And at the sight of this most adored face his heart began to beat rapidly and the smile that transformed his face from mask to man broke out. Then fate, that most cruel mistress, took away his moment of delight, for out of the shop stepped forth another man and they both turned as one to move away, so that he would be able to walk past them. Of a sudden, the man stopped and his face broke into a wide smile as he recognised Joey, then turned to raise his hat to greet the lady by his side in a mannerly fashion. When he saw who it was he forgot his manners and took hold of her arms, smiling delightedly into her upturned face.

"Oh my dearest Sarah-Jane, how wonderful it is to see you again!" he enthused as she gazed rapturously at him. On the sight of it, Joey felt such pain cut through him as the memory of all his wasted protestations burned into him, warning him that her love for Paul Trevarthen - like Joey's love for her - had never died.

Paul turned his smiling face from her to Joseph Bolitho and as he did so caught the expression on his face. For once in his life, his naiveté failed him, recognising Bolitho's despairing look for what it was. A long forgotten conversation echoed through his mind and he knew then who the prim and proper damsel had been that would not have Joey for a husband. He smiled hesitantly at Joey and determined to excuse himself at the first opportunity that presented itself, but he had fallen into a predicament with his obvious delight at seeing Sarah-Jane again and it could not now be turned to cold formality so easily.

"How remiss of me, Joey, for you appear to know each other and I have blundered into your meeting. Forgive me my bad manners, both of you, but I was overcome at seeing my oldest friend after all this time. Perhaps I could walk with you both a little way, for I will be leaving for home soon. My wife is expecting me," he added pointedly and smiled at Sarah-Jane in his usual sunny fashion, hoping that she interpreted his delight at seeing her as not extending further than the friendship he had always felt towards her.

Sarah-Jane intuitively took her lead from her old friend and said she had not far to walk, but would not object to their company. Paul, with unusual presence of mind, insisted on taking the package she was holding and carrying it for her. Although it was not large, he succeeded in holding the package awkwardly and in such a manner that he was unable to proffer his arm, ensuring that it fell to Joey to offer his. And so they walked together down the street. Paul talked about his family in great detail; Joey and Sarah-Jane were meant to perceive and indeed, did have it to understand, that he was taking great pains to point out that he had a secure and happy family life. After a tentative enquiry from Joey, she informed them that she had been widowed within a year of her marriage and, although they both expressed their sympathy, it was her inquisitor who felt an igniting of the hopes that he had always cherished towards her. When she stopped at a large, imposing house they stood bemused by her side until she informed them that it was where she resided. They turned as one and admired the property - both her companions presuming that she worked there as a cook or housekeeper - but she surprised them yet again when she informed them that she owned it.

"It is not so big as the one I own in Falmouth, but Penzance is my home town after all, so I was delighted when the opportunity to purchase it came about," she said. Only then did Paul notice the quality of her clothes and smiled to himself for imagining that, when she had married, it was to some poor old salt that had hardly a penny to his name.

"Please to come in and take some tea with me, gentlemen, for I am so overjoyed to meet . . . to meet you both again," and she smiled at them in turn, hoping that he would accept her offer at least. Paul expressed his disappointment that he was unable to do so, but gave her his card and informed her that he and his wife would be delighted to call in the near future. He returned her package, doffed his cap and, turning to Joey, asked if he could attend on him the following afternoon, for he had a matter of great importance that he wished to discuss with him. Joey, blind to anything other than her face, did not notice the slight frown on Paul's, but told him he would come as directed and they shook hands and parted from each other. They both watched as Paul sauntered off towards a local inn to collect his horse from its well-maintained stables and, when he had disappeared, they turned and regarded each other again.

"You are most welcome to take tea with me should you wish to do so, Mr Bolitho," she said, smiling. But there was not the delight in this smile, for now it shone on a different subject.

"Bes' not, Sarah-Jane," he said softly, "fer I am still not as you would 'ave me be, 'een tho' I would most dearly like t' be fer me feelings towards you 'ave never changed, me dearest." A little sigh escaped him.

She put her head on one side and stared at him for a long while before saying gently: "Should you wish for it, Joey, you could be more than you are, for 'tis not so very hard to rise above adversity, you know."

"If fer one minute, I could believe that in so doin' I would be able to receive one look that could ever match the look you got fer 'e, Sarah-Jane, believe me I would," he answered sincerely.

A becoming flush flooded her cheeks and she bowed her head, and when she lifted her eyes she searched his face calmly before saying sadly: " I'm sorry, Joey, that it should be me your fancy alighted on, for a good woman would have been the making of you."

"A good woman?" he mused, then smiled despondently before adding, sadly: "yes, my dearest, she is that." Then he took up her hand and, lifting it to his lips, left a soft kiss on her fingers. With a last smile at her astonished face, he wished her farewell, before turning abruptly from her and hurrying back the way he had come.

Sarah-Jane watched as he walked down the hill and enormous sadness flowed through her, for well she recognised the sorrow that lay within him for love of her, as she carried her own unhappiness at her own unrequited love. She had been surprised that Paul should have him for a friend, for Joseph Bolitho was not the sort of person that she would have thought an acceptable companion for him. From his request for Joey to call on him on the morrow, it was quite obvious to her that their friendship was recognised but then - and she smiled fondly at the thought - Paul was ever the man for committing himself to anyone he considered a friend. Even with all his money and fine learning, he had spent many an hour in her family's little cottage and had been a great friend to all of them. He held his head high, but he never lost sight of the common man and she probably loved him for that more than any other reason. Slowly she turned and entered her house. Laying her parcel on the table she moved into the elegant but quietly furnished withdrawing room and rang the bell for tea, then sat down to await the entrance of her servant in solitude.

"Do 'e knaw where 'e's gone, Mrs Skewes?" he asked, smiling down at her upturned face, although his expression was wasted, for Likky's mother had been blind for many a year.

"Dunno, Joey," she replied, "fer 'e didden 'ave much say fer 'iself, but 'e's worried 'bout somethin' 'cos I could 'ear 'en tappin' 'is foot on the floor an' 'e d' only do that if 'e got somethin' on 'is mind."

"Well, tell 'en I called, Mrs Skewes, if you would be so kind," said Joey, "but I 'spec I'll find 'en roun' town somewhere."

"Right you are Joey," she replied and they wished each other farewell. As she heard his footsteps receding, she returned to her chair by the fire, sat herself down in it and wondered what it was that had worried her son, for it had worried Joseph Bolitho also. His voice, although pleasant, had an edge to it that she had never heard before.

Joey searched fruitlessly through the town, looking in all of Likky's normal haunts, but the man was nowhere to be found. It was only when he bethought himself to take the road that led away from Penzance and towards Newlyn that he finally ran him to ground. Sitting on a wall, his hat pulled down to shade his eyes from the sun, Likky was idly surveying the horizon with the heel of his foot continuously kicking the stonework. Joey sat down beside him and merely said: "Likky," by way of greeting. Without turning towards him, Likky replied: "Joey," in return. They sat for a while in silence, watching the sea and its little ships beating their way through the waves, until finally Likky coughed and asked: "Bin' away Joey?" although he knew full well that this was not the case for Joey had no trade in hand at that moment.

"No," replied Joey, slowly, "Bin' up at Trevu. Did a bit a' shootin' at rabbits 'gain, an' 'ad a bit too much t' drink, so stayed the night."

Likky's foot continued to tap the wall but he said nothing. He could have told Joey that Hudson had knowledge of his activities and knew where Joey had spent his time. But a strange feeling was growing within him and, not recognising that it was jealousy, he interpreted it as anger and decided that he would speak to Joey again when he was in a better frame of mind with him. They had spent their lives together being so careful of who was watching their every move, putting all their trust in each other. Now Joey was turning his head away from what he should have been doing and spending his time with that damn darkie. 'Fair enough,' Likky thought, 'Trevarthen had money but so did many another that Joey knew, so perhaps Hudson was right after all and Joey was chasing after Trevarthen's wife now. Joey's besetting sin had always been women and, after he could not fix himself with that Williams' maid and she had moved away, there was no stopping him'. If Likky had been in a better frame of mind he would have laughed at his many memories, for Joey had bedded many a woman over the years and there were plenty of tales to tell about his conquests.

"Goin' fer a drink, Likky?" asked his companion quietly.

" 'Ess, might as well," replied Licky nonchalantly, so they got off the wall and searched out a nearby ale house. After a few drinks, Likky considered he ought to tell Joey of his suspicions about Hudson and that he had set another man on to him but, as yet, he had no knowledge of who it was. He turned his head, leaned towards his friend and was about to speak when Joey announced that he would pick him up in the morning on the morrow, for he had something to do in the afternoon and would not be in the town.

"Got some work on fer we then, Joey?" asked Likky, a spark of interest in his eyes. But they dimmed as Bolitho shook his head and merely said: "No, not yet Likky - goin' up see Trevarthen 'bout a bit a' business he want discuss wi' me." Draining his tankard, he suggested that they make their way back to Penzance. Calmly, Likky finished his own drink, rammed his hat down over his head and followed in Joey's wake as he strolled out into the sunshine. But a bitterness had settled on his features and he stared resentfully at the back of his old friend.

"Is your watch repaired, Paul, for I know full well how you have been missing it, as your mother gave it to you and you seemed so lost without it?" enquired Chloe as he came into the parlour and bent to kiss her cheek.

"Yes, all is well again," he said, "but you will never believe what a sight presented itself to me in Penzance. Indeed, such a surprise was it that I find I can hardly believe it myself."

She looked up at him and noticed his mischievous grin, but shook her head and told him that she was not going to attempt to guess. So, if it please him, she would prefer that he told her at once instead of keeping her in suspense.

"Well, dearest," he said excitedly, "when I came out of the watchmakers I walked straightway into Joseph Bolitho, for he was standing outside of the shop, talking to a woman." He waited in expectation of her look of surprise, but none was forthcoming, for she would not play his game and merely said, sardonically: "How unusual! I presume you wish to tell me her name, for that would explain your look of barely suppressed excitement."

"I should say so, Chloe," he continued boyishly, "for it was none other than Sarah-Jane Williams that was, you know, John Williams' daughter, he who used to be the mine captain at Wheal Sankey when I was a boy."

Chloe put down her book and regarded him calmly. She knew of Sarah-Jane, for there were many who had spoken of her and her attachment to Paul. She knew also that her Paul, as ever, had never understood the poor girl's devotion to himself, but she was aware of it; some of the servants had said that she had moved away with a broken heart, because the man she loved did not return her affection.

"I expect he knew her from when she lived here before," said Chloe serenely.

"Oh he knew her right enough, for I have never seen his face so before, Chloe. He is besotted with her," he announced elatedly, "and from something he said to me some time ago, I have deduced that she was the girl whose hand he sought in marriage years ago." His wife raised her eyebrows in surprise, so he plumped himself down in the chair by the fire and continued to tell her of all he had seen and noticed. "She would not have him though because . . . because . . . well," and he faltered slightly, then continued in a rush of eagerness: "Methinks would it not be fitting if, after all this time, she should become enamoured of him? For that would be the making of him. He angers me so that he is so stubborn and will not change his ways for, although I hate to have to admit to it, I have a great fondness for him and consider he has the makings of a fine man."

She smiled at him and noticed how his face glowed with enthusiasm, but shook her head at the suggestion that she should invite them both to dine at Trevu.

He looked ludicrously disappointed as she continued: "It would be for the best if Joey does his courting without our assistance, Paul. After all, if she is still adamant in refusing him he will not thank you for attempting to interfere on his behalf," she pointed out wisely.

"I merely think that some . . . assistance would be beneficial to both of them," replied Paul sullenly, for he wanted desperately to ensure that both his friends - his newest and his oldest - should find the happiness that he enjoyed himself.

"No, Paul, it would not be right, for if the consequence of your intentions should not be the result that you, or they would wish for, then it would be to you that one or both of them would look with their recriminations," she informed him with her usual sagacity.

She could not forebear a smile, for he looked so downhearted at her observations. But she advised him that, if he wished to help Joey to win himself a wife, then he should concentrate his efforts on leading him away from his smuggling activities and attempt to make him follow a lifestyle that would prove more acceptable to Sarah-Jane.

"After all," she added, "she would not wish to have a smuggler for a husband, surely?"

"No, you speak the truth there, my dearest, for Sarah-Jane was brought up with a great moral sense and she is not without some wealth; her first husband had obviously left her well provided for, as she has one property in Falmouth and has now purchased a fine house in Penzance." He studied the fire in thought and after a while added: "I shall discuss with Joey, when I see him tomorrow, the sort of things he likes to do, and endeavour to set him up in some occupation that could lead his footsteps along a more law abiding path. After all, no crime has been proved against him, 'een though there are many known." He sighed deeply, but after a moment's quiet reflection, continued determinedly: "For giving me back my life, surely it is only fair that I should attempt to provide him with a better one, don't you agree, dearest?"

He raised a worried and uncertain face to her and she smiled reassuringly back at him, before telling him that it would be quite in order for him to attempt such an action on Joey's behalf and that this course would no doubt prove more beneficial to Joey's attempts at courtship than Paul's original intent. A look of relief flooded his face and he smiled brightly back at her. His grin broadened when she rang the bell for tea: a tantalising smell of baking had assailed his nostrils on his return to the house, so he knew full well that a plate of fine cakes would accompany the tea tray. Chloe, catching his look of delighted anticipation, smiled and shook her head. Then laughed and said: "Oh Paul!"

A wicked easterly blew across the field, howling and moaning and shaking the bare trees most roughly, causing the two hunters to seek shelter in the lieu of a hedge. As they sat with their backs against the stones, the tallest reached into his pocket and produced a flask and a small linen bag. The flask contained brandy and the bag, barley cakes, so these were offered to his companion along with his wide, happy smile. Refusing a cake, Joseph Bolitho took a sip of the brandy and was glad of it, for the wind was most bitterly cold and it put warmth into him. In spite of his sadness, he watched with a half smile on his lips as his brother happily consumed the barley cakes.

"Apart from yer wife an' family Paul, I d' believe that food is yer next greatest love," he remarked, and had to smile in response to Paul's happy grin.

Paul Trevarthen nodded in agreement and remarked cautiously that he was a most fortunate man, for he had the benefit of a good home and a happy family life. He considered for a moment how to continue and then, after taking a fortifying mouthful of brandy he swallowed hard, coughed and launched himself into his attempt at delivering Joseph Bolitho from his unlawful ways.

"I have often thought, Joey," he ventured, "that you have many talents that could be so better used in a more fitting way. Your skill at organising your smuggling activities is most remarkable, for you have employed yourself in that profession for many years and have never been caught." Looking up, he noticed the smuggler's sombre expression, but he had taken the first step and so ploughed on regardless. He talked at great length, making both observations and suggestions on Joey's lifestyle, but he was aware of a tangible silence from his companion and his speech faltered to a stammering decline. Finally, he brought himself to a halt by saying: "If money is your object then . . . I . . . I have more than enough for my needs and could quite easily . . . set you up . . . um . . . I mean provide the finances if . . . if needed for you to become a . . . a law abiding member of . . . of society." His companion made no comment. Paul nervously ran his tongue around his lips, then finally summoned up the courage to look Joey in the eye. He had expected to see anger in his face but, although Joey did look annoyed, there was a hint of amusement dancing in his eyes as well and on noticing it, Paul's brows creased in puzzlement.

"Well?" asked Paul tentatively, "have you nothing you wish to . . . um . . . say to me?"

"Not at all, Paul, fer I think you 'ave said enough." replied Bolitho, smiling grimly. "But don't look so worried, boy, fer I idden goin' thump 'e one over it. I appreciate yer concern on me be'alf, but I never 'ave asked 'e fer money an' I'm not goin' start now."

"But Joey . . .," he began, and was silenced by a raised hand.

"I said I will 'ave none of yer money, Paul," he said firmly.

Another silence fell over them, but Paul was nothing if not determined and so started up again, attempting to point out to Joey that with enough money behind him, he could lead a more respectable life. He added unguardedly, that in so doing, the possibility would arise that some suitable female would find him more than acceptable as a husband.

"This suitable female that you d' speak of, Paul," remarked Joey icily, "she 'as perhaps got a name?"

If the situation had been different, Paul's blushing face would have made him burst into laughter, but the tightening of his heart would not allow for such levity. He stared wrathfully at him instead as Paul tried desperately to extricate himself from the pit he had so unthinkingly cast himself into.

"Well I did notice that you were . . . I mean it was most apparent that . . . that Sa. . . the woman we encountered yesterday . . . um . . . I mean . . .," but again Joey raised his hand and stopped him.

"Tha's enough, Paul," he cut in angrily, "fer 'tis none of yer business." Then he caught himself up, as Trevarthen was so obviously trying to help him with his predicament. So, after a moment, he added softly: "I knaw you mean well, Paul, but fer the sake of our friendship yer to stop now, you understand me?" and he raised his eyes to Paul's and gave him a hard stare.

Paul looked uncomfortable and lowered his gaze. He had the unnerving feeling that time had whirled about and he was being put into his place by his father for some youthful stupidity, so he mumbled an apology and lapsed into silence. Joey turned his face away from his brother and studied the landscape, noticing in particular how barren the countryside looked, when normally he had always seen something in it that filled him with pleasure. He sighed heavily and was aware of Paul's eyes upon him, but he refused to look at him and kept his gaze steadfast upon the scene before him, lest the turmoil within him should burst forth and he take his anger out on the poor fellow who was trying so hard to help him. Understanding came to him of the predicament that Bert Pendray had found himself in with Paul's attempts to help that poor man. For Paul, who had never been without secure finances, money was of no use unless it could be used to help another. But to Joey, who had to struggle so hard to get any security at all, money was the proof of his abilities, the standard by which he had held up his head in his particular society. Amongst the fishermen and criminals he habitually conversed with, it gave him status, almost as much as their fear of him gave him protection. However, to the woman he loved it counted as nothing and, even if he could have allowed Paul to burden him down with his money, it would in no way have altered the smile on her face at sight of the man she actually loved, the one that displaced any feeling for him that could have blossomed into love.

Paul, detecting the simmering anger in his voice, swallowed hard and made a lengthy apology for his unwanted advice and remarks. Eliciting no response, he turned to Joey and held out his hand, then fretted again as it appeared he would not accept it. Finally Bolitho stirred and, after a moment's hesitation took hold of the proffered member and shook it firmly but briefly, telling Paul in a flat, dispassionate voice that he wished for no more interference from him on his behalf. Paul looked relieved and disappointed at the same time.

"I did not mean to offend you, Joey," he said lamely, and his crestfallen face bore witness to how guilty he felt.

"I knaw, Paul, I knaw," replied Joey softly. Sighing, he moved to get up and told Paul that they had better head for the lowest meadow, where they and the rabbits would find the most shelter.

So Paul scrambled up to his full height and followed in his wake, but his head hung low and his heart was troubled, for he desperately wished his good intentions had not gone so disastrously askew; Joey had made him well aware that Paul had need to interfere with his friend's pride most carefully.

CHAPTER 19

SHE looked at the posy that he held so incongruously in his large hands and smiled up at him, with laughter in her eyes.

"Joey, did you truly walk through the town carrying flowers for me? Methinks the townsfolk would have stared at you agog," she chuckled as he shamefacedly admitted that he had actually hidden them under his coat until he obtained entry into her house.

She led him into her withdrawing room and indicated a seat, which he went and stood before, waiting for her to seat herself before lowering his long limbs into the chair. A servant took the posy and returned after a few moments with it arranged in a small vase. They chatted companionably and he felt most relaxed in her company, for she was making great efforts to put him at his ease.

Their conversation continued, but she noticed that Joey's sentences were becoming more and more shortened and, when finally he looked her full in the face, she knew that he had come to ask something of her. She was full of trepidation for she could not fail to be aware of how nervous he had become, and imagined she knew what his question would be. Finally, he braced himself and launched into a speech of great length, assuring her that his love for her had never waned. Although he could not describe himself as a man of good habits and law-abiding ways, he determined to change his life for love of her. This was not the first time he had asked this question of her, but he had never wanted another in place of his beloved Sarah-Jane and had waited faithfully for her hand in marriage. If refused again, still he would take no other and, looking her directly in the eyes, he added: "Fer there is no other that can come to the place in my 'eart, fer you are in possession of it, my most dear love, and cannot be deposed."

She sat calmly, with her hands folded in her lap, and waited for him to finish his proposal. When he finished speaking, she raised her eyes to his and noticed how anxious he looked. Sarah-Jane was touched with his love for her, but that could not change her answer, so she refused him as gently as she could.

"Am I to be given a reason, my dearest?" he asked stoically.

"I know it is only right that I should, Joey, but all I can tell you is that I do not feel for you as a woman should when contemplating matrimony," she answered simply, and hoped her explanation would suffice.

"As you felt fer yer first 'usband, no doubt!" he retorted sharply.

Colour flooded her face, but she took a deep breath and continued calmly: "Captain Polmear had many fine qualities, Joey, and he offered me security. As a single woman I had only two choices. I could marry him or remain a spinster. I chose to marry him for what he could offer me and not for any love I felt towards him. He understood that, but I endeavoured to show him care and kindness at the end of his life."

"I can offer you security, Sarah-Jane, an' there is nothin' I wouldn't do fer you, my dearest love. You do knaw it surely?" he urged desperately.

"I am sorry, Joey, but I cannot accept your most kind and sincere offer," and she shook her head and looked down at her hands.

An angry glint came into his eye and he announced bitterly:

" 'E'll never be yours, Sarah-Jane, no matter 'ow long you d' wait. 'E' loves 'is wife an' will look fer no other. You can sit 'ere sighing over 'en to yer dying day, but 'e won't come fer 'e so you'd better make yer mind up to it, first as last, my girl!"

She flashed him an angry look, whether because of his rudeness towards her or for the reason that he had so obviously understood her lack of love for him. Looking at him, she noted the tension in his face and saw a muscle twitch in the side of his cheek, but as he knew the truth she would have been a fool to counter his accusations with lies. So she took a deep breath and plunged on:

"Do you think I don't know that, Joey?" she answered desperately, "for I have loved him from the first day I met him, but he has never noticed. For my sins I cannot take another now, and you will have to live with the disappointment of that fact as I have had to live with mine." She averted her face from him and stared sadly at the little vase of flowers that sat in isolation on her little table.

"Bleddy 'ell, Sarah-Jane," he swore, unable to stop himself, "I love you woman an' 'ave loved you from the moment we first met! Must we both suffer because of 'im?" He stood up suddenly, and moved towards her, taking her hand and roughly pulling her from the chair and into his arms. He should have held her tenderly and professed his undying love for her, but Joey was a man of action and sought her approval as directly as he knew how, so bent his head and kissed her fiercely and passionately. She struggled desperately until finally he released her. Mortified, she pulled herself away and shouted at him: "How dare you, Joey!" then, in a gesture of loathing, put her hand to her lips and wiped his kiss from his mouth. Turning her back on him, she stormed away to the side of the room.

"Oh God!" he cried, full of contrition, "Fergive me, Sarah-Jane, my dearest soul, fergive me!" He came and stood shame-faced behind her, tentatively putting out his hand to take her gently by the arm. But she swung around to face him at his touch and her beauty shone out at him in her anger.

"I will not!" she blazed at him, breathing heavily. "Now get out of my house, Joey, get out, for I will never marry you, never!" and she turned her back on him again and covered her face with her hands. He stood mute, unable to express his feelings to her. Finally, he dropped the hand he had extended towards her, bowed his forsaken head and turned away. She heard his soft footfall recede and the door open and close behind him. Only when her front door had slammed shut did she begin to cry and when she did, sobbed as if she would never stop.

Likky had to run to catch up with Joey for he was striding so quickly, but when he did catch him by the arm the face that was turned towards him was almost unrecognisable to him. Never had he seen such an expression of anger on it, for Joey kept a tight control over his feelings and one would more often catch sight of his cold smile than any other emotion.

"Joey," panted Likky, "Where 'e goin', Joey? Am I s'pose come too?"

"No," said Joey and turned on him wrathfully, "I don't need you."

Likky drew back as if a whip had caught him, but he had been Joey's lap dog for most of his life, so like a faithful canine he continued to follow him. He could not be spurned, so he tried again:

"I'll go with 'e, Joey, no trouble, you knaw me, Joey." He thought his friend would not stop, but he turned to look at Likky and some of the anger melted from his face at the sight of his troubled expression. Then Joey sighed and said softly: "I got see someone Likky, fer I got somethin' I want t' do, an' I don't want no other with me, understand?"

"But where 'e goin', Joey? Where 'e goin?" he cried in desperation. He watched as Joey disappeared into the stable and, after a moment, returned with his horse and swung himself into the saddle.

Angry though he was, Joey respected Likky enough to shout over his shoulder as he galloped from the yard: "I've got go up Trevu, Likky. Business! I'll see 'e 'gain when I get back to town."

"When 'll that be?" shouted Likky, but Joey had gone past hearing and there was no sound except the receding clatter of his horse's hooves on the cobbles.

Likky's shoulders drooped and he turned and headed to his home, but then thought better of it and instead took the alley that led towards the inn, for he felt he needed a drink. He had almost gained the entrance when a voice behind him said sneeringly: "Left you again, Likky? Joey must be fond of his Trevu friends indeed." Likky heard Hudson laugh mirthlessly and turned to see his dark shape disappear down the lane towards the harbour.

When Joey's horse thundered into Trevu's yard, Davy came running to take it and flashed Joey an angry look as he caught hold of the poor, sweating beast. But he kept his thoughts to himself, for one look at Bolitho's face told him he would brook no arguments with anyone.

In answer to his feverish knocking, a surprised looking Lizzie informed him that Mr Trevarthen was not in. With that information he was suddenly at a loss as to how to continue. Aware of a movement, he looked up and saw Mrs Trevarthen descending the stairs and would have turned to go, but she saw him and called his name. Lizzie stood back as he walked into the dark hallway, removing his hat before greeting her.

"Mr Bolitho!" she said kindly, "How nice to see you again. Please to follow me into the withdrawing room, for I do not expect Paul to be away for long."

When the door was closed behind them he shook his head at her suggestion of tea, so she indicated a chair and went to sit opposite to him. Joey was too agitated to sit, so he walked up and down the room until finally Chloe asked quietly:

"Something is troubling you, Mr Bolitho? If I can be of service in any way, please do not hesitate to ask. However, if your need is to converse with Paul, he is at the lower farm helping with a cow that is having difficulty calving, but I do not expect that he should be gone for much longer." She smiled her sunny, open smile at him and he felt again the twinge of excitement the sight of her always gave him. He studied her for a while and considered how he had fondly imagined that he could have fallen in love with her, but when he saw her with her husband and family he knew well that no man would ever displace that which she held most dear. Even more understanding had come to him when he had been reunited with his lost love himself, but for him there was to be no happy solution, for his own dearest love loved another.

"No one can 'elp me now, Mrs Trevarthen," he said despairingly and sat down, dropping his head into his hands.

Chloe was shocked by his actions, for he had been such a rock to her in her troubles that she could not believe the sight she had now of his dejected figure.

"Please to tell me, Mr Bolitho, for I hate to see you so dispirited," she said gently.

She thought he would make no reply, but at last he took his hands from his face and, staring woodenly at the floor, detailed the events of the afternoon, but he took great care that he kept her husband's name out of his narrative.

"My actions were unforgivable, Mrs Trevarthen," he said in shame, his face flooding with colour at the memory of it, "but I couldn' 'elp myself, fer I do love 'er most dearly!"

The sight of his distress troubled her, for she considered that he deserved to have better fortune in his love. But she knew why Mrs Polmear would not accept Joseph Bolitho for a husband, even though Joey himself had not mentioned the name of the man who had come between them. She studied his face quietly but was most composed when she asked him her next question, lest her own face should betray her emotions.

"What do you wish for Paul to do on your behalf, Mr Bolitho, for surely you have not ridden all this way merely to tell him of your troubles?"

He glanced up quickly into her wise eyes, then stood up and snatched up his hat, saying: "I should not 'ave come, Mrs Trevarthen, fer 'tis not right that I should burden you with this, or yer 'usband either, fer there is nothing either of you can do. I'll take my leave, ma'am, and would wish you goodbye." He would have bowed, but she was on her feet herself and moved quickly to stand in front of him.

"Mr Bolitho, well I know the reason Sarah-Jane refused you. I know also that Paul has never sought her love and when he saw you together and realised your . . . your love for her, he wanted to do all in his power to help you both. If he thought he could enable you to have Mrs Polmear for your wife, he would be more than willing to try to advance your suit with her," she told him, and her hand came out and took hold of his, squeezing it gently.

He looked down at her little hand, which lay so trustingly in his, and sighed heavily, then gave a sad, resigned smile.

"Fool that I am, Mrs Trevarthen, I thought if 'e told 'er he could never love 'er she would turn to me in 'er despair an' learn to love me as she does 'im," he told her simply. But then his ire got the better of him and he said angrily: " 'E 'as so much, Mrs Trevarthen, a wife an' family that he adores, a 'ome 'e loves. I jes' wanted 'er fer meself, but even that is to be denied me, fer she thinks she belongs to 'im. Is it fair, ma'am?" he asked huskily, "Is it fair?"

"No, Joey," she said sympathetically, pained by his evident unhappiness, "it is not fair as I know well, for when I married Paul he loved another and it took a long and painful time for him to realise that he had fallen in love with me. But you should ask Paul to intercede on your behalf, for you would find him most understanding." Then, taking a deep breath she said resolutely: "but he would be even more understanding if you told him who you are."

He turned from her suddenly and shouted: "No!" and went to move away from her, but she put her hand on his arm and whispered his name softly, then said: "You must tell him for both your sakes, Joey."

He sighed and faced her again, shaking his head sadly. If only the woman he loved could have shown him a tenth of the kindness and understanding that was being shown to him by his own brother's dear little wife. Reaching down, he took hold of her hand with both of his and cradled it gently against his breast for the comfort he could draw from her compassion, then said softly but clearly: "It must never be, fer 'e must never knaw the secret we share between us, my dearest Chloe. Methinks it would kill 'im to 'ear of it."

The slamming of the withdrawing room door made them spring apart guiltily and they found themselves looking into the hurt and anguished face of Paul Trevarthen.

"P.. Paul!" said Chloe and a blush flooded her face, "I . . . I did not hear you enter the house, dearest."

"So I would understand, Wife!" he snapped angrily, his eyes flashed at Joey and he took a hasty step towards him.

She realised that Paul had misinterpreted what he had seen and rushed towards him, crying out distressfully:

"No! It is not what you think! Please Paul, listen . . ." but he pushed her aside and, when he was standing in front of the shocked and unbelieving Joey, he hit him with his fist so hard that he staggered and fell back.

"So!" Paul roared, breathing heavily, "You are not content to have my friendship, you must needs cuckold me as well!"

"Paul!" Chloe screamed, terrified by his words, "No Paul! It is not as you would have it be. Please, Joey, tell him, please!" and she ran towards her husband and gripped his coat in desperation, pleading with him to listen to her. But Paul was beyond listening, for with what he had seen he felt as if he had been stabbed through his loving, adoring heart, such was the pain within him. He caught her again by the arm and flung her to the floor with all his strength. She lay like a crumpled doll and sobbed at his feet.

"That's right, madam, cry if you will! For what you have so manifestly been about, you can gain no forgiveness of me now!" Of a sudden he moaned and bent over her, then catching her arm he wrenched her to her feet and slapped her hard across her face. He had time to hit her only the once, for Joey was upon him, landing such a blow upon his brother that it sent him backwards against a small table, which gave way under his weight and spilled him to the floor with a crash.

"Damn you, Paul! Listen to us fer God's sake, fer . . ." But Paul, maddened beyond reason, sprang for him and had him by the throat. To stop him, Joey thumped his ribs so hard that Paul grunted as he felt the force of the blow and released him. But undeterred, he came for Joey again. Chloe placed herself between them and gripped hold of Paul's coat, refusing to let him go.

"Paul! Paul!" she sobbed, her tears falling unheeded down her face, "Listen, please, listen!"

"Get out of my way, you damned harlot," he raged and tried to throw her from him again, but she clung to him in earnest.

Turning her bruised face to Joey she called his name, but the sound of it and her use of it so angered her husband that he wrenched at her hands and pulled her away.

"Tell him, Joey!" she screamed, "for both our sakes! Tell him!"

"I will hear nothing of him!" shouted Paul, "lest it be that he pleads for me not to kill him!" and advancing on his brother he delivered another blow that made him stagger back. Seizing upon his advantage he came towards him again, but this time Joey was ready for him and knocked him to the ground. Once more, Joey tried to speak to him, but Paul would have none of his words, letting his fists testify to the anger that consumed him. They fought on, unheeding of Chloe's desperate cries, until Paul, the stronger, caught Joey another blow to his head and sent him sprawling to the ground. Paul stood over him and kicked him viciously in the body, but something within him stopped him from delivering further blows, for the man was down and even in his hatred he could not continue to hit him. Holding his ribs, he picked up Joey's hat and then, catching hold of his coat collar, pulled him to his knees. Joey, breathing with great difficulty, raised a bruised and battered face to his.

"Now, you bastard, get out of my house, and my life!" and Paul pushed Joey away and threw his hat at him.

Slowly, painfully, Joey dragged himself upright, even though it felt as if every bone in his body screamed in agony.

"Paul," he panted, "I must talk to . . ." but Chloe rushed to him and turned him from her husband, lest they should fight again, crying desperately: "He will not listen, Joey! Please go, please! I beg of you, for I will talk to him and make him understand! Please, Joey!" She pleaded and coerced him and pushed him towards the door, and all the while her husband's hurt and anguished eyes never left her.

"I'll be back, Paul," he gasped, "fer you will listen to me. An' I warn you: if you have hurt her I will take my knife to you an' spit you like a dog."

Joey wrenched upon the door and made his way painfully from the house under Lizzie's horrified gaze. When he got to the stables, Davy took down the water bucket and untied his own neck cloth, then soaked it before applying it to Joey's bleeding face, which helped in a small way to revive him. He gasped his thanks and Davy helped to heave him onto his horse. Joey kicked him on and slowly made his way to Penzance. At the turning, the tall figure hidden by the wall knew himself blessed with an unforeseen turn of events, so allowed himself an evil, contented smile as he watched the broken man make his way painfully along the road.

With Joey's departure, Paul turned to his wife and told her in a shaking voice to go to her room, for when he had composed himself he would have words with her.

"Paul! Please I must . . . ," but she got no further as he shouted for her to get out of his sight.

With her tears streaming down her cheeks, she fled the room and made her way to their bedchamber, then threw herself upon the bed and sobbed into the pillow. She could not believe how such a disastrous tragedy could have occurred in so short a space of time. But she would make him understand, for she determined that he should know all at last in spite of her promise to his brother.

172

So when a little later the door opened, she turned her head to face him with all the resolution she had left in her little body, pulled herself to a sitting position on the bed, and between racking sobs, began to speak: "You have misunderstood what you have seen, Paul, my dearest. For Joey is not my lover, he is . . ." But at the sound of that cuckolding word something snapped within him: he caught hold of her by her hair and she cried out his name in pain as he twisted her face to his.

He looked down at her bruised cheek, her tearstained face, her shocked and bewildered eyes and saw only the woman who, in spite of all his protestations of his love, had so wilfully deceived him. An anger consumed him so fiercely that he could not control his emotions.

"For the last time, Wife, for the very last time!" he hissed viciously. Before she could stop him, his hand had hold of her dress and he ripped at it with his strong hands until finally he tore it away from her trembling body. Deaf to her cries and blind to her tears, he pushed himself down upon her and took by force that which before she had always willingly and lovingly given to him.

CHAPTER 20

SITTING in the garden, the spring sun warmed his skin but not his spirit. A blackbird sang of it's pleasure with life but he could not recognise its meaning, for the bird and the man had experience of two different emotions. He heard a whispering behind him and knew that the children were come into the garden, so he asked them what they wanted in an indifferent, hard voice.

"Father, may we visit the Bosanko's this afternoon if you please, for we have not been to see them for such a long time," asked Daisy bravely.

"Are you both to go?" he asked coldly.

"Yes, Father," she replied, "for Grace would like to take some sewing she has done for Mrs Bosanko and so I will be pleased to go with her."

"Very well. You may go in the carriage and you are to return at four. You had best take care to be no later, for I will have words with you if you return here after the appointed hour, do you understand?" he said grimly.

"Yes, Father. Thank you, Father," said Daisy woodenly and he heard, but did not see, Grace's frightened whispered thanks.

He was left to his garden in peace, but the bursting spring life brought him no pleasure. So, after he had heard the departing wheels of the carriage on the drive, he got up and entered the house, taking himself to his study where he kept his books. Then he picked up some paper, jabbed his pen into the inkwell and began to write. Mechanically, he translated the words from the book to the page. He did not stir from his seat when, later, he looked out of the window and saw the carriage return. Tomorrow his son was to come home from his school, to the house where no child laughed and no face registered pleasure. He would instruct George as he had the others: that there was to be no mention of her name or even of her very existence. But in spite of all his instructions she came to him at every twist and turn, pushing her way into his mind and, although he would not believe it, his heart. Closing his eyes, he tried to blind himself to her image, but she rose up before him like a Fury that was bent on his destruction. He shuddered as he remembered all he wished to forget: finding them holding hands, Joey's soft words, and the fight that ensued. But worst of all were his actions to her that night, to the one who had been his most beloved. He shook his head and tried to free himself from the thought of what he had inflicted upon her. But even as he did so, her outstretched, pleading arms reached out to him and held him fast by his heart still. When he had finished his assault upon her body he left her bruised and sobbing, then locked her in the room and let no one in to her. He made hasty but cold calculations for her dismissal from the house and from both his life and the children's also; so consumed with anger was he that he would have her punished as much as it was in his power to do. By nightfall of the next day she was gone. She had money, clothes and a servant with her, for Lizzie surprised them both by refusing to have the mistress despatched so cruelly alone in the carriage that took her on her long, distraught journey to London. Sardi's London house was to be her new home, where she could live in quiet elegance, and reflect on the crime that she had committed against her husband. Even at the last, when she had begged him on her knees to see the children, he had taken a cruel pleasure in not allowing her sight of them, even though they could both hear the girls' distraught sobbing and little Jack's frightened screams. Servants and workmen stood and stared aghast to see the way he dragged their mistress from the house and pushed her into the carriage, before shouting at the coachman to: "Get that damned harlot fast away from here!" And of all those assembled, there was only one who believed she was such a woman as that, for he had given voice to the terrible word.

As the carriage had bowled up the lane to begin its journey, Jack - escaping from the nursery - and the sobbing Miss Clavering, rushed from the house and tried to chase after it. But his father ran after the child and caught him and, although he kicked and screamed, he was not to be released. The poor, heartbroken little boy could only scream the more for his 'Mama'. And the only comfort his father had to offer was to shake him roughly until finally, in his own distress, Paul could stand his cries no longer and he slapped his tearstained face so hard it left an ugly, red mark all down one side of it. Since that day little Jack had hardly spoken and, if he drew at all, it was only a picture of his mother's face. And when his father caught sight of one of them, anger consumed him and he took it from him and burned it on the fire. Her letters also - and there had been so many of them, to him and the children - were despatched, unopened, to share her picture's fate. They flared up like the passion he still felt for her, but even their fierce glow could not warm his cold hatred.

The following morning, the bright spring sunshine could not lighten the poor lad's heart as George descended from his father's carriage. He thanked Davy, as he arranged for his trunk to be carried it into the house. Davy, like all the other servants, had little to say, for a gloom hung over everywhere.

"I'll send it to yer room, Master George," said Davy sombrely but kindly, adding: "You'll find yer father in the withdrawing room sir, an' 'e said you was to go in to 'en as soon as you arrived." George facing the door with trepidation, took a deep breath and knocked resolutely, then heard a hard and, to him, almost unrecognisable voice telling him to enter.

At the sight of his father's face he suffered his first shock, for he had never seen such a hard, cold look on it and, although he received a welcoming smile, there was no warmth in it.

"Well, George, how good it is to have you back with us again," Paul said. He walked towards him and shook him firmly by the hand, then moved away as if touching him further would have caused him pain.

"You know, of course, that . . . that she has been sent away and why, for I wrote to you of it?" he asked coldly, turning his face away to stare blindly at the window.

"Yes, Father," replied George sadly.

"Her name is not mentioned in this house, George," he said, icily, "and you are to remember that, for I will not have the sound of it here again. Is that understood?"

"Yes, Father," mumbled George, and he felt it difficult to breathe, so strong was his desire to cry.

"Thank you, George. That is all that I wish to say to you at present. We will see each other later when we dine," and he strode towards the window and looked at the garden unseeingly, before adding in his frozen voice: "You may go."

"Yes, Father," and he let himself out of the room with his tears clinging to his long, dark eyelashes. He ran for the nursery and, when he arrived, flung himself into Miss Clavering's protective and understanding arms. She soothed him gently and crooned over him as if he was her youngest charge. But he cared not, for he had need of someone to show him comfort and let him know that love was not completely destroyed in his disrupted home.

So George was in their midst again and it was to him that the other children turned when they needed someone in their sadness, when Nurse had charge of Alice or could not be with them. Young Jack, in particular, was often with him, more often then not clinging to his hand. He could not understand why, of the three dearest adults in his life, two had disappeared and the third, the one he had always adored, had become like a stranger to him.

The children talked amongst themselves, and well away from their father about what they knew of what had happened, and took it upon themselves in consoling Jack to the best of their abilities, who was too young to understand but who felt the loss so painfully. To be in the company of their father was an almost impossible task for them, so cold and distant as he had become, for he had always been their adored and adoring parent. Their meals were consumed in silence, for when they sat down to dine with him it was most oppressive for them all. They could not fail to notice how thin he was becoming, for he had not the appetite to eat as he was used to do. Their melancholy days passed and soon George would have to return to school, so Miss Clavering bravely and nervously requested permission of George's father to take him to Penzance, for Paul's eldest son had grown so much that he would need new clothes and this necessitated a visit to the tailors. Paul agreed and surprised her by suggesting that, if she felt it within her capabilities she should take all the children - with the exception of the youngest - to the town and ensure that their wardrobes were refurbished.

"Yes, Mr Trevarthen sir," she complied in a docile manner and dropped a curtsey, then fled back to the protective cocoon of the nursery.

The following day, the children dutifully followed their nurse as she conducted them on a tour of the various establishments that would provide them with the articles of clothing she acknowledged that they required. The traders appreciated her, for the Trevarthen children were always dressed in the finest, and with four to provide for and another at home, the purchases were soon piling up on the floor of the spacious carriage. She felt much sympathy towards the quiet group of children and, when all the shopping had been done, she looked at her timepiece and realised that they had time to spare, so suggested that it would do them all good to go down to look at the sea. She arranged with the coachman that he took the himself off to a suitable establishment, charging him most forcibly that he was not to imbibe too freely before collecting them from the appointed place that would allow them the best view of Mount's Bay. He touched his forelock and turned the carriage in the direction of his cousin's inn, knowing he could tell him again of all the troubles that had been experienced at the big house and still not have to pay for his bowl of soup and the jug of ale that would be provided for him. His retelling of the latest Trevarthen scandal was all he needed for payment, such was the desire for gossip amongst the townspeople.

Meanwhile, Miss Clavering assumed her role of a mother hen and directed Paul's offspring down the hill towards the sea. They were relieved to be from their home and began to relax in the freedom that they felt, but out of respect for their caring and obliging nurse behaved themselves. They were most careful not to do anything that would upset and annoy her, for well they knew what effect their bad behaviour would cause that poor woman if their father should get to know of it. So when George caught sight of Joseph Bolitho striding from an inn that backed on to the road along the sea front, he held on to his brother's hand tightly and prayed that he did not notice him. Miss Clavering, conversing with the girls, was occupied in pointing out to them a particularly fine sailing ship that was breasting the waves and heading across the bay, having no knowledge that the gentleman who had been the cause of so much heartache in her little world was at that moment less than twenty feet away from them. Jack, looking up from contemplating his boots, caught sight of Joey but was too afraid to call to him, for nothing was as it had been in his little world. Joey stopped when he caught sight of the little group huddled together and hesitated. He saw the little boy's face, with his eyes welling up with tears and he could not bear to see his sadness, so he walked across to them, doffed his cap and greeted Miss Clavering. The poor lady jumped to see who it was, with his melancholy face and tight, grim smile.

"Why, Mr Bolitho, sir," she twittered nervously, "I did not think to see you here."

"Nor I you, Miss Clavering, ma'am," and he continued sombrely: "an' I would 'ope that you an' yer charges are all well?"

"Why yes, sir, we are all in good health and . . . and . . ." but she knew not how to continue and her voice faded away.

He understood her predicament and so told her he had best be moving on, but he asked permission to greet little Jack, "fer I 'ave missed 'im greatly, ma'am."

She knew she should not, but she took a deep breath and nodded for, of all the children, she knew it was her dearest little rogue who had suffered so much and was suffering still. Night after night he had awoken crying from his disturbed rest and she had cradled him in her arms, knowing full well that she was no substitute for what he had lost.

"Thank you, ma'am," he said softly and, replacing his hat, went down on one knee and opened his arms to the boy, who immediately flung himself against him. The storm broke and he sobbed and sobbed, and sad though it was it helped to heal a small piece of his broken heart.

George did not believe the whispered accounts he had been told of what had transpired between his mother and this man, and in the Trevu household at least, apart from one, nor did any other. But he was the eldest and to him fell the responsibility to ask, so he said clearly and simply:

"It is not true, Mr Bolitho, sir, is it - what they say of you and . . . and Mama?" and he looked fervently into Joey's eyes.

"No, Master George, you are in the right of it fer none of it is true, an' if yer father would only let me see 'im, I could tell 'im. Fer yer mother is the kindest an' dearest of woman an' she loves only yer father and no other," and at his words George felt an overwhelming relief. He believed every word, for it had been spoken with such simple sincerity.

"Thank you, Mr Bolitho, sir, thank you," and he held out his hand and clasped Joey's. Then the girls in turn, who had held on to and treasured every word he had uttered, came forward and took him by the hand. Lastly, Miss Clavering herself stood before him with her hand extended. Joey stood up, lifted Jack into his arms and held him against his broad chest as he shook hands with her.

"So beautifully expressed, Mr Bolitho, sir," she said, pulling out her handkerchief and dabbing at her eyes. "And so true, so very true." She sobbed a little, then blew her nose and said prosaically that it was for the best that they went their separate ways. He nodded and had some comforting words with Jack, then put him back down on the ground and, taking out his own handkerchief, wiped Jack's tearstained cheeks.

"Now, young Jack, what is it I d' always ask you t' do fer me, eh?" he said with a semblance of his old smile.

Little Jack smiled bravely back and said: "Behave myself," and gave a watery sniff.

"That's my good fellow," said Joey. Leaning forward, he planted a light kiss on his black curls, before turning abruptly and walking from them. When he got to the alleyway he faced them again and raised his hand in farewell, from that distance none of the assembled group could see the tears in his own eyes. He marched purposefully on and when out of sight of the little group, dashed his hand across his eyes. He was as lost and distressed as the rest of the Trevu household for he had known, as no other could have, the circumstances that had led to such a disastrous outcome.

In the evening of the day Mrs Trevarthen had been sent away, Jonas Hampton had come to his door to tell him that he was never to call or visit at Trevu ever again, for the master would not have him on the place.

"I could write 'im, Jonas," Joey said anxiously, staring bewildered into Hampton's equally sad eyes, but Jonas shook his head.

"He will not listen to anyone, Joey, so consumed with anger and hate as he is, neither would he read anything you could write him. There is not a servant or workman at Trevu who believes a word of what he believes, but there is not one amongst us who would go to him and tell him so. He looks like a man about to do murder and there is not one out of all of us brave enough to confront him. The bravest of us all was Lizzie, for she stood up to him and would not let the mistress depart alone and in such distress from the house," and he sighed sadly. Jonas watched as the bruised man made his way painfully to a chair and sat down heavily, before dropping his battered face into his cut and damaged hands.

"Why wouldn' the damn fool listen to we?" he mumbled in distress.

"Because he's too big a fool and too angry to hear anything other than what he wants to believe, Joey!" replied Jonas. Crossing the room, he took a chair beside Bolitho, then placed a hand on his shoulder and continued: "Best to wait and see if his attitude to her should soften, Joey. He can't go on hating her this way, he'll see sense before long, you mark my words."

Three months had passed and still Jonas's prophesy had not been realised, and Joey well knew that his brother had not softened in any way towards his wife. He never came into town and if he had business with any of the townspeople it was conducted through Jonas or another. Mr Pawley, the librarian, took a carriage to Trevu if there were discussions to be had over the Library. And if his solicitor wished to see him, as he had frequently to do in the beginning, he too took a journey to the sad, lonely house to converse with its withdrawn occupant. Joey, not wishing to make Chloe's situation any worse than it could possibly have been, bided his time. But he would confront his brother, for he could not have her innocence on his conscience and he determined to put all right.

Pulling his mind back to the present with a sigh, he continued on his way into the town and was soon in the midst of a throng of people busily occupied with their shopping in Market Jew Street. Some people looked and sniggered but his reputation went before him, so they avoided any eye contact and made sure their guffaws were not heard by him. He came to a clear space and stepped aside to let a woman pass, not noticing who she was and only lifting his cap in a mechanical gesture, but she called his name and he stopped. On recognising her, his eyes lit up for one moment and then almost immediately dimmed again.

"Joey," she said, "How . . . How are you?" and her eyes searched his sad face with concern.

"Sarah-Jane," he returned crisply, "Well, I would thank you. An' yerself?"

"I am well also but I am . . . I am most saddened to hear of your troubles . . . and those of some others," she said falteringly. She lifted her green eyes to his cold, blue gaze and was shocked to see the despair in it.

He bowed his head and she had to lean forward to hear him say: " 'Tis not as it 'as bin' told, Sarah-Jane."

There was a long, awkward silence and then she said softly and with a gentle tone that she had never used with him before:

"Joey, I have known you for such a long time; known you for the rogue you are. But even so I am aware that this terrible thing did not happen, for when Paul brought her so proudly to meet me I knew the way she felt about him, because I recognised it in myself. I know that she had love for only the one man and that neither you nor any other could take his place. If I waited for a thousand years I would still sit alone," she said with sadness and resignation. "For he will not come to knock on my door; the distress he is suffering now is for love of her. I should have listened to you, Joey, for what you told me was the truth and I should have believed it then, for in some way I think I have been the cause of the trouble between you."

He stared at her grimly, but he could not find the words to say. She smiled at him and said brightly, if only to see an answering smile on his face again: "Would you kindly give me your arm, Joey, for the street is so full of people today and I would not go home unaccompanied." After a moment's hesitation he offered her his arm and they walked through the town. This time, eyes opened even wider at the sight of them, but they held their heads proudly for neither of them cared; their rejection by their loves gave them a mutual understanding and companionship. Stopping at her house, he doffed his cap and wished her farewell. She made no attempt to impede him because she knew as well as he did that they had only walked a little way, and neither was sure if their path was to continue further. His heart lifted a little higher though, for after all his dark days of despair a little light had crept into his life to illuminate and soften some of his darkest feelings.

Meanwhile, Miss Clavering sat in the coach and whispered urgently to her charges: that on no account were they to mention to their father who it was that they had encountered in the town, for he would be most angry should he hear of it. After they nodded their agreement, she put her hand into her reticule and pulled out the letter that had been sent to her for collection at Penzance, warning them most particularly that they were not to tell him about what she was now to show them, for it would have disastrous consequences for them all. It was not a long letter but it gave them all immense pleasure, for Miss Clavering read it softly and beautifully, and so Chloe's dearest love was delivered to all her most adored children. They communicated just what they wished for Miss Clavering to write in return and she promised faithfully that, when next she went to Penzance, it would be posted to her. The letter was passed around amongst them all. Even Jack, who could barely read it, but liked to think he was touching something that Mama had touched, for it gave him great comfort. Then it was returned to Nurse, who hid it away again and smiled lovingly at them as they entered the lane leading to the forbidding house, and away from the brightness that had just touched them.

When the carriage pulled up before the house they noticed a little group of customs men sitting on their horses: one of them holding the bridle of a rider-less chestnut. They surmised correctly just who their father's visitor was, and they did not need the new maid, Beth, to tell them that Mr Hudson was with Mr Trevarthen in the withdrawing room. So they each carried some parcels, and quietly took the stairs to the nursery, then busied themselves with unpacking their various purchases.

In the withdrawing room the two men faced each other, the one with a hard, set face and the other with a sardonic smile.

"Most disturbed to hear your news, Mr Trevarthen, sir, most disturbed," and he smiled, and could not keep all the joy from off his face. His host regarded him with a stony countenance and had nothing to say, so his visitor continued, for he would turn the knife until he could turn it no more, purely for the pleasure of knowing he was inflicting pain upon him.

"I would have called before but thought it best not to intrude upon your distress. To think you made a friend of him and this is how he should repay you, such a dog as the man is, for you have shown him nothing but kindness and have worked so hard on his behalf." With every word he uttered, his heart sang the louder. For Trevarthen's expressionless face told him how deeply the man had been hit by what had happened to him.

"I do pity you most profoundly, sir, to have been . . .um..." and he paused for a moment, noting the wary flicker in the sad brown eyes, "...cuckolded, and by the likes of Bolitho too." He shook his head in mock sympathy and sighed. "Such a shame that you did not know what they were upon and how devious they were with your . . . um . . . trust." Again the pitying smile was directed at Trevarthen and he noted how Paul's hand clenched as if he would hit him, but Hudson knew himself secure, so he waited briefly before continuing:

"Of course, I am not aware of your wishes, but should you require details of dates and times, sir..." and he lowered his voice as if he was about to utter an obscenity: "for a . . . divorce." Paul's mask cracked as Hudson saw him flinch at the word. "I can supply you with all you would need." He produced a small book and waved it in Paul's face. "For 'tis all here and you, no doubt, could supply me with much that I . . . that I would know."

Here Mr Hudson had made a mistake, for Paul had not contemplated divorce; his wife's disgrace had been broadcast throughout his little realm, but he could in no way contemplate the shame such an action on his part would cause if published to the world. His blood ran cold at the thought of the damage that such a public revelation would have upon his young family.

"I have no wish to receive communications from you on any matter, Mr Hudson," he said coldly and brusquely. Turning, he presented his back to him. "If you have nothing further to say, I suggest that you leave. Good day, sir."

"I can understand your position in such a serious matter, Mr Trevarthen, sir, but as I have so often told you, one word, only one word, and he will be gone." "Left to swing for his sins," he continued, in his insinuating fashion. "All of them, and you will have the satisfaction of knowing that the felon who has brought such distress to you and your family is no longer left to plague you on this earth."

He saw the shoulders tighten and waited anxiously for Trevarthen's next words, but he was doomed to disappointment yet again.

"Good day, Mr Hudson," was all he was to hear. But he was a determined man and would come again, for he would have out of Trevarthen what he wanted to know. He was down now, and weakened. It would not take much more to break him.

"As you wish, Mr Trevarthen, sir. My condolences once again," he said as if Paul had suffered a bereavement, which in some ways he had, so he merely added: "Good day, sir." The Preventative Officer let himself from the room, unable to wipe the gloating smile from his florid face, and on the way back to Penzance at the head of his troop of men, laughed aloud at the joy of the unforeseen events that had played themselves into his outstretched hands.

"Seth says Captain MacGregor needs your answer before the week be out, Joey!" said Likky urgently. " 'E wen't wait ferever an' we need a good 'aul soon. Our last cargo is near exhausted an' we 'ave orders to meet."

"I knaw, Likky," replied Joey, but his mind seemed elsewhere, and Likky felt his rising disgust, for the man no longer acted so directly as he had been wont to do. Ever since that trouble with Trevarthen's wife - something he had brought on himself, for he would always chase the women - he had not been the same man. He seemed to have lost all interest in smuggling and to Likky this was almost unbelievable, for this had been their sole occupation for so many years. During the war against the French they had braved the navy on both sides of the channel to get the illicit booty through and had received good money for so doing. Joey contacts were legion, he could sell to the best in the land and they were willing to pay whatever price he charged them. Never had Likky seen his friend as he saw him now, for he was hesitating and to see him so brought a tremor of fear to Likky's heart. Well he knew that you needed a cold head and swift decisions to run their game with any degree of success.

"Tell 'im, I'll meet with 'im on Wednesday, at seven a' the clock, in the usual place," he said in a lowered voice. "If I am followed then I will contact 'im again by the Thursday in Marazion, but will send another in my place tho' the hour will be the same." Finishing his ale, he raised his arm in farewell to Josh and the crowd at the bar, then strode from the inn. Likky raced to finish his drink and left the inn in a hurry, such was his haste to keep up with the man, although Joey seemingly cared not whether he was beside him or no. In the house opposite, the man finished writing in his notebook and moved away from the window, then made his way slowly but confidently down the stairs and took the alley that led down to the harbour. Soon, Hudson thought to himself, he would have him an agent that would deliver that man to him. For he was certain his hunch was right and that the fellow would not be able to overcome his disgust and mistrust of Joey, and so would finally seal his fate and help to push the filthy rogue's neck into the noose.

A week later and Likky was rummaging in his pocket amongst his few remaining coins to pay for his next tankard of ale. He did not often drink in St. Just for it was away from his usual haunts, but he had begged a lift on a farmer's cart returning from market, having no wish to remain in the town that day. His anger with Joey knew no bounds, for their meeting with MacGregor, that he had been at such pains to set up, had come to nothing. Joey would not agree to the man's demands, which Likky considered were reasonable enough; the customs men were becoming ever more noticeable and the Captain would need good money to undertake the voyage. As they had walked away from the inn he had not been able to contain himself and so had told his friend of his disgust.

"I will not set myself up to deal with 'im," Joey had told him softly but calmly, "fer the man is 'ot 'eaded and will lose all 'ere long, fer 'e is not careful enough with 'is crew or 'imself. Did you not see the way 'e shouted aloud 'is intent just so to make the crowd drinkin' with 'en laugh?"

"We knew every one of 'em, Joey, there was nothin' to fear," replied Likky indignantly.

"Nothing to fear!" snorted Joey, in disgust.

"No, nothing to fear!" returned Likky, hotly. "Seems to me you lost 'eart in the game, Joey," and then uttered bravely: "Yer not the man you was, Joe, perhaps Trevarthen's thrashin' made 'e go soft." There was a brief moment when he thought that Joey was to beat him to the ground. His hands clenched and in the moonlight he could see the anger in his face, and the hot sparks in his eyes, but then his body relaxed and his face resumed its impassive mask.

"Stop now, Likky, fer you don't knaw what yer talkin' of," he advised him calmly, but Likky was annoyed by the implication that he was no longer Joey's confidante and carried on recklessly:

"No! I 'aven't got no idea wha's goin' on, 'cos ever since you bin' playin' the 'usband with Trevarthen's missus seem to me that . . ." But the world was never to hear his revelation, for a blow caught him so forcibly that he was knocked to the ground, unconscious. He awoke a considerable while later to find himself bruised and wet in the bottom of the muddy ditch bordering the deserted country lane.

So the following day he drank alone, but the ale that he was consuming in vast amounts could not quench the bitter fire burning within him. Rocking slightly, he pushed some coins across the counter, and picked up his ale and began to drink. Not caring how fast the liquid was flowing down his throat, for it mattered not.

"A brandy, my good sir," announced an oily voice at his elbow, "and one for my good friend here. Your finest, mind, landlord, for we will have nothing but the best, eh Likky?" The smile that accompanied these words did not fill Likky with joy, but in his despair it held a certain charm. There were a handful of shining coins on the counter and Likky wished to consume more in spite of his own lack of finances.

He took up the glass with the glowing amber liquid and, raising it to his companion in a silent toast, found himself grinning foolishly when the gesture was returned and heard the sneering voice whisper, before tossing back his brandy: "To absent friends!"

CHAPTER 21

SHE had taken up her pen only when she was recovered enough to do so. Attempting to show her granddaughter a dance step that had been the fashion in her youth she had fallen, damaging her hip, and had been advised by the doctor to remain in her bed. She was most frustrated at having to follow his command for she thought him - and informed him quite sharply, on more than one occasion - that he was an old woman to be fussing over her so. When almost recovered from this infirmity, the grandchildren had paid a visit and the youngest, suffering from a heavy cold, could do no better than to pass it on to her. Weakened by the length of time she had spent abed, her body had little resistance to another illness, so once again medical assistance was called for and this time she was overjoyed to see the doctor, for the cold had made her weak and listless. Her struggle against its effects took much of her remaining strength and it took its toll both mentally and physically. Slowly recovering, she was dimly aware that no letters had been received from either of them and this was unusual for they both wrote frequently, but she felt too unwell to pay overmuch attention. Consequently, it was to be awhile before she felt well enough to write a letter to her nephew which contained, in the most part, a catalogue of her recent woes and very little else. But she did remark, towards the end of her missive, that a letter from him would have helped to lighten her days and would no doubt have lifted her from the fit of the dismals that she had suffered as a result of her debilitating illness.

Within a week she had received a reply, and the shock of reading the contents had the effect of recalling the doctor to her bedside yet again. That evening she lay in her bed, propped up by her lace edged pillows, unable to comprehend the enormity of the calamity that had befallen her family.

"I cannot believe it, Cecily," she whimpered and sniffed at her sal volatale to fortify herself, before continuing: "for there is no way that the dear sweet girl would ever have done such a thing. Leastways with him, she has been besotted with Paul ever since she met him, for when he first introduced her to me it was writ all over her face."

"I know, Mama," her daughter replied consolingly, "but she has had a most trying marriage, for 'tis well known he could not see the love she had for him. And when he returned with his love child for her to take in, well, methinks she could have died, for well I know I would have done." She rolled her eyes heavenwards and shook her head in disdain.

"Well I know what you would have done, Cecily!" snapped Caroline tartly. "But dear Chloe is made of firmer stuff, for she had ever the ability to maintain a sense of decorum and after all, he grew to love his wife once he had seen the error of his ways. As for Daisy coming to live with him, if I know Chloe she would have demanded that he bring the child to her. He is much like his father and would have kept her hidden, were it not for the strength that he acquired from the woman he married." She frowned and considered for a moment, before announcing in a strong voice: "Well, as I cannot go to him at this present time, for I will have need of all my strength for that, I will write to Chloe and beg of her the truth of the matter."

"Mama, you cannot!" cried Cecily, shocked. "For well you know that he has most expressly forbidden you to communicate with her in any way, look!" and picking up Paul's discarded letter from the counterpane, pointed to the relevant script. "He says so here, and he goes on to state he will brook no interference from any in the family!"

"Humph!" snorted Caroline, "as if Paul can tell me what I should be about! I should like to know who he thinks he is?"

"He," retorted Cecily firmly, "is the head of the family, Mama, and you have no right to go against his wishes."

Her mother regarded her with a withering look before embarking on a speech of great length, detailing her knowledge of her nephew and of his past misdemeanours, the details of which so shocked her daughter that she covered her ears, lest she should be in some way contaminated by the information ripping so viperously off her mother's tongue.

"Mama! You should not speak so of him."

"I am only speaking of him that which I know, Cecily, and I do wish you would stop behaving in that prudish way. Your cousin and uncle followed the same path, at one time in their lives, and it was only their foresight in marrying such exceptionally fine woman that saved them from falling into complete degradation. Then for Paul to throw it all away and believe that of her! It shall not be, for I will not have it so! No, I shall write to Chloe and demand the truth of her and I will tell her also of that which I know and she does not. When I have had my reply of her I shall know how to act and you will not stop me!"

"Mama! I will not allow you to do this thing, an' if you will not listen to me then I will inform my dearest Nathanial that he is to talk to you and show you the error of your ways," her daughter announced primly and with as much authority as she could muster.

Her mother shot her another of her withering glances before announcing, in a voice that left Cecily quivering in her pretty little satin slippers:

"If you suppose that I shall be in any way deterred by that simpering fool of a husband of yours, then you are much mistaken my girl!"

"Mama!" said Cecily, tears sparkling in her eyes. "How could you speak so of my dearest Nathanial. You have always maintained what a fine and upstanding husband I had married!" and she burst into loud sobs.

"Well, and so he is a fine husband," returned Caroline testily, "an' well I know how grateful I have been that he wished to marry you, for his income and standing is quite exceptional. But I will brook no nonsense from him an' I doubt he dare to countermand me an', if he should do so," she added thoughtfully, "I do believe I would think the more of him." She picked up Paul's letter and with only a brief shudder regarded it with equanimity, before folding it and placing it on the table at the bedside.

"You may leave me now, Cecily, for I have much to think of," she announced dismissively. Her daughter bravely attempted again to protest that her mother should obey Paul's expressed wish but her mother's hard, dark stare reduced her resolve. So with a succession of loud, watery sniffs she left the room and went in search of her beloved. When Cecily informed this stalwart what he was to tell his mother-in-law; that she was not to follow any action that had been forbidden by her cousin, he looked appalled. Then, summoning up all his courage, he announced that he had business in the town and would return later to escort his wife to their home. He moved as quickly as his portly frame allowed him to do, lest his wife should stop him. Picking up his hat and cloak he hurriedly fled his wife's mother's house, almost as if that redoubtable lady herself had risen from her sick bed and was even then pursuing him down the street.

"I dunno, Likky," said Seth, shaking his head sadly. "I'd rather it were Joey. Felt safe with 'e fer 'e never let a man down if he could 'elp it."

"Whose t' say I will?" retorted Likky, stung by the implication that his prowess could not match his erstwhile friend's.

" 'Cos Joey wouldn' a fool wi' drink when there was business afoot, fer a start!" rapped Seth, casting his eye upon the glass and tankard that were nowadays never far from Likky's grasp.

"I bin' as many years doin' the job as 'e," announced Likky proudly, "tidden nothin' he can do that I can't. 'E idden such a man as all that. An' anyway look at 'en now. Moonin' roun' town like a dog with 'is tail 'tween 'is legs. What chance would 'e 'ave save yer necks with a man who 'aven't got 'is mind on the job."

Some of the other men nodded and agreed with Likky, but Seth remained steadfast. He felt uneasy, for although there was nothing that he felt Likky could not do that Joey could, there was something about Bolitho that gave a man confidence. He had a way of leading men, with firmness and authority, that made you want to follow him, to do his bidding without question. For, above all else, he looked out for the welfare of the people under his command and would abandon an enterprise if he felt it was in any way detrimental to their safety. Likky, on the other hand, saw only the gold of the prize and could easily lose sight of the needs of those around him.

He shook his head again and made to turn away from him, but Likky caught him by the arm and asked him if he would think about it.

"I'll give it some thought, Likky, but I d' make 'e no promises fer I don't like it an' tha's a fact," he told him soberly. Then with the briefest of farewells he made his way from the inn, his troubled mind showing in his dejected posture as he strode slowly up the hill to his home.

"Don't worry, boys," announced Likky with a confidence that he was far from feeling, " 'e'll come roun' to it. Now, who's fer another drink?" The jingle and clatter of the coins he slapped on the table were drowned in the shouts of the crowd assembled around him.

An hour later, Likky, stumbling slightly, pushed open his front door to be told by his mother that a gentleman had come in by the back entrance and had expressed a wish to see him. For a moment his fuddled brain felt alarm, but then he relaxed. For all the men apart from one, who lived well away from Likky's home, were still drinking happily in the inn.

"Well?" his caller said brusquely, then remembered to smile in a friendly manner, for he was close to his prize and could not afford to lose it now.

Likky shot a nervous glance towards his mother, but she sat regarding the fire with her unseeing stare. He relaxed and turned to the man, announcing proudly: "I 'ave all but one of them, fer Seth is wary. But I reckon 'e'll come roun' to it too, fer money is precious short an' 'tis unusual to 'ave a chance of such a trade as this'll be at this time a' year." He spoke as clearly as he could, for the drink slurred his words.

"Good!" came the succinct reply, "I will be in touch," and he dropped the small purse on the table, turned on his heel and left the way he had come, without acknowledging either the mother or the son.

Likky stumbled to the table and picked up the leather bag, stuffing it into his jacket with a satisfied smile on his face.

"What about Joey?" asked his mother when she was certain they were alone.

"What about 'en?" asked Likky angrily. "I don't need 'e," and finding the remains of a pie on the shelf he took it to the table, sat himself down and began to eat noisily.

"You bleddy fool!" she swore, "Joey's the only man can see 'e all safe. You 'edden no bleddy good fer yer always too full a' liquor. Bes' stop now afore you do lose all, Likky," and her voice took on a pleading note as she added: "fer all our poor sakes."

Her son merely swore at her and told her to shut her mouth because she did not know what she was talking about, so she sat silent and wrung her hands whilst she worried in silence.

The curricle dashed up the drive, pulled by a pair of sprightly, high stepping greys, and came to a halt in front of the house. A very distinguished gentleman, with his slightly lined and dissipated face enlivened by a most attractive smile, descended and greeted Davy cheerily as if meeting a long lost friend, which indeed he was.

"Damn me, Davy, do you never age man? For you are as sprightly now as ever I can remember you to be!" and he clapped him affectionately on the back. Davy beamed up at the tall, finely built man, but then he remembered the cloud that sat so heavily over the house, and frowned as he greeted him in return.

"Why, 'tis grand to see 'e 'gain sir, grand, but you d' come 'ere upon sad times, sir," and he shook his head worriedly before saying again: "very sad times, sir."

"Not a bereavement, Davy, surely not?" asked the man in a shocked voice.

The old servant shook his head again and, lifting his wrinkled face to the man, announced: "T'idden fer me to say sir, but there's bin a mort a trouble 'ere." Then, in acknowledgement of the visitor's raised eyebrow, said slowly and in a lowered voice: "The mistress is from 'ome, fer 'e sent she away 'cos 'e do believe she 'ave disgraced 'erself with another man."

There was a hastily curtailed shout of laughter, then the man reached out and caught hold of Davy's arm, looking again into the troubled face.

"But this cannot be, not Chloe . . . I mean not Mrs Trevarthen, for she idolises him. There is no way, Davy, no way and surely he must know it?" he said in horror.

" 'Course 'e should knaw it, sir, fer we all do! We knaw 'ow she d' feel 'bout 'en but 'e's too damn mad knaw anything, the silly beggar," and he turned and spat in disgust before directing one of the men to carry the man's baggage into the house.

"Is he at home?" said the gentleman, giving the care of his curricle to another of the men.

"At 'ome. 'Ess 'e's at 'ome sure nuff, fer 'e d' never leave it these days 'cept fer when 'e got business on the farm." They walked together towards the house, before the aged servant stopped at the door and said sadly: "You'll find 'en changed sir, most changed." Shaking his head sadly, he led the way into Trevu's dark and forbidding hallway.

The new serving girl would have announced him, but on being told that the master was in the withdrawing room, he thanked her gracefully and told her he knew the way and as an old friend would announce himself. Noting her worried look, he smiled at her kindly and repeated softly: "An old friend, my dear, and methinks he has need of them now." Leaving his hat and cane in her care, he strode forward and approached the withdrawing room. With the barest of knocks, he entered and then closed the door firmly behind him.

The figure, silhouetted in the light from the window, spun around on his heel and turned his haggard face towards him. His visitor could not believe the sight he saw, for never could he remember his friend to present him with such a countenance as he was seeing now.

"Hello, Paul," he said softly, and walked towards him with his hand extended in greeting.

"Peter! You, here . . . but how . . . I had no letter," he stumbled, clumsily, before adding blankly and unconvincingly: "How good it is to see you again." Mechanically, he caught hold of his old friend's hand and shook it briefly.

"I only arrived in Bristol last week and hurried home to see the old man before coming on down to Cornwall. I did think to write but considered you would not turn me away if I arrived unannounced." He lifted his bright eyes to Paul's dull ones, before saying cautiously, "An' I hope you will not turn me out now that I am here."

"I would not . . . I would not dream of it, Peter, but . . . but . . ." and he swallowed hard before announcing: "Things are not as they . . . it is a . . ." Unable to explain, he came to a faltering halt and could not look his friend in the eye.

Peter waited patiently for Paul to continue but realised that it was impossible for him to unburden himself. So, considering how best to use the information given to him by Davy, thought it best to lead him gently.

"And dearest Chloe, she is well I hope?"

Paul flinched like a man receiving the first lash of punishment from a whip.

"She is no longer here." he snapped coldly. "I have sent her away, for she has most grievously . . . for she has . . ." and unable to continue, he turned away and withdrew to the window with his back turned to his old friend.

Undeterred, Peter strolled quietly to his side and prompted gently: "She has ...?" He waited patiently for a resumption of Paul's explanation.

Taking a lungful of air, Paul said quickly and in a quivering voice: "She has taken a lover and has been sent from this house!"

"Fiddlesticks." said Peter, calmly.

Once again, Paul spun around on his heel. He stared at Peter, amazed that he should respond so dismissively to his admission.

"How dare you!" he blazed, "I have told you nothing but the truth! How dare you to come here and take her part!"

"I dare, old friend, because I know full well that she would never do as you say. From the minute I first clapped eyes on her, I knew that there would never be another man in her life, no matter how young a child she was when first she met you. When you left Berkshire and returned to Cornwall she moped around London like some poor, abandoned waif until finally, when she came to visit you with Sardi, you had the wit to propose to her. Lady Wrothford was almost in despair that you should not ask for her hand in marriage, for throw as many suitors at Chloe as she could, the dear, sweet girl had her eyes and her heart fixed only on you," he told him without rancour.

"Time has passed, Peter, and I believe she must have grown tired of me for I caught her with her hands held fast by another . . . another man and if you could have seen the look on her face as she looked into his eyes as he was . . ." He stopped and bit his lip, unable to continue.

"I presume that she gave you some explanation of this occurrence?" he asked quietly, and noticed how discomforted Paul looked by his question, so much so that Peter sighed and enquired in disbelief: "You did ask her for an explanation, surely?"

"Well . . . no . . . no, I did not for I was justifiably enraged and with his words to her and . . . and I knew full well what he meant for he is a man renowned as a common rogue and deceiver," he announced bitterly.

"And may I enquire what a man with such a reputation as that should be doing under your roof, let alone, talking with your wife?"

"He was . . . he was a friend of mine," he answered defensively.

Peter sighed and rolled his eyes heavenward, before walking to the sideboard and raising his eyebrows in a mute question.

"Please to help yourself," sighed Paul and went to the settle, then sat down dejectedly.

He shook his head when his friend enquired if he required a drink, so Peter poured himself a solitary brandy. Taking a seat opposite to his friend, he regarded him quietly, although to all intents and purposes he appeared to be studying the colour of the amber liquid in his glass as the light from the window played upon it.

"Paul," resumed Peter softly, "all the time I have known you, I have recognised in you your compassionate nature and your complete disregard for any man's station in life. But I find it impossible to believe that this fellow of whom you speak should be allowed to come here and talk freely with your wife if he is now to be portrayed in as bad a light as you have given him. Surely you would not have allowed him into your home if you did not in some way regard him as a person to be trusted. I think I have to hear more of the fellow before I judge him. Would you . . . could you bring yourself to tell me what you know of him?"

Paul sighed loudly, then launched himself into the tale of how first he met with Joseph Bolitho and, hesitatingly at first, recounted all that he knew of him and all that had happened to him because of Joey's entrance into his life. He left out not one single moment, including the acknowledgement that the man had undoubtedly saved his life, then finished his speech with the details of the tremendous fight during that fateful day. But of his wife, Peter noted, there was little mention, almost as if he could not bear to name her.

"During all this time, I assumed he was a friend of mine. But he was, in reality, attempting to entice . . . entice my wife away from me." Drawing a long breath he lifted his sad eyes to his friend's face.

"And you made no enquiry as to the meaning of the words he uttered before beginning your altercation with him?" Peter enquired.

"No, why should I? They both had such a guilty look about them that I knew the truth at once!" answered Paul hotly.

"Paul, Paul," said Peter softly. "On many an occasion I have known your own face covered in guilt, were it only for stealing some of Hannah's cakes! I think it best that you try to rectify this drastic situation by discovering the meaning of this fellow's words, before this tragedy be allowed to plunge your life into a pit of despair out of which you will never be able to crawl."

"I am in that pit now, Peter, and any explanation of theirs will do nothing but confirm to me that they have both worked to deceive me, for his very words confirm that they wished to keep a matter of great import from me," he announced coldly.

"Nevertheless, Paul, it is not fit that you continue in this fashion, unsure of exactly what has occurred, for you have no proof," he told him firmly.

"I need no proof, for I have seen their faces and no further evidence is required," he snapped. Then, without feeling, said: "If you have finished your drink please to follow me, for it is close to the hour for dining and I expect you will require to refresh yourself before you sit down with us," and he stood up and signalled his friend to follow him. But on reaching the door he paused, before turning to Peter and informing him flatly that he was not to mention her name in the presence of any other in the house, for he had expressly forbid the sound of it to be heard. As far as he was concerned she had no longer the right to a place in his home.

"Out of sight, out of mind, eh Paul?" asked Peter derisively, and had the satisfaction of seeing a hot blush flood into Paul's cold face.

Joseph Bolitho watched dispassionately as the tall, well-dressed man talked at length with various fishermen on the quay. He had no knowledge of the stranger in their midst, but by their guarded expressions he was aware that they were being asked questions they had no wish to answer. A puzzled frown fell across his normally enigmatic face, but he kept himself in the shadows and waited until he saw Seth Mankee break away from the little group and head towards his own home. Following him discreetly, he caught up with him by the top of a dark alley and whispered his name loudly. Seth spun around and searched the gloom until he caught sight of Joey, half obscured by the shadow falling from an overhanging roof.

"Seth," he greeted him again.

"Joey," said the fisherman warily, for Joey coming upon a fellow in the dark usually meant only the one thing.

"Stranger in town, Seth? Seemed most keen to talk to all of 'e down by the 'arbour. What did a' want knowledge of?" and he lifted his cool, cold eyes to Seth's worried face, waiting calmly for his reply.

Seth licked his lips nervously before replying: "You!" and seeing Joey's eyebrows lift in surprise, continued hurriedly: "Seems 'e's a friend to

Trevarthen an' 'is tryin' to find yer whereabouts, fer 'e says 'e wishes to have speech with 'e."

"About what?"

"Wouldn' say. Jes' said he wished speak to 'e 'cos there was somethin' 'e wished to knaw," and he coughed nervously before adding: "Nobody telled 'en nothin' Joey, fer you knaw you can trust we."

He thought Joey was not to say anything, but slowly he moved into the light and looked down into Seth's worried face. Smiling grimly, Joey sighed and then said: " 'Ess, I knaw you boys wouldn' cut me throat, Seth." Then, clapping him gently on the shoulder, he asked how things were with them all, as he had not seen them in an age.

Looking worriedly up and down the street, Seth finally leaned forward and whispered hoarsely to Joey, "Likky got a job in 'and Joey, an' there's a fair few of they fools goin' to 'elp 'im with it."

"Yer not one of 'em I take it, Seth?"

"Damn right I idden, fer I told 'en I didden trust no one but you with me life, Joey. Likky's drinkin' 'ard an' 'e'll lose sight of what 'e's about if 'e idden careful," he hissed. Then looked over his shoulder again, lest someone should appear of a sudden.

"Drinkin' 'ard you say?"

" 'Ess and damn me if I d' knaw 'ow 'e can afford it, 'cos 'e must be as low in the pockets as the res' of we." Seth sighed and shook his head, before grasping Joey by the hand and avowing he and the others would have a care what they were about with the stranger. After confirming that Joey wished no more of him, he breathed deeply with relief and hurried on his way.

Joey watched as he disappeared out of the alleyway, but he stood for a long while in silent contemplation before saying softly, under his breath:

" 'Ess, Seth, an' I d' wonder where Likky is gettin' 'is money from the same as you. But the difference is, I fear I d' knaw." Turning abruptly on his heel, he headed back towards the harbour and, regaining his post, settled down to watch the stranger once again.

Joey observed the man shrug his shoulders resignedly and turn to leave, then followed him back to where he had stabled his horses and watched as he had them harnessed to his curricle. He turned away after seeing all he wished to see and headed off, using every short cut available in the direction of his own house. That he should have to travel across Penzance was in no way surprising, for his residence lay across the town in the poorer area and the stranger had stabled his equipage at Penzance's finest inn, a far more salubrious establishment than Joey's beast had ever seen the inside of.

Finally, when a myriad of ostlers had finished their work with the man's horses and his equipage, he tossed remuneration of no mean value to all of them. They pulled their respective forelocks in enraptured thanks and advised him of their best endeavours should ever he call again, before retiring to the stables in delight, to remark upon their good fortune at having a gentleman so keen to distribute his largesse in their establishment.

Bowling along the road to Trevu, Peter Fleetwood could not keep the frown from his face and told himself what a fool he had been to think he could arrive amongst the fishermen, introducing himself as an old friend of Paul

Trevarthen, and expect them to confide in him. Naturally, the men would assume that in some way Paul had sent him to locate this Joseph Bolitho, perhaps to finish him off for the shame he had brought upon the Trevarthen household. He wondered idly how he was to find the fellow if these men would not be forthcoming with him. As he took the corner where the road narrowed, his thoughts were driven from his mind as he caught sight of a tall man sitting astride a sweating horse, which stood resolutely full-square in his way.

He swore loudly and struggled to bring his team to a halt in time, for it was most apparent that the man had no intention of moving. He found himself sweating as profusely as the stranger's horse, for he only just managed to stop his team from cannoning into the obstruction.

"Damn you!" shouted Peter, desperately trying to control the frightened pair that were now threatening to kick over the traces, for they were high spirited and easily excitable.

"Have a care what you are about fellow, for your stupidity could have caused a most serious accident!" he said in an indignant tone, before finally lifting his eyes to the face of the man who still sat solidly astride his horse, so quietly and without concern.

Peter Fleetwood had spent many years in the diplomatic service, had been trained to look at the demeanour of any man and to recognise within it all that there was to see. In this man's face he noticed his features: the colour of his hair, his cold eyes, the firm set of his lips, the way he sat his horse. But most of all he noticed the lack of expression. Unlike his friend, he immediately recognised in it something that Paul had never been able to see.

"You bin' lookin' fer me?" asked the man slowly and dispassionately. Even the sound of his voice, so different in its accent but so similar in tone, brought back to Peter's ears the echo of another's, now long departed.

"Oh my God!" proclaimed Peter, feeling a shiver run down his spine. Summoning up the courage of his convictions, he said: "I presume that I am addressing Mr Joseph Bolitho. And if it indeed be the case, sir, I cannot tell you how much pleasure it gives me to see you, for the very sight of you has brought a great relief to my troubled mind." He descended from his curricle and tethered the reins of the quietened pair to a hawthorn stump in the hedge, before striding forward with his hand outstretched towards the forbidding man, who sat still and regarded him so coldly.

CHAPTER 22

JOSEPH Bolitho, finding an elegant hand extended towards him, frowned, for he was not sure that he wished to shake the stranger's hand. But he was puzzled by the man's attitude towards him for he expressed no fear. If he was acting in an official capacity, as he supposed him to be, he certainly bore none of the hallmarks of a man from the Preventative's Office. He appeared to be in a most friendly attitude of mind and so Bolitho leaned forward and grasped the hand lightly. He was surprised by the man's enthusiastic handshake and his delighted smile as he introduced himself, before saying happily:

"Well, Mr Bolitho, 'tis many a year since I made use of the inns in these parts. Correct me if I assume wrongly, but is there not a most fine establishment about two miles in . . ." and he caressed his chin whilst he mused for a moment, "in that direction," and he pointed across the fields towards the little hamlet of Trewint.

"There is, Mr Fleetwood, sir, but 'twas not to 'elp you find an inn that I made efforts to stop 'e," announced Joey threateningly for, unsure as he was, he did not wish to be cajoled into a false sense of security by the jovial visage that regarded him.

"I can well imagine that it was not the case, sir. But unless you wish me to talk about your..." here he paused and regarded Joey with an excited and amused expression on his face, "...relation on the common highway, I think it best we depart for this establishment. For judging by the look on your face and the feeling within myself, we have much need of some alcoholic fortifications." He had almost burst out laughing when the poor fellow jumped at the mention of the word 'relation', but Peter had controlled his features admirably, mentally noting how useful a life in the diplomatic office could become in the hurly-burly of the real world.

"Tie your horse on the back and climb aboard with me," he commanded. Then he turned back to his curricle, collected his reins and, climbing back into his equipage, waiting patiently for Joey to follow his instructions, watching with glee as he noticed a flicker of Paul's mulish expression cross the man's face. But, slowly and hesitatingly, the man did as he was told and, as soon as he was seated beside him, Peter cracked his whip over the horses heads and they sprang forward. When he reached the fork in the road for Trevu, he turned away and in no time they drew up in front of a fine alehouse. Upon entering the inn, Peter requested a private room. On sight of the bills that were flashed under the landlord's nose, his wife and her sister found themselves evicted from the front parlour and deposited in the kitchen without ceremony. Noting the knowing look in her husband's eye, the landlady announced to her sister that this sort of thing happened most frequently, for the gentry were most fond of their humble establishment. Had she known that one of her visitors - now ensconced before the fire in her best parlour - was none other than the notorious Joseph Bolitho, she might not have been so happy to oblige her husband. But she was well aware that money was to be no object, for the gentleman had asked for two tankards of good ale and a bottle of the finest brandy, along with two glasses and a tureen of her best soup with fresh bread.

The two men sat in silence whilst the landlord and serving maid busied themselves with fulfilling their client's orders. The landlord received his payment immediately and blinked gratefully at the largesse pressed into his hand, for he had made more in this one transaction than he had done with all his trade of the past week - and it had been by no means a poor time. The serving maid received a coin of her very own along with a wink and a wicked glance from the gentleman dispensing the money, so gave him her thanks, along with a saucy smile as she departed in the landlord's wake.

"Damn me, Joey," he announced, "I've always said there are some damn pretty maidens in this part of the world and I have seen a fair few of the finest, I can tell you."

His guest regarded him without expression but had nothing to say, so Peter took a sip of his brandy and smacked his lips together in appreciation.

"My God, this is a most fine vintage! Try some, Joey, I think you'll be most impressed with it," he urged enthusiastically.

"Possibly," responded Joey dourly, "fer I sold it to 'em."

Peter tried hard to control his expression, but it went from shock to amusement and he tilted back his head and roared with laughter. His glee was infectious and even his guest allowed a small smile to play upon his lips. Noticing it, Peter announced that he was pleased to see his new acquaintance had a sense of humour at least. He got up and quietly opened the door to ensure that no one was listening in the hallway before returning to his seat. Then, picking up his spoon and bowl of soup, he blew on the steaming concoction and began to eat. Joey watched him warily, but he had not eaten since morning and felt in need of sustenance himself, so began to eat tentatively. His eyes never left his companion's face and all the while his mind was engrossed in his attempts to understand this strange man's behaviour towards him. It was obvious that indeed he did know Paul and knew him well, to see in himself his likeness to his brother. No other could have told him of it unless he had acquired his knowledge from Caroline Crebo. A frown creased his brow as he tried to fathom exactly what is was that the man knew, and from whom he had acquired his information, and more importantly what it was he thought to obtain from him.

As soon as they had finished eating, Peter filled their glasses again, then sat back and breathed a sigh of satisfaction before resting his gaze on Joey's fathomless face.

"My God, man!" he exclaimed, "but you have such a look of your father about you with that expression on your face, 'tis most uncanny!" Then, abruptly, he asked: "Paul has no knowledge of it, I presume?"

Joey shook his head and Peter nodded.

"Mmm, I thought not, else why would he make such a cake of himself?" Not expecting an answer, he continued with barely a pause: "Do you intend to tell him, for 'tis this knowledge that I presume you described as your 'secret' when Paul surprised you holding hands with his wife?"

Joey nodded and tilted his chin up, before replying severely: "You seem to 'ave great knowledge yerself, sir, of what occurred?"

"Years in the diplomatic corps, Joey. That teaches a man to find the story behind the words, don't you know? Still, wouldn't expect a fool like Paul to think his way through it. Hasty tempered fellow, always was, and innocent as the day is long. Yes, my God, known him since his early twenties and he was as big a fool then as he is now. Hear you took a thrashing from him too, so don't suppose he gave you much opportunity to explain yourself, did he?"

Once again Joey shook his head, and said tersely: "Wouldn' listen to either of we. Silly beggar was that mad. Mind you, I was fair enraged meself fer 'e treated Mrs Trevarthen badly. I only went fer 'en 'cos 'e upped an' slapped the poor liddle soul."

Peter winced and said feelingly: "He can be an ugly tempered devil when he is angered, although most times he will control himself, but then I suppose it was a bit of a shock to him to see you talking so . . . er... closely." Lifting his astute eyes to Joey's, he waited patiently for an explanation.

Joey looked uncomfortable, but after a moment cleared his throat and explained the situation that had arisen between himself and his lady friend, and how he had come to Trevu with the intention of seeking his brother's assistance. And how, upon realising the futility of it, had decided to leave again.

"Mrs Trevarthen wished me to tell 'en who I am, fer she said if 'e knew of it 'e would do 'is best to 'elp me, but tidden that easy, Mr Fleetwood." He then proceeded to explain to his companion various details of his sordid past that affected or involved Paul.

"My God, Joey, you've had an exciting life and no mistake, man!" Peter exclaimed, smiling, then placed his fingertips together and thought long and hard.

"Well, there is only one answer to it." Noting Joey's enquiring look, he stated, baldly: "He'll have to be told, but how to tell him? That is the problem. He is in a foul mood with Chloe, for all her letters are thrown on the fire unopened, but she would be the very one to tell him."

"Easy enough to say, Mr Fleetwood, sir, but even I, with all my contacts 'ave no knowledge of 'er whereabouts."

"London!" announced Peter firmly, "The servants have told me Paul sent her to London, to his mother's old home. Big house, plenty of servants, he's made sure she had got more than enough money for her needs. He's been most thorough, don't you know." He pondered again for such a long time that Joey shifted uneasily in his seat, when suddenly Peter sprang to his feet shouting: "Eureka! Aha, Joey! I know what I have to do and I shall not hesitate to do it." He turned quickly to face Bolitho and smiled gleefully at him, before asking him if he could keep himself away from Paul for a while longer.

" 'Twould not be a problem, Mr Fleetwood, fer 'e'll not 'ave me on the place, although I am determined to see 'im an' I will, but I 'ave stayed my 'and 'til I could see the bes' way to do it. I couldn' abide to cause more trouble to either of 'em see, Mr Fleetwood, sir, fer it has never been my intent to wreck his life. I lie awake nights with the misery I 'ave brought upon both of 'em, fer 'twas not the way I wished that particular day to go," he said sadly.

"I know, man, I know," and Peter gripped him firmly by the shoulder before giving him an encouraging shake, stating: "Patience, Joey, a little patience and I think all will come right. Now, there are two more things that must be done."

Joey lifted his brows at him in silent enquiry.

"Firstly, we must finish this most excellent brandy," he announced and filled their glasses.

"An' the second, sir?" asked Joey with a hesitant smile.

"The second?" asked Peter in surprise, "Ah yes, the second, Joey. You will do just as your brother has always done."

"Sir?" said Joey, confused. Then, finding himself with Peter's extended hand thrust towards him, heard his cheerful, easy voice say: "Why, you will call me Peter, of course," and this time Joey shook hands with the man as if he had been his oldest friend.

Peter arrived at Trevu late in the evening. Paul would have asked him where he had spent his day, but his life was so wrapped around with his own troubles that he cared little for how others entertained themselves, so his friend was spared the necessity of an explanation. It was apparent that Peter had been drinking, but this was not an unusual occurrence for he had a great love of alcohol. In the past, the two friends had often frequented the local inns and whiled away a pleasant evening therein. However, even in Paul's uncaring state he was still surprised to be told that Peter wished to leave on the morrow.

"I suppose, all things considered, my company is not what it was used to be," said Paul, abruptly.

"Well, you have not been at your friendliest, that is for sure, but after what you have told me I admit that one could not expect you to be at your most companionable," said Peter with a sigh.

"I have not told you all, Peter," announced Paul in a quiet voice.

"Well, come on, old friend, unburden yourself and let me hear what is it you wish to tell me." Sitting down in the chair by the fire, he waited patiently for Paul's next revelation.

Slowly and shamefully Paul told him what had occurred on Chloe's last night in the house. Even saying the word caused him pain for, of all the treatment she had received at his hands that day, he knew that deed to be the foulest and the most unforgivable.

When he had finished he looked up at his friend's face, whose expression made him quickly lower his head again.

"My God, Paul! How could you do such a thing? Only the lowest blaggard could commit such an horrific act upon any woman!" Peter cried in disgust.

"I know! I know, for God's sake! I cannot forgive myself for it. She did not deserve that for all the disaster she has brought upon me by her own uncontrollable lust," and he hid his face in his hands.

"Pray to God that she can one day forgive you, Paul, for of all the people you have hurt, you have need of her forgiveness above all!" Peter rose from his chair and hurriedly left the room, slamming the door behind him and leaving his old friend to wallow in his shame alone.

Early the next morning he left, after taking an almost silent breakfast with his subdued host. They had few words of farewell and Peter lost no time in cracking his whip at his steeds when departing from Trevu, as if his greatest desire was to shake the dust of the place from off his heels as quickly as was practicable.

Later that morning, a letter from Aunt Caroline was placed on Paul's desk. When he read it, his eyes opened wide at her request. Picking up pen and paper, he wrote hurriedly that he had no wish to receive a visit from her. And that, if she could not communicate her sentiments to him by letter, then she would not be given the opportunity to discuss them with him face to face, for he did not desire her presence in his house. Then he added for good measure that she was not to expect the carriage, 'for 'twould not be calling for her in either the near or distant future'. Sealing his letter, he called to Beth to make sure that it caught the post from Penzance, then stamped angrily away to his study, where he sat and looked at his Latin text before picking up the blameless book and hurling it across the room in temper.

"I can't get Seth to go, but I 'ave all the others," said Likky to the closed door.

"That's all right, Likky," came the muffled reply, "and Bolitho has no knowledge of what is afoot?"

"No, none at all sir," replied Likky proudly. The door opened a fraction and a small purse was passed out through the narrow opening. Likky snatched it gratefully, for he had a great thirst upon him.

"Thankee, sir, thankee." But there was no reply and he assumed, correctly, that the man had departed.

Likky had gone down but a few alleys from home when he noticed Bolitho standing with his back to a wall, nonchalantly regarding his approach.

"Af'noon, Likky," Joey said with a smile.

"Af'noon, Joey," Likky replied warily.

"Got much on?" he enquired conversationally.

"Who me? No, Joey, no I 'aven't!" he announced nervously, then enquired of Joey, "You?"

"No, me neither," replied Joey easily.

"Well, I'd bes' be goin' on then," said Likky before adding, "Cheerio, Joey!"

"Cheerio, Likky! See 'e roun'," and he nodded his head to him before moving slowly up the alley and away towards the town.

That night, Macgregor's man met Likky in the inn at Newlyn and told him the times that he would need to know in order to arrange the collection and transportation of the shipment. On the way out of the inn, the two men, having imbibed freely of liquor, almost fell over a dirty, smelly old tramp. He sat huddled on the floor by the open door, drinking from a broken jar that the landlord had kindly tipped some ale into from a discarded tankard. They kicked him viciously and laughed as he grunted in pain and indignation.

"Get out me way, ya filthy bastard!" shouted the seaman, kicking him again for good measure when he did not move fast enough to clear their path. They walked back towards the road for Penzance, arm in arm and in high good humour with themselves. Neither of them noticed as the tramp lifted his filthy face, and a pair of cold, calculating blue eyes watched their every step.

A week later and the self same laughing seaman and others from the little boat, along with all of Likky's band of men, were rounded up by a large group of preventative men with hardly a shot being fired. They were easily accosted for the full moon could not hide their actions in the sandy little cove. Bolitho, holding his horse by the reins, stood in the shadow of an overhanging rock looking on dispassionately. He noted that one of them was making his way unhindered from the scene, and knew him by his walk, for they had been friends since boyhood. Likky had escaped and made his way back to the security of Penzance and to his own home, but within two hours he entered a disused cottage and found a purse and a cask of brandy, illuminated by the moonlight, on the broken chair by the window. He lifted his head as he heard a familiar voice call his name.

"Remember, Likky: to Trevu with it. Hide it in the lower barn, where they keep their old harness. When you have done it, return to your home straightway, for I do not wish you abroad tonight. Meet me here at nine of the clock tomorrow morning and tell me if you have accomplished it, for I would know it safely hidden. And remember, Likky, not a word to Bolitho, mind!"

"No, sir, I'll not say a word, sir."

"There's some extra for you today, for well I know how hard you have worked on my behalf and you have deserved it. Now I must away and list the men I have in the lock up, for without their names I can make no charges against them," and Likky heard a low chuckle that turned his blood to ice. Now he was alone, holding tightly to the purse in one hand with the cask under his other arm. After taking a quick look outside of the cottage he made his way hurriedly to the stables. Acquiring a horse, he strapped on the bundle wrapped in his course jacket and paid the hire of the beast, before spurring the ungainly animal in the direction of Trevu. He rounded the corner where the patch of undergrowth grew around the trees by the unconcealed pathway and, like his provider before him, did not see the tall man gazing at the road from within the midst of the green, twisted foliage. Within an hour, Likky's mission was accomplished He returned minus his bundle and headed back along the road from Penzance, the thought of the alcohol he would now be able to consume with the money in his purse uppermost in his mind. Mindful of Hudson's message not to roam abroad, he decided to buy himself a bottle of brandy on his way homewards. After all, a drink could be enjoyed wherever one found oneself, he surmised happily.

Fifteen minutes later, Joey Bolitho sat his horse at the fork in the road leading to Trevu and pondered the problems that faced him. He had promised Peter Fleetwood that he would not attempt to see Paul. So to go to Trevu now, boldly demanding entrance, would not be the wisest course for him to follow. In all probability, Paul would refuse to see him - if he did not attempt to start another fight - and more importantly his men would have been told to have nothing to do with him, so he would not have a chance to tell either Paul or any workman of his suspicions. Hudson wished there to be contraband hidden on Paul's property, to be found at a later date no doubt. It was obvious to Joey that this was then to be used as evidence of his brother's involvement in the smuggling trade. He needed to warn Paul that Hudson had not forgotten his hatred for him and was determined to have him pulled down. That the Customs Officer wished to do the same in his own case did not bother him. When the time came, he would be able to act in his own defence and he was quite prepared to forget his promise to his brother that he would never kill again. He sighed and considered some more, for then there were the men that had been taken, all old friends. Bolitho had a plan to set them free but to do that he needed to be in Penzance, not here on the road to Trevu. Suddenly, inspiration came to him, for he knew where to go to save his brother. He spurred his horse on away from the road to Trevu and headed at a gallop towards Bert Pendray's cottage. He stopped some way from the building and waited patiently for the person he wanted to see. Joey had not long to wait and as the light dimmed in the cottage window, the door opened and he heard whispered voices. After a moment he could make out the figure of a man making his way slowly down the road towards him, so he hissed his name. The man started, surprised to be accosted and even more astonished as he realised just whom it was who had called his name.

An hour later, in Penzance, walking up the alley towards the darkened cottage he considered how best to wake the man. Finding an old discarded besom by the side wall, he picked it up and made his way to the back of the building, then began to tap vigorously on the window of the linney.

After a moment the window was pushed open and a voice shouted angrily: "What the 'ell do 'e think yer doing, you beggars. This 'idden no place fer a ³shalall, you fools!"

"Seth!" hissed the man softly.

"Joey!" came the surprised reply, "What you doin' 'ere?"

"Come down 'ere. I got talk to 'e. S'important so be quick, man!" ordered Bolitho in an urgent whisper.

As quickly as he could manage, Seth threw on his clothes and after a whispered explanation to his wife, picked his way over his sleeping children and made his way to the back door, leading to the small yard set on to the back of his house. As soon as Seth stepped outside into the cool night air, he felt his arm grabbed and he was pulled away from the house, soon finding himself at the bottom of the alley.

"Whasamatter, Joey?" he asked, still half asleep.

Joey cast a swift look up and down the alley, before turning to Seth's worried face and saying bluntly: " 'Udson's got all of Likky's boys. Took 'em all cleanly an' a couple of MacGregor's men as well. They're all in the lock up an' the cargo's in the Custom House store."

"Bleddy 'ell!" swore Seth, before asking: "Likky too?"

There was a momentary pause before Joey said quietly: "No . . . No 'e managed to outwit 'em an' got away."

"What 'e goin' do then, Joey, fer there's nothin' can be done fer the poor beggars now if 'Udson's got 'em?"

"I'll 'ave to leave they where they are, but get 'old of as many men that you can trust as soon as you can 'an meet me down by the inn next to the customs place. I'll see to the rest." Joey gave him a little push and disappeared into the dark.

By the time the sun was struggling to rise, all had been accomplished according to Joseph Bolitho's wishes. Seth turned to him with a half smile on his face:

---

3 ³shalall: Riotous celebration by friends and neighbours outside of the bedroom window of a honeymoon couple on their first night together.

"Dammee, Joey, but tha's a neat trick. Pity 'bout all that trade tho', 'twould 'ave gladdened a few 'earts. What 'e want me do now?"

"Go home, Seth, an' should anyone come a' callin' make out you 'ave 'ad a night of uninterrupted sleep. Warn Esme not to say anythin'," Joey informed him.

"Don't 'e worry 'bout the missus. 'Er family bin' smugglin' all their lives - she'll keep 'er mouth shut," and he grinned and waved a hand in farewell before returning to his home.

Joey watched him depart and yawned slowly, for he was most tired. He had had no sleep since the previous day, but he knew where he would be able to snatch a couple of hours of rest at the very least, so headed purposefully away.

Likky stumbled noisily into the dusty room, knocking against a discarded shovel and bringing it crashing down on to a broken chair lying on its side. A dog began to bark outside. Skewes, annoyed by the sound of it, looked around and found a loose stone in the wall, then pulled it out and, opening the door, glanced up and down the alley until he had spotted the noisy animal. He threw his missile expertly, which caught the poor canine in his painfully thin body. The dog let out a loud yelp as it felt the stone's hard impact in its ribs and hastily retreated to a safer part of town. Likky laughed at the sight and then turned away. Testing a bench to see if it would take his weight, he grunted approvingly and sat down heavily, calmly awaiting the arrival of his benefactor. He had not long to wait, for a man's footsteps could be heard approaching the front of the cottage. Suddenly, the door was pushed open and the tall man stooped his head and entered the cottage, smiling at Likky as he did so.

"All done, Likky?" Hudson asked, an oily grin on his full, loose lips.

Hastily Skewes stood up and removed his hat as his employer advanced into the room.

" 'Ess, sir, jes' the way you wanted," replied Likky, with no small note of pride in his voice, for he did not believe that even Joey could have arranged for all to go as smoothly as the work he had accomplished the previous night.

"Good! Good!" exclaimed Hudson, before adding softly: "and you have told no one of your extra mission for me last night and of our meeting here today?"

"Dammee no, sir, fer I d' knaw 'ow keep me mouth shut," he replied smugly. Noticing the man's look of approval, he smiled broadly. The smile became wider as the officer reached inside of his coat and withdrew another leather purse - considerably larger than the one he had received on the previous evening - and held it aloft.

"For you, Likky." Hudson smiled broadly himself as he watched Likky hurriedly head towards him with his hand outstretched towards his booty. As he reached him there was a flash of silver, Likky grunted and fell forward before ever he had the chance to take hold his prize, for now he needed both his hands to attempt to hold back the blood that was pouring from his chest.

As he pitched onto the dust of the floor he heard the man swear angrily: "Damn! I have his filthy blood on my hand!" Hudson took out his handkerchief and fastidiously wiped it away before discarding it. Stained and crumpled, it fluttered to the ground and lay beside the poor man's body, as the door closed firmly behind the departing assassin. There was silence for barely a moment. Then the broken door leading to the tiny space that had once served as the house's larder fell forward and thumped to the floor. The man concealed behind it hastened to the body lying inanimate in the dust.

"Likky! Likky, my old pal!" he called urgently. He fell on his knees and gently turned the body, then lifted him into his arms and carefully brushed the dirt from his contorted face.

"Aah!" cried poor Likky as the pain increased, "Joey! Aah, Joey, my 'ansome! See what the bastard 'as done to me?"

"I knaw, Likky, I knaw," he said and his tears coursed unheeded down his face as he cradled his dying friend in his arms.

"We . . .still . . . pals . . . Joey?" his companion stuttered anxiously.

"Course we are, you bleddy fool!" answered Joey on a sob, "Fer I never 'ad none better then 'e, Likky, all my life long."

Likky smiled and felt his pain ebbing away as he looked up into Joey's concerned face, then a worried frown appeared between his brows and he asked: "Mother, Joey? Wha's to 'appen ....?"

"I'll take care of 'er, don't 'e worry 'bout that Likky. She'll want fer nothing an' I shall tell 'er to be always proud of 'e," he promised faithfully.

"But . . .I done a bad thing, Joey. Fer... fergive . . . me, fer I was took in by greed fer money an' anger at you fer . . . fer . . ." and Likky swallowed hard on the warm blood that was filling his mouth.

"Ferget it, Likky, 'tis not important now," whispered Joey reassuringly. Then, grimly smiling down at Likky's relieved face, he said earnestly: "I'll get the bastard fer 'e, Likky, I'll get 'en, pard', fer what 'e's done to you."

"Joey, thankee. Thankee fer all you bin' to me an' fer all you..." but his last words remained unspoken as his life's blood drained away from him and his body slumped lifelessly.

Joey, on his knees in the dust, pulled the dead man towards him. He held him fast in his arms and with his head bowed rocked him gently to and fro, as if encouraging a fractious child to sleep, crooning his name softly over and over again.

.

CHAPTER 23

THERE had never been a guard placed on the door where the illicit goods were stored at the Customs House, for in most cases the men who had handled those self same goods were themselves locked away. As it was situated on the ground floor of this imposing establishment, at the bottom end of one side of the building along a dark passage, it was thought unnecessary. The padlock was still in place and its key dangled as usual from the guard's belt, so no one felt the least concern regarding the safety of the items that were kept from time to time in the room. The men that had been captured were still safely imprisoned in the town's lock up, so the horror felt by the guard as he opened the door - to add three casks of geneva that had been found floating in the harbour at Lamorna that morning to the contents already stored - knew no bounds when he could find not one cask left from Mr Hudson's most successful raid ever. So amazed was he that he pulled the door shut and opened it again, in the desperate hope that what he had not been able to see the first time should mysteriously reappear. There was no magician on hand to help him, however, and only an empty space stared forlornly back at him. Hurriedly, he left the men holding that morning's meagre catch, turned towards the stairway that faced away from the almost empty space and raced up the stairs to an office on the first floor, shouting over his shoulder that they were to make sure that no one went into the room.

He knocked loudly on Mr Hudson's door, but when he entered he wished himself in any other place than the one in which he stood.

"Well, Carveth, what is it, man?" barked Hudson angrily.

" 'Tis gone, sir," he announced simply.

"Gone! What's gone, you fool?"

"Tuesday's goods, sir! All that we took up from Winnerd's Cove!" the guard said quickly, believing that the sooner the disastrous news was uttered the sooner his torment was to be over.

"What!" shouted Hudson, his florid face growing red in temper and his bulging eyes almost starting from their sockets in shock. He stood up so quickly that his chair tipped over and clattered on to the floor behind him. Not caring, he pushed the guard aside and fled the room, taking the stairs two at a time. Finally, he stood in the middle of the cellar and stared around at its depleted contents, unable to fathom what had happened.

Arthur Carveth hastily followed him into the room, explaining as he did so: "I unlocked the door sir, to put in the Lamorna goods we obtained this morning and 'twas all gone sir, every one of them." He cast a swift look at his commanding officer's face and took a prudent step backwards at the sight of it.

"Who has keys to this room?" Hudson bellowed.

"Why, only me and yourself, sir, and I keep my keys about my person at all times," Carveth uttered as stoutly as he felt he was capable of doing, for his legs were shaking beneath him.

"Are you implying that I do not?" Hudson glowered down at the terrified guard.

"No, sir. No, sir! I only meant for you to know what great care I do take of them sir!" He gulped as his superior grabbed him by the throat and began to shake him violently, before casting him aside in disgust.

Hudson paced up and down the room, until finally he turned and faced the cowering guard once more.

"Assemble the men, every damn one!" And as the poor fellow hastened to obey his command, shouted after him as if he needed to be told: "And be quick about it, man!"

Running as fast as he could, a rising annoyance grew within him for it was obvious that Mr Hudson himself had mislaid his keys. Most unfairly it was to his door that the blame was to be laid for the catastrophe that had befallen the service. Carveth was never to know that his liking for a certain Polly Vingoe, a rather buxom damsel, who had often entertained him on many a lonely night, could have helped to explain the remarkable disappearance of the casks. This delightfully obliging female had been instructed some time ago to make a wax impression of both of his keys, by another more exciting man that she habitually shared her favours with. So, when the poor guard had been under the influence of her attentions and the rather strong brew with which she plied him, her skilful fingers had carried out her secret work. Many a blissful night, spent fast asleep in her arms, had been his reward for providing Joseph Bolitho with the only other set of keys to the cellar, that was kept so dutifully locked at all times.

When the men were assembled, Hudson stood before them and issued his orders. The prisoners in the lock up were to have their homes searched from top to bottom, along with three others: Seth Mankee, Likky Skewes and last but not least, Joseph Bolitho. The men muttered amongst themselves at the burden imposed upon them, for sixteen men had been picked up that night and all but two of them had homes in the locality. With the additional houses to search they were set for a strenuous time.

"And search thoroughly, men, for I will have nothing missed, every part of every house, every outbuilding if they have them. Tap every wall, pull up the floorboards and heave off the thatch if you have to, but I will find this stolen brandy and when I do, they will pay again for their outrageous behaviour towards the law!" He slapped his whip angrily against his boot, slammed his hat on his head and led his men away towards the town. They searched diligently as instructed and suffered the hoots and catcalls of many a disgusted wife as her home was turned into a shambles. Esme Mankee swore at them as she gathered her children around her skirts and threatened them most vilely, but the men were more afraid of Hudson then anyone else they had encountered in the little houses, so they searched on. In Likky's house, his mother was unable to see the destruction that they caused; her neighbours had returned after the troop of men had departed and patched the thatch that had been displaced, returned the furniture to an upright position and swept away the shards of the broken pots. Sitting in her chair, her sightless eyes looking upon a different scene, she stroked Likky's old battered hat and merely said: "I'm some proud of 'en, some proud," over and over again. Her neighbours shook their heads and tapped their foreheads significantly, before one of them placed a bowl of hot broth in her hands and left her quite alone.

At Joseph Bolitho's house even the bravest hesitated, but when it was realised that there was no one at home they burst in with false bravado and took each room apart. Bolitho had few possessions, but what he did have were either broken or ripped and Hudson took a sadistic pleasure in destroying, or overseeing the destruction, of everything he came across. But like every other house that they had searched that morning, it was devoid of the treasure they sought. They left the door swinging on its hinges and returned, dejected, to their base. On the way they were subjected to much derision; one unfortunate fellow was hit on the head by a flying kettle and staggered under the blow, which sight only added to the laughter directed at them.

Back at the Customs House, Hudson dismissed the men angrily and stomped up the stairs to his office, then sat moodily regarding the window that gave him a view of the road along the harbour side. His eyes widened with interest as he watched Joseph Bolitho walk nonchalantly up the road, but he smiled grimly as he thought of what he would find when he returned to his home. He had an impulse to follow him but thought better of it, for he remembered dismally that the letter to Sir Reginald Bonython had already been delivered, which informed him of Hudson's glorious success at Winnerd's Cove and hinted at even more triumph to come. Gerald Hudson had no knowledge of the manner in which Bolitho had achieved his aim, but he was convinced that it was to his door that the blame was to be laid for the missing casks. Following him now would be falling into his trap, for he had no doubt that Bolitho had timed his walk past the Customs House in the full knowledge that he would be seen and, having been seen, would be followed.

"Well, damn you, Bolitho, I'm not going to do it!" ranted the officer to himself. And so he sat on, moodily staring at the wall, forgetting even to return home for his lunch.

Jonas walked away from Paul's office and decided there and then that he would not go, but would send his deputy in his place. It was about time the lad learnt how to negotiate with the farmers over rents and disagreements between them and the estate office, and there was none wilier than old Percy Eustace for trying to obtain more than was his due. He smiled as he imagined poor Nicholas Greep having to contend with Percy; his sighs and head scratching, whilst all the while complaining of his poor harvests and telling him that his ground "wouldn' fittee 'nuff fer growin' nothin' but stones" and he with some of the best land in the parish!

Returning to the building on the end of the barn that served as his own office, he smiled at the youth and informed him what it was that he wished him to do that afternoon. Young Greep's face paled, but he nodded, then sat down and listened studiously as Jonas emphasised just what he would be allowed to offer Percy and exactly at which point he was to refuse any more. The boy announced that he would follow his instructions to the letter and within an hour was on his way across the fields towards this old adversary's farm. He felt a mixture of trepidation, excitement and pride, for never before had he been charged to undertake such a responsibility on his own.

Meanwhile, Jonas offered to take the mail into Penzance as he had some business to conduct there, so he saddled his bay mare and made his way into the town. He partook of a frugal lunch in the inn before deciding to return to Trevu, but by chance he overheard a conversation relating to certain events of the morning. What he heard made him head hastily for Joseph Bolitho's home. The door was still hanging as it had been left by the troop of men and at first he thought the house empty, but as he poked his head inside he saw Joey standing by the remains of his meagre wardrobe, picking up and discarding the ruined clothes one by one.

"Joey, has that man done all this?" he asked in awe as he walked in unannounced, staring around him at the broken furniture and other items that lay strewn round about the floor.

Looking up, Joey's brows furrowed, then he smiled grimly at Jonas. Righting the bench that lay on its side in the middle of the room, he lifted it back and set it against the wall and, finding a piece of the cupboard, wedged it underneath to act as a replacement for its broken leg.

" 'Fraid so, Jonas! Well, 'is men at least. I don't think they 'ave left any piece unbroken in the place. Still," he laughed, "could 'ave bin' worse fer I could 'ave bin' asleep in me bed, an' tha's only good fer firewood now."

He tested his weight on the makeshift repair to the bench and, after announcing that he thought it would hold, offered a seat beside himself to Jonas, who crossed the room and gingerly lowered his body down beside him.

"What's the fellow doing now?" he asked, and correctly interpreting who 'he' would be, Bolitho told him Hudson was in his office and mad as fire into the bargain. He allowed himself a hollow laugh, and proceeded to tell Jonas of the events that had occurred during the night.

"What if he finds the brandy?" asked Jonas worriedly.

"He won't do that, fer 'tis all thrown down a shaft, where no one is goin' find 'em," and then he turned anxiously to Jonas and asked: "You seen to the other one fer me?"

Jonas nodded and said succinctly: "Different shaft tho'," and he grinned.

"I've got a man to watch 'en 'cos his tail's up an' 'e'll be after Paul next, so I need to knaw of 'is movements to warn 'en," said Bolitho, a grim expression on his face.

"Don't be a fool, Joey!" cried Jonas, "For Paul will never let you on the place. I'll warn him for you."

"Tha's a clever idea, Jonas, but I think even Paul might be tempted ask 'ow you come by yer information," he retorted, grinning sardonically at him.

Jonas looked at him nonplussed, for until then it had never occurred to him: Paul would realise that there would be only one person with the knowledge and resources to know of all that was happening in the customs service, apart from Hudson himself.

"Take care, man, for Paul is the one person amongst all of us who could cause the most damage to you and your friends. Let us hope for your sake that you have no need to go," Jonas told him earnestly.

"Oh, I 'ave to go fer 'tis my destiny. [4]Proverbs, chapter 18, verse 24, Jonas, you understand. I 'ave to save 'im from 'Udson's coils if not from 'imself," he said softly. He turned to a bewildered Jonas and asked if he would be prepared to do something of a most serious nature for him and explained exactly what that task would entail. The estate manager looked horrified at what he was being asked to do.

---

[4]A man that hath friends must show himself friendly: and there is a friend that sticketh closer than a brother

"I would do it myself but I think that, maybe, I won't be around to see to it. I knaw 'tis a 'eavy burden I'm asking of 'e, but there's no one left I can turn to," Bolitho said seriously.

Jonas shook his head vehemently, for he could not countenance such a thing, then turned to Joey on a sudden thought and said: "What about Likky?" and noticed the dejected look that came over the smuggler's face.

"Down with the brandy, Jonas, poor soul," and he heaved a great sigh.

The estate manager moistened his lips and asked tentatively if that was some of Joey's work.

"Not all of it, Jonas, I only buried 'en as it were. 'Udson saw 'en out a' this world," and he swore, then spat in disgust onto the dusty floor.

"Why?" puzzled Jonas, "for I thought him his henchman. After all Licky arranged to give the men up to Hudson and 'twas he himself who hid the brandy on Paul's property."

"Tha's right, Jonas, he was. But he was also 'Udson's only witness so he wanted rid of 'en. I should 'ave seen it comin', but even I never thought he would commit such a dastardly act as that," and he swore loudly. After a moment's quiet reflection he turned again to Jonas, smiled his charming smile and said softly and coaxingly: "I idden askin' fer meself, Jonas, you d' knaw that."

When Caroline Crebo had read Chloe's letter for the third time she finally burst into tears, saying: "Oh! The poor, sweet child!" over and over again. Cecily attempted to be of comfort to her but was brusquely told that, as usual, she was of no use whatsoever. Her mother sat down at once and dashed off a briefly worded letter to her nephew, telling him to send his carriage for she wished to call and impart news of great importance to him. When his reply came she looked in danger of suffering a relapse, so drastically did her colour fluctuate, but poor Cecily was once again harangued by her now irate mother and was promptly instructed to send for her husband, for his mother-in-law had great need of him. He arrived looking flustered and very red in the face. When he heard just what it was that his wife's mother required of him he agreed at once, in spite of Cecily's protestations. Being of a practical nature, he foresaw two advantages to her scheme; the one involving Caroline's removal from the locality and the other the restoration of his peaceful lifestyle. He had married his wife for her docile nature, not realising that Mrs Crebo's more robust society would be added to his sedate world as part of the marriage settlements.

So it was that a week later Caroline Crebo, comfortably ensconced in her son-in-law's best carriage, found herself heading in the direction of Trevu, busily working out how best to tell Paul all her news. That her nephew would not be in an accommodating mood to listen to her did not bother her in the slightest, for she had usually been able to handle his more recalcitrant moods. She settled back against the squabs, idly watching the countryside passing by at a sedate pace, and contemplating the actual time of day when she could expect to arrive, when there was a jarring thud and the carriage gave a loud crack before suddenly tipping sideways into the ditch. That she received no hurt physically was remarkable, but her renowned fiery temper was able to be vented, fuelled by the assault upon her dignity, when after some difficulty she was rescued from the inside of the carriage. The coachman and guard hung their heads as she lambasted them most cruelly. They attempted to explain that the broken axle was not a fault that could be laid at their door, but she would have none of it. As they were in open countryside they would have need of both a conveyance for their passenger and assistance to mend the axle and damaged wheel. So the guard was dispatched to find the first of their requirements, for Mrs Crebo was not of an age that she wished to be left standing on the highway. When help arrived, she suffered the indignity of being carried to a local hostelry on the back of a farm cart that smelt suspiciously of pigs, but by this time she was almost beyond care. Fortunately, she was met at the inn by a most understanding landlord and his wife: a humble woman of great kindness, or so thought Caroline. It was not long before some restorative tea and any amount of comforts that she required were offered to her. After a most delicious repast, she mellowed somewhat and only blanched when she was told that it would take another two hours for the carriage to be made ready for the road again. After the allotted time she set forth, along with some hot bricks and a small hamper packed with some delicious pastries that the landlady had baked that very afternoon, especially for Mrs Crebo's delectation.

Sitting back once again in the comfort of the carriage, she sighed heavily, for the afternoon was well to fore and she realised with exasperation that she would not arrive at Trevu until well into the evening.

"Let us hope Paul has dined well," she said to herself, "for with my news methinks he might lose his appetite somewhat!" And she settled back once more to enjoy the second half of her journey, fervently hoping that it would prove less eventful than the first part had been.

The children had dined with their father, the meal consumed in almost total silence as usual, and when they had finished they dutifully said goodnight and filed quietly from the room. Paul studied the port but did not wish for any, so he rose from the table and left Beth to clear the away the remains of the meal. In the evenings he now sat in isolation in the large, lonely withdrawing room, for the back parlour held too many memories for him and he never used it now. He preferred to stay in total silence amidst the cold splendour of one of the largest rooms in the house, for here his memories did not crowd in on him so painfully. They would not stay away from him completely, for no matter how hard he tried her face came to him at every hour of the day. And when he took to his lonely bed, his longing for her clawed at his body. Unable to forgive her still, Peter's visit had unsettled him enough that he had gone over and over in his mind Bolitho's words to her, trying to see another meaning. But he could find no other reason than his original conclusion. Perhaps Joey had used his charm on her, and innocent as she was, she had turned away from her husband because of the smuggler's appeal and the quality of excitement that always seemed to be around him. The way she looked at Bolitho as he looked down into her face, her smile with its almost pleading look - did the fellow so taunt her with his desire that she had almost to beg him to love her in return? Unable to find an explanation, he got up and wandered into the library to find a book. He returned some minutes later with one in his hand and closed the door quietly behind himself, before resuming his seat on the settle and commencing, half-heartedly to read.

"Good evenin', Paul," said a familiar voice from behind him.

Paul jumped to his feet, throwing down his book and turned wrathfully to face the intruder.

"How the hell ...?!" he began to ask.

"Through the window," came the calm reply as Joey strode across the room. Paul swung back his arm, but it was grasped in a firm grip and twisted so that his arm was held tightly behind his back. He tried to move it, but it was contorted painfully, then Bolitho's other arm came around his chest and held him tight.

"You will listen this time, Paul, fer I will not leave until you do," the hated voice hissed in his ear. "Now, we 'ave two choices: I can 'old you tight like this until I 'ave finished what I 'ave come to say or we can sit an' face each other an' talk man to man. 'Tis fer you to decide."

Paul tried to struggle but his strength had dissipated since he had sent his wife away, and he was at least a stone lighter than when the two men had last fought. He had barely left his house and rarely rode or indulged in much physical recreation, but although not a weakling, the man who held him pinioned had still all his strength and the advantage of him. After some futile struggling he realised that he would gain nothing so, breathing heavily, he said in cold anger:

"Very well, you blaggard, it shall be as you wish. But nothing you have to say will alter my attitude either to you or to . . . to her!" Almost as soon as the words had left his mouth he was released and Joey stood away from him.

Paul spun around and looked at him, his face seething with anger. But Bolitho seemed not in the least perturbed and walked in front of him, then nonchalantly sat down on the settle and calmly waited for Paul to do the same. After standing his ground for a moment, he stamped to his seat and sat down sulkily. Joey could not help smiling at him in spite of himself.

"Have you come here to laugh at me for the tragedy you have caused to my life?" snapped Paul.

"You caused yer own disaster, Paul, fer you wouldn' listen to either of we, so determined you were to believe what you 'ad thought you'd seen," Joey told him calmly.

"I am well aware just what it was that was being paraded in front of my eyes when I saw you both, and hearing your words only served to confirm it," he told him coldly.

"Your wife was never in love with me, Paul," Bolitho told him quietly, "an' you d' knaw full well who it is that I am in love with, 'ave been since I first met her. Your wife 'as only ever bin' in love with you an' no other, you bleddy fool! I came 'ere that day to see you, not yer wife."

"I do not believe you!" shouted Paul. "For you want only to fool me as you both did before, but I am wiser now and will not be so beguiled!"

Joey sighed heavily and began to speak again in his soft, calm voice, which was so at variance with Paul's bitter, angry tone.

"I 'ad come to ask yer 'elp, Paul, fer Sarah-Jane would 'ave none of me. I wished fer you to intercede in the matter, fer if you told 'er she meant nothing to 'e then I 'oped she would turn to me fer comfort an' so grow to love me. At long last, Paul, I 'ad reformed myself fer she wouldn' 'ave me any other way. But it 'ad been of no use and when I asked fer 'er 'and, it was refused. Yer dear Chloe was only trying to console me in me sadness at sufferin' Sarah-Jane's rejection."

"And your secret?" asked Paul acutely, "Have you forgotten your own words to her? For I have not! They plague me every day and have ripped the heart out of me. Tell me, Joey, what it is that you share with my wife and perhaps then I can begin to believe your far-fetched tale? For to me it sounds like a man trying to lie and cheat his way out of the foulest crime that one man can perpetrate on a fellow who took him for a friend!"

Joey lowered his gaze and could no longer look steadfastly into his brother's eyes. He shook his head and said carefully: "If I told you, Paul, you would not believe me, an' I think if you ever get to knaw of it you will not wish to believe it."

Paul stared at him angrily, his words only confirming that the man had come to reel out a parcel of lies, and for no other reason than to fool him again.

"I have listened to you, Joey, but nothing you have said has made me believe any of your lies. No doubt she has contacted you to try that you should win me over, but I am not the fool you think me! You had best leave, for there is nothing more I want to hear of you and the sooner your filthy carcass is out of my house the better!" Paul told him viciously.

"I 'ave told you the truth, Paul!" Joey announced desperately, "believe me fer her sake if not mine, you fool!"

"No!" he shouted, "Now get out!"

Joey sighed, then stood up and walked slowly towards the door. He hesitated with his hand on the doorknob and looked as if he would say more, but at that instant there was a commotion in the hallway. Raised voices and shouts and the next moment the footsteps of a running man. Recognising one voice, Joey stood back and, after a quick glance, positioned himself to the front of his brother as the door burst open.

"Damn me!" cried a voice joyfully, "I have both of you caught in my net at last!" and Hudson's sadistic smile swept over his face in cruel delight.

"How dare you burst in upon me so!" said Paul wrathfully, "I would demand an explanation of your behaviour, for you had better have a good reason for this intrusion."

"Oh! A most good reason, Mr Trevarthen, sir, for I have come to arrest you, as you have hidden contraband on your property. I shall be able to prove, Mr Trevarthen, sir, that you are a common smuggler just like Bolitho here," and he leered maliciously at both the men.

"You can't prove I bin' smugglin' 'Udson an' you knaw it, an' in a little while you will 'ave no case 'gainst Mr Trevarthen either," announced Joey calmly.

"Your very presence here, under the circumstances, proves you are involved with the goods that are hidden on Mr Trevarthen's property, Bolitho, so I have your neck ready for a noose at last," and he cackled delightedly.

"I tell you 'gain, 'Udson, there are no goods 'idden in Trevu. Search as much as you d' want, you will find nothin', fer you 'ad only Likky's word that he 'ad done what you asked of 'im." Joey allowed himself a grim smile as he saw the consternation in Hudson's flushed face.

"How do you know that Likky was. . ?" then he stopped, realising what he had been about to say.

"The situation can be solved most expeditiously, Mr Hudson, for if you ask Likky he will no doubt be able to tell you the truth that I do not and never have had anything to do with the smuggling trade," announced Paul coldly and calmly.

For one moment Hudson looked unsure of himself, but his prize was almost in his hands and could not be left go.

"No need, Mr Trevarthen, sir, for he admitted your guilt to me yesterday when I had speech with him, for you see he has been in my employ for a considerable time now," and he smiled at Joey with sinister pleasure.

"Ah! Yesterday, Mr Hudson, 'ess, yesterday, I remember it well," Joey said coldly, and reaching into his pocket he produced a blood stained handkerchief, holding it up for the man to see.

The effect was dramatic, for the blood drained from Hudson's face. He took a step towards Joey and cried: "Where did you get that?"

"Why!" answered Joey, "Next to Likky's body where it was left, of course. Trouble was you didn't manage to kill 'en straight away, an' 'e 'ad some words fer me afore he died. Told me 'e 'adn't done as you told 'en to after all!" As if to corroborate this statement, Carveth came panting into the room and announced: " 'Tis not there, sir! We 'ave searched all over the barn but there is nothing to be found. Shall we search here, sir?"

Hudson, white with anger, shouted at him to get out and await further orders. When they were alone again, he turned to Joey and stared at him nervously. Then, a crazed grin spread across his face and with both hands he reached inside his jacket, removed a pair of pistols and pointed one at each of them. To him, words were immaterial now, for he had lost and he knew it, but still he had another plan and this time he would not leave his witnesses alive to tell of what they knew.

For now he had become the accused and they the accusers. However, he knew his men would believe anything that he told them to believe, so he had only to say that Bolitho and Trevarthen had attempted to overpower him and he had fired in self-defence. Keeping the pistols trained upon them, he moved around them so that now they were between him and the door, the better to make their escape. When his men came back into the room he would be found on the floor, feigning injury, with two dead criminals lying in front of him. He smiled, first at Joey and then at Paul, before saying in a smug and righteous tone: "I see you thought to outwit me, Bolitho, but your plan has failed for I have a better one. Attempting to escape me after most foully attacking me, I had no choice but to fire on both of you afore you made your escape. You first, Trevarthen, for I would save Bolitho to the last. He will be worth the wait, so long has it been that I have sought to catch him." He raised his pistol and fired, and Paul fell back against the wall. Almost immediately a second shot rang out and another body pitched forward and lay full length along the floor, his blood seeping into the carpet to meet the other river of blood that was flowing as freely towards it.

CHAPTER 24

DENZIL DUNSTAN worked steadily and quickly, for there had been a severe loss of blood and the man was very weak. When Jonas Hampton had come knocking at his door with his white face Dunstan knew that, whatever had happened at Trevu, it had been of a most serious nature.

"The ball will have to come out and it's in deep. The blood loss is what worries me the most, for in spite of all your efforts ..." and he indicated the blood stained cloths that lay in the bowl, "... he lost a powerful amount of it. Still, the poor fellow will not know much about it for he is not conscious." As the doctor began his work, the man holding the bowl swallowed hard at the awful sight, but kept his hands steady and did not move from the doctor's side. When Dr Dunstan had removed the piece of lead he applied basilicum powder freely and began to pack the wound with clean lint, then with his helper's assistance bound it tightly. After he had finished with the bandaging, he poured out a strong smelling liquid into a glass and announced the patient would have to be lifted. When this was accomplished, he prized open his patient's mouth and poured some of the liquid down his throat in a rather rough and ready manner. But most of it disappeared and he had to assume that the drug would have the desired effect. Crossing the room, he washed his hands and wiped them dry on the cloth provided.

"I will stay for a while to see how he does," said Dunstan, "but you had best go down and get yourself a brandy," he continued with a smile, "for you have the look of a man who has great need of one."

"I ought to stay for . . ." but the man was cut short and this time Dr Dunstan ordered him from the room in a firm voice. So with another look at the figure, lying like a dead man in the bed, he made his way slowly down the stairs.

As he crossed the hallway he heard the sound of the cart, with the dead body wrapped in blankets rocking lifelessly on it, slowly make its way down the lane and begin its journey home to Penzance. He almost went into the withdrawing room, then he remembered all the blood that was spattered about, so he turned and found his way mechanically to the back parlour and entered quietly. Instead of getting himself a drink, he stumbled to a chair, sat down and sank his head in his hands.

He was aware that someone was pouring some liquid into a glass and, after a moment, he felt his hand grasped. He looked up to see saw a rather large brandy had been procured for him. He raised the glass to his lips with his shaking hand, took a large mouthful of it and swallowed. Its familiar, warming burn had not the slightest effect for he was still in shock.

"Well?" asked Caroline Crebo softly, "Will he live?"

"I do not know, for he has lost so much blood that Dr Dunstan cannot say. I cannot believe what happened, for it was all so fast. One moment he was standing defiantly beside me and the next he was in my arms with his blood pouring all over me." He glanced down at his bloodstained jacket and crimson stained trousers, and took another gulp at the brandy.

She sat in the chair opposite him and regarded him calmly, for she had regained her composure and could face the prospect of another death now, although the loss would sadden her greatly.

"He did what he wished to do, Paul, if he . . . if he should not survive you have to remember that," she told him calmly.

"I know, Aunt, I know but I do not understand why, for twice he has saved my life and this time he was prepared to lose his own in order to do it." A sob escaped him, for the horror of what had happened began to engulf him.

He could remember it all so well for it was engraved upon his mind. When the first shot was fired he was suddenly aware that Joseph Bolitho appeared directly in front of him, as if from nowhere. He fell back into his arms and his weight brought Paul crashing to the floor. The second shot was accompanied by a crash of breaking glass and took Hudson cleanly between his shoulder blades. His face warped into a caricature of his sinister smile and he fell forward with his head almost touching Paul's feet, who watched, horrified as blood poured from the wound in Hudson's back. Pandemonium broke out around him: he heard a woman's screams and men came running, some his servants, but mostly men from Hudson's troop. They had to pull Bolitho off him for his weight was pinning Paul to the floor.

Thinking quickly, he was ready for them when they asked what happened of him and, even as he was packing the wound in Joey's shoulder, he was aware of the smile that the badly injured man was directing at him.

"Mr Hudson heard a noise in the garden and took out his pistols to go and investigate. He turned around to advise us to move back against the wall and as he did so a shot rang out and he fell. Unfortunately, as he was hit, one of the weapons discharged and Mr Bolitho received a wound in the shoulder," Paul muttered as he struggled to staunch the blood that was seeping through his neck cloth. He had wrenched it off to make a pad with which to put over the gaping hole caused by the shot.

" 'Tis Likky Skewes," announced Carveth, "Has to be, for all the rest of the gang is in the lock up. He must 'ave come after Mr Hudson, followed 'en all the way up 'ere and then come through the garden an' shot 'en like a dog. The dirty bastard!"

"Well, we never seen 'en," said his companion suspiciously, and then turned and nodded at Paul. " An' we don't knaw that Trevarthen 'ere didn't do it," and he levelled his own pistol at Paul.

"Don't be so bleddy daft!" Carveth told him vehemently, "How did he get outside and back in 'ere in the time? And he couldn' even get Bolitho's body off 'en on 'is own, fer we 'ad 'elp 'en."

The other man frowned for a moment in consideration of what Carveth had said and then nodded, saying: " 'Ess, tha's true 'nuff Arthur," Then, casting a look at Hudson, he remarked matter-of-factly that they had best get his body back to the town.

Beth, her eyes averted, brought cloths to Paul, and he used one after another. But gradually the colour drained from Joey's face and slowly he drifted into unconsciousness without saying a word. Jonas, rushing in from outside with a very white face, shouted to Paul that he would go for the doctor and sped from the house towards the stables. By the time he returned with the doctor they had moved Joey to a bedroom in the new wing of the house, far away from the nursery so that the children should neither be disturbed by Bolitho or be a disturbance to him, but not before Caroline Crebo had walked through the open doorway and almost fainted at the sight that met her eyes. Her nephew, covered in blood, was carrying the body of Joseph Bolitho towards the stairs with the help of several of his farm workers. Another body, wrapped in a blanket, was being removed from the house by a group of customs men. A hat placed ignominiously on the top of its lifeless chest.

Mrs Gurney, at the top of the kitchen stairs, immediately rushed to Mrs Crebo's assistance and helped her to the back parlour, for Davy had said the withdrawing room could not be used as: "it was in a helluva mess!" Mrs Gurney managed to calm Caroline's shattered nerves and sent for Davy. He explained to the best of his ability what he had gleaned from Hudson's men and the farm hands as to what had happened. The information, - that an intruder in the garden had shot through the window - set Caroline's nerves on edge again. But when she was informed that the late officer's men had searched the garden and had found not a trace, surmising that the man was long gone, she was greatly relieved. Paul was away for a long time, but she had managed to compose herself before he entered the parlour. When she saw his face she determined that she would not give in to her nerves, for this haggard, shocked man needed some calm in the storm that had erupted so violently around him.

So she sat quietly with him and, after a while, he began to feel better and recounted the exact events that had occurred in the withdrawing room. When he had finished, he got up and said he would go back to Dr Dunstan to see how his patient fared, then wordlessly left the room.

The doctor smiled as he entered the spacious bedchamber, but shook his head when Paul asked quietly if there had been any change.

"Difficult to say what is to happen, Paul, for he is most weak. If he goes into a fever I fear we will lose him. He will not withstand that, for he will not have the strength," He looked sympathetically at Paul and asked if it were possible to stay the night; he thought it best because his skills would be needed for a while yet.

Paul nodded dumbly and, feeling helpless, went off to find a servant to make up a bed for the doctor. Then he realised he would need one for his aunt as well and so made arrangements to accommodate her. When he had finished, he returned to the back parlour once again and sat down heavily in his chair.

"There is no change, but Denzil has told me he will stay the night to render all possible assistance." Paul ran his hand through his hair and stared blankly in front of him. Realising that now was not the time to talk to him, Caroline feigned tiredness and said that she had much to say to him, but it would save for the morning. Then she got up and kissed his cheek lightly before moving towards the door. She hesitated as she was struck by the thought that, if Bolitho did indeed die in the night, Paul should have been put in possession of the facts, for the sake of his own tortured soul if for no other reason. She made her way back to where he sat and put her hand on his shoulder.

"Paul," she said softly.

"Yes, Aunt," he answered and looked up at her sympathetic smile. He watched as she reached into her reticule and withdrew a letter, whose distinctive script he well knew.

"You have to read this, Paul, for it contains nothing but the truth, and although what she says may cause you great pain, you have to be told. How you wish to act afterwards is entirely up to you, but you have great need of this knowledge at this time and it will explain that which you cannot understand." Taking up his hand, she gently placed the note into it.

He stared at the letter, fearful to open it, long after she had left the room. So afraid was he of what it contained that he could not bring himself to look. But his aunt's words echoed in his head until finally, he mastered his fears and with shaking hands spread open the single sheet. Upon reading it once, he went back to read it a second time, so unbelieving was he of its contents. He stared at the words as they burned their meaning into his brain, whilst his tears fell slowly down his cheeks and dripped onto the blood that so heavily stained his clothes.

In the hour before dawn, Dr Dunstan got out of his bed and made his way quietly to his patient's side, but was surprised to find another there, sitting quietly with his hand holding Bolitho's in a tender clasp.

"How does our patient?" he asked gently, then came to the bedside and made a brief examination.

"He does not move. Were it not for the fact I can see him breathing I would suppose him dead," replied Paul in a despairing whisper.

" 'Tis a good sign, Paul, for were he restless I would fear a fever, but bear up, for I have him under the influence of a most strong drug. Rest yourself easy; the worst is not yet over, I know, but he is holding on to life most tenaciously." With a gentle squeeze of Paul's shoulder, Dunstan left the room and made his way back to his own bed.

However, Dr Dunstan had his worst fears confirmed when, within twenty four hours, Bolitho was caught in the tight grip of fever, and such a fever that all feared for his life, for even the doctor could not believe that such a weakened body could sustain the attack that was being made upon it. For Paul it was a nightmare of despair, for he could have no speech with him. During the brief moments when Joey appeared conscious, he had no knowledge of where he lay and could recognise none around him. His delirious pronouncements ranged from agitated pleas to his mother to respond to him - always followed by his anguished screams, which took the efforts of the both the doctor and Paul to hold him down, so violently did he struggle - to the softest of endearments addressed to his dearest love. He fretted himself unbearably, lest some unnamed person should be told a secret, and at such times Dr Dunstan brought his distress to a swift conclusion by drugging him with as strong a potion as he thought his poor body could withstand. Joey's brother's distress could not be alleviated in the same way and he sat appalled, day after day, by the bedside of the man that previously had subjugated, from everyone who knew him, all his innermost emotions. But now, all unknowing, Joseph Bolitho laid bare his personal torments for his brother to witness, and such was depth of the sick man's anguish that Paul himself felt as if he was experiencing the hell that comprised his brother's nightmare. The good doctor struggled hard to sustain Joey's life for the sake of his own pride and, as he had been made aware of the relationship that was now known to exist between the two men, he could not bear the thought of Paul Trevarthen finding and losing his sibling before he had even a chance to call him 'Brother' to his face. At all times he sought to comfort Paul, whilst he sat in such despair at the injured man's bedside, and when finally the fever broke and Joey showed signs of improving he smiled encouragingly into his brother's distraught face and told him quietly that at last a chance existed for his patient's recovery.

The household was subdued and quiet, as it had been for so long, but now there was a tremor of excitement present whilst Bolitho's struggle for life was being played out. Even when Paul returned his wife's letter to Caroline, and although they had sat and talked quietly together in the back parlour, he had little to say for he found the events almost too momentous to comment upon. She was most understanding and advised him to slowly come to terms with the sudden news that he had received, for she knew what a dreadful shock it had been to him.

"He never wanted you to know for he knew you thought badly of him," Caroline told Paul with a worried frown. "As you have read for yourself: as soon as Chloe realised, she pressed him to tell you but he never would, for he was determined that you should never be made aware of it. It was not from shame of his father but of himself. You do understand that, Paul?"

He nodded his head and smiled grimly. As usual, he said, she was in the right of it. And although he could now comprehend so much of what had happened in the past, the discovery that he had a brother and the knowledge of who that brother happened to be, was something he had never foreseen. Paul had instructed his aunt to take charge of the running of the house, for he could not put his mind to it, and Jonas Hampton was ordered to oversee all that needed to be done on the farm and was not to come to him with any problems whatsoever. The children had been told all that the adults thought it best to tell them and had been instructed to keep well away from that part of the house, and at all times to be quiet. The arrival of George was of considerable help, for he had grown taller again and had an air of authority mixed with a childish sense of humour that the younger ones responded to. He was able to reassure Jack when he needed to be comforted and the girls were slightly in awe of him, for he looked so different from the young boy that had left them at the end of the Easter holidays. His voice had altered as well for it had more resonance. He had even spoken privately with his father, for he had been called to Paul's study the morning after he had arrived and had been informed of all the facts as far as Paul himself knew them. Looking more relieved than shocked, he tentatively asked his father if they could now write to their mother, for it was obvious that she had done no wrong. Paul raised his eyes to his son's face and nodded, but lowered them again when George bravely asked if he had written to her himself.

"No, George, not yet for I have much to be forgiven and I must consider well what it is that I should say to her and to . . . ask of her," he replied gently. He then smiled at his son and assured him that when the time was right he would do it. George smiled reassuringly and merely said: "Of course you will, Father," then returned to his self-imposed task of being a comfort to his siblings.

Almost a week after being shot, Joey awoke and found himself in a strange room, but he recognised the doctor who was leaning over him and he knew himself alive for his shoulder was in great pain.

"Soon be over now, Joey," Denzil said soothingly, "just have to tighten this bandage a little," as he did so a sharp pain made Bolitho clench his lip between his teeth.

"There we are," said the doctor encouragingly and Joey became aware that someone was gently lowering him back against his pillows. Turning his head, he looked into his brother's serious and concerned face.

"Paul?" he croaked, for his voice was dry with lack of use, "What are you doin' 'ere?" and he saw him smile before telling him he was in a bed at Trevu. Joey looked around in wonderment for he did not recognise the room, its appearance being so different from the house he had grown to know.

"You are in the new wing that Mother had built when she married Father. I rarely use it for I prefer the original building, but it was felt that you would be best served by being in the quieter side of the house, away from the children, so we brought you here." He would have said more, but Dr Dunstan silenced him and ordered Paul to lift his patient again, then directed Joey to drink from the glass that he was pressing against his mouth. He did as instructed, but the foul taste made him grimace and Paul winced in sympathy, for he had a loathing of medicine himself.

"He will sleep now, Paul, but when he wakes he will need to . . . ." and the doctor's voice droned on but Joey, in his weakened condition, was reacting quickly to the drug and soon he fell into a deep sleep again.

Slowly, as the days passed, Joey began to win back his strength. Dr Dunstan oversaw his convalescence and supervised the preparation of the meals that were cooked for his consumption. Weakened though he was, Bolitho began to improve almost by the hour and the doctor commended him on his remarkable constitution, but brought himself up short from uttering the comparison that hovered so dangerously on his lips. It would be his brother's duty to tell him what he knew of Joey's past. When Paul thought him well enough, he had sat down and explained to Joey how a shot from outside had killed Hudson, but he said not a word about the realisation he had of their relationship. Joey made no comment about Hudson's death, but he asked for Seth Mankee to visit him. When he arrived, he spoke to him privately and was astonished to discover that Paul had already been in contact with him, arranging monies for the wives and families of the imprisoned and ensuring that Seth had organised care for Likky's mother.

"Jonas Hampton come see me the day after you got shot, fer Paul give 'en a great pile of money an' said I was to make sure the people you d' take care of was looked after 'cos you wouldn' want 'em go without," Seth said in wonderment. Then he added: "Likky 'as become quite a 'ero, fer he was the one that fired the shot that killed 'Udson. Course 'e's gone to ground somewhere, took ship to France or somethin' but they can't stop talking 'bout 'en down in the town. They're goin' 'ave leave our boys out soon as well, 'cos they 'aven't got no case 'gainst them. They're tryin' find a way keep 'em in but there's nawthin' they can do," and he chuckled gleefully at the predicament that the authorities now found themselves in.

When they had finished talking, Paul took Seth back to Penzance in his curricle, but declined a visit to Josh's in his company, instead passing him a handful of money for the boys to "raise a brew to Joey's recovery" as he informed him with a gentle smile. Leaving his curricle at the livery stable he set forth into the town, impervious to the many glances he received and only briefly acknowledging the greetings of numerous persons that he met on his way. He conducted some business with his lawyer, and called on some acquaintances in the town before returning to his home, but once in his office, sent word for Jonas Hampton to come to see him.

As Jonas entered the room he greeted Paul in a hesitant manner, for his employer had a most serious expression on his face.

"Sit down, Jonas, for it is most important I talk to you," said Paul, curtly, and he pointed to a chair that was positioned directly in front of him.

Warily, Jonas did as he was directed and waited for what his master was to say next. When he began to speak, the colour drained from his face at his employer's first question.

"I have been wondering how it is that a dead man could kill another, Jonas?" asked Paul softly, and expecting no reply continued in the same tone: "But I have come to realise that the man who did kill Hudson, would not wish such a question spread abroad, would he?"

"No, Paul, he would not, for 'twould be very difficult for him should it become known, even though the man believes he was attempting to stop the officer from committing a foul murder," answered his estate manager in a subdued voice.

"He did not think to do this deed himself, I presume?" asked Paul, with his eyebrow raised.

"No . . . No he did not but your bro... another man said he could not offer full protection to . . . to . . ," and he halted, unable to find the words to continue, but Paul merely nodded.

"I understand what you are trying to say, Jonas and I think it best we never discuss the matter again, for 'twould be better if we both forget what we have seen and what we know, do you not agree?" and he smiled. Jonas gratefully nodded his agreement and got up to leave the room, but when he reached the door he heard his name called and turned to face Paul again.

"I almost forgot, Jonas. Excuse me my bad manners, for I do most sincerely thank the man who fired that shot, for well I know if he had not I would have lost my life." Paul looked directly into his eyes. Jonas mumbled his acknowledgement and gave a brief smile before turning and letting himself out of the room.

Jonas returned to his office but his mind was elsewhere. Although what he had done plagued his conscience, he firmly believed that if he had not undertaken the act then his master would have indeed been murdered. Bolitho had asked him, after all, to take particular care of Paul and had told him who the man would be that would cause the most trouble to him. Well, he had done as Joey had asked of him and Paul knew what that had meant.

When Hudson had arrived at Trevu that fateful night he had hidden himself in the garden and, as the events unfolded, had acted in what he had considered to be his master's best interests. From his vantage point he had realised that whatever was being said in the room, that Hudson, by his action in taking out his pistols and aiming them at the two men, intended to kill one, if not both of them. Jonas has fired his gun to protect the Master of Trevu.

The tale that had been spread around: that Likky Skewes had pursued Hudson because his gang were in the lockup, would do very well and the estate manager's sudden appearance on the dreadful scene had not been questioned by any of Hudson's men for, after all, he had a right to be there.

Jonas shook his head and thought instead of the tale that had also come to his ears concerning the two men. Now he understood why it was that Joey had shown such a fondness for Paul and his family. With Trevarthen finally aware of the truth, perhaps it would lead to a renewal of the friendship between Paul and Joey, for it had saddened Jonas greatly when the two men had become estranged. The only thing that was needed now was for Mrs Trevarthen to return and then perhaps some happiness would come back into the lives of all the residents of Trevu.

The following day, after confirming to his own satisfaction that Joey was well on the road to recovery, Dr Dunstan left Trevu for his home. On the road out of Trevu he met Edgar Bawden, the local barber, bowling along the road in his gig. 'Poor Bolitho to be spruced up no doubt,' he thought, shaking his head and allowing himself a loud chuckle. He could imagine the talk he would soon be hearing, for he well knew that the news had been allowed to spread around the town deliberately. When the barber presented himself, Joey did not object to being shaved, although he raised an eyebrow when Mr Bawden began to trim his hair, but he was most surprised at his attitude. He had never been shaved by the gentry's barber, for that was the position Edgar Bawden held in Penzance. In spite of Joey's ruthless reputation he would not have attempted to use Bawden's premises for he knew it would have meant a rebuttal. To say Mr Bawden was obsequious did not do justice to his manner, for he treated Joey as if he had been the Mayor. When he had finished he made a polite farewell and left. It was not long after he had departed before Paul's head appeared around the door and asked him if he could bear to have a visitor. Joey looked surprised, but when he heard a stifled whisper his face broke into a smile, for well he knew whom it was that wished to call on him and he nodded his agreement. Jack bounded into the room, talking all the time and, after receiving instructions from his father as to how he was to conduct himself in the sick room, was left alone with his hero for a quarter of an hour. When his father came to tell him that he had best to leave, he frowned heavily. But on being told that he might make Mr Bolitho unwell again if he outstayed his welcome, he promptly said his goodbyes but promised to come again on the morrow. The invalid laughed to see him skip out of the room.

"I could get used to this life, Paul," laughed Joey, after Mr Bawden had left for Penzance on the third successive day that he had dutifully arrived to be Joey's barber. He looked up and noticed a serious look on Paul's face, but it lasted only a moment before he caught sight of a brief, tentative smile. Paul did not stay long in his company, and when he did their conversations were minimal: although Joey's every need was seen to, he thought it best to assure his host that as soon as he was well enough be would be returning to his home.

"As you wish," replied Paul enigmatically, and making no further comment, left Joey in peace.

Later that day, with his head resting comfortably against the soft pillows at his back, he was engrossed in a book when he heard heavy steps along the corridor. His brow furrowed, for he could not recognise the sound and it was obvious that more than one person was approaching. When Beth opened the door to admit Dr Dunstan and another rather large and richly dressed gentleman he looked momentarily surprised, but apart from greeting the doctor did not attempt further speech until he knew exactly to whom he would be speaking. It was as well he was reticent, for when he found himself introduced to Sir Reginald Bonython, the head of the Customs Service, he felt his mouth go dry of a sudden.

"Well, Bolitho, caught at last I see!" boomed the rather corpulent gentleman. He sat himself down in the chair next to the bed and looked around in wonder at the furnishings of the room.

"Dammee man, but this is a fine establishment an' I mistake not!" he mused. Then almost immediately he turned his bright blue eyes on the occupant of the bed and regarded him with a grim smile. Joey kept his face impassive and waited for what next the man would say.

"There will be no more of your smuggling, Bolitho," he boomed, "For if there is, all of Denzil's work here," and he pointed to Dr Dunstan, "will have been in vain." He stared Bolitho in the eye before asking abruptly: "Do you understand me man?" Sir Reginald found himself the object of a firm, calculating stare and his lips twitched slightly at the man's undoubted audacity, but after a moment Bolitho replied that he did.

"Good! Denzil here tells me you nearly died, so I will not keep you long lest I tire you. Also, Trevarthen has told me his cook has prepared a most excellent repast upon which I am shortly to dine," he said, his face lighting up in anticipation of the forthcoming meal.

"I believe that Hudson had tried to entrap you and Trevarthen as smugglers, for with the information I have gleaned from his men it appears that way to me at the very least. Trevarthen is stoutly denying that he knows anything and to a certain extent I believe him. I doubt the poor fellow has ever had to do with smuggling in his life, whereas you have known no other existence. My problem is that Trevarthen appears wary of explaining to me how exactly you found yourself on the receiving end of Hudson's pistol shot. Perhaps you could enlighten me?"

"I don't remember what 'appened, sir," replied Joey, after a moment's hesitation.

"Humph! You don't, eh? Perhaps if I told you, as I have told Mr Trevarthen, that I believe that Hudson tried to murder you and would not have spared Trevarthen as a witness. As you can imagine, this is not the sort of tale the Excise Office would like to have laid at their door. Whilst we are happy enough to catch you blaggards fair and square, 'tis not in our interests to have our officers hide evidence on people's property. Nor to attempt to have anyone killed should those plans go awry. We are not such a highly regarded service hereabouts to play any underhand games, for should we embark upon that course the local populace will mistrust us even more than they do now. As it would be in everyone's interests to concur with Mr Trevarthen's statement to Hudson's men: that the pistol was discharged accidentally when Hudson was shot by an intruder in the garden, I would hope that your version of events will agree with this story." He paused and searched

Joey's face shrewdly for a sign of understanding. When he had convinced himself that Bolitho knew what it was he was being prompted to say, he posed his question again: "Perhaps you can advise me as to what happened in the light of my explanation," he said. A roguish smile played on his lips as he leaned forward in expectation.

"Mr 'Udson was shot an' 'is gun discharged as 'e fell forward. I felt a pain in me shoulder but I passed out not long after an' don't remember no more," Joey announced firmly.

"Good man! Denzil, you heard that. And, dear friend, you will note it matches exactly with what Trevarthen had said the night Bolitho here got himself shot. And when I pass him the information Mr Bolitho has just given us, perhaps he will say to my face what he had stated previously. For his ingenuity then would, if repeated, make for a clean ending to what could have been a nasty business, a very nasty business! We have men abroad scouring the countryside for Skewes, the presumed murderer. And when he is finally brought to book he, unlike you, Bolitho, will be shown no mercy. From what has been heard it is believed that he has got himself to the continent, an' if he has any sense I doubt that he will set foot in the county ever again. Good friend of yours, I was led to believe, so if you have knowledge of his whereabouts it might be as well if you should get a message to him and advise him of the consequences of returning to these shores. A court case might be prejudicial to the standing of this office, sir, for in the interests of justice the whole of Hudson's activities would be brought to light and . . . er . . . I am sure that neither yourself nor Mr Trevarthen would wish for that to happen." He paused before advising Joey pointedly, that he had given orders to the effect that Mrs Skewes was not to be questioned or harassed concerning the whereabouts of her son in any way whatsoever.

"Mr Trevarthen asked me expressly that she was not to be worried by my men for she is old and infirm and, being blind, could have little information to give us in any case, poor soul." And so saying, with much creaking of the corsets restraining his corpulent frame, he heaved himself to his feet. When this feat was accomplished, he leaned over the bed and offered his hand to Joey, who regarded him suspiciously, yet with a hint of admiration in his eyes. Both men shook hands, satisfied that they each understood the other very well indeed.

"Wish you good fortune, Mr Bolitho, but remember..." and he subjected Joey to a calculating stare, only leavened by the slight smile that would not leave his lips, "...step one footfall the wrong side of the law and I shall not hesitate to arrest you, is that understood?" A pair of cold, blue eyes looked into Sir Reginald's face, which could barely contain its amusement, but Joey nodded and said: "I understand perfectly, sir."

"I thought you might. After all, Bolitho, you would be a fool indeed to throw away the status you have now attained." He saw Joey's eyebrows rise in surprise, so he hastily added: "Well . . . um . . . I would not be late to sit down to dine," and with a swift word of farewell he hurriedly left the room. Dr Dunstan informed Joey that he would call to change the dressings on his wound before he returned to Penzance and Joey was left alone, to wonder exactly what it was that Bonython had meant by his remark concerning his status. Perhaps the townsfolk envisaged him as some sort of hero for saving the life of the Master of Trevu? He shrugged his shoulders - which made him wince - and considered how best to find out.

When the doctor returned, Joey thought to ask him what Bonython's last statement referred to, but having always to be a careful man with his speech and with whom he spoke, considered it best to broach the matter with Paul instead. In this he was frustrated, for when, later that afternoon his brother came to his room, he had little Jack by the hand and so he could not talk to him privately. He spent a restless night, for now it was beginning to be borne in upon him that, although he was having his every need attended to, he was unable to direct his own life and would have to wait until he had the strength to leave his bed and subsequently, his room, before he could again take control of his own affairs. It was obvious that Paul had no wish to sit down and talk with him, for he would not stay long when in the room and it was apparent that the man was ill at ease in his company.

There was much Joey wished to know, but to ask Paul outright was an impossibility for his brother had a noticeably wary look about him, so he resigned himself to concentrating on improving his health. In the afternoon, when the servant had removed the remains of his lunch, he picked up his book, settled back against his pillows and resumed his reading. He had not the chance to finish his chapter for a knock on the door heralded another visitor. His eyes opened wide with surprise when he saw who it was that Beth was showing into the room.

"Sarah-Jane!" he gasped. Attempting to sit upright he moved so quickly that, forgetting his injury, he inadvertently caused himself pain and let out a sharp gasp.

Quickly, she crossed to his side and, placing her hand on his, advised him to lie quietly, informing him that she did not expect him to look as well as he did. Spreading her skirts elegantly, she sat at his bedside and looked at him critically with her clear, green eyes. From the day following the shooting, both Jonas Hampton and Paul had kept her informed of Joey's progress. At first she was stunned by the news of Paul's relationship to Joseph Bolitho but, sitting in her lonely house, she had time to consider how like the Captain Joey actually was. He could stare at the world from behind the same mask-like face as Paul's father would so often do and, in spite of his wretched beginnings, he had developed into a man with surprising talents. She smiled fondly in remembrance of her dear father on his sickbed and the pleasure that the tainted man's readings from the invalid's bible had brought to him. As her oldest friend had sat in her withdrawing room it had been a revelation to her, for Sarah-Jane found that she shared Paul's distress as he recounted the details of Joey's raging fever. She listened to the man's fervent prayers for his brother's recovery, all the while offering up silent prayers of her own. When Paul had called with the news that the fever had finally broken, the joy she had felt was not for the sake of seeing her visitor's relieved face, but was deeper and more significant. Memories of Joseph Bolitho as a young man: his determined pursuit of her and his many unsolicited kindnesses on her behalf ranged against her harsh treatment of him and her cold-hearted refusals to marry him. She had believed herself in love with another man and had clung to her desire for this idol who, by word or deed, had shown her none of Joey's constant adoration. Her dismissive treatment of the smuggler plagued her guilt-ridden conscience. For years she had been blinded by the adoration she had carried in her heart for Paul, impervious to the love that his own brother had so unreservedly given her. Now her vision had finally cleared, allowing her sight of the one man above all others who had so steadfastly loved her from the first day upon which he had made her acquaintance. For his years of devoted worship, the man deserved more than her cold dismissals of his protestations of his love for her. Observing the worried expression that he was so desperately trying to hide from her, she smiled comfortingly at him and began to speak.

"I would have visited before, but Paul has been advising me on when he thought that you would feel well enough to have callers. I was to come yesterday but apparently you had a most illustrious visitor, so Paul came to tell me it were best if I waited another day." She spoke in a clear and controlled tone, but he noticed how a delicate smile played on her lips as she looked at him and Joey felt his heart quicken at the sight of it.

"Paul seems to 'ave been most protective on my behalf," announced Joey ruefully, "fer I 'ad no knowledge that he was regulating the number of people that I am to receive visits from." She laughed at his words and the sound of it made him smile broadly in return.

"He has been doing more than that, Joey," Sarah-Jane told him and, at his enquiring look, she went on to explain a great deal of what had been happening. He learned that as soon as it was possible for him to do so, Paul had gone to Penzance and had been instrumental in having the men released from the lock up. For as his lawyer had pointed out, no proof existed with which to convict anyone of a single misdemeanour. Furthermore, a fund had been set up for Hudson's widow and a substantial contribution made to it by an anonymous donor, the poor woman was then able to accept the condolences of her friends and acquaintances adorned in Mrs Martin's finest black silk. During the same visit to his solicitors, Paul had made it known that he wished to make over certain of his properties to Joseph Bolitho - much to Mr Rodda's obvious amazement - and had set everything in order for it to be done. He had then bethought himself of another matter and had visited the late Squire Tregurthen's wife, informing her exactly what the relationship was that existed between Joseph Bolitho and himself. At the mention of this final piece of information, Joey felt the colour drain from his face and knew himself unmasked at last.

"Of course, as Paul well knew, he had not even left Penzance before the news was spread abroad. He had come to call on me after leaving the 'dear gazetteer' as he rather rudely called her and told me of all he had done and . . ." she paused. As she marked the anger in his face, she hesitated for a moment before continuing calmly: ". . . and why he had taken the course he did."

"An' what was 'is reason?" asked Joey stiffly, his simmering indignation apparent in his voice.

"He said he had to, for it was what his mother - and by that he meant his stepmother - would have wished him to do. As he said: 'if dearest Mama had known of Joey's existence he would have been welcomed as lovingly as I had been'. Understanding Paul is not difficult if his stepmother was known to you, for like him she had the kindest of hearts," she explained gently. Drawing a deep breath she continued bravely, for an incensed scowl had settled on Joey's face: "Paul considered that it was not your fault that Redvers never knew of your existence, for your mother never informed him of your birth. Perhaps if she had and his wife had discovered it you would have had a better life. Who can say?"

"I 'ave done what I could with what I 'ad an' do not wish to be given anything as if I were some old retainer offered charity!" he snapped angrily.

"Paul told me that he has divided as much as he can, that which Redvers left to him. Although that does not include the properties and incomes from his mother's estates, for he states that they are not part of your inheritance," she advised him cautiously, for she could see how infuriated he was becoming with his brother's actions.

"And you are sent as 'is deputy no doubt," Joey fumed passionately, "for 'e 'as said not a word of this to me!"

"Probably," she reasoned calmly, "for until now I could not be sure if you had been told of what he had done." She regarded him quietly for a while and waited patiently as she observed his angry flush begin to dissipate. Taking another deep breath, she continued in the same composed tone; "Paul has told me that he finds it difficult to speak to you now, because your relationship is placed on a different level, so he prefers to keep himself away from you. I know how difficult he finds it to make friends with people and how sensitive he is to their reactions to him. Although he has never mentioned it to me, I have always believed that he feels that the colour of his skin makes people dislike him."

"Fool!" said Joey, and then furrowed his eyebrows and began to think deeply. When he lifted his eyes to hers, he noticed that she was looking at him in a manner he had never seen before and had begun to smile again and, on the sight of it, he felt his body tremble and a flush filled his face.

"I . . . I 'ave not thanked you fer callin' on me, Sarah-Jane. 'Twas most rude of me an' I do beg yer pardon," he muttered awkwardly, not daring to hope for more than his beloved had ever offered him in the past.

She laughed at his embarrassment, but after a moment regarded him solemnly as she remarked: "Were it not for your actions Paul would have been killed. I had to come to thank you for that at least, Joey." She noted how sad his expression became at her words, but continued proudly: "I have much to admire in the man who would throw away his life knowing that his brother would never know of him. "With an ironic laugh she added: "Paul was ever a fool when it came to recognising love, Joey."

Seeing a fond smile play on his lips, she seized her opportunity and told him urgently: "You can still help him, Joey, if you will. For he is distraught that, because of his actions, his wife will never return to him. Tell him it is not the case, Joey," and she leaned forwards and clasped his hands in a tight grip, "for he has much need of reassurance in this matter to enable himself to ask her pardon."

He shifted uncomfortably in the bed and cleared his throat before announcing that he would indeed be having words with his brother, whether he would wish to hear them or no. Looking down at her little hands, grasping his so tightly, he determined in spite of further rejection to attempt another proposal. He raised his eyes to look again at the dear face regarding him so sympathetically.

"I still wish fer yer 'and in marriage Sarah-Jane, but I tell you now that I will 'ave none of Paul's gifts an' I am as you see me, a man with a wicked past an' an uncertain future," he said quietly, and he lowered his guilty eyes. He coughed again and began humbly saying: "An' I 'ave been most . . . um . . . There 'ave bin' many women in my life but I . . . I 'ave loved only you an' I 'ave never . . ," but he was unable to continue, for she rose from the chair and sat beside him on the bed. She took his face in her hands and searched it with her clear eyes. With a glowing smile on her face that set his heart racing, she told him gently: "Paul has not been the only fool when it comes to recognising and appreciating the value of love, Joey. I have not always thought myself in love with you but I began to understand, slowly at first, that you are a man of good qualities. Your love of Paul and your willingness to die for him opened my own heart to you. As you have good cause to know, I have loved him for many years now, Joey, and probably a part of my heart will always belong to him, but no matter, for well I know that a part of your own heart is in his possession as well."

"Sarah-Jane!" he whispered, his face flushed with excitement at what he so hoped was the significance of her words. "Does that mean you will accept me fer yer 'usband, my dearest?" he asked nervously, and his blue eyes opened wide with delight as she smiled lovingly at him and placed her lips on his for answer.

When Sarah-Jane kissed him goodbye at last and made her way from the room, ordering him to rest as she did so, Joseph Bolitho allowed himself a long, contented sigh and lay back against the pillows, unable to stop himself from smiling. Before leaving to return to Penzance, Sarah-Jane had sought out Paul and told him that she had finally accepted his brother's proposal. His delighted response was to hug her to him and to offer her his sincerest congratulations.

"My dearest friend," he told her, "I am so delighted for you both, for no other held a place in Joey's heart the way you have done all these years."

In the evening, Beth came to bring Joey his tray for dinner and so he seized his opportunity and asked her if it were possible to speak with his brother. She told him he had dined early and was writing in his room and did not wish to be disturbed, so he merely bade her to pass on his message when next she saw him, for he wished to talk to him most urgently. So it was much later that evening that his brother entered his room, regarding Joey's enigmatic face with a nervous smile.

"You wished to see me, Joey?" he asked tentatively.

"Damn right I do!" snapped his newly discovered brother forcefully and motioned him to the chair at his bedside. Paul sat down obediently, looking for all the world like a schoolboy caught out in some prank that merited a severe punishment.

"What is this I 'ere from Sarah-Jane about what you 'ave bin' about regardin' me an' my affairs?"

"Well . . . I thought it only right, Joey, for . . ," he began nervously, but was cut short by an angry expletive that issued from his brother's lips.

"I 'ave never asked fer nor wanted any money or . . . or recognition from you, Paul. An' now, stupid fool that you are, you 'ave spread abroad the knowledge of yer . . . our father's conduct to every tittle-tattler in Penzance! I imagine every 'ouse from the top to the bottom 'as nawthin' better to talk about than we two an' our father!" he snapped.

"Yes, I imagine that is the case, Joey. But as we have, all three of us, given them plenty of gossip to chew upon in the past, some more will not hurt them surely?" and he smiled briefly at Joey before quickly lowering his gaze.

There was a short, angry silence before Joey announced that, if he were fit enough, he would like to give his brother the thrashing that he thought he deserved.

"Best to wait until you have regained your strength, Joey," advised Paul, and his mischievous smile appeared on his face as he added: "if you believe you could."

Joey controlled his own smile and then informed Paul brusquely that he would accept none of the properties or income that was being made over to him.

"They were father's to leave to his son, and they would have been divided if he had knowledge of you. In fact if he had known of you I doubt very much if I would have been here to have this conversation with you," he announced simply.

"That would 'ave been a great pity, Paul, fer I couldn' 'ave wished fer a finer brother," said Joey, not without pride. Then his angry frown returned and he said abruptly: "but I will not 'ave 'e leave yerself short fer you 'ave a family to think on, so I will not accept yer money."

"I have not given you any of my mother's money, which I do consider rightfully to be mine," he said and then added thoughtfully: "Have you any idea of how much I am worth from my mother's estate alone?"

Joey shook his head, so Paul told him exactly what sort of income he received from his mother's various properties and businesses. Joey looked thunderstruck at the huge amount quoted and Paul laughed as he added informatively: "Father was always considered one of the richest men in the county, but even his estate paled into insignificance against the amount Sardi accumulated in her short life, and she acquired all her wealth after beginning with nothing. She was a most remarkable woman," he said proudly, and smiled fondly to himself.

"Paul, were it not fer me your dear mother would be alive still. You can't abide to live with that knowledge, surely, an' . . . 'an still want me fer a brother?" Joey pronounced softly, in a guilt ridden voice.

Unable to look into his face, his brother lowered his gaze and stared at the carpet for a long time, saying not a word. Then he took a deep breath and began to speak in a measured tone:

"What you did, Joey, you did to protect yourself and your friends and could not have known then what you know now. I have never condoned the way you lived your life, but Edwin told me how upset you were by Hudson's revelations and the disaster that your actions had brought down upon my family. We are both the sons of . . . of murdered mothers, I think that should draw us closer together Joey, not push us further apart." Then he gave a long sigh before stating firmly: "and that is my final thought on the matter," and raising his eyes to Joey's, he regarded him with a worried expression. His brother returned his glance impassively and Paul found himself smiling reminiscently, until finally he admitted: "I have to tell you, Joey, that now I know of your heritage, I can feel dear father looking at me all over again. I find it wonderfully reassuring that I have gained a brother for, growing up, I did most sorely miss the company of one."

Joey, his hidden heart beating rapidly at Paul's words, regarded him inscrutably for a long while before finally speaking.

"We will 'ave words again, Paul, about dividing the property. Fer I tell you most assuredly, I do not want it, an' as to 'avin' you fer a brother," replied Joey sternly. He then paused, noticing how immediately Paul's worried look appeared on his face. He found he could not help but smile at the sight of it, so he concluded with his mischievous grin: "Well, I could wish fer nawthin' better than to 'ave a more 'onest an' generous man than you fer mine."

Paul's face confirmed his gratitude at his words and he leaned forward impulsively, hugging him so forcibly in his pleasure that Joey had to let out a gasp of pain. Immediately, his brother released him and began to apologise profusely, his face such a picture of contrition that Joey had to laugh.

"You bleddy fool, Paul!" chuckled Joey and lifted his hand to dash the tears from his eyes, hoping that his brother would think he was crying with laughter alone and not from the sentiment, which brought a warm glow to his heart from the regard he bore him.

CHAPTER 25

"Surely, he has written to her by now?" enquired Dr Dunstan, his eyes open wide in surprise.

Joseph Bolitho shook his head, and now that his shoulder was at last free from its burdensome bandage, he stretched his arm and grimaced as his wound protested, warning him not to be too adventuresome.

"You had a clean wound there, Joey, and it has healed fast. More quickly than I would have thought. As soon as you have all your strength returned you will be free to go about again. I would advise you not to try to hold the reins of your horse just yet for that frisky beast of yours will pull your arm too roughly." Having finished with his examination, the doctor packed up his bag, then turned again to his patient and brought him back to his original question: "Has he had no communication with her at all?"

"Not that I am aware of, Denzil, an' at the moment I think I am closer to 'im than many, apart from the children that is. An' now that George 'as returned to school I can see 'im becoming more withdrawn," sighed Joey sadly.

"But there is no need, man, for all he has to do is pick up his pen and write her! He is the county's greatest living author, so surely he of all people can manage that?" the doctor cried in disbelief.

"It appears not," replied Joey and remained thoughtful, eventually saying, in a voice full of conviction: "I think 'e is too full of fear."

"But what has he to be afraid of? Mrs Trevarthen sends letters to the children all the time, and they reply to her. I heard Jack read his mother's letter to Paul only the other day, and so proud was he that he could read every word," he reasoned.

" 'Ess. I seen it too but I never seen one of the children say she do send 'en 'er love, Denzil. There is never a mention of their father in any letter that I d' knaw of," remarked Joey, shrugging himself into his coat.

"The servants have told me how badly he treated her. Insane with jealousy I imagine, for I have never known him behave in such a fashion ever before in my life. Perhaps she cannot forgive him after all?" the doctor suggested pensively.

"Perhaps she can't," replied Joey sadly, "but I wish fer 'is sake that she could, fer he is pining away fer love of 'er. Sarah-Jane tackled 'im 'bout it but 'e turned angry an' left the room sayin' it was 'is business and 'e would not talk of it, so we 'ave not spoken of it since. Mind you, I 'ave seen my Sarah-Jane bursting to 'ave words with 'en time an' time again," and he smiled proudly at the remembrance of those moments.

The doctor coughed and made the suggestion that perhaps someone else could write - on Paul's behalf as it were - and make Chloe realise how her husband was a true penitent and how much he was suffering, and he looked hopefully at Joey. He received an aloof stare for his answer and thought there would be no speech. But slowly, Joey said: "If I thought I could achieve anything I would take 'im by the neck an' shake 'im 'til 'e see sense, but Chloe once told me 'e do brick 'imself in with a wall a' sadness. Well, tha's what 'e's doin' now, Dr Dunstan, an' none a' we got Joshua's trumpet to blow down this

Jericho's wall. All the time I was lying sick an' 'e thought me asleep, I could see 'en sittin' in that chair an' knew 'en fer a man with a broken 'eart. 'E does not expect to be fergiven an' if she will not write 'en perhaps he is right. You d' knaw what he did, an' you d' knaw Paul. 'E don't expect 'er fergiveness, fer 'e cannot believe she will ever be able to, after what 'appened that night. Now you ask fer someone to write on 'is behalf," and he stared at him, suddenly belligerent with impotence. "What would you 'ave me say?" And as Dr Dunstan looked embarrassed, Joey snorted and thumped the top of the chest of drawers angrily.

"Well, someone should do something, for your new found brother will pine himself away 'ere long," lamented the doctor. Wishing Joey farewell, he left the room and made his way slowly and resignedly from the house.

Joey stared at the closed door for a long while, then adjusted his neck cloth as simply as he could, for his arm was still stiff. He made his way down the stairs and, hearing the sound of a piano, found his brother in the music room playing a sad, gentle tune. They smiled at each other. Paul would have stopped, but Joey asked him to continue, for he liked the sound of it, then went to a settle and sat down to watch him at the piano. The afternoon light cast him in silhouette and you could not tell the colour of his skin, for Paul appeared dark against the light, but his profile showed his father's face more clearly to Joey than ever before. He wondered what Redvers would have said and done to help his cherished son, for he could not believe that he would have let him go into such a decline without trying of his best to help him. Well, he thought to himself, as the elder, to him fell the responsibility of ensuring that his brother stepped back from the brink of despair, so he took a deep breath and asked him directly.

"Well, 'ave 'e 'eard from Chloe, yet?"

He watched as his brother's shoulders stiffened, but kept his face impassive as Paul turned and regarded him angrily.

"I will not discuss my private affairs with you!" Paul snapped, and he slammed down the lid of the piano and made to stand up.

" 'Pon my life, Paul, tha's rich comin' from the man who 'as done every damn thing 'e could to tie up my own affairs. I 'ave acquired property, position an' am shortly to acquire a spouse, all thanks to my own brother's efforts. Now I'm ferbidden to even talk 'bout the problem that besets 'im lest 'e like not what I would say to 'en. Well, damn you, Paul, I shall say what I bleddy well want to say to 'e!" As he watched his brother stride angrily across the room, he said softly: "Always knew 'e fer a fool, Paul, never knew 'e was a coward as well."

Paul swung around angrily and in a raised voice told him again that the matter was none of his business.

" 'Course 'tis my business!" retorted Joey, swiftly. "If I'd told 'e 'fore that I was yer brother, you and Chloe would still be together, you knaw that. Now yer so full a' fear of what yer wife d' think of 'e you can't even write the dear soul a letter tellin' 'er how you d' feel 'bout 'er, an' askin' to be fergiven fer what you did."

Joey did not turn in his seat to look at Paul, but knew intuitively how he was struggling to overcome the emotion that was welling up within him. After a moment, he heard his brother release his breath and to say softly: "I . . . I realise that you are only trying to help, Joey but . . . but for the sins I committed against Chloe I do not expect forgiveness."

"You aren't the first 'usband to sin against 'is wife, Paul," announced Joey, sympathetically, "even . . ," and he paused for a moment, before continuing frankly: "even our father did the same," adding thoughtfully: "more than once if we be anything to go by."

"I . . . I have sinned worse than father ever did, Joey," admitted his brother guiltily.

"I knaw, Paul, I knaw. Yer servants d' think the world of 'e but that didn't stop 'em talkin' 'bout what went on, but if 'e don't ask 'er to pardon 'e you'll never knaw if she'll come back to 'e," announced Joey, reasonably.

"There is no possibility of Chloe ever forgiving me for the crime I committed against her, Joey. What wife would want such a monster of a husband as I have proved myself to be?" He turned again and walked across to the window, staring sightlessly out of it, before announcing decisively: "No, I will not write, for I would only put more agony on her and she has suffered enough. If she wishes to come to see the children I will go away rather than that my presence offend her, for the sight of me must appal her."

"How noble!" remarked Joey sarcastically, "I'm sure she'll be most impressed with yer attitude."

He waited for his brother to reply, but exhaled noisily as it became clear that Paul had no intention of continuing the conversation. So he rose and silently left the room, leaving his brother to contemplate his bleak future in isolation.

During the following days, he watched in frustration as Paul became even more withdrawn. Even though he made further attempts to persuade his brother to write his wife, all his efforts came to nothing, for Paul would not change his mind, no matter how persuasive Joey made himself to be. There were heated words and long sulking silences, but try as he would, he could not move his brother to write. It was no surprise to his affianced, therefore, to find Joey sitting at the table in the withdrawing room, attempting to write a letter, for he was determined that Chloe should know of her husband's deep repentance and of his churlish stupidity. When he explained to Sarah-Jane precisely what it was that he was about, he had the grace to blush when she pointed out that his own reluctance to explain himself to Paul concerning his identity, was an example of what appeared to her to be a family trait.

"That was a different matter!" Joey snapped, annoyed.

"Nonsense!" she rejoined, tartly, "for the more I see you together the more alike you appear to be, you can be just as blindly determined in your attitude as Paul. You persist in not accepting your father's inheritance, but I can see why Paul should wish for you to inherit your share of Redvers' estate. What nonsense to refuse his offer to give you the security he thinks you deserve. As to your future: without that money, what do you propose to do?"

"I 'ave some money of me own. 'Tis not all gone fer I was at my trade since almost a boy," he muttered defensively.

"Trade!" she said, peremptorily, "Trade! Your name for your smuggling activities seems hardly fitting to my ears."

He blushed again and raised his blue eyes to hers, noticing how her cheeks were tinged a rosy red in temper.

"I 'ave never told you 'ow delightful you d' look when yer annoyed," he tried cajolingly, but Sarah-Jane was determined that he would not win her over and turned her shoulder to him. However, Joey was not a man to be deflected and, after a while, she felt his hand on her arm and turned her head to look at him. She noticed that his eyes had their coldness warmed by the expression of regard on his face. Sighing, she caught up his hand and squeezed it before saying softly: "Write to her, Joey, in the simplest terms of which you are capable. Tell her how much her husband needs her, for no one else will ever be able to take her place in his heart, and if she has any care for him at all she must come back to him. He fears her rejection more than anything, else 'een now he would be at her side, on his knees, asking forgiveness for his sins."

Slowly, Joey picked up the pen and passed it and the ink together with another sheet of paper across the table towards her.

"You write to Chloe, Sarah-Jane, fer 'twill be better to come from you," he suggested firmly.

She would have refused him, but in her heart she knew he spoke the truth and her avowal would prove more to Chloe than anything another person could write or say to her. So she set her pen to the paper and, as each sentence spread across the page, she knew that Chloe would understand the exactness of what she wrote. She spelt into each word her own acknowledgement that her love for her husband's brother had become the more complete. In spite of Paul's kindness to all around him, it was to Joey that she had looked for compassion, and received it, for he understood the pain of rejection. She ended her letter with a request that Chloe attend their wedding, stating that she bethought it only fitting that the family be complete after so many years of unknown division. When she had finished, she passed it to Joey for his perusal and, when he had read it through, he looked at her with his eyes shining, and a proud smile resting on his lips.

"Beautifully eloquent, my dearest," he said proudly. He took the letter and, sealing it with a wafer, passed it to her and furnished her with the direction. On completion, the letter was tucked into her reticule so that it could be taken to catch the mail in Penzance that day, thus ensuring that it would not go with the Trevu mail, in case Paul should observe it.

"Did you say . . . did you write so fer me, dearest?" Joey asked after some thought, and a look of disappointment crossed his face as she shook her head.

"No, I did not," she replied swiftly and then smiled, so that he caught sight of the dimples in her cheek, before she told him sincerely: "for both our sakes."

Joey smiled broadly and his response to her teasing was to pull her into his arms and kiss her passionately. He noted how she gave herself freely to him, as if a link in a chain had finally and irrevocably been broken. They sprang apart as they heard the door open and Paul Trevarthen was presented with the picture of two adults, regarding him as sheepishly as a girl and boy being discovered at an illicit tryst. Although his heart was gladdened at the sight of their love for each other, his own despair increased on perceiving their happiness. He made to withdraw, but Joey called his name and asked him if he wished to speak with him. Then, noting the hesitant look on his brother's face, he stood up and walked towards him.

"I did not realise that you had company, Joey. Good morning, Sarah-Jane. My apologies for not greeting you before, for I was unaware that you were here; I was engaged with some writing in my room," he explained.

"Writin' to anyone in particular, Paul?" asked his brother hopefully, but Paul flushed and said that he meant he had been occupied with a translation. They regarded each other awkwardly for a moment, then Paul said that he had wondered if Joey would wish to ride with him in the afternoon, for he had a quiet bay mare in his stables that was up to Joey's weight and would not be too taxing for him to manage with his injured arm. Joey regarded his brother's face calmly for a while, but then he admitted he would be glad to be free from the house, for he sorely missed not being able to go and ride as he was wont to do. So after lunch, Joey, mounted on a rather placid horse, accompanied his brother on a slow progress around the estate. Paul took the opportunity to point out to his brother the parcels of land that had been made over to him, mentioning that the lower farmhouse was empty and would be, as it was part of Joey's inheritance, an ideal home for himself and his wife. An annoyed look crossed his face as Joey shook his head and refused again to accept anything from Paul, giving for his reason that he had no wish to break up the estate.

"That house is usually given over to the estate manager, Paul, 'twould not be right fer it to be mine an' I will not accept it," Joey told him firmly.

"Jonas Hampton is a single man and he has no need of such a large house," replied Paul, and was surprised to see his brother throw back his head and roar with laughter.

"Maybe 'e don't want it today but it 'idden goin' be long 'fore 'e will be glad of it," chuckled Joey and, noting the look of surprise on Paul's face, told him that his estate manager was courting strong.

"Jonas? Courting?" cried Paul, and laughed himself at the absurdity of it.

"Yer estate man spends 'is evenings with 'is feet under Emily Bosanko's table, Paul. Did you 'ave no idea?" and on sight of his brother's astonished look, realised that the information was a complete surprise to him. Joey proceeded to tell him that Jonas and Emily had become great friends after Bert's death and slowly they had become attached to each other. Seeing Paul's obvious consternation, he proceeded to tease him for not realising that a man he had contact with every day should be able to conceal from him the details of his private life.

"And they intend to marry?" asked Paul.

"Well, if they don't tie the knot soon they'll 'ave to 'cos they got quite a passion fer each other," answered Joey sagely.

"I wish them happy, for a good marriage is a thing to be treasured," pronounced Paul, blushing quickly as he realised what he had said.

"Indeed it is, Paul!" said his brother and eyed him speculatively. Unable to return Joey's gaze, he turned his horse away from the property and they both began slowly to cross the fields to Paul's side of the estate. The Master of Trevu, unlike in the past, avoided all contact with any person seen working in the fields and, although he still rode around the farms on his estate, he rarely visited any of his tenants. He was accompanying his brother only because Dr Dunstan had called to see Joey and after had sought out Paul, to advise him that his brother was capable of riding and that some sensible exercise would be of great benefit to him. After an hour's gentle exertion, he looked at his brother in astonishment when Joey suggested that they put the horses to the gallop. An expression of consternation swept across Paul's face and his brother found himself on the receiving end of a lecture on the stupidity of jeopardising the excellent progress he was making on returning to fitness.

"Well, damn it, Paul, this is tedious stuff!" complained Joey.

"I care not, Joey," returned his brother swiftly and continued with sanctimonious censure: "Dr Dunstan said you were not to over tire yourself and I am merely following his advice."

"As you will, Paul!" snapped the convalescent, annoyed by his tone, "then follow this as well!" Joey slapped his mare into a gallop and took off across the fields. When, finally, Joey reined in his horse and halted, he waited patiently as his brother galloped up, unable to hide his smile at the thunderous expression on Paul's face.

"What damned foolishness, Joey, after all the care that has been taken of you!" stormed Paul as he pulled up his grey beside the winded mare.

"Well stop treatin' me as if I were an old spinster, Paul, fer 'tis more than I can bear an' so I tell you!" replied his brother with a wide, beaming smile on his face, completely at variance with Paul's angry expression.

"You could have broken open your wound again with your stupidity," snapped Paul, in no way mollified by his brother's smile.

"Fiddlesticks!" cried Joey, but he turned his horse and suggested compliantly that they made their way home.

"Best not to try that trick again with me," said Paul testily, still annoyed by his brother's unreasonable behaviour.

"Oh stop goin' on, Paul," said Joey tersely, "fer yer just as bad! You 'ave taken no notice of all the advice yer friends 'ave been givin' 'e."

"I shall not tell you again, Joey! Best for you if you were to refrain from interfering in my life!" he suggested angrily.

Joey regarded him inscrutably before pointing out to his brother that, as the elder, he felt he had an obligation to advise Paul when he considered him to be in need of guidance. Paul's shocked expression bore testament to the fact that he had never considered him in a position of authority over him.

"I . . . I . . ." Paul began, but his brother, seizing his advantage, swiftly interrupted him:

"As yer determined that I'm to be included in yer family, then I think 'tis only right that my brother's wife and the woman who 'as become a sister to me should receive some communication from you, fer yer attitude is selfish, needless and childish," he announced severely.

Paul blushed, but then his mulish expression settled on his face and, forgetting his previous desire not to do anything to prejudice his brother's recovery, he laid his whip into his horse's sides and headed back to Trevu at a gallop. Joey watched with a grim smile, then sighed, shook his head and set off after the disappearing figure.

The following day, Paul sought out his estate manager and tentatively asked him if he would wish to remove from his cottage to the Lower Farm. Jonas, blushing fiercely, replied that he had been considering it but, when it became known that parts of the estate were to be divided between his master and Joseph Bolitho, he realised that this would make a difference to his plans.

"Joey is still steadfastly refusing to accept anything from me, he has even told my solicitor that he does not wish to have any part of the lands and monies I have divided between us," sighed Paul. "Yesterday we rode over the estate and even when I pointed out all that was to be his, he would have none of it. I will not let him leave here to go to Sarah-Jane with no more than the clothes he stands up in, for he has promised me faithfully not to go to the smuggling trade again. But with no knowledge of anything else, what can he do?" and Paul presented a worried face to his estate manager.

"Set him up in a business he can follow, for Joey is not like you, Paul. He'll not be content to sit around on his farm. He's a man for the company of people. Since he has been up and about, he's been down with the farm hands and stable lads, desperate for company. As soon as he is allowed to go he'll be touring the inns of Penzance, as usual, and if he has enough money, wider afield as well," Jonas informed him. He coughed and looked at the floor, but continued staunchly: "You are the brother for the estate, Paul, not Joey; for he has not the temperament for it and he, at least, is wise enough to know it."

Paul nodded his head in agreement before announcing: "I know you speak the truth, Jonas, but I cannot let him go back to his foul trade, not only for his sake but his dear wife's yet to be. I have a great regard for both of them and I could not bear that."

"Then buy him a property and set him up in a business that will involve him in enough work to keep him out of trouble, but not so much that he cannot enjoy the benefits of his endeavours," Jonas said sagely.

"I would be quite prepared to do that if I knew of any trade that he could follow. He knows something of farming, something of the sea, a layman's knowledge of mining and, considering his precarious upbringing, is remarkably well read, but that accomplishment will not serve him either as a teacher or a librarian," said Paul despondently.

Jonas could not help but laugh at the thought of Joseph Bolitho as a librarian and his amusement even brought a smile to Paul's lips. They lapsed into silence and sat deep in thought, puzzling on Joseph Bolitho's future, whilst the subject of their deliberations sat with just such a troubled mind and considered if there was any other way in which he could help his brother and his family.

CHAPTER 26

PAUL descended the stairs leading down to the hallway with a thoughtful expression on his face, only looking up as the big main door slowly opened. He noted the care that the man took as he closed the door softly behind him and watched silently as he walked cautiously into the hallway.

"Good morning, Joey," said Paul, a look of annoyance on his face.

"Ah, Paul!" said his brother with a start. "Good morning, I . . . I didden expect to see you," he muttered sheepishly.

"That I can well believe and judging from your appearance, I should imagine that you would wish to wash and shave before joining me in the dining room," said Paul sternly. He looked into his brother's unwashed face and, observing his crumpled clothes, advised him that he would also find a clean set of clothes laid out in his room.

Bolitho had the grace to blush. "I thought it best to stay with Seth fer I was well into me cups, after meetin' up with the boys at Josh's. Didden' think I could get 'ome anyways," said Joey, grinning mischievously at his brother.

Paul pursed his lips, but merely said that he was glad that his brother had enjoyed his visit to his old friends, but would have thought it better if he had sent a message to Trevu to explain his absence.

"After all," he added, severely, "You have been away for two nights and apart from Jonas meeting with Nat Roscorla yesterday, no one here had any idea of exactly what had happened to you or indeed where you were. Jonas said your house was locked up, so we knew you were not at home. And when Sarah-Jane came to see you yesterday, I had great difficulty in explaining to her that you appeared to be visiting your old friends and that I had no knowledge of when exactly you would be returning. I will see you at breakfast and tell you what your affianced had to say about that," he said brusquely and passed him by, making his way towards the dining room.

Joey swore under his breath and, once in his room, lost no time in removing two days growth of beard and making himself presentable. Consequently, it was not long before he joined his brother at the big dining table, looking almost back to normal, or as normal as he could be, bearing in the mind that he had spent two days of conviviality in Penzance, enjoying his freedom from the oppressive atmosphere that now pervaded every part of Trevu. He studied his brother's serious expression, but was unable to raise a smile when he mentioned that Paul would have made a good schoolmaster with his strict ways.

"I have made allowance for the fact that it is difficult for you to adapt to living in this house after the sort of life you have led, but I think you should show some consideration for others," remarked Paul in a unyielding voice. But Joey, completely unabashed by his brother's sermon, suddenly announced that he proposed to leave soon and return to his own home. Paul stopped in the action of raising his tankard to his lips and looked at him in disbelief.

"Surely not?!" he cried. "You cannot wish to return to that hovel when you have every right to live here until your marriage. You will not go to church from Penzance but will leave from Trevu, for Sarah-Jane wishes most particularly to be married in St. Martin's, as it was the church in which she was baptised and her parents are buried in the cemetery. Whether you wish to or not, you will return to Trevu for your wedding breakfast an' so I tell you!" He raised his hand as Joey opened his mouth to interrupt him and continued firmly: "Oh no, Joey. You will remain here, for the whole of Penzance knows you have come into a fortune and should you spend a night in your old home, you will likely be murdered in your bed by some fool thinking to rob you."

"Jes' 'ang on a moment, Paul!" returned Joey, in an annoyed tone. "I'll decide whose roof I'm to sleep under I'll 'ave you knaw, not you. I've no desire to spend longer in this 'ouse than necessary an' I think I'm near 'nuff fit to go now, so you can stop makin' schemes fer me. I don't want yer property or yer money, fer I 'ave some of me own left an' Sarah-Jane knows it afore you start goin' on 'bout me 'aving nothin'. Once I'm married I can look 'round fer a way of earnin' a livin', an' I can do that without any 'elp from you," and he slapped his hand down on the table in temper.

If he expected that his brother would now withdraw his objections he was mistaken. Paul had spent two nights of worry; for he had a great fear for his brother now that his financial and social circumstances had changed. Joey could no longer go abroad with Likky for bodyguard and had to rely on his own instincts. And now, given the knowledge that he had spent his time away from Trevu, happily drinking himself into what Paul imagined was a stupor, for his appearance that morning gave him that impression, who would there be to look after him? Paul's newly acquired fraternal instincts were aroused and he determined that his brother should accept his position in the new society in which he found himself, so he drew a deep breath and continued unabashed.

"You will stay under this roof until you have come to your senses, for I will not have you turn into a drunk and layabout because you have no occupation to follow to fill up your days, now that you have promised not to go back to the smuggling. If the life of a farmer does not appeal to you, then your money can be used to set yourself up in some . . ." but he was forestalled from saying more as Joey swore at him.

"Damn you, Paul, stop now before I 'it 'e one! You can't go 'round buyin' people's lives. Bert didden' want money from you an' neither do I!" he shouted, thoroughly annoyed by Paul's sanctimonious attempts to organise his life. He noted the shocked and pained expression that swept across his brother's face, but Paul's attitude had made him lose his own temper and he refused to be swayed by his brother's arguments.

"What's all this 'bout me bein' a drunk, anyways?" he snapped, angrily, "I'll admit I couldn' ride me 'orse but I've seen you in a worse state, an' I stayed over to Seth's place so with his beard I didden expect 'ave the use of a razor. My 'ouse is still in a mess, but it can be done up fer God's sake an' made 'abitable."

"I am sure Sarah-Jane cannot wait to get over the threshold and begin to order the furnishings," scoffed Paul sarcastically, "for she must be sorely tempted to leave her house for your dwelling, and in such a salubrious location as yours is to be found!"

Joey clenched his fist in temper, but Paul stared at him boldly and would not withdraw.

"Sarah-Jane may 'ave done well fer 'erself but she's not the pompous ass you 'ave turned out to be, Paul!" he hissed.

"I am not and never have been a pompous ass!" shouted his brother angrily, hurt by Joey's remark. "I do not regard myself to be better than any other man, but if you think I care so little for my father's son that I will let him throw away an opportunity to accept his rightful place in society, then you are much mistaken. I care enough of you for that, and as for my dearest and oldest friend Sarah-Jane, well I will not have you drag her down to living amongst thieves and vagabonds as you seem happy for her to do. I have enough concern for her that I would wish for her to be comfortable in her marriage, and not to have to live with a man who imagines that he can provide her with everything she desires from an address that even the lowest of the low would think himself impoverished to live in."

"Damn you, Paul, I'll not 'ear any bleddy more from 'e!" swore Joey and rose to his feet, his temper lost. Paul, just as enraged, stood up so quickly that his chair fell over backwards onto the floor with a loud crash.

"Well, well!" said a cool voice from the doorway, "I see you have become well acquainted with your brother, Paul."

Both men whirled about and found themselves looking into the amused countenance of Peter Fleetwood. He smiled at their shocked expressions, then turned to Beth, who stood behind him with a worried look on her face and asked her most charmingly if she would very kindly bring another tankard to the table and, if possible, procure some coffee for him. She glanced nervously at Paul - who nodded his assent - and then rushed to the kitchen to supply the distinguished gentleman's needs.

Meanwhile, Peter walked nonchalantly into the room and clapped Paul on the back in greeting, before turning to Joey with his hand outstretched and saying: "Delighted to meet you again, Joey. I see you are recovered from your injury." Then he shook his hand enthusiastically before adding: "And I would thank you most sincerely for saving your fool brother's life, even though I can understand that he can be the most trying of individuals especially when, as now, he is attempting to impose his way upon others. In spite of his wayward life, he occasionally wraps himself in the garb of a saint, and when he adopts that attitude he can be the most infuriating man, can he not?" and he beamed wickedly into Joey's angered face.

"Damn infuriatin', Peter," agreed Joey. His temper quickly ebbed as he looked into the smiling face and felt no small measure of relief to meet again with Paul's old friend.

Beth returned with a tray, containing a coffee pot along with another jug of ale and a tankard and set them down on the table. She blushed rosily at Peter, who expressed his thanks and watched in admiration of her face and figure as she turned and left the room.

"Damn me, Paul, that young woman is the most delightful creature," enthused Peter knowledgeably, before turning his attention to his consumption of breakfast. Paul and Joey exchanged embarrassed glances, then Paul picked up his chair and, along with his brother, resumed his seat.

Peter made polite conversation with both of them; Paul was intrigued to find how it was that Joey was known to his old friend and so was informed of the circumstances under which they met.

"When I told you to stay your hand, Joey, I was not aware of how fast things were moving against Paul as regards that customs chap, whatever his name was. Damn lucky for you, Paul, that your brother was keeping an eye on things for you. Knowing you as I do, I can imagine that you had no knowledge of the plot the man had hatched to embroil you. Oh! Before I forget, Joey, Chloe sends her best regards on your impending marriage and her thanks for all your kindness you have shown to the children."

Paul started as if he had been stung and cried: "Chloe! Have you . . . have you seen her?" and turned a desperate face towards Peter.

"Good lord, yes," replied Peter, and took a long drink from his tankard before adding quietly: "I have made frequent calls on Clifton Court. She it was who has been informing me of what has been happening at Trevu, for she has had letters from the children and Miss Clavering, who understandably has been able to supply her with much needed information regarding the children's welfare and all the happenings here. Caroline Crebo has also been a most enthusiastic correspondent as well."

Joey, glancing at his brother's face, noted his stunned expression and quickly asked if all was well with his sister-in-law.

Peter lowered his gaze briefly, and then looked up with a determined expression on his face.

"She has not been in the best of health, no, but the doctor has said that with care and kindness she may be able to have the roses bloom again in her cheeks," and he turned to Paul as he heard a low moan from him. There was an awkward silence, until Paul whispered that he hoped that she had called in a reliable doctor to attend her.

"Naturally," replied Peter, " your mother's practitioner and the best in London, but even he could not perform miracles."

He withstood Paul's worried and guilt ridden expression for only a little while, before informing him softly: "Even the most experienced doctor has no medicine at his disposal when it comes to mending a broken heart, Paul."

"Perhaps . . . perhaps if I sent the children to see her," began Paul after a long pause, during which time he tried to master his tortured feelings, "then . . . they might be of help to . . ." but Joey told him to open his eyes to what his friend was trying to tell him.

" 'Twas not losin' touch with 'er children that 'as so saddened 'er, 'tho' God knows tha's bad enough fer 'er, but 'tis not 'avin' any word from you, you bleddy fool!" he cried in exasperation.

"Beautifully expressed, Joey, and I can imagine that you have been uttering similar sentiments for quite some time now," Peter remarked. Then he sighed as he added: "But my old friend and your new brother can be most obstructive when it comes to accepting good advice," and he noted Paul's darkening skin as a flush swept across his face.

"Better for Chloe if she should see you, Paul, for 'tis not the children who have lost their love for her," he informed him.

"I have . . . I have never stopped . . . even when I thought . . . She is ever all about me," Paul announced finally, "in my head and my heart."

"Then tell her, you fool, for she has great need of that knowledge," urged Peter desperately.

"I cannot, for I have destroyed the sanctity of my marriage and for that she will never forgive me! My actions will never be pardoned, for there is not a woman alive who would bear to have me in their presence again!" Paul rose swiftly from the table and fled the room before either could say a word to him, slamming the door behind him.

"Have you ever noticed, Joey, that when Paul is at his most despondent, he will run and hide his hurts like a beaten dog?" Peter noted calmly, and shook his head before smiling at Joey's worried countenance.

"Paul 'as convinced 'imself that she will never fergive 'en. Nawthin' I 'ave said will make 'im write 'er because 'e is afraid of 'er answer," sighed Joey in a sombre voice.

"I imagine he has been the most trying of hosts, and knowing him of old I should imagine that you have had a hard time of it with him," noted Peter sympathetically.

Joey grinned but then said seriously: "Damned frustratin'! An' 'e will not leave off tryin' to set me up as 'is equal. Still, my refusals have kept 'im schemin' an' plannin' on my be'alf an' that has been a 'elp to 'im fer I don't mind tellin' 'e Peter, there 'ave bin times when I thought 'e would blow his brains out, such as bin' 'is despair."

"I can imagine, for he looks a shadow of his former self," admitted Peter worriedly.

"Will she . . . will Chloe come back to 'en?" asked Joey desperately.

"She does not say, but she looks as ill as her husband. It is almost as if without the other they are unable to exist, but she is the wronged person in this case and will not bring herself to pardon him for he has not asked her forgiveness. I have come to see what I can do to bring about a reconciliation between them, but Paul is going to make that difficult because his intransigence will not allow him to make the first move," said Peter.

" 'Tis not intransigence Peter, 'tis fear. 'E 'as made 'imself believe she will not 'ave 'im back, so if 'e does not ask 'e will not be 'urt further," Joey told him, before adding vehemently: "Bleddy fool!"

"Just so," Peter agreed sadly.

Peter sat at the writing desk in the library, and wrote quickly and precisely in his elegant script. He sealed his letter with a wafer and tucked it out of sight into his coat pocket, then got up to leave the room. But just as he was replacing his chair, Paul opened the door and, catching sight of Peter, smiled briefly and strode towards him.

"I was wondering if you would be going into Penzance, Peter, for I have some documents for the mail and I would much appreciate it if you could take them for me," he asked simply.

"Certainly, old fellow," acquiesced Peter jovially.

"I would go myself but I . . ." Paul attempted to explain, but his friend smiled sympathetically and merely said: "I know, Paul, for Joey has told me you rarely leave the house these days."

"My brother is ever on at me to visit my old friends, but in truth I rarely go in. I had to when I discovered what relation Joey was to me, for I wished the news spread abroad as quickly as was possible; he was in no position to stop the gossip from diffusing throughout the locality, laid up as he was. He wished that father's indiscretion should not be known, but I have always maintained that, if father had knowledge of his firstborn, he would have seen him well endowed with money. If my dearest stepmother had heard of his existence she would have desired that he should have been brought to Trevu, an' methinks his mother would have been glad to have been rid of him. She plied her trade quite happily, apparently, but he thought none the less of her in spite of her lack of care of him," and he proceeded to tell Peter the tale of his brother's young life and the struggle he had to maintain his existence.

"I could never come to terms with the way he led his life, but even I have great sympathy for many of his actions," Paul said sympathetically. They both turned as the door opened again and admitted the subject of their discussion. The look on their faces was proof enough to Joey that they had been spending their time talking about him.

"Sarah-Jane 'as called, Paul. I thought I should let you knaw an' I was wishful fer Peter to meet with 'er, fer I understand that they 'ave never been introduced." He spoke sharply, for it annoyed him to be spoken of in his absence.

"Delighted to make the lady's acquaintance," said Peter quickly and smoothly, "for I have often heard the family speak of her but it has never been my pleasure to meet her," and he followed Joey to the withdrawing room.

Peter's pleasant manner soon set Sarah-Jane at ease and he sat and conversed with her in his usual friendly fashion. They exchanged fond memories of Redvers and Joey devoured their reminiscences hungrily, for he was always most keen to hear of his father, as all his life he had felt the lack of one. When it was time for Sarah-Jane to leave, Peter said his goodbyes and, after Paul had wished her farewell, he linked arms with Peter and led him off to the library again. It was there that Joey found them, after he had seen his fiancé safe into her carriage and had waved her off the premises.

"Did Sarah-Jane have words with you about your exploits, Joey?" asked Paul with a slight grin, and his brother's raised eyebrows and answering smile made him laugh out loud. He proceeded to explain to a bemused Peter what their amusement had been about, but Peter soon wiped the smile from his face by giving details of Paul's own activities as a young man.

"Well, who are you to talk?" responded Paul sharply to his friend, "for we hardly had time to dine when you took me on a tour of those houses in London that summer."

"Lord, what a time we had! A girl for each arm and sometimes another to kiss, as well," laughed Peter, wiping the tears from his eyes.

"If you could 'ave 'eard the sermon I got from 'en this mornin', over the breakfast table," and Joey waved his hand to indicate his brother, " you wouldn' believe 'twas the same person," he told him, "an' all I was about was 'avin' a few drinks with me friends."

Their jovial company began to improve Paul's disposition, and it was a far more relaxed man that saw Peter off in his curricle to Penzance.

The following morning, Paul and Joey were surprised to find Peter already at breakfast and busy exchanging pleasantries with Beth. Paul noted her high colour and, as soon as she had left the room, advised Peter that he had better not be contemplating any of his horse-play with her, for her father was one of his tenants and a local preacher into the bargain.

"Trevu's reputation is mired enough, without that my friend should attempt any indiscretions with the servants," Paul told him solemnly.

" 'Pon my soul, that's rich, coming from you, Paul, for there was nary a girl safe in the locality, so Hannah, bless her, informed me when I first came to stay. You were after them all, so she told me, and you certainly showed no shyness when you took me to Penzance and . . ."

"Peter!" said Paul sharply, and looked quickly at his brother. But Joey merely grinned and told him not to act so righteously, for he knew full well the sort of life he had led back then.

"Well," remarked Paul defensively, "that was in my youth, and unlike Peter I have outgrown such exploits. Best for you if you had married and settled down, Peter," he added and frowned at his friend.

"Fiddlesticks!" replied Peter unabashed, "I am not the marrying kind, Paul, for I would soon become bored with just the one woman to amuse me and anyway, unlike you, I never found one that I loved in the way that you love Chloe."

Paul was stricken into silence and lowered his gaze to his plate in consternation. His brother began to regale them with a tale of Jack's latest exploit, which had been recounted to him the previous evening and involved the necessity of an apology to old Davy.

"Poor Davy woke up with a start an' grabbed fer his jacket, not knawin' the young rascal 'ad looped string down through the arm an' 'ad attached it to the 'andle of a bucket a' water placed on the beam above 'im. Fair drenched 'e was, an' Jack said Miss Clavering give 'im what fer an' no mistake fer what 'e 'ad bin' about." His gleeful laugh was infectious and soon both men had joined in the merriment but, as soon as Peter had consumed a fortifying breakfast, he announced his intention of leaving Trevu for the day, as he had made arrangements to visit someone. Smiling apologetically, he informed Paul that he would not be returning in time for lunch.

"As you wish, Peter, but take care on our country tracks for you know how easily you can be caught out, an' I should not wish you returned on a pallet with your head broke," Paul told him seriously.

"I should have a care yourself, Paul, for you are becoming quite a cantankerous old bore, you know," rejoined Peter swiftly. Smiling serenely, he nodded farewell to them both and swept out of the room before his host could think of a suitable retort. Joey's suggestion of a ride around the estate found favour with his brother, for although it was a cold day the sun was shining brightly. This time, Paul did not fear that his brother would damage his arm and so they made good progress. On the way home, they chatted easily to each other and when lunch was set before them, Joey noted with pleasure that Paul made a better meal than he had been known to do of late. They were in the library, happily discussing books when the children returned from school. Joey was soon led away by Jack, for he had much to tell him and Grace headed for the nursery to play with little Alice, so Paul found himself alone with Daisy. She smiled at him brightly and went to sit by him, then leaned her head on his arm and sighed.

"You seem in a much better frame of mind today, Father. Quite the best you have been for a long time now. Have you . . . have you had good news perhaps?" she asked hopefully. She felt him stiffen and heard the sudden intake of breath, but he did not lose his temper and snap at her as he was wont to do if she said the wrong thing. Instead he told her that his friend, Mr Fleetwood, had been to see Mama. Then Paul asked if she would like to see her mother again soon.

"Oh, Father! Is Mama to come home? Oh! I must run and tell the others for how pleased they will be," and she made to get up, but Paul caught at her arm and turned her to face him. It almost broke his heart to see the sadness that crept over her shining face as he explained that he meant that the children should go, in Miss Clavering's care, to visit their mother.

"You would like to visit her, would you not, Daisy?" he asked nervously.

"Yes, Dada," she answered honestly and then added: "but I would much rather you asked her back to be by your side, for you have missed her so and to see you all alone is a great sadness to us."

Paul, completely taken aback by her sudden pronouncement, turned his head aside in an effort to blink away the tears that sprang to his eyes. His daughter gently placed her arm around his neck and softly whispered into his ear: "Please ask Mama to come home, Dada, please," and dropped a kiss on his wet cheek. Paul hugged his daughter to him, but could find no words to say to her. So, when the door to the library swung open soundlessly, they were still locked together in their embrace and consequently unaware that they were being observed.

"Paul?" a soft voice called, and he recognised at once the sound that he thought never to hear again.

"Mama!" shrieked Daisy delightedly. She rushed from her father's side, flung herself into her mother's arms and felt a soft kiss on her curls. But when she looked up into her mother's face, she was not looking at her daughter, but was staring at her husband and Daisy could not understand the hurt expression that lay across her features. She turned slowly and realised that her father had not moved from his seat, but still sat with his head turned away from the door, unable to look at his wife.

"Daisy, dearest Daisy. I will come to the nursery to see you all soon, but please to leave your father and I alone for a while, for it is most important that we should talk," Chloe told her quietly in a firm voice.

"But . . . but you have come home to us, Mama? You will not go away again, will you?" asked Daisy, suddenly aware of the sadness in her voice and the tension in the air.

"Later, Daisy, later. I will see you all later but please, dearest, to leave us alone now," she said again.

"Yes Mama," Daisy replied sadly and made to leave, but of a sudden turned back to her mother and whispered impulsively in her ear: "Please forgive him Mama, for he has suffered so." Then, before her tears fell, she rushed from the room and her footsteps could be heard running across the hall and up the stairs.

There was a long silence, then Paul heard the silk of her dress rustle as she moved across the floor towards him. He desperately tried to control his shaking hands as her perfume filled the air around him.

"Paul?" she said again, "Are you so ashamed that you cannot even look at me?"

"I have no right to expect you even to speak to me, Chloe, even less that you should wish to see me ever again," he answered slowly, his voice trembling as he spoke.

"I have to sit down, Paul, for I am so very tired," she announced wearily and, as she moved to a seat, he stood up immediately and looked at her for the first time. His heart leapt at the sight of her, even though he could see that a worn and ill woman stood before him and not the vivacious wife that he had known of old. The sparkling eyes were dimmed and, although short of stature, she had never stooped as she did now. Her cheeks had lost their colour and there was no smile to be seen on her lips. He procured a chair for her and as he took her hand to help her to the seat, he felt a sharp sensation shoot through his whole body at the touch of her.

"Oh!" she sighed, "That is so much better, for I have not been used to standing for so long."

"Peter . . . Peter said that you have been ill," he told her awkwardly, an unbearable pain in his heart to have her again in his company, but so removed from it.

"Yes, but the doctor has told me that I will recover, if the circumstances needed to improve my health are followed," she told him softly. Her eyes poured over his face, drinking in every feature and, like her husband, she was aware of how careworn his face had become and the sadness that overlay it.

Aware of her gaze, he lowered his eyes for he was too ashamed to look at what he had wrought in her.

"I can go away, Chloe and . . . and you can stay here with the children for they have missed you so . . . so dreadfully and . . . and 'twould not be right for them to be denied your presence," he muttered clumsily.

"Have you missed me, Paul?"

"Missed you? Missed you? I have burnt up my nights longing for you and my days despairing that I would never see you or hear your dear voice ever again!" he cried in an anguished voice and tried to cut short a bitter sob.

"Peter says that you cannot ask to be forgiven, for you do not believe that I could ever pardon you your actions that day," she told him quietly, watching as he hung his head in shame.

"I have no right to expect to be pardoned, Chloe, an' I would not ask that you should so demean yourself to me, for well I know that I have lost all the love you held for me because of my monstrous behaviour," he said slowly. Then, turning his face away, he began to stand up to move away from her. She reached out her hand to touch his arm but, unaware of her action, he was on his feet and had moved across the room to stand at the window, staring bleakly at the fields and valleys that stretched away across the winter landscape. Slowly, she withdrew her hand and let it fall. They remained silent for a long while, until he heard her soft voice again and forced himself to return to her side. He smiled sadly into her sombre eyes and asked how she had suddenly appeared in the house again.

They sat beside each other on the hard-backed library chairs and talked softly for a long and agonising time. He learnt that she had travelled from

London in Peter's company and, although she had Lizzie to care for her, by easy stages. She had rested for two nights at his Aunt Caroline's until Peter had come to fetch her. He had told Chloe that it was her choice if she wished to see her husband, for he could easily travel back to Trevu and explain to Paul that his wife wished to see her children and only her children. As she talked of them, tears fell softly down her cheeks. When she said that she would like to see them again, Paul looked discomforted for a moment, then bent and gently lifted Chloe's slight body, carried her to the withdrawing room and sat her on the settle. Noting how cold her hands were, he sent for Beth to get a rug to lay over her legs and he put extra logs on the fire to warm the room. As he stood up to go to the nursery and collect the children, there was a knock at the door and Peter stood in the doorway, asking if he might come in. But, on being told about Chloe's wish to see her children, he advised Paul to stay with Chloe and offered himself to go and collect them. But Joey, already informed by the servants that the mistress had come home, overheard him and called from the hallway that he would go instead. The children were so excited to see their mother again, that Paul worried that they would be too boisterous for her in her state of health, but she waved aside his protests and seemed to begin to blossom with their tears and kisses. Grace sat at her side with a rapturous expression on her face, Jack's eyes glowed, snuggling into her other side. Little Alice crawled onto her lap, chuckling happily although she had no clear recollection of her mother. Daisy sat and stared in wonder at the happy group and could not keep her beaming smile from her more often inscrutable face. Miss Clavering sat in a chair by the settle and hid her face in her handkerchief, snuffling loudly. It was a moment before Paul noticed that his brother was in the room and when he looked at him, he became aware that he was holding something in his arms. It was only when the bundle emitted a cry of rage that he realised with a shock what exactly it was that Joey clutched against his chest so tenderly.

"My latest nephew," announced Joey proudly. Smiling at Paul's astonished expression, he strode towards his brother and carefully placed the tiny baby into his arms.

Too shocked to speak, he stared at Chloe open mouthed and she lifted her head, watching for what his reaction would be. In spite of her heavy burden of sadness, she could not forgo but to giggle back at him irrepressibly at the sight of his astounded countenance.

"A rather strong willed little man," smiled Chloe as two minuscule dark fists thrashed the air and a series of strong yells emitted from the bundle.

"Has he a name?" Paul asked in wonder.

"Not yet, Paul, for I was unsure what you wished to call him," she told him. At her words he looked at her hopefully, but dreaded to wish for more than she had already given him.

Turning his attention to his son, he studied the child for a long while and as it quietened in his firm, rocking clasp, he carefully announced the name that he wished to call him by.

"Samuel," then he looked up and caught his brother's smiling face and said softly: "Samuel Joseph Trevarthen." He saw Joey's face flush with pleasure, then turning to Chloe, his heart leapt to see her nod in agreement. Noting her tired smile, he announced in a firm voice to the children that their Mama needed to rest, then he passed his son to the outstretched arms of Miss Clavering and, lifting his wife in his arms, carried her to the bedroom. Once Paul was satisfied that she had all she needed for her comfort, he told her he would leave her to rest, then awkwardly advised her that he had returned to sleeping in his old room and went on to explain his reason:

"For I could not bear to lie alone here after you had left . . . " then he lifted his chin and admitted guiltily: "after I had so mistreated and wronged you and sent you from your home."

She regarded him inscrutably, and then said in a soft but firm voice the words that filled his heart with a crushing pain: "Perhaps it will be for the best, Paul, if you should remain there."

From the depths of his despondency he dragged up a feeble smile, then advised her to rest and withdrew, closing the door quietly behind him.

CHAPTER 27

ONCE again, Penzance had another Trevarthen scandal to contend with. But this time the house flooded with visitors, overjoyed to have Chloe back in their midst once more. If they noted how awkward the couple seemed to be in each other's company, they had nothing to say to either of them concerning their private life, but in their withdrawing rooms they happily dissected every look and word that they saw and heard.

"After all," announced Mrs Penrose, the eldest daughter of the late Mrs Carter, "I think it only right that Chloe should return to her home 'een though Paul had treated her abominably."

"Perhaps," mused the old Squire's widow, "but although she is back amongst her family, it is obvious to me that he has yet to win himself back into her good graces. Why, he has the look of a desperate suitor 'bout him! 'Twas most apparent I thought, did not you, dear Mrs Hudson?"

From the midst of her widow's weeds, Mrs Hudson was heard to say pointedly that Mrs Trevarthen was most fortunate to have a husband at all for, as she proudly stated: "It is thanks to my own dear Gerald that Mr Trevarthen should be alive today, for if my dearest had not been the one who was shot then I do believe that that dreadful felon, Skewes, would have killed them all. He has the reputation of a most dreadful murderer. I was only saying to dear Mr Pawley, when he so kindly came to call with a book that I had expressed a desire to read, that I dread to think of the consequences if my poor Gerald had not so heroically laid down his life to save them. I am convinced that dearest Gerald had realised that Mr Bolitho was more to Mr Trevarthen then merely a friend, for he was ever the most astute of men. Mr Pawley says I must be most proud to have had such a man for a husband and indeed," she continued with a fond smile, "it is so. I often think of him, for dear Mr Pawley has said it is only right and proper that I should do so. Dear Mr Pawley is such a kind and understanding gentleman," and she sighed loudly and lowered her gaze to her black gloved hands. Two pairs of eyes exchanged shrewd glances, and although Mrs Hudson was unaware of it, the quiet, well mannered, unassuming bachelor librarian and the young, rather empty headed but kind hearted widow were having their future designed for them, although not a word had been said.

"Well," said Mrs Penrose, after a long silence, "we shall have to see if Paul can win back the devotion of his wife. 'Twill do him good to have to make the attempt, anyways." A baffled look from Mrs Hudson elicited the explanation that, for probably the first time in his life, Paul Trevarthen would have to win the affection of the one woman who would not fall at his feet in undisguised admiration. "For most times he has only to break into that enchanting smile of his, and there is not a woman whose heart does not flutter wildly at the sight of him," and all three ladies sighed and nodded their heads in confirmation of her perceptive remark.

Meanwhile, in Trevu, the object of their admiration set about his task to regain his wife's love, ignorantly imagining that no other was aware of his predicament. However, Lizzie and Beth ensured that the household was informed of how well he was faring in his attempt. Beth youthfully wished that all would soon be as it should be, but Lizzie, saddened and wiser, was unable to forgive her master so easily.

"An' she'll run 'en ragged afore ever 'e's allowed near she 'gain, Mr Bolitho," Lizzie informed Joey vehemently as he sat alone at the breakfast table, "an serve 'en right!"

"Paul is sufferin' mortal bad, Lizzie, surely you can see that, an' all the time the poor dear was away 'e was nearly out of 'is mind with despair," Joey pleaded softly. For well he knew that Lizzie had the ear of her mistress at all times, so close and fond had they become of each other during their enforced absence from Trevu.

For answer, Lizzie gave a derogatory sniff, but he fervently hoped that his words would be conveyed to Chloe. He glanced up at his brother as he quietly entered the dining room and saw his face darken as he was subjected to a withering stare from Lizzie's dark eyes. Looking suitably chastened, he took his seat and said not a word as the servant noisily set about her task of serving his breakfast. He thanked her humbly but was rewarded with only another loud sniff, then he watched her stiff, unbending back as she marched proudly from the room and closed the door behind her with a crisp click. Paul looked into his brother's sympathetic gaze, but Joey had nothing to say, for now that Chloe had returned to Trevu not one member of the household had enquired of the couple if all was well between them, and so the two brothers consumed their meal in almost complete silence.

However, life in Trevu had been improved by Chloe's return and Paul had never given up on his attempts to improve his brother's situation, for his wedding was fast approaching. Joey, still adamant in refusing the acceptance of any part of his brother's estate, was surprised one morning when Paul offered him one of his houses in Bristol.

"Not to own but to rent, although I will not be actually charging any money for its use," said Paul, with a twinkle in his eye.

"What would I do with a 'ouse in Bristol?" asked Joey bewildered, and watched his brother's slow smile break across his face.

"You will need to use a residence there to enable you to follow your new profession," Paul informed him, with a satisfied grin.

Joey's eyebrows signalled his confusion, so Paul explained that Chloe and Peter, in consultation with Sarah-Jane, had thought Joey would make an ideal wine merchant. For in his life the acquisition of alcohol, albeit by illegal means, had been a mainstay in it.

"And this time 'twill be legitimate, Joey," Paul told him firmly, with a forbidding expression on his face. But his enthusiasm returned as he continued: "What other profession could you follow, for you have a host of contact's already so I have had my agent in Bristol seek out a business suitable for your needs. Furthermore, I have been furnished with the name of a gentleman who wishes to sell out and retire in the new year and have begun the process of buying it in your name. He will be willing to explain the business to you, although you will have the advice and assistance of a manager who has been working for this gentleman for many a year." Paul noted with contentment that his brother appeared to be showing some interest in his proposal.

"Sarah-Jane is in favour of this?" he asked cautiously.

"Why yes, for she says it would be most beneficial to the inns that she will be running," answered Paul, and Joey was surprised to catch a mischievous grin playing on his brother's lips.

" 'Old 'ard, Paul, you go too fast fer me! What inns?" he asked, thoroughly confused.

"I have purchased two of the packet inns for Sarah-Jane's wedding gift. She is also considering turning her property in Falmouth into a hotel, for she says it is being wasted as it is and she much enjoyed helping her brother to maintain his inn many years ago. Of course, she will have to set up landlords to run them and has informed me that she has already appointed people to one of the premises," his brother informed him.

"She 'as mentioned none of this to me!" expostulated Joey angrily, and he frowned heavily before announcing defensively: "an' anyway I 'ave a lot of contacts in France, so 'aving the use of a 'ouse in Bristol might not be as useful to me as you d' think!" He glared at Paul and was dumbfounded to hear his brother agree with him, then reeled as Paul explained that a house had also been purchased in Dover.

"I'm to pay no rent fer this one either I s'pose?!" snapped Joey, unnerved by his feeling of having the ground disappear from beneath his feet.

"Certainly not, for 'tis my wedding gift to you," said Paul simply.

"Damn you, Paul, will you never stop interfering in my life?!" Joey fumed and he swore in frustration.

For answer, Paul walked to his brother's side and clasped his arm around his shoulder. "Joey, I promise faithfully that I will never interfere in your life again, an' if I should 'twill only be on two accounts."

Joey looked at his brother's smiling face suspiciously and asked succinctly: "An' what be they?"

"Why! That you are always to remain as faithful a brother to me as you have been since first you knew of my existence, and that when I purchase my brandy and Chloe's Madeira from you, that you do not overcharge me, of course?" Paul beamed at Joey, then grinned even wider to see the rueful smile that slowly broke across his brother's face.

"You bleddy fool, brother," laughed Joey, then shook his head and hugged him briefly and fondly.

The preparations for the wedding were unfolding in earnest and Paul sent to London for his tailor, to fit his brother with suitable attire that would proclaim to the world Joey's new status. Although Joey tried to overrule him, Sardi's son was adamant that he should be suitably clothed for such an important occasion and, even though Mr Murdoch could produce a fine coat and pantaloons, he could in no way match the talents of Mr Goldstein, Paul enthused. Joey attempted to remonstrate with his bride to be, when he visited her that evening, that once again he was being subjected to Paul's overbearing ways. But Sarah-Jane laughed off his complaint, for his brother was obtaining much pleasure from his actions. She informed him that she herself was to have her wedding dress - as well as a quantity of other modish outfits - made for her by the lady who ran Sardi's renowned establishment in London and that all the costs were to be placed on his brother's account. This respected lady had arrived in Penzance that very afternoon, along with six of her best seamstresses, and were at this moment resting in the finest hotel that the town had to offer.

"An' mark my words, 'twill not be long, Joey, before my establishments will rank alongside the best hotels in the county," she told him proudly and tilted her chin at him, then laughed at his expression of surprise. She reached up her hand and caressed his disbelieving face before planting a loving kiss on his lips.

"Methinks you'll 'ave me workin' all 'ours, Sarah-Jane, to 'elp maintain the quality of the refreshments served to yer guests," he told her in exasperation, but not without pride.

"Oh no! Not all hours, Joey!" she mocked him provocatively, then chuckled heartily as he pulled her to him, whispering her name softly into her brown curls. Then she allowed herself to be gripped in his strong embrace and had her teasing rewarded with his fierce and passionate kisses.

Peter arrived for the wedding celebrations, after stopping at Truro to call for Caroline Crebo and dutifully escorting her to Trevu. If he was somewhat irked at the pace at which he had to travel, his charming manners showed not a trace of it and Caroline descended from Paul's carriage with her face covered in a most contented smile. She was not so old that she could not appreciate the care and attention that had been shown to her, especially when the delivery came from that of such a personable younger man. Mr Fleetwood's many tales of his experiences around the world, suitably abridged for Caroline's ears, kept her enthralled throughout the journey. However, on being greeted by her nephew it was most apparent to her that, although he looked in better health, as did his wife, and that their latest addition to the family was turning into a most lusty child, all was not well. It was even more noticeable that an air of gloom still lingered in the house, mingled paradoxically with the excitement generated by the arrangements for the forthcoming marriage. Saying nothing to either of them, she greeted Joey and Sarah-Jane warmly and delivered her gift of exquisite chinaware to them. But, in spite of the happiness surrounding the engaged couple, she watched carefully and was made aware of how matters stood in her nephew's marriage after only a brief time at Trevu. Observing them together, she noted that her nephew was desperately trying to atone for the sins he committed against his wife. He obeyed Chloe's every wish and his eyes followed her everywhere like those of a discarded puppy. But most noticeably: when he smiled, he could not hide his sadness. Caroline watched his futile attempts to appease his wife, but took time also to study the object of his endeavours and saw what Paul, in his despair, was unable to acknowledge. Forthrightly demanding of Paul an explanation, she made him admit to the true situation that existed in his marriage. Much to his discomfort, she laughed to scorn his protestations that he was patiently attempting to reawaken his wife's regard for him.

"Reawaken!" she snorted, "Reawaken! What tomfoolery you do speak, Paul! Too much Latin, my boy. Get that silly head of yours out of your books, for Chloe will love you till the day she dies an' if you are too blind to see it you must be the most complete fool." She studied his worried face before announcing, firmly: "This has gone on long enough and I say that it shall stop now!"

Opening his mouth to attempt another protestation that all was lost, Caroline immediately ordered him to be silent, before issuing a further instruction: "Now, summon up your courage and go and tell your wife that you have come to plead forgiveness of her," she ordered sternly.

"But Aunt, what if she refuses even to listen to me?" he pleaded, sick with his desperate fear. For a moment she hesitated and considered his situation, but she was convinced that she was interpreting what she had seen correctly, for she had known Chloe since she was a young girl of seventeen. Caroline had been sure of her then and believed herself right to be as certain of her strength of character now. If she were wrong, then she was condemning her nephew to even more purgatory than he was already suffering, but she was determined that he should be made to talk to his wife, for it was his not knowing that was so undermining him.

"Paul! Paul!" she sighed. Moving towards him she took his hand in a remarkably firm grasp for such an old lady, before telling him firmly but gently: "Ask her now, unless you wish to spend the rest of your life frightened to speak at all for fear of the result. Summon up some of dear Sardi's courage, for of all of us in the family she was the strongest and had to fight the hardest to win her goals."

Reaching up her hands, she rearranged his neck cloth and gently patted his cheek with her hand, before slowly turning him and giving him a firm push in the direction of the door. He walked hesitantly forward, but when he reached the door he heard her call his name softly and he turned his head towards her.

"And Paul," she said roguishly, "When you have plucked up your courage to ask, do not forget to smile," and her eyes twinkled with girlish delight. He smiled back bravely, feigning resolution, but he knew his wife hurt beyond measure and could not believe in the success of his venture. However, his aunt, as usual, was right to order him to try, for he could not continue to live in the personal hell that his actions had created. If the woman he so loved should spurn him, so be it, for in his anguish he considered that he deserved no better of her.

At the entrance to the back parlour, he waited anxiously for a moment, but finally he mastered his emotions and knocked lightly at the door. Her answering voice sounded so sweetly in his ears that he almost lost heart again, but he was here now. He opened the door and strode purposefully into the room. His wife stood with her back to the door, looking out over the garden. She turned to face him and, when she saw him striding into the room, studied his face for a moment before turning back to continue her contemplation of the garden. Outwardly calm, her heart was fluttering excitedly at the determined expression she had seen on her husband's sombre face. She knew what it was that he wished to ask of her, had known even before the moment of her return. Peter and Sarah-Jane had told her how frightened he was to ask, for dread of her reply, but she had decided not to help him, for even now the pain of his beliefs and actions on that fateful day had bitten deeply into the love she had always had for him. He came and stood beside her and she felt herself tremble at his closeness. Such a giant of a man, and she shuddered again at the remembrance of the beating and suffering he had caused her, he who had always been so kind and gentle with her. It was the husband's right, she well knew, to exact authority over his wife and no court in the land would have convicted him of mistreating her, but she understood her husband well enough to know in what light he now saw his behaviour. He had been attempting to earn her forgiveness ever since she had re-entered Trevu's portals, but the words she so desperately desired to hear had never been uttered. Had he come at last to give voice to them?

"Yes, Paul, you wish to see me?" she asked quietly but resolutely, and she turned and looked boldly, but without a semblance of a smile, at his frowning face.

"Chloe, I have come to . . ." he began strongly, but with his head bowed. As he spoke, fear enveloped him, for now he was in her presence he could not bear the thought of her rejection of him. So he stumbled on clumsily, until his endlessly practised, and until that very moment, unused, speech fractured and was discarded. "I am here before you because I must make you aware of my abject . . . It is only right that you should be made aware of how I have . . . I never intended to cause you such . . . pain and . . . and I . . . I . . ." He put up his hand and pulled at his necktie, as it had suddenly become too tight for his neck. He coughed and continued on, as bravely as he could: "My stupidity and unwarranted jealously made me blind . . . I acted so unjustly and . . . and . . . treated you so . . ." and finally he lifted his shamed head and looked desperately into her face.

Chloe stood as if made of stone and made no movement toward him. He found himself staring at a beautiful but icy mask and his heart sank within him, but his fear made him desperate and he could not turn away now.

"Chloe!" he whispered softly, "Please, I beg of you, my dearest, if only for the love we had for each other in the past, the love that would not set me free from you then and will never release me from its hold 'een now. Please, my beloved, please forgive me." And, remembering his aunt's advice, he essayed a small smile, which trembled nervously on his lips.

At sight of his distraught face with its tragic smile, something within Chloe weakened and she found her hands outstretched towards him. Unbelieving of what he was seeing, he stared at her open mouthed, but in a moment he shouted her name in an exultant cry before crushing her to him in his strong clasp. But he was not so lost in his own jubilation that he was not aware that she was sobbing gently in his arms.

When the children returned from school, they were directed by their great aunt to go to the nursery. Grace took Jack by the hand and led him, protesting all the while, up the stairs. But Daisy stood her ground. Raising her impassive face to Caroline she asked directly if all was well.

"I am given to believe, Daisy, that all is very well indeed, for your mother and father are at this very moment together in the back parlour. They have been together for most of the afternoon and, therefore, I do not wish their . . . their conversation to be interrupted," She raised her eyebrows over her distinctly twinkling eyes, giving Daisy a very direct and conspiratorial look.

For answer, she received a flash of her niece's brilliant smile, so like her father's, and was surprised by the knowing look that was directed at her. As

Daisy made her way dutifully from the room, Caroline surmised that at least one of Paul's children was, in many ways, more of an adult than her poor father would ever be. Peter, returning from a visit to Penzance, entered the withdrawing room and Caroline lost no time in advising him as she had with Daisy. His reaction to her information was to cross the room and bend his head, before raising her gloved hand to his lips and planting a kiss on the fingertips.

"Why! Mr Fleetwood!" she said, blushing merrily.

"The very least I could do, Ma'am, for such a wise and capable lady deserves to be appreciated. How you inveigled that poor foolish nephew of yours to finally lay his ghost I know not, but you are to be congratulated most heartily for what you have accomplished. Joey and myself have spent long hours with him, but nothing we said could move him," and he smiled into her glowing eyes.

"Well, 'tis many years since I had need to break him to the bridle, dear Mr Fleetwood, but I have not forgotten the way of it. He learnt to do then as I told him and he recognised in my voice today that I would brook no argument from him," she told him proudly.

"I must admit that, like Paul, I feared Chloe would refuse him, for her face appeared so set against him," said Peter wonderingly.

"Just like a man, my dear Mr Fleetwood, but 'tis the eyes mirror the soul, and that was where I searched for confirmation of what I was so sure she felt in her heart," confirmed Caroline.

Peter was about to say more, when the door opened and they both turned their heads, to see the Master of Trevu framed in the doorway, unable to control the beaming smile on his face for the light-headedness of his relief. He strode across the room and, seating himself by his aunt boisterously but as gently as he could, hugged her to him and placed a warm kiss on her cheek.

"Paul!" she berated him, blithely. "You foolish boy, you have knocked my cap all askew!" but the relief she felt made her as light-headed as her nephew.

Word that the master and mistress had become reconciled spread through the house like a wildfire and, although nothing was said to them directly, their servants smiling faces greeted them everywhere they were to be seen. Lizzie, hurrying from the back parlour to procure some tea for her mistress, had nothing to say to Paul as she met him in the hallway, but she could not keep her own smile at bay for relief at seeing Chloe's happiness. His brother was told the news by old Davy, who winked at him as he took hold of his horse, when he returned from visiting Sarah-Jane just before the dinner hour. Joey's surprised look was answered by Davy's irreverent comment that: 'twas best you d' 'urry in 'cos Paul won't be moping an' wastin' time over 'is dinner 'night, if 'e can eat at all wi' that great grin 'e got stuck on 'is face." So Joey hastened to the dining room, and was met by the sight that he had waited desperately for and so hoped to see again. The host and hostess smiled nervously at each other across the dining table and seemed impervious to all others in the room. And when the meal was over and the men were left to their port after the ladies had retired, Paul threw back the ruby liquid at one go and rebuffed Peter's suggestion of another so quickly that Joey and Peter could not forbear to exchange knowing grins. However, when the time came for all present to retire for the night, not one person there could fail to notice the shy smile that Chloe directed at her husband as she and Caroline left the room. Paul became as nervous as a bridegroom, so Joey linked arms with him and led him up the stairs, talking all the while of the latest gossip that had come to his ears in Penzance, and when Joey saw him pause as he turned towards his room, he slapped him forcefully on the back and merely said: "I'll wish 'e goodnight brother." And if he did push him slightly towards his bedchamber, Paul seemed too bedazzled to notice. Joey walked slowly away to the new wing, smiling to himself and wondering idly if, in a very few days, he would be as nervous as Paul when his beloved Sarah-Jane finally became his wife and their life together was to begin.

In the midst of the celebrations of his wedding breakfast, Joey, resplendent in his new clothes, did indeed feel nervous but the actual ceremony had gone without a hitch. His brother, acting as his best man, seemed incapable of wiping the broad grin from his face and, when the groom caught sight of his bride, escorted by his nieces Grace and Daisy as bridesmaids, his heart swelled with pride at the sight of her.

Sarah-Jane advanced down the aisle, her beauty enhanced by a splendidly worked dress of embroidered cream silk over a peach satin petticoat, and held the arm of her eldest brother, William John, who gave her away with great dignity and unconcealed delight. In years past, Joseph Bolitho would not have been the man that he would have wished for his sister to marry. But now, with Bolitho's changed circumstances, he had become a most eligible addition to the family. Wealth and position could not entirely obscure his past, but with his actions in saving Paul Trevarthen's life, the townsfolk of Penzance were willing to forgive him much of what had gone before. And throughout his life, the one thing Joey had never lacked, when he chose to use it, was charm. The guests at his wedding were proof, if any were needed, that Bolitho had no need to fear rejection from society. They ranged from the Trevarthen family, the Tregurthen's and even the daughters of the late Mrs Carter, as well as many another of Penzance's notables, through to Josh Pascoe who was accompanied by most of Joey's friends and their families. The only member of the gathering not to appreciate the vista of the assorted classes paraded before their eyes was old, blind Mrs Skewes, but even she could relish the comfort of her surroundings. And if she was unable to see the irony of her beloved son's best friend having his back slapped by Sir Reginald Bonython, she knew full well that the money allocated to her by Leviticus' lifelong companion had improved her own life beyond measure. Peter Fleetwood shook Joey's hand with great cordiality and, after a few words to the newly married couple, betook himself to a corner of the room, where he had espied a particularly fetching black-haired damsel with flashing dark eyes and a cupid's bow of a mouth, which he determined to kiss before the celebrations were over. Delighted to be a part of the festivities, Dr Dunstan congratulated Sarah-Jane on her choice of husband, he beamed at Joey as he did so and kept repeating "Damn glad to see the change in you, Joey, damn glad!" The tables groaned with exquisite food and an endless supply of drink, but Paul laughed to scorn his brother's attempts to thank him for all he had done for him on this day and in the recent past. Paul merely wished him a happy marriage and would have spoken further, but they were interrupted by Jack, who wished to have speech with his uncle. The brothers exchanged rueful glances at the sight of Jack's furrowed brows, but Joey dutifully accepted his nephew's invitation to walk with him in the garden and they strolled hand in hand towards the seat that was bathed in the soft sunlight of a winter's day. They sat together and Joey waited respectfully for Jack to unburden himself. After some fidgeting, Jack raised his face, upon which the remnants of a rather sumptuous custard tart still remained, and brought himself to the point of asking his question.

"Uncle Joey?"

"Yes, Jack," replied his uncle, with a soft smile playing on his lips.

"Will Aunt Sarah-Jane let you come and see me sometimes?" he asked worriedly.

Joey threw back his head and laughed, but recovered himself quickly and enquired of Jack why he had thought he would not see him again.

"Well, I heard Dada tell her that he wished her every happiness and that he hoped that she was to have a wonderful marriage with you, and she said that she hoped so too but if you was any trouble she would keep you under lock and key until you was too tired to wander." Jack looked in wonderment at his uncle as, at his words, he laughed all the more. When finally he stopped, he reached out his arms, then hugged his nephew to him reassuringly and told him that he was not to worry, for now that he was a married man he intended to be the best of husbands and a good provider for his wife, so that she would never have to worry about anything ever again.

"So you will come and visit me?" Jack said brightly, his eyes shining with relief.

"Of course, I'll be comin' see 'e, an' yer Aunt will come with me, don't you worry. I'm goin' be livin' in Penzance same as always. Perhaps, if you d' be'ave yerself, you can come an' stay with we in Chapel Street, sometimes," he told him.

"Honestly?" cried Jack, delight written all over his face.

"Damn right!" Joey told him.

Jack hugged him excitedly before thinking seriously for a moment.

"Uncle Joey?"

"Yes, Jack?" his uncle replied with a gentle sigh.

"You will be good and behave yourself just like you are always tellin' me to do, won't you? I only ask because I think Aunt Sarah-Jane might do as she says if you are naughty," he informed him in a serious tone.

"Well," said Joey determinedly, "I shall jes' 'ave be'ave meself," and winked at Jack before adding: "like you d' do!"

Jack drew a deep breath and said proudly: "I am good sometimes, Uncle Joey, especially if you tell me to be."

There was more laughter, then Joey took out his handkerchief and deftly wiped the stains from Jack's face. And all the while his nephew, with an uplifted face, gazed at him in adoration, so different from when his poor nurse attempted to accomplish the same exercise with him.

Watching from the window in the withdrawing room, Paul smiled to himself and turned as his wife joined him to see what it was that had captured his attention in the garden.

"Joey looks a different man from the one I met that day in Josh's tavern, and even with all his friends about him here today I could see the change in him. He had always an air about him, Chloe, even then. But I do believe most sincerely that the Joseph Bolitho of old has finally been laid to rest," and he sighed, "and the man that has taken his place has many of the qualities of which Father would have been so proud."

Placing her arm around him, she leaned against him and smiled up at his relaxed face, but said nothing. Discovering the existence of the unknown brother had been an agonising journey for all of them: Paul, Joey and not least herself, but through it all they had come to a better understanding. Paul had been humbled by his treatment of his wife and had sworn never again to so mistreat her. Joey had finally acquired the status he should have had from birth and had carried his new position with dignity and authority, without losing friends or acquiring enemies. And as to herself, she sighed unknowingly; her silly, beloved husband was still trying to prove by every thought and deed how grateful he was to her for her forgiveness of him. In her heart she had forgiven him his sins, but she was woman enough to revel in the attention he continued to lavish upon her. She felt Paul's arm around her shoulders as he squeezed her protectively and they exchanged a smile of shared but, in consideration of their surroundings, muted passion. Comforted and reassured equally, they turned to gaze again upon the scene before them in the garden.

The man and the boy on the garden seat were joined by another as Sarah-Jane, elegantly attired in her peach and cream wedding dress, and looking far younger than her age, crossed the lawn and came to sit beside them. They laughed together as they talked until, as one, they rose to return to the withdrawing room. Jack, preceding them, skipped gleefully towards his brother George and his sisters, talking happily with Harry and Dick Pendray, noting with satisfaction that Miss Clavering was busily engaged in showing off his young brother to various of the assembled ladies. He stopped abruptly and turned in surprise when the happy couple entered, for a great cheer went up from the assembled family and friends. He stared in disbelief at his uncle and his new aunt, unable to comprehend why their entrance should cause such a commotion.

Joey slipped his arm around his wife's waist, which elicited some ribald comments and caused Sarah-Jane's colour to fluctuate rapidly. But Joey only laughed and smiled proudly until, finally urged on by Seth's recommendation that he kiss his bride, he took her in his arms and kissed her soundly. The cheers and whoops that the assembled company emitted were so loud that Trevu's walls almost shook at the sound, but the old house had seen such sights before. And a winter breeze that had suddenly blown up from the sea gently rustled the branches of the trees, so that they seemed to sigh in contentment with the gathering within.

Printed in the United Kingdom
by Lightning Source UK Ltd.
115823UKS00001B/148-189